D1291580

The Gossip Boats

Kathleen Wallman

Copyright © 2022 Kathleen Wallman

ISBN: 9780692104675

DEDICATION

Some stayed in the West of Ireland; others left to start
different lives in America. Here's to the bravery of them all.

ACKNOWLEDGMENTS

Thank you to everyone who read earlier drafts and encouraged
me to press forward.

FOREWORD

The Harte family, my family, comes from the west of Ireland. The Irish of the west are reputed to be a melancholic people, and a visit there explains why: the vast gray skies, the rain, the nothingness between villages, the distances between the houses in the villages.

Across this landscape bounded a young William Butler Yeats, glowing in the dawn of the Celtic Revival, pumping householders to share their stories, the ones they remembered from as early as they could. He found the west rich in mystic, folkloric beliefs and provoked many stories of ghosts and fairies - not the dainty, spritely type, but rather tall, elegant mysterious men and women living along side regular folks in magical places and in the night shadows.

Yeats published several collections documenting this ethnographic work, and I came to know about it through a Penguin-published collection called Writings on Irish Folklore, Legend and Myth. I devoured the book, reading and re-reading it until it almost fell apart. Through its pages, I began to see a way of posing a question that I had wondered about for a long time: What makes some belief systems mainstream and others marginalized? What makes my belief system true and yours preposterous? These questions are at the heart of so many conflicts that have spanned generations.

In crafting a story to explore these questions, I have relied on Writings on Irish Folklore, Legend and Myth as a roadmap, retelling and sometimes revising the stories collected from my family's homeland — including Michael and Biddy Hart (an alternative spelling of the family name; we still fight about it) who show up as sources in Yeats' writing — to move the story forward. So many of these stories are not my original confabulations; they belong to the millennia, and I am grateful to Yeats and his sources for making them accessible today.

1.

Father Pádraig was old school: sober every day for the morning mass, but not much longer after mumbling the dismissal and waving the devoted out the door. The village's lone public house, Beach Club, didn't officially open until eleven o'clock, but Willie, the first and only barman ever employed there, was a friend. He'd let the priest in early through the delivery door around back from the street, as soon as half past eight some mornings, to have an ounce of Bushmill's with his tea.

"It's a bad business going on at the Gunning place," Willie called over his shoulder, sweeping down the pockmarked dance floor. A wet mop was what it needed, Pádraig thought, after the sudsy dousing the floor had weathered last night. But he bit his tongue. A good guest suffers even humble hospitality silently, his mother said.

Pádraig knew just what Willie was talking about, but pretended not to. The confessional was sacred, after all, and ignorance was a good strategy in a village as small as Mullaghmore. Knowing too much was at least awkward, and could even be dangerous. Not that anyone would dream of hurting a priest.

"By which you mean what?" he inquired innocently,

setting his cup down gently to minimize its wobble as it neared landing.

"Ah, you know as well as I do, the whole village knows, there's something not right going on between the man and his daughter. It's a shame, that's what it is. A damn shame." He stood upright, surprised by his own infraction. "Sorry, Father," he mumbled.

"Three Hail Marys, and don't let me hear it again," Pádraig growled. He'd heard a lot worse right here last night and, truth be told, said a lot worse in some of his darker moments, which were no longer rarities. But there were appearances to keep up. Seeming too lenient would not do.

"Well, everyone's talking about it, and no one's doing a thing about it," Willie said defensively. "I heard he beats his wife, too."

Pádraig slapped his open hand on the bar top. Hospitality or not, this was a place to put a foot down. Willie snapped upright again, startled by the sound and stung by the rebuke it carried.

"That's enough of that!" Pádraig said, raising his voice to sermon volume. "You don't know, you just don't know, what happens when a man closes the door to be with his family. You don't know what holds them together." He drained his cup and stood. "Look, Willie, stay out of this, and don't spread these rumours. It's a sin just as well and truly as it is to tell a lie. That's what gossip is – it's reckless, baseless lies and it stains this village like filthy soot." He strode out the door too quickly to hear Willie's plaintive retort: "But what if it's true?"

He hadn't stayed long enough at Willie's for a full treatment, which would have involved another two cups of tea and an elaborate ritual of first refusing the bottle as Willie passed it over the cup, then relenting and looking away as Willie sweetened his tea. The feeling of relative sobriety at this hour emboldened him, and the flare of adrenaline that his burst of anger had given him fueled his pace down the main street of the village, Castle Road. He forced himself to smile and wave at those he passed, almost all of them parishioners. His determined stride signaled that no, he couldn't possibly stop and chat just now. He pressed on toward the post office.

On a spring morning like this, wet and cold, with the teasing hint of later sunshine, there were only a few places out of the damp for the villagers to gather outside their own homes. The pub was still officially closed, so that left the shops, some with space and a homey feel welcoming enough to invite lingering. There was the little book shop, but the proprietor was a book worm and frowned on conversation above a whisper as if the books themselves might be disturbed. And there was An Post.

In a proper town, the post office would be a marvelous government building with stone steps and mailboxes with compass-pointed combination locks. But here in Mullaghmore, it was a much more casual affair. There had once been an iron grate to separate the postmaster and the cash box from the customers, but it began to pull away from the ceiling a few years back, and rather than risk having it fall on a customer, or on himself, God forbid, the postmaster took it down.

It suited him better. Martin O'Flaherty couldn't stand, truth be told, the separation from the customers, his fellow villagers, that the grate necessitated. The accusation that the grate implied, that they were not to be trusted, embarrassed him. So he was relieved when it starting coming down, separating itself a bit at the ceiling, and a few villagers who had known him longest whispered among themselves that they saw him yanking on it to hasten the necessity of its removal. Strictly speaking, without that grate, the place wasn't up to even minimal government standards any more, and it might even be said, and some did say, that Martin had destroyed government property, but it would take years for anyone to come around and take official notice.

It was no surprise, then, to Pádraig to walk in upon Martin holding court that morning from his clerk's chair behind the counter. They were mostly women at this hour, the men recuperating at home or already at work in the shops and the dairy barns, but a few men in sweaters and caps stood about. The caps came off when Pádraig entered. Martin hopped to his feet even as Pádraig shooed him back into his chair with a wave.

"G'morning, Father," the group said in parochial school chorus.

"It'll be fine this afternoon, the news reader said this morning, Father," Martin offered. As a postal agent, he got a free antenna subscription, and while he resisted bragging about this, he enjoyed the special status it gave him as a source of information for villagers without the privilege.

"I expect it will be, then, if he says so. Though it may be he was talking about Dublin, did you think of that Martin?" Pádraig asked Martin. Martin looked flummoxed a moment until the priest's raised eyebrows gave him permission to laugh at the joke, or what he thought was a joke, at least.

"How's your mum, Father, does the weather bother her much these days?" Claire McGettigan, baptized Claire Kennedy, lived at the end of the street where the village trailed off into the countryside and had the distinction of owning the most reliable bread oven in the village.

"She's well, thanks, Claire, you're kind to ask after her." He patted her shoulder as he stepped up to the counter. The conversation in the tiny post office had ceased. Tom Whalen stood halfway upright to toss another peat brick into the stove and eased himself back into the chair closest to it. Pádraig's arrival, as unremarkable as it was, was new and entertaining. Pádraig realized there was no hope of doing what he came to do discreetly.

"Martin, I'm here after the post for the Gunnings. Ned may not be in town for a few days, and I told him I'd look after it for him."

Martin's face went somber. "Well, Father, um, I'm actually not supposed to give out the post except to the party to whom it's addressed. "

Officious prig, Pádraig thought, and smiled nonetheless. "Well, Martin, I wouldn't want you to bend the rules at all, but it would be a kindness to the family, not to require them to come down here, with the daughter sick and all. There could be something important from the doctor."

The part about Fianna being sick he hadn't meant to mention, but the situation required more persuasion that he had anticipated. He halted himself from saying more, staring an amicably as he could manage into Martin's eyes. He usually won this type of showdown with a parishioner.

Martin's left hand moved slightly behind him to a small stack of mail he'd already evidently set aside. He picked it up without looking at it and handed it to the priest. "You might be right about that, Father. I didn't mean to look, but of course I have to sort the post, and I couldn't help seeing that there's a letter from the hospital, St. John's in Stillorgan. Close to Dublin, I think it is."

Pádraig took the mail and tapped the edges of the letters together so they rested evenly in the crease of his palm. He looked sidelong at Martin, a silent reprimand for the gossipy discussion he was trying to provoke, but uttered no rebuke. He waved good-bye with the letters aloft in one hand and began his exit. He was almost to the door when Claire could stand it no longer.

"Father, what's wrong with the child?" she asked.

"Send up your prayers for her, Claire," he called over his shoulder. "She'll be no better off with them than without, but no worse either," he said only to himself.

The road up to the Gunning farm was rutted and potholed. A version of macadam once was applied here, part of a public works project, but it had long since crumbled and deserted the roadbed. I'd not like to be coming out here at night on foot, Pádraig reflected, weighing the chances of a turned ankle on a road rarely travelled at a point more than two miles outside the village. He could have taken the car, a little gray Ford Escort, functional and sufficiently modest for a village priest, but his head was still buzzing a bit from his morning tea, even at reduced dosage, and the walk would clear him up, he thought. Best to be bright eyed and clearheaded when handling this delicate business, he resolved.

The morning was cool and misty, and his breath formed clouds as he covered the distance to the Gunning place at a brisk pace. He was still a quarter mile away from the house when the dogs, two Springer spaniels, caught his scent and charged toward him, barking. They posed and pranced around him as Pádraig reached into his jacket pocket for a stub of shortbread which he broke in two and gave to the dogs.

"You've a good memory for bringers of treats, the both of you," he said, tousling their ears with his free hand.

The dogs' commotion brought Ned out on the porch, now mostly given over to storing peat bricks under the eaves of the house and out of the rain. A lone rocking chair took up the space between the door and the woodpile. It had the look of a sentinel's post.

Ned stood on the porch with hands on hips, watching Pádraig approach. His look was hard, gaunt and tired, an affirmation of the stress visiting this house. Pádraig stopped at the foot of the porch, looking up at Ned. "And how is she today?"

Ned shrugged, "She's the same today as she is every day. Mad as a March hare in a field of carrots." He crossed his arms. Pádraig mounted the porch steps, tapped the packet of letters on Ned's forearm. "Patience, man, more patience. I think I've brought good news." He shuffled the letter from the hospital to the top of the stack and handed it to Ned. "Go on and open it; they'd only have written if they found a bed for her."

Ned snorted. "What kind of good news do you call that? We haven't the money for that kind of thing. Who's going to pay to put her in a fancy hospital all the way down to Dublin, for pity's sake? And how will she even get there? I can't be walking away from the animals and the work." Pádraig shook his head and reached for the kitchen door. "One thing at a time, Ned, one thing at a time."

He let himself into the kitchen, dark even in the overcast morning light. The lone light bulb over the table would not be switched on until hours later when the setting of the sun finally made working or eating in the room impossible. It was Ned's rule.

His eyes adjusted as Bertie moved toward him and clasped his right hand in both of hers. Her voice caught and the room's scarce light rippled across the moistness in her eyes. "Father, I heard you say they have a bed for her? They have a bed for Fianna? Is it true?"

"I think so, Bertie, I do think so. We'll know when Ned opens the letter." They both turned and faced Ned, who tossed the stack of letters on the table and ripped open the top one. He turned it to the window to read it, then thrust it back at the priest. "My eyes are not good," he growled, "and there's too much fancy language in there. Why can't people speak plainly?" He slouched against the icebox while Pádraig took his place near the window. "Yes," he said after a moment, "they do have a place for her." He paused for a moment and looked more closely at the print. "What? They say that she has to be there today between noon and three." He looked at the date of the letter. "This is dated a week ago yesterday. Damned An Post. They get slower and less reliable every year." He glanced at his watch. "We'll have to leave no later than an hour from now."

Bertie clapped her hands together and gasped. "Thank you, Lord," she said, with an upturned gaze and rushed to embrace the priest. "We'll have some help for her, finally!"

"You all are dreaming!" Ned shouted, slamming his fist on the table and making the tea mugs jump. "We haven't a penny for this, not a penny! She needs only one thing, I'll tell you, and I'll give it to her with my own belt." He began undoing the clasp as he strode toward the staircase. "Fianna!" he yelled, summoning his daughter. "Come down here!"

Bertie flung herself upon him as he set foot on the first stair tread and slowed his progress enough for Pádraig to loop his arm through Ned's and turn him back toward the kitchen. He knew Ned's misbehavior would only go so far while he was in the house, and was eager to establish Fianna's going to St. John's before going back to get his car to start the trip toward Dublin.

"Now, Ned," he said as calmly as he could muster, "I know it's a strange thing, this ailment, but it is an ailment, an illness, and we must treat it as that."

"I'll have none of it, none of it, I tell you. She is willful and bad, just willful and bad, that's all. If she's coddled, she'll never leave off of it."

"Ned, that's enough!   We have to see to her getting better." He paused to deliver his finale: "After all, Ned, she's your daughter now."

2.

Bertie insisted on sitting in the back seat with Fianna, as much, Pádraig thought, to comfort the girl as to distance herself from the windscreen. Not a mad idea, Pádraig thought, since she's no doubt seen me driving about now and then. Pádraig never drank in a place he couldn't walk home from, but even sober, his constant reminders to himself to drive carefully were readily derailed upon seeing someone or something more interesting than the road before him.

They drove south to Sligo and then on to Dublin on the N4. Pádraig paid casual attention to the speed limits. He wanted badly to be at St. John's within the prescribed window, and there was an important stop to make beforehand. Besides, his experience was that it wasn't difficult for a driver in a Roman collar to charm a garda out of writing a summons.

Bertie spoke periodically to Fianna in a low voice, the kind he'd heard her use when soothing animals around her barn. "You'll be fine, a chuisle. We'll get you into the calm for a little while, let you rest. You'll see it's not so bad. And then you'll come home again, and everything will be all right."

Pádraig smiled faintly at Bertie's endearment. Hardly anyone used the old Irish phrases any more. Too old fashioned for people, now that the turn of the century was less than twenty-five years away. More's the shame, Pádraig thought, it's often so perfect. A chuisle mo chroí, the pulse of my heart. Bertie had made a good home for the girl and loved her, in spite of and sometimes in defiance of Ned's misgivings about Fianna.

Fianna sat silently for most of the trip. Pádraig glanced at her now and then in the rear view mirror. She glanced up for a moment and their eyes intersected for a moment or two until Pádraig reminded himself to watch the road.

"He hates me," she said.

Bertie gasped, "He doesn't hate you, you mustn't think that. He loves you, only he doesn't ..."

"He hates me," Fianna repeated, a bit louder and more insistently. "There's no point in covering it over, Mum. He wishes I'd never been born." Bertie began to cry. Pádraig glanced as often as he dared at the pair in the back seat using the mirror and now and then turning his head. He was torn between intervening and letting the two sort it out on their own. He decided it was too complicated a situation to deal with at full speed on the motorway, and pulling off to calm everyone down was out of the question in view of the tight schedule.

"We're almost there, hang on, you two. If there's time we'll have a cup of tea and chat about it, but let's first of all make sure we get there on time. All the more so since I've absolutely got to stop at the Chancellery before we go on to St. John's."

Bertie asked no questions about Pádraig's insistence on the stop at the chancery; Fianna stared back at Pádraig in the mirror, then turned back to studying her hands in her lap.
Pádraig found curb parking and turned himself out of the car and into the rain. He leaned back inside to assure Bertie and Fianna that they wouldn't be delayed long. "I need a word with just one person here. It will only take a few minutes."

Inside the Chancellery, he spoke quietly to the reception secretary. "Good morning, I wonder if you can help me find Monsignor Hargadon for a brief word."

"Do you have an appointment, Father?"

"No, no," Pádraig chuckled in a way he hoped would seem disarming. "I'm just an old acquaintance from his former parish in the west, St. Molaise in Mullaghmore."

The secretary smiled politely. "I'm sorry to say I've not heard of it, but my people are from County Mayo, so...."
Pádraig smiled broadly, "That's understandable, but I'm surprised that Monsignor Hargadon hasn't filled your ears with tales of his pastoral work there! He was the pastor before me, and let me tell you, he left some big brogues to fill!" He had the secretary laughing along with him now. He leaned across the desk to speak confidentially, "Frankly, I'm here because I need a word with him on some delicate matters in the parish. No one has more experience with such things than Monsignor Hargadon." Every word of this is literally true, not a single lie so far, Pádraig consoled himself as he continued to con his way into seeing Roger. He had thought of calling ahead, but that seemed more likely to make Roger remember a conflicting engagement away from the Chancellery.

The secretary still looked dubious. "I should think that his having been gone from the parish for so long, it must be fifteen years, he'd be a bit removed, wouldn't he?"

"Sixteen, in fact. But nothing ever changes in Mullaghmore. No one ever moves out, all the same families and characters as when he was there. Listen, if you don't mind, I could really use a word with him."

She paused for a moment, then pushed her chair back from the desk. "I'll have to go see if he's free. He doesn't like the phone ringing on his desk unless it's absolutely necessary." She paused and turned back toward Pádraig, "I'm so sorry for not asking earlier, but whom shall I say is visiting?"

Pádraig smiled warmly. "Please tell him it's Father Hart."

The secretary disappeared down a hallway and behind a door. It had barely closed when it flew open again, with Roger in the lead and the secretary following at a distance.

Roger strode across the room to Pádraig, his hand outstretched. "Paddy, so good to see you." Pádraig forced himself to continue smiling during this unwanted infliction of familiarity. No one ever called him Paddy. "You should have written or called. I had no idea you'd be in Dublin."

"Nor did I until this morning. It's a trip on short notice." He stared silently at Roger. "I think we should talk in your office."

Roger chuckled, "My office is a mess, which won't surprise you. You remember my study back in Mullaghmore. I'm no better at housekeeping here than there!" The secretary smiled in affectionate confirmation of his self-assessment.

Pádraig had stopped smiling. "Roger, I really think we should talk in your office."

Roger paused, considering one more attempt to cabin Pádraig's visit to the lobby, then turned away from Pádraig abruptly. "As you'd have it. Follow me."

Roger closed the door to his office as Pádraig briefly looked around for a chair not laden with books and papers, then gave up. Roger dropped the veneer of charm. "What do you want, Pádraig?"

"It's the Gunnings. They need your help."

Roger grimaced and waved Pádraig's words away in the air. "I've told you over and over that I'll have nothing to do with that family."

"Roger, listen to me. The girl is sick. I know you have the means to help the family with her treatment. She has bulimia."

Roger laughed. "Bulimia? The one where the teenage girls throw up perfectly good food so that they can fit into tight trousers? That's considered a disease now, is it? If it is, I'd say that the best treatment is to deny her the attention she's seeking and let her grow out of it. And it won't cost a penny." Roger picked up a cup and saucer from his desk and sipped his tea.

Pádraig shook his head. "Never much of a man of learning, were you, Roger. Yes, it's considered a disease, and one for which there's a very good treatment program at St. John's in Stillorgan. If they can get the money to pay for it."

"Look, I've told you that I'll have nothing to do with that family, because I've never had anything to do with that family and I'm not going to start now acting as though I have some

12

responsibility to them."

"Consider it charity, then. An act of mercy."

"Absolutely not. These things get misinterpreted. I have a reputation to protect. You know, I'm up for a very big promotion to a position at the Vatican." He smiled and rocked on his heels. Pádraig suppressed an urge to punch him.

"Well, then, we might as well have this out. You do have a responsibility to them. And if you won't own up to it, I'll tell the chancellor. I'll tell him everything. You'll never go to Rome. You'll stay here in Dublin."

Roger walked slowly to the window and looked down into the Liffey. "Pádraig, what do you really know? What do you personally, actually know about all this? Think about it. Before you start asserting my responsibility to the family, I should mention that while I haven't been in close touch with many in Mullaghmore since I left, I do have occasional conversations with…I probably shouldn't say whom. But the consensus that they report to me is that the daughter bears a striking resemblance to you." He turned to Pádraig with a thin smile and arched brows.

Pádraig fumed. "You really are a bastard, Roger."

Roger gestured lightly with his hand. "I may be a bastard, but not the one under discussion." Pádraig took a quick, light step toward him, and slapped his cheek and ear with his open palm. Roger stepped back, cracking his head on the window frame on the recoil. His hand touched the place reddened by Pádraig's hand. "I think you'd better leave now," he said coolly.

Outside in the rain, Pádraig turned up his collar and shrugged his coat in against the drizzle. He walked a block away from the car to compose himself. He let a few minutes pass before drawing himself together and heading back to the Escort.

"What did he say, Father?" Bertie's hands were sweeping away the drops of drizzle on his shoulders as soon as he got into the car. "Can he help us?"

"No, he can't, Bertie." He wanted badly to vent his anger by telling them the more hurtful truth that it wasn't at all that he couldn't help, only that he wouldn't. But it could do them no good to hear it. "He's leaving for Rome, a new position, very important. The Holy Father himself requested his services. He's no time left to work things out for us at St. John's."

Bertie pressed a crumpled tissue to her mouth. Pádraig glanced in the rearview mirror for a glimpse of Fianna; her ashen face and cracked lips propelled him to action. "We'll go there ourselves, we will, to St. John's then and make the best of it."

3.

The hospital should not have been difficult to find, but Fianna's evident decline worried and distracted him from following the landmarks the receptionist at the hospital had told him to watch for when he'd called. Finally, frustrated with himself, he stopped at a petrol station for directions. Even in Dublin, the occasion of a priest asking for directions inspired people to go the extra mile, and in a moment the station's owner had sent his son running to the tow truck with instructions to "show Father the way".

The tow truck led them to the gates of the hospital, and with a honk of the horn and some vigorous pointing over the cab of the truck toward the hospital on the right, the truck took a u-turn and sped back to the station.

If a place can be imposing and inviting at the same time, this was St. John's. It was a place not meant to be left easily..

Wrought iron gates wrapped the grounds as far as the view from the entrance permitted. A little guard box at the entrance produced an ancient, bristled-mustached man who touched the brim of his hat and stepped back deferentially upon seeing Pádraig at the wheel. He pressed a switch to make the gates groan open.

Inside, the driving path wound through curved lanes of

trees with broad trunks of old age. Benches and terraces here and there suggested outdoor leisure, but there was no one enjoying these seats at the moment in the chill of the drizzle.

Pádraig parked the Escort a little past the entrance, and the three of them went in. The entrance vestibule was surprisingly quiet for its cavernous size, and made Pádraig lean in to the receptionist at the desk and whisper his introduction.

"Good afternoon. I'm here to see to the admission of a patient," he said gesturing to his left and behind him. "The girl. She's not well."

The receptionist leaned out to look around him. "Yes, Father, I see. You've called ahead about the arrangements?"

"Yes, the family had a letter just today confirming you've a place for her. It must have been delayed by the post. We rushed to get here as soon as we could."

"Right, then. I'll just call our admissions office." She murmured into the phone, and momentarily a woman arrived, announced by the echoing of her heels on the black and white tile of the vestibule. Her hand outstretched, she greeted the priest with a stiff handshake and nodded crisply toward Bertie and Fianna.

"Hello, I'm Mary Weller, director of admissions. Let's have a seat over here and talk over the paperwork." She herded them toward a cluster of drawing room chairs, more or less presentable apart from their worn armrests. They sat. She affixed a practiced smile, and began, "First things first. Form of insurance?"

Bertie cast her eyes down. Pádraig said, "Well, that's the thing. There is no insurance, and the family has not been issued a medical card because too many people have already gotten them in County Sligo so they're overallocated for the country. And there are no family funds. We hoped you might be able to extend some help nevertheless." He paused to assess his progress with her. Her smile had faded and was replaced with pursed lips. He pressed on. "Or perhaps payment could be deferred for a time and the parish could raise some funds." He blushed a bit, knowing that he was close to a lie; there would be no help for the Gunnings forthcoming from the hard hearted at home.

Mary Weller crossed her hands in her lap. "Father, perhaps we could speak privately for a moment." Pádraig had barely even turned to Bertie to voice the request when Bertie was on her feet ushering Fianna to another corner of the lobby. He turned back to Mary Weller with the most pleasant smile he could manage. "Father, we do sympathize with families in this situation, but I'm sure you understand that we must balance our finances. If we take charity cases, it raises the cost of treatment for our other patients, and that's not fair to them. I'm sure you see." Pádraig stared blankly at the woman. If she was going to say no, he was determined to make her say it out loud, plainly. "I'd suggest that you take the step you mentioned of canvassing the parish for contributions, then reapply. Perhaps the diocese out in the west – Achonry, I think it is – could help. Or you could try the Dublin diocese."

Pádraig guffawed and stood up. "Thank you for those helpful suggestions. I think the Dublin diocese is a dead end, though. In fact, I've just come from there. But we'll pursue the other ideas and reapply." He bent toward her and whispered, "unless she dies in the meantime."

The drive back to Mullaghmore was silent. Pádraig could think of no words of comfort that weren't tainted by dishonesty. He offered a stop at a tea house off the road in Longford, but Bertie shook her head. "Best to get her home, I think, Father, if it's all the same to you."

It was dark by the time they pulled into the village, and Bertie pled with Pádraig to leave them off near the rectory. "It isn't far, and we could do with a good walk, being in the car all day." Pádraig disregarded them and drove as close to the house as he could. The muddy road made him cautious about going all the way up to the porch. He parked and left the headlights on so that the three of them could see their way to the house. The bright lights brought Ned out on the porch. Ned swayed a bit as he walked out the door, which confirmed to Pádraig how Ned had spent the day. He was relieved he had insisted on seeing Bertie and Fianna to their door.

"So you're back, the both of you." Even drunk, Ned

avoided embroiling a priest in his recriminations. "Well, that was a triumph of a success, wasn't it? I told you it was a waste of time. Don't tell me. Let me guess. No money, no hospital. Am I right? Tell me, am I right?" He continued his harangue as Bertie and Fianna tried to squeeze by him in the doorway. Ned did not yield, and as soon as he saw the jostling start, Pádraig stepped in. He gave Ned's elbow the tight grip he used with unruly students and pulled him back on the porch to clear the entrance for Bertie and Fianna. "Leave off of it, Ned. Let them in, then let's get you settled for a long sleep in the parlor."

Ned leaned against the wall and steadied himself. Pádraig heard Bertie and Fianna go straight up the steps. He peeked in the doorway to confirm that they were out of sight, then hustled Ned into the parlor and dumped him on the divan. He summoned up the voice that he used when he wanted to instill obedience and told Ned, "Sleep here tonight. Do not go upstairs. We'll speak of this when you're recovered."

Leaving the darkened house, he spotted the glint of Ned's whiskey bottle, the shape of a flask, two-thirds empty, perched on the hallway table. He wondered for a moment whether it would fit into the inside pocket of his suit coat, then discovered that it did.

4.

Pádraig wandered through his Saturday morning routine. Early mass was lightly attended; the daily mass goers, all women, had men at home on Saturdays, off from work, to wait on. He had his usual visit to Beach Club, but no whiskey this morning; he was off to visit his mother. Purely as a matter of respect, he refrained. That, and the fact that he knew she didn't approve. She'd pushed him into signing the teetotal pledge as a teenager, and mistakenly thought his joining the priesthood protected him from missteps. It was convenient that she no longer came into town, Pádraig thought, to see him stepping into the pub every day.

He'd collected her post during the week and piled on top of that the day's newspaper and a copy of Craic magazine, which she loved to have read to her, though Pádraig puzzled over why. Even the name is distasteful, Pádraig thought, but at least the publisher's honest enough to call it what it is - gossip for fun. The primping starlets and their never-ending dramas and divorces were a million miles away from her experiences. But maybe, Pádraig reflected, that was exactly why she enjoyed it.

He put the mail and news in the front seat of his Escort and drove up the Castle Road, past the turn where the Red

Islands came into view on the shoreline below, and up and over the crest of the hill by the boarding stables at the horse farm. His mother's house, the house he had grown up in, was on the far side of the head, the south side. On a clear night, the lights from Sligo Town sparkled in the distance. When her vision was better, his mother had enjoyed the view many nights from the porch, wrapped in a shawl so old that it had begun to unravel into the skeins it had been knitted from.

It was close enough to the rectory that Pádraig could have walked, either along the road he'd just driven or cutting through the middle of the head. He often relied on the privileges of his uniform to hop over a few fences for the short cut, but did it often enough and without objection that he no longer felt he required permission. But taking the car was easier, and there was always the odd chance that his mother or her sister, who had moved in when Pádraig left for Hong Kong, would need a lift to run an errand or might just enjoy a ride.

He had just turned off the engine when the door flew open and Stella saluted from the door, her raised hand cinching a cigarette between two fingers. He waved back and made his way up the steps. "Well, hello, Father, welcome to our humble abode!" Stella ramped up her western accent and mimicked the kind of bowing and scraping reception he received at most homes he visited. He grinned back and tapped her gently on the shoulder with the stack of letters he carried. "Two Hail Marys for your lack of respect and sarcasm. And make sure I see you at mass tomorrow." They went into the house together.

He lowered his voice. "How is she today?"

"She's happy as fish and chips and has no idea what day it is. All in all, she's fine. Pleasantly confused is the medical term."

Stella was trained as a nurse in Baltimore and had intended to stay there for good without looking back. But as the older siblings in her family aged and became infirm, she felt tugged back to help. There was a span of almost thirty years between the ages of the Stella and Pádraig's mother with

20

seven more sisters and five brothers in line between them. His mother, though the eldest, had already outlived five siblings, each of whom Stella had taken care of through their final days.

Pádraig nodded toward the cigarette. "I thought you were not smoking around her."

Stella took a deep drag and shrugged. "She's forgotten that she hates it. Besides, I can't be stepping out on the porch every twenty minutes. Come on through. She's in the room with the telly."

Pádraig could hear the television booming out a laugh track. He followed Stella to the back of the house.

"Margaret, the priest is here," Stella said, competing in volume with the television.

"Oh, send him right in! Can you close the telly for me, dear?" She turned to Pádraig. "I'm so sorry I can't get up to greet you properly. My legs are not cooperating, I'm afraid."

"Not a worry, dear." Pádraig reached down to give his mother a hug and a kiss on the cheek. "How are you feeling?" He sat down next to her on the sofa nearest her chair. She leaned over to him. "Well, I'm fine. But I do worry about Stella. She introduced you as 'the priest'. Do you suppose she's forgotten you're my son?"

Pádraig suppressed a laugh. "I think she's all right, Mum. Just make sure she doesn't steal your Craic magazine before you're done with it. She's a dodgy one when it comes to that sort of pilfery."

He visited for half an hour more, then said his good-byes and checked with Stella about supplies she needed now or later in the week.

"We're fine on milk, fine on porridge," Stella said opening the refrigerator and cabinet doors. "We need eggs and rashers. And cigarettes."

"You need cigarettes, not 'we'. And haven't you heard -- those things will kill you."

"So they say. But she's the sixth of us Murrans I've taken care of. I've seen how it all ends for us. First your legs don't work, then you lose your mind. It ain't pretty, as they say in America. I figure I should have some fun while I can still remember that that's what I'm doing." She inhaled again and smiled mockingly. "At least it's not a sin, as far as I can tell. Unless they've changed the rule book lately."

Pádraig kissed her lightly on the cheek. "How would you know? You haven't been to mass in ages. Come for Easter, at least. We'll get one of the sisters to come up for a couple of hours to relieve you."

"Ah, Pádraig, I'll think about it. See you soon." She saw him out the door. "By the way, the phone is working again. Thanks for whatever you did to get them to come out."

"You're welcome. I think they were surprised to hear a priest use some of the words I deployed to persuade them. I feel a lot better knowing that you can ring me up at the rectory if something comes up." He waved and turned the car back out on the road.

On his way back to the rectory, he passed the stub of road that led out to the Gunnings' house and slowed while he debated stopping by. His fingers drummed the wheel while he considered hiking up the path. But he decided that letting the family alone for a full day to come together around Fianna's problem and how to solve it was the best thing to do. His conscience bothered him as he drove on, but he consoled himself by noting that it was only a little, and there was always tomorrow to attack the problem afresh.

5.

The mass on Palm Sunday was a long one, but the reading of the Passion was one of Pádraig's favorite performances. He read the long version this year, ignoring the sighs of the parishioners in the front pews as they realized that he was not going to omit the sections marked as optional by brackets in the missal.   He plowed on nonetheless.   Sometimes, he thought, you have to take it on the chin to teach the faithful. Whether they like it or not. This recitation, after all, told the story at the heart of the faith, and it began with the humiliation and self-sacrifice of someone who might have chosen otherwise. On this last point, Pádraig privately admitted some doubt. He wondered beneath the words he read aloud, Is selflessness noble when it's fate, not choice? How noble is it to just give in to fate, not choose sacrifice?

He had plowed on, unperturbed, when Willie Gillooly, his friend from the Beach Club, and a normally reliable deacon hadn't shown up. It was nine years now that he and Willie had been doing the Passion reading together. Willie made a fine Jesus in the reading, and Pádraig was content to read the role of the narrator as it was more instructional in nature. They didn't even need to rehearse any more, though Pádraig had come to look forward to the private drink they usually had together on the Saturday night before, just to run through it one more time. Willie hadn't shown up for that either, but Pádraig toted it up to a misunderstanding.

The parishioners followed along for their part, voicing the Jews who had played out the welcoming of Jesus into Jerusalem as a hero, then as Pilate's scapegoats in Jesus's crucifixtion. The narrative called for no waving of the palms, but Pádraig's eye vaguely caught Fianna, next to Bertie, swaying absently with the palm fronds raised above her shoulder in her left hand.

Pádraig recycled his usual homily for this time of year, exhorting a deepened reverence for the holy week observances. "I might mention in this regard that Our Lord would be equally welcoming of the men of the parish at our masses as well as the women who attend so faithfully," he said, smiling at the congregation. "And I note that the introductory matter to today's mass, as found in your missal, urges that a good confession, as early in the week as possible, not waiting until Holy Saturday, will clear the way for a more meaningful observance." He distributed his gaze over the full measure of the congregation. The few men standing in the back shifted uncomfortably, anticipating the raising of the same subject at tea at home later in the day.

Finally, he dismissed the parish and walked to the back of the church to shake hands, deliver short blessings and say good-byes. He dodged the odd stray palm cluster, its sharp edges more of a weapon than a toy in the hands of a toddler raised to eye level in the arms of his mum.

Bertie was one of the last to shuffle past him in the line, her arm hooked through Fianna's. She leaned in to speak to Pádraig, and he realized she had deliberately trailed to the back of the line for a more private word.

"Father," she began, he voice already cracking, "Fianna just wanted to, I mean Fianna and Ned and I just wanted to say how much...." She was in tears before she could complete the sentence. He enfolded her in his left arm, tucked her up under the wing of his purple vestments. He smiled at Fianna. "I'm glad to see that you're looking better, Fianna." He drew a small sign of the cross on her forehead with his right thumb and touched her cheek with his palm. She cast her eyes down; no smile came to her face and she said nothing. "Why don't you run ahead to home, tell your da that mum will be home directly. We're just going to have a word and a prayer here, your mother and I."

Her shoulders drooped and her small frame shifted forward as she pushed toward home.

Once Pádraig was sure she was out of earshot, he asked Bertie, "Is it any better then with Ned?" Bertie's face twisted and she began crying again. "No, Father. I can't say that it is. I don't know what it will take to make him soften his heart toward her."

"Give it a little time and a lot of prayers, Bertie. It will come to him." She shuffled off in the direction of home.

Pádraig rushed to the sacristy, eager to disburden himself of the heavy vestments. The altar boys who had just finished service, twin brothers, Jeffrey and Gregory Garrity, leapt to their feet upon his entrance. They had changed into their street clothes and awaited Pádraig's inspection of their effort to put the sacristy in order. He flipped the purple vestment over his head and into its place in the armoire and glanced about the surfaces of the sacristy, nodding and smiling. "You lads have done a fine job, here and on the altar today. The only remark I might make is that whichever one of you was the crozier," he paused and looked quizzically at the two; he hadn't a clue which boy was which. "'Twas me, Father, Jeffrey."

"Ah, Jeffrey, I know that giant cross is a bit heavy, but try to hold it up a bit higher so the bottom edge doesn't hit the steps of the altar as you go up." He smiled to make sure that the correction was received as gently as he intended.

"Yes, Father."

"You might tell your mum you need an extra rasher on mornings you serve mass to give you a boost of energy." He patted Jeffrey's shoulder, and the boy smiled. "I'll ask her to give one to Gregory, too, in case we switch places," he said.

"Good idea!" Pádraig exclaimed and saw them out the door.

He walked briskly back to the rectory, looking forward more than usual to his Sunday dinner. The main perquisite of rectory life was that the best cooks in the village vied for the position of housekeeper to the pastor. The most recent effort to fill the position, already seventeen years past, found Mrs. O'Flannelly. She reliably produced roast beef and root vegetables on Sundays and a rotating wheel of chicken and lamb throughout the rest of the week. When Pádraig began agitating a few years ago for more frequent salads, she melted in tears, thinking he had all along silently disliked her longstanding menus. It had taken a week of coaxing for Pádraig to convince her to discuss the matter and allow him to explain that he merely wanted to add the salads to her undeniably delicious meals, purely to satisfy his emerging understanding of the importance of greens in a man's diet.

He was just standing behind his chair, forming a prayer of thanks for food and health, when Mrs. O'Flannelly rushed in, wiping her hands on her apron. "I'm so sorry, Father, to interrupt your dinner, and me still in my apron, forgive me, but Bertie Gunning's at the kitchen door, all upset and wanting to talk to you. I told her you were at dinner, but she's looking just tortured. Will you see her?"

Pádraig replaced his napkin. "Yes, of course, I'll come right away." He followed Mrs. O'Flannelly through to the kitchen. Bertie stood by the breakfast table, supporting herself with one arm. She was pale, and her supporting arm was shaking.

" Father, she's gone."

"What do you mean, 'gone'? We both just saw her, not thirty minutes ago, headed for home."

"I know, I know, Father. I went home, straightaway, after a short stop at the shops for Ned's newspaper. No more than five minutes. Maybe ten at the most. I asked Ned 'where's Fianna?' and he said he hadn't seen her since we both left for church. He said she never came home after mass."

"But that's impossible. There just aren't that many places for her to go between the church and your cottage. Does she have friends between here and there she might have stopped to see?"

"No, no friends, Father, no friends at all."

"That's very strange, Bertie. Is Ned sure she didn't come home at all? Could she be in the house but hiding from him?"

"He says not. He says he was sitting on the porch in the front for the whole of the morning and she didn't come up the path."

"It just doesn't sound right, Bertie. Why don't I drive out there with you. We can peek up some lanes along the way, see if she might have taken a longer way home so that she wouldn't arrive before you. And I can talk with Ned to see whether he might have taken a break from his vigil on the porch, diligent though I know him to be about such things as sitting around, when she might have slipped into the house."

"Oh, Father, but you must have your dinner, I can't take you away from that."

"Nonsense, Bertie. Mrs. O'Flannelly's cooking is timeless -- by which I mean it tastes just as wonderful whenever you get to enjoy it." He smiled at Mrs. O'Flannelly to head off her exasperation over another meal that would have to be reheated.

6.

Pádraig rolled the Escort slowly through the village as both he and Bertie swiveled their heads to try to spot a clue of Fianna. Not a sign emerged before they were at the foot of the path to the Gunning's home. Still reluctant to try to nudge the Escort up the rutted path, Pádraig parked as far off the main road as he dared without tipping into the ditch off the shoulder and went around to open the door for Bertie. They picked a careful route up to the house in the grass, staying out of the tracks made muddy by Thursday's rain.

The front door of the Gunning cottage stood open, and Pádraig made out Ned's figure pacing back and forth in the hallway, one hand clutching the other. They climbed the porch steps, Pádraig striding ahead toward Ned. He glanced at the rag Ned was using to cradle his left hand. It was red with blood, soaked through. Bertie saw it at the same time. "Ned, what have you done to your hand?" she asked, rushing forward to unwind the bandage to inspect the damage.

"It's nothing," Ned insisted. "One of the goats bit me."

"A goat? Which one?" Bertie asked as she worked to rewind and tighten the bandage.

"Sheebah did it. Was trying to give her a nibble of carrot and she bit me." He stared at the bandage as Bertie worked.

Pádraig glanced around as much of the house as he could see from the hallway as he waited for the moment when they could turn back to the business at hand. As sorry as he was for Ned's hand, Fianna's disappearance seemed far more urgent. His eyes turned back to Ned, whose trousers sagged at the knees, fairly covering his shoes. He can't have been going about like that in the yard, Pádraig thought. He'd have tripped and broken his neck in the mud.

"Ned, where's you belt?" he asked.

"Oh, I...I'm not sure I put it on this morning." Bertie looked up at Ned. "Sure, you did. You came down without it and I went up and got it for you." She looked back at Pádraig in puzzlement.

"Well, where is it now?" Pádraig asked quietly.

"What the devil does it matter where my belt is? My hand is bitten, right down to the bone!"

Pádraig stepped forward, his face inches from Ned's. "If you had it earlier, and don't have it now, I want to know what you used it for in between times, that's the matter."

Bertie stepped out on the porch and returned with the belt, its edge, toward the middle of the loop, slick with blood. "Oh, Ned! What have you done? Where's Fianna?"

Ned sank into the hallway bench, still clutching his hand. "She's no good, that one. She needed a good smack with the belt, she did. Still does! She came at me like a banshee. She bit me as soon as she saw the belt come off. She bit me!"

Pádraig clenched his jaw and examined the belt. "But you did hit her and you split her skin, didn't you, Ned? Where did you hit her?"

"Right here in the hallway, I hit her."

Pádraig threw down the belt to prevent himself from lashing Ned with it. "No, you idiot. Where did you hit her? From what part of her wasting body is she bleeding?"

Ned fell silent for a moment. "The forehead. Near her eye, the right one."

"You let your child run of the house bleeding from the head?" Pádraig asked incredulously. Bertie began a low moaning. Pádraig took her arm. "Come on, Bertie. Not a

29

moment to lose." He rushed her, quickly as he could, back towards the car.

7.

Pádraig rolled off Mullaghmore Head and onto the straightaway into Cliffoney. Mullaghmore was too small to merit its own garda station, and even too small to earn a passthrough by one of the patrols more than twice a week. Cliffoney was the closest place to obtain official help, . Bertie fretted along the way, barely convinced that she and Pádraig were doing the right thing.

"Are you sure, Father? Is it the best thing to involve the police? Mightn't they just dismiss it as a family quarrel?"

"I doubt it, Bertie. Regardless of why she left, which they no doubt would regard as a domestic squabble, she's gone away with her head bleeding. We need their help to find her. There's no telling how much she's bleeding or whether she'll look for help on her own. We're here on the disappearance, not on the events leading up to it."

"I suppose you're right. Though it seems a fine line to me, Father. I haven't the mind you do, but it seems a bit risky thinking we can raise one without the other coming up."

"We'll do the best we can, Bertie. We need the help. They can fan out and help us find her much more quickly than we can on our own."

Pádraig pulled in along the curb near the garda station.

There was little competition for parking on a Sunday afternoon, so Bertie would have little distance to walk, good for her in her worried condition.

The garda station had a musty smell that wafted out at Pádraig as he pushed the door open for Bertie. She hesitated for a moment, unused to putting herself ahead of a priest at a doorway. Pádraig smiled gently and urged her ahead with a nod.

The lone garda looked up from his desk over his reading glasses as they entered. He bounced to his feet when he saw Pádraig's collar. "Good afternoon," he called out, approaching the service counter.

"Good afternoon, Officer Finney," Pádraig returned the greeting, glancing down at the man's name badge above his shirt pocket. "We're over from Mullaghmore, in need of your help. I'm Father Hart from St. Molaise back up on the head and this is Bertie Gunning. Her daughter's gone missing. Sixteen years old. Named Fianna Gunning."

Finney reached to his right for the top page on a stack of forms. "I'm sorry to hear, Mrs. Gunning. I'll just take a report then we'll see what we can do. When did you notice her missing?"

"This afternoon, after church."

Finney looked up sharply. "She's only gone missing this afternoon? That's hardly missing at all for a sixteen year old girl. You've checked the shops and such, I assume, the usual places she might go, friends' houses?"

Pádraig stepped in, "It's a small village, Officer, not many places for her to go and we've checked them all. Most establishments are closed, it being Sunday afternoon. And she keeps to herself after school. No close friends to speak of."

"Still, it can't have been three hours yet. That's just a long walk in these parts, you know. Or she might have hopped on a bus, over to Bundoran or down to Sligo Town. The fare's not dear on Sundays. Most likely that's it. It's small comfort to you until she's back under your roof, but I'll tell you that we see this all the time here in Cliffoney and about these parts. The teenagers get restless. Not enough to do, not enough to entertain them. It's worse out in your village, I imagine. In fact, I've heard some of the cheekier lads call the place 'Mulla-bore' there being almost no diversions over there as I understand it." He stopped and smiled blandly. Pádraig's palm rubbed the counter, giving his hand an alternative to slapping the man. Pádraig lit up his own smile.

"Well, I hope you're right. You may very well be right on the money, but still we'd like you to take a report and send some officers to help us look for her." He leaned in confidentially. "Officer, the matter is that she's not been well lately. She may be in need of medical help."

Finney stood quietly for a moment. "By the by, where is the girl's father? Is he not concerned for her? It's not a domestic row, is it, that sent her on her way?"

"No, no, nothing at all like that. He's waiting at home in case she should come back," Bertie said, louder and more quickly than Pádraig thought Finney might find convincing. It was a delicate act, this, giving enough information to bring the garda out, but not so much as to cause another firestorm in the House of Gunning. Finney slowly replaced the form on the top of the stack to his right, untouched by his pen.

"Listen, Father, Mrs. Gunning, with great respect, I think your alarm is premature. She'll be back by tomorrow if she's like any of the other teenagers I've seen careen through Carbury Barony in the last ten years. Oh, I think you'd find her to be unique, entirely unlike the crowd you're thinking of, Pádraig thought. "There's nothing I can do today, anyway," Finney continued, obviously eager to get back to his newspaper. "I'm the only one on duty. I'd have to call in help from Bundoran, and we only do that in an emergency. You won't like to hear it, but a person fifteen years of age or older isn't even officially considered missing for seventy-two hours."

Bertie's face tightened and she began to cry. Finney patted her hand. "Now, Mrs. Gunning, I know it's difficult, but try not to worry. Give another pass through the village, take look here and there and you may find her yet today. If she's not back by Wednesday next, come back and see us and we'll take a report." He patted her again. "But I'm certain that's not going to be necessary." She continued to cry and Pádraig put his arm around her and glared at Finney, deploying his most effective gaze of rebuke and hoping he'd relent. Finney opened his mouth then shut it. Finally, he said, "Maybe I can make this a bit easier, ma'am. We can't start looking until Wednesday, that's the policy. But if she's not back by tomorrow, Monday, let's say by noon, give us a call and we'll drive out to your home and take statements from you and the husband and make a report out there. Save you the trip back to Cliffoney and we'll have the paperwork done in the very unlikely event that we need to start searching on Wednesday. How would that be?" He smiled, happy with his own helpfulness.

Bertie stood bolt upright. "No, no, that's not necessary. Not at all. We'll come back if she's not home by Wednesday, come back and ask for help then if that's the way the law handles it. Thank you, but we'll come back. Father may be able to give me a ride, but in any event, it's not a far walk." She gripped her purse. "Father, if you don't mind, I think it would be better to head back to the village and look around as Mr. Finney says."

Pádraig said a perfunctory word of thanks to Finney and hurried to catch up with Bertie. He found her on the sidewalk outside the building.

"Bertie, I don't understand. Why wouldn't it have been better to take him up on the offer of coming out to the house to give things a head start in case we need the help?"

"Father, don't you see? If they come out to the house, they'll take the measure of Ned, and that will be the end of the whole thing." She was crying again. "Why shouldn't she want to run away from such a one?" She looked around to see who might be witnessing her humiliation. She struggled to breathe evenly and regain herself.

Pádraig had a slow dawn of what he was hearing. "Bertie, has he hurt her before?" She nodded. "Has he hurt you?" She turned away from Pádraig. "I don't want to talk about that, Father, I'll be all right. I need Fianna back at home, and I can't have the garda asking too much about what he's like as a father and a husband. What if they come by when he's taken a drop too many? I can't lose him, too, Father!" She was whispering, but fiercely.

Pádraig stood rooted to the sidewalk for a moment. I have a knack for this, it seems. Making things worse by trying to make them better, he thought. "Come on, Bertie. Let's get you back home." He enclosed Bertie in the Escort. "Home," he added to himself as he walked to the driving side of the car. "Such as it is."

8.

Pádraig drove Bertie back to Mullaghmore. They argued all the way about whether he'd take her to the end of her lane, which he insisted he do, or whether he'd let her off in the center of the village near the quay across from the church. She insisted she needed the walk back the rest of the way home to clear her head and compose herself for whatever Ned might have in store for her. In the end, she prevailed, and Pádraig added it to the list of arguments he'd had with women, and lost.

He parked the car behind the rectory, but didn't go in. He pocketed the keys and walked across Castle Road to Beach Club. The official name of the establishment, Beach Hotel and Leisure Club, made it eligible, because it offered overnight accommodations, to operate a residents' bar This exempted the pub from the closing hours law, and allowed it to remain open until the single-digit hours of the morning. Technically, the residents' bar was only available to persons paying for lodging in the hotel, but at this geographic remove from the law, no one seemed to care.

The availability of the residents' bar also gave Beach Club the flexibility to offer Sunday drinking hours earlier than the usual opening time after tea. All of this meant that Pádraig knew exactly where to go mid-afternoon on a spring Sunday to recruit his search party.

He pushed open the door to the jingle of tiny bells meant to alert a busy barkeep of a new patron. Heads bobbed up above pint and shot glasses to meet his entrance, then came the slow scrape of chairs pushed back from tables as the patrons stood to observe the arrival of clergy. The men at the bar slid off their stools, and stood leaning upon them for safety's sake, except for one man who glanced over his shoulder at Pádraig and then curled back over his book and his cider. Mary O'Neill half rose from her table.

Pádraig surveyed the room and cleared his throat. "Gentlemen of the parish, and Mary,I need your help. Right away. Fianna, the daughter of the Gunnings has gone missing this afternoon. The garda will do nothing until Wednesday according to their policy, which they adhere to against common sense. That's too long to wait. I need a search party, all of you, to cover the ground of the head, street by street, field by field and building by building. Door to door. Check below decks of every boat at the quay. We must start right away and make the best use of the remaining daylight." He turned his shoulder to the door to initiate the deployment. No one moved.

"Begging your pardon, Father," ventured Martin O'Flaherty, "but is it really all so urgent as that? Won't she likely come home on her own by end of day?"

Pádraig squared his hips toward Martin. "Yes, Martin, I believe it is urgent. As you are aware, being so well informed about the issues of the village, Fianna has not been well. We can't have her about somewhere in her condition."

"And what condition is that, Father?" asked Mary Curran from her table near the fireplace.

"We needn't go into that now, Mary. Suffice it to say she's not well and needs our help."

The men shifted about uncomfortably, looking one to the other. A few sipped their drinks as they stood. Darren O'Conor drained his pint and put the glass down on the bar loudly. "Well, right then. Let's get about it." He gestured to a group of four men nearest the door. "You lot, take a walk.

Cover the streets. All of them. Knock on every door you pass and ask have they seen the Gunning girl or any sign of her." He collected his cap and nodded toward three men leaning against the wall near the fire exit. "You fellows come with me down to the quay. We'll poke about and see what we find." The bar was quickly cleared except for Willie behind the bar with Ellen O'Rourke, the proprietor; the unfamiliar man at the bar remained hunched over his book. Pádraig wondered whether he might be deaf. Mary had finished her lager and slipped out with the men, avoiding any particular assignment. Willie removed his apron and rolled down his sleeves.

"Where do you think you're going?" Ellen asked, glaring at him.

"I'm going to help Father look wherever he's going to look."

"No, you are not. You're on the clock here. Do you expect me to polish the bar glasses myself? And serve the drinks on top of that?"

Willie looked down at his hands. He was used to this treatment, but not in front of others. "Well, I hardly think it'll be busy for the rest of the afternoon with everyone out helping Father look for the girl."

"'Everyone'? Just the few who were here, I'd say. I doubt the town will be pouring into the streets to help the Gunnings," she snorted. "Apologies, Father. I know it's your job to be charitable to everyone in the parish. But the Gunnings? In any event, I can't spare Willie. And goodness knows I can't leave myself. As soon as I turn my back he starts the long pours, even when I'm still on the premises." She exited past the loo and into her office near the kitchen.

"Sorry, Father," Willie said retying his apron.

"It's not your fault, Willie. I understand. I suppose it was something of the same that kept you away from Mass this morning. We missed you." Willie shrugged and turned back to work, holding pint glasses up to the light to see which needed polishing. Padriag approached the stranger at the bar.

"Excuse me. I wondered if I might introduce myself." The man looked up from his book giving Pádraig his first good look at him. He was past thirty years in age, Pádraig judged, but not much more than that. His hair was sandy colored, and longer and fuller than then fashionable in the west, thick with waves. His beard was light, almost invisible, but hadn't been shaved in a few days, Pádraig could tell when the man turned his head. The most memorable part of that first look, Pádraig would later recall, was the man's eyes, which were a bright, wolfen blue and seemed to transmit their own light rather than reflect the glow of the room.

The man hesitated a moment as if he objected to the interruption, then stood and extended his hand. "Attergood. Stephen."

Pádraig shook his hand and noted it was smooth and uncalloused. "Pleased to meet you. I'm Father Hart, the priest of the parish."

"So I gathered," said Stephen, smiling slightly.

"I don't suppose I could persuade you to join the search party?"

"Well, I don't see what I could add, being so new here. I don't know the girl or the family at all. I wouldn't know where to begin to look, and it's not likely many people here would open their doors to a stranger as I am to them."

"Perhaps not. But still, every pair of legs and arms can help. And some fresh thinking could be useful. I think you can tell, if you were listening, that the Gunnings are not well loved here."

Stephen sighed and boosted himself back up on the barstool. He was shorter than Pádraig by at least half a foot, perhaps nine inches, Pádraig judged. "I did hear that part. It would be nosy for me to ask why that's the case at this point, so we'll leave that be. Why don't you tell me something about the girl and let's see what comes to mind?"

Pádraig slid onto the adjacent barstool, elbows on the bar. "Her name is Fianna, and she's fifteen years old as of last December, the twenty-first."

"A winter solstice child," Stephen said.

"What? Yes, I suppose that's right. She's enrolled in the

school, has good attendance. A very quiet girl. Intelligent, but keeps to herself. Her marks are good, but from what I see, teaching religion and Irish, she's distracted. You can't tell if she's listening to the lecture or something far off in her imagination."

"Friends? What are they like?"

"Nonexistent. She's the class stand off. Eats lunch by herself, walks home by herself. There's a boy named Aidan whom I've seen try to speak to her a few times, but it didn't look successful."

"Churchgoer?"

"Faithful to it. She comes to mass with her mother on Sundays, takes communion, never looks me in the eye. She was part of the confirmation class last year, which was a trial. She never quite got all the words down for the Apostles' Creed. The concepts, yes, but the words, no. If I hadn't been the examiner myself, she'd have gotten failing marks for it, but I couldn't see the reason to do that and make her wait another four years until the bishop got around to us again."

"Gets on well with her family? Parents? Siblings?"

"An only child. Her mother holds her dear and would do anything for her. She's only home now because I insisted she look after her own exhaustion."

"What about the father? I assume there is one?"

"Yes. The father. Ned. That's a bit more complicated. He's got a temper. And no patience for a teenage girl's moods, I'm afraid.

"And the illness you referred to, if you feel you can tell me?"

"Yes, in discretion, if you don't mind. The last thing I need to do is fuel these gossip mongers around here with too much time on their hands."

"Of course."

Pádraig glanced around to ensure that Ellen hadn't crept back into the room and that Willie was distracted with the washing up of the bar glasses that the search party had left behind. He lowered his voice. "It's an eating disorder. Bulimia. And anorexia to boot. You're familiar with these illnesses?"

"Ah, yes. Only too much so. I assume that it's the usual reaction she's getting from her father and those in the village who've figured it out? What's wrong with her, must be nutters, serves her right, blame the victim, that sort of thing?"

"Yes, more or less. But her mother and I have been trying to help her get treatment. So far unsuccessfully."

"Good on you for trying to assist," Stephen said, taking a swig of his cider. "But too bad your faith demonizes illness. That can't be helpful to her around here."

"What? We don't demonize illness. Where did you get that daft idea?"

"Oh, sure you do. Illness is punishment for something, isn't it? Isn't that how it goes?"

"Not in my book. But listen, are you planning to be helpful, or are you just going to pick a fight? Because I've got something important to do." Pádraig rose to leave. Stephen put his hand on Pádraig's arm. "Sorry, please don't go. My fault. It's just that I haven't had an intelligent dialogue on anything that matters since I got here a month ago." He finished his cider and pushed the glass away. "So. Tell me where her hideaway is. We'll start there."

"Hideaway? What makes you think she has a hideaway?"

Stephen cocked his head as if he suddenly doubted the priest's intelligence. "Well, Father…I suppose I really do have to call you that, don't I? Anyway, you've just told me about an alienated, probably very angry teenage girl who has no friends and doesn't get on with her father, who may be abusive to her for all I know, but that doesn't matter at the moment. She's the dreamy sort who lives in her own head a lot and is not having much fun at home. In fact, her whole situation upsets her so much that she's apparently decided she doesn't deserve to eat food, or keep it down once she's eaten it. Of course she has a hideaway. Who wouldn't want a place to run away to in those circumstances, Father?"

Pádraig blinked, dumbed by the analysis. "Okay, makes sense. But I wouldn't know where to start in looking for it."

"Is there a place on the head where no one is supposed to

go?"

Pádraig thought for a moment. "The grounds of the castle, Cassiebawn."

"Right, then. Let's start there." Stephen shoved his book in his rucksack. "Lead the way, Father."

9.

Pádraig set off for the castle at a brisk pace, but quickly realized that Stephen was having to make the walk more of a trot to keep up with him in compensation for the difference in their heights. He smiled to himself about this unexpected advantage, and slowed down discreetly.

"How far is it to the castle grounds?" Stephen asked, regaining the rhythm of his breathing now that Pádraig had slowed down.

"Not far," Pádraig said. "Perhaps a half mile. We can see if there's a gap in the fence at the nearest point. But if we have to circumnavigate the whole property, that's a big walk, I'm afraid, and overland across some rugged fields."

"Oh, no problem for me. I've done nothing but hike since I got here, trying to get to know the place. I'm a bit limited, of course, by the property boundaries. I'd hate to discover I was unwelcome on the inside of a fence by meeting a bull. Or the sparky end of a rifle."

"Well, perhaps we can walk together one of these days. I know which fields have a bull in residence and anyone walking with me is unlikely to to see the wrong end of a weapon." They walked on a bit in silence. Pádraig opened a topic, hoping his curiosity would sound friendly. "You said you've been here for a month, I think."

"That's right, I did say."

"What brings you here?"

"Family."

"Oh. You have family here?"

"I do now. I helped my mother move up from Chapelizod near Dublin. Staying on with her for a bit."

"I see. I don't know your mother, I'm sure, and I don't know of any Attergoods otherwise in the parish."

"I suppose you're asking why anyone would choose to move here. Middle of nowhere, et cetera?"

"It's my home, too, no need to disrespect it. But yes, that's more or less what I'm asking."

"Uncle Randall. My mother's brother. Last name Connell on her side."

"Ah, yes. I did know Randall. Nice fellow, saw him from time to time at the post. Not a churchgoer, though."

"No, not at all. Runs in the family. Except for my mother. You might see her in the pews from time to time."

"I didn't know he'd passed, sorry to say."

"Well, he didn't ask for your professional services, so I can understand how it might have passed notice."

"All the same, I'm sorry for your loss."

"Very kind of you to say."

They walked past the shops and the church and onto the stretch of the road that parallels the marshes off to the west of the quay. Not a stick of building ever went up along the marshes, where the muck would suck down the footings of a house sooner than a family could move in. The south side of the road was clear of buildings, too for reasons that no one remembered for certain, but some thought it had to do with the occupants of the castle insisting upon a clear view to the water.

Soon enough, they arrived at the gates of the castle, two towering iron grills bound together with a giant lock and double-secured with a chain and padlock. Stephen surveyed the arrangement "I guess we won't be walking up to the front door and ringing the bell. There's an intercom, though, we could..."

"Actually, I wouldn't do that just yet," Pádraig said quickly before Stephen's finger touched the button. "The caretaker, Edward Larkin, he's a bit prickly. He's unlikely to let us in unless we've got good reason to believe that she's in there. For that, we need a bit of evidence. I suggest that we take a walk around the grounds, on this side of the fence. If she's in there, she'd have had to find a way in, which isn't easy, I assure you. Larkin has been caretaker here since we were teenagers together here in the village, and his father had the job before him. They've made it a point of pride that not a single poacher has been on the land in decades, a credit to how they've cinched the place up. We'll see how secure it is against an angry teenager, and if we find a way she might have gotten in, we'll talk to him about looking inside the grounds."

Pádraig and Stephen started off in a southerly direction around the curved wall of the castle. It was a drystone fence up to eight feet, made of carefully placed, interlocking stones with out an ounce of mortar, but the drystone technique ensured a wall as strong as concrete. Above the drystone wall were hedges planted inside the wall and running up to a total of twelve feet. Stephen judged the combination reasonably impervious.

Stephen managed to focus his attention mostly on the task of finding gaps in the wall, but couldn't help being distracted by the view over the fields to his right. They rolled and lifted, until they finally swooped down to the rocks and the sea. Cattle and horses dotted the pastures, some penned in by fences, but some apparently left to their own good sense not to wander too far away.

They finished their circumambulation of the south and west portions of the wall, and turned left to inspect the north wall, which was furthest from the entrance they had first approached. On this wall, they found another entrance, apparently meant for tradesmen's and merchants' trucks as it had a wider road bed and more modest gates, but equally well secured as the main entrance.

A tenth of a mile past this entrance, as Pádraig and

Stephen walked together, they were suddenly and oddly separated as Stephen's path, hugging more closely to the wall than Pádraig's sloped down into the earth.

Stephen looked up at Pádraig. "What the hell is this? Did you know this was here?"

"No, I didn't. I have no parishioners in this direction, so I never come this way, and I never played here as a boy."

"Of course not. It was against the rules."

"What is it then? What do you see?

"It's a tunnel, made of stone, as if it's going into something else, a chamber of some sort." Stephen reached into his rucksack and pulled out a battery operated torch. He switched it on and let it play against his hand to check that the batteries were still good. He flopped his rucksack up to where Pádraig stood. "No reason to take more than necessary into a tight space." He crouched and duck-walked into the space. Pádraig suddenly envied him his slight stature.

After a few minutes, Stephen's torch beam reappeared, playing on the insides of the stone archway at the start of the tunnel. Pádraig had moved down from the berm above the slope into the tunnel and was waiting, hands on knees, for Stephen at the mouth of the tunnel. Stephen looked at Pádraig solemnly. "You've got to come in. I think this is the place."

"Will I fit, do you think?" Pádraig asked as Stephen turned back into the tunnel.

"I think so," Stephen said, his voice muffled by the stone. "Try walking on your heels, down low. I don't think you'll need to crawl. Just keep at it, a little distance at a time."

Not crawling sounded fine to Pádraig, so he crouched down low as he could and worked his way down the tunnel, which took a sharp turn to the right before culminating into a beehive-shaped chamber of corbelled stone, capacious enough for him to stand up in. In fact, it looked as though a dozen people could crowd into the space. Stephen had lit some candles on his first pass in, and Pádraig could see clearly the ornate Celtic carvings in walls of the chamber.

"What is this place?" Pádraig said with astonishment.

"If I'm right in my history, this is an ancient pagan worship place that probably also served as a tomb. You can see the indentations in the shelves along the wall. Those would have been sinks where cremated remains of the clan associated with this place would have been laid to rest. The Druids, or their forbears predating the naming of them, dug out these places everywhere. This style is called a crown tomb because of the shape of the interior. They also come in a wedge style, which I'm sure I'd find frighteningly claustrophobic. The ceiling comes down as the walls narrow. Passage style, cruciform, all pretty tight. We got lucky ending up in a crown tomb." Stephen walked up close to the walls to examine the carvings more closely with his torch."

"I suppose they're all below ground?"

"They were build that way, although sometimes they were built by making a giant mound of earth, then burrowing into that. With erosion taking away the manufactured mound over time, sometimes all you get to see is the stone entrance, with a giant rock placed above two pillars to serve as the lintel. But yes, they all started out underneath. Below ground seemed more in touch with the nature the Druids were uniting themselves with, it seems. These places are a dime a dozen around this part of the country, if you're looking. Carrowkreel is the most famous one nearby, excavated enough for tourists to visit. But don't try driving out there in winter. You'll get stuck in the field, and there's not a soul about willing to help you."

"You speak from experience, it appears."

"I'm afraid so. It was a long walk back. On Christmas Day, no less."

"Sorry to hear. I suppose we should look around. You evidently think there's signs of Fianna here?

"Clearly signs of someone who's spent -- or is spending -- a great deal of time here," Stephen said gesturing to a table and chair arrangement at the far end of the chamber from the entrance tunnel.

"The chair looks familiar," Pádraig said. "Like one I've sat in at the Gunnings." He turned it on its legs a bit. "Yes, this is the same style. Not to say that other families haven't bought just the same, but this is what they have at the home."

Stephen walked the perimeter of the tomb, taking inventory. "A cooking kettle, looks like it's been used here. There's fireblack on the bottom, and it does smell a bit smoky in here. She'd have to stick to a small fire since there's no ventilation to speak of here. Looks like a bedroll over here, rolled up and stowed away rather neatly. This looks like a little desk. I wonder where she'd have gotten that." Pádraig joined Stephen near the desk. "It's from the school. We replaced a few of them last year for broken hinges beyond fixing and the like. You'd be surprised what a licking our young men and women of the village can give the furnishings." He lifted the lid of the desk to show the broken hinge and Stephen's torch light fell on a small stack of composition notebooks." Stephen scooped them up. "There are three of them. Do you recognize the handwriting?" Pádraig flipped through the book on the top of the stack. "Yes, it's Fianna's hand, I'm sure of it. It looks just like her homework." Stephen tucked the notebooks under his arm and gave the tomb one last going over with his flashlight. "I think we've done all we can here for the moment. This is definitely her hideaway. But she's not hiding in it at the moment, and we can't be sure if she's visited here this afternoon since she went missing."

Pádraig licked his thumb and forefinger and pinched out the flames of the three small candles Stephen had lighted. "I'd noticed a few of these votives missing from the church in the last little while. I guess it's harmless enough to let her keep them." He took a last look around the tomb. "At least there's no blood. That's a good sign."

"What?" said Stephen sharply. Pádraig quietly rebuked himself for telling Stephen more than he'd intended. "You were expecting to find blood?" Stephen demanded.
"Not expecting, more fearing. When last seen she had a cut on her forehead and appeared to be bleeding."

"You might have mentioned that. It does put a certain urgency to the search. You might have gotten more cooperation back at Beach Club if you'd told them."

"Then they'd be wanting to know how was she hurt, and who did it to her, and isn't her father a drunkard, aren't the Gunnings all a worthless sort, why should we help them? I doubt it would have helped."

"I see your point. Let's get back out in the daylight and see more about what's in these books." They hunched and wriggled back out through the low, narrow passage way. Stephen and Pádraig simultaneously took a deep breath as they emerged.

"God, what a confining place. If you weren't depressed before you went in, you'd be layered with it by the time you came out if you spent as much time in there as she appears to have. Let's have a quick look at the notebooks and we'll decide whet to do with them, leave them here or take them with us." He handed one of the notebooks to Pádraig, opened one himself and put the third under his arm. They read silently for a moment.

"It looks like a journal, a diary of some sort," Pádraig said quietly. "But it's not a chronicle, not like girls like to do. Not 'dear diary, here's what happened today.'"

"No, it's not that. It's all written in verse, but it has daily entries as if it corresponds somehow to the days of her life here. We'll need to read it more closely, We should take it with us."

"Are you sure that's the right thing to do? Obviously, they're very personal to her if you're right about what they are. I'd feel terrible if she came here and couldn't find them and it sent her into a panic of some sort."

"I see your point. I know what we'll do. You can leave her a note in the desk. We'll borrow a page from the back of this notebook, and you'll write her a kind note telling her that you took the books for safekeeping and she should please come home right now." Stephen handed Pádraig the paper and fished a Bic pen out of his rucksack. He gave Pádraig the book he'd been reading at Beach Club to use as a writing surface.

"I have to go back in there?" Pádraig said as he wrote.

"What, you think I should do it for you?" Stephen asked.

"Well, I was only thinking that it's a bit easier for you because of your...compactness."

"Great, here come the jokes about being short."

"I wouldn't dream of it. I'm merely pointing your God-given advantage in this situation," Pádraig said, smiling and handing Stephen the note

Stephen eased himself back through the passage, leaving Pádraig a moment to look around the place they'd just discovered. How could it have been here all this time and none of us knew about it but Fianna? How did she find it on her own? How long had she been coming here? He glanced down at the book Stephen had loaned him as a field desk. Yeats, Writings on Irish Folklore and Myths. An odd selection for barroom reading, Pádraig thought, but then realized he had never seen anyone in Beach Club anything at all.

Stephen's head appeared at the mouth of the entrance. "I left the note. But as I've been thinking about it, I don't think it will make much difference."

"Why is that?"

"If she left of her own will, she'd have had time to run by here and pick these up, precious as they seem to be to her. You can see here," Stephen said, leafing to the middle of one of the notebooks, "that this is the last entry in the one notebook that isn't full. It's dated yesterday." He tucked the notebook under his arm and opened another notebook. "And you can see here that the earliest entry goes back over a year ago. These notebooks were dear to her. She wouldn't have left without them if she had half a chance to grab them."

"And you're sure we should take them?"

"Absolutely. We may very likely learn something important from them."

Pádraig paused for a moment, then nodded. "Okay, we'll bring them along. We can always bring them back if that seems the better choice later." Stephen hustled to keep up with the priest. "Right, but if we do, it will be your turn to walk like a duck, I'm sure of that," Stephen said.

10.

Pádraig and Stephen walked back to the village square. As the curve of the road straightened out along the quay, they could see a small crowd, just about as numerous as the gathering in the bar two hours ago, milling about in the sun near the tables in front of Beach Club.

"What the devil are they doing back so soon," Pádraig demanded, scowling and quickening his step. Stephen gave up on the pace, and Pádraig shortly realized he'd left Stephen behind. He turned to him. "Put those notebooks in your rucksack, if you would, Stephen. They don't need to know what we've found."

Stephen rolled his eyes and complied. "Again," he said, "selective dissemination of important information. Why do you even ask for help if you won't bring them in on what you know?"

"Shh! Not now. We'll discuss it later. I have to deal with this lot."

Pádraig looked over the group. "How can you be done so soon with a thorough search? You can't have looked everywhere. Can't have knocked on all the doors as I told you to do. The circumstances are grave, gentlemen, and...."

Darren Healy stepped forward to interrupt him. "Begging

your pardon, Father, but we've looked all we need to look."

Pádraig stopped short, not sure whether to be elated or mournful, trying to read Darren's face for what news he had.

"What do you mean, Darren? Have you found her? Is she safe?" Stephen took note of the anxiety in the priest's voice. Understandable, he thought, when you have so few parishioners to begin with.

"No, no, Father, nothing like that. But we checked the quay and the moored boats as you said."

"And what did you find?"

"Well, Father," Darren said hitching his thumbs under his belt, "it's more a matter of what we didn't find."

"Darren, for the love of Mary and all the saints, tell me what it is you have to say!"

Darren looked to his left and to his right at his friends. "We accounted for all the boats, commercial, recreational, even the rowboats. Except one. Ned Gunning's boat is missing."

Pádraig stood silent for a moment. "Well, does anyone know, did he take it out this afternoon?"

The men looked among themselves, shifted, exchanged glances, looked back at the ground. It grew so quiet that Pádraig could hear the slumbered breathing of Orlando, the collie mongrel, mascot of Beach Club, lying in the sun. Connall Harris spoke up. "Father, isn't it obvious what's happened here? We all know the man drank and he did it."

Pádraig turned a deep crimson from the neck to the ears and forced himself to take three breaths before speaking. "Connall, we know nothing of the sort. And all of you hanging about a pub on Palm Sunday, let one of you who is free from sin cast the first stone against a man out here in the middle of nowhere, son of our melancholy ancestors, who lifts a glass to sip from time to time." He turned to Stephen and said quietly, "We've got to get out to the Gunning house quickly, before this mob soaks up more drink and heads out there."

here. Insert chapter ten text here. Insert chapter ten text here.

11.

Pádraig trotted back to the rectory for his car. He swung by the square and pushed the passenger side open for Stephen, who jumped in with the car still rolling.

"Thanks for slowing down," Stephen said as he settled himself in and looked for the seat belt.

"It's broken," Pádraig said, noticing Stephen's futile casting about for something to snap into the fastener. "Been meaning to get it seen to. Just hold on to something. Brace yourself against the dash."

"Brace myself against the dash? Are you mad? Let me out of the car," Stephen said, but Padriag was already picking up speed to climb the hill on Castle Road and skidding into the turn above the lookout over Red Islands. "No, I need you to come with me. If Ned's in a lather, an unfamiliar face may force him to be hospitable nonetheless. That's our nature in the west. Hospitality to a stranger always comes first. Your being there may make him a bit more reasonable."

"What am I, a lure? Why don't you just tie me to a stake in his front yard and see if he beats me or feeds me? This chap sounds like an ogre. What are you getting me into?"

Pádraig leaned forward to make sure he was staying off the margins of the road. They were still soft with the rain, and at this speed it would be easy to turn a small mistake into a disaster that would take them hours to dig out. "It's not as bad as all that. Let's just say I could use the help and a fresh set of eyes and ears on the situation. Bear with me."

Stephen endured the rest of the ride in terrified silence and was relieved when Pádraig stopped short at the end of a muddy, rutted lane. "We walk from here," Pádraig said briskly as he launched himself from the car." Stephen looked up the lane and down at his shoes. "I guess this is the last of these shoes," he said wistfully. "And I just bought them last month. In London." Pádraig called over his shoulder, "We'll find you some new brogues. Hurry now."

They walked the half mile up the lane and began to hear the shouting, faintly at first, but growing louder as they approached. No dogs greeted them, but Pádraig could see two pairs of eyes shining from under the porch where they were weathering the storm of anger ensuing in the house above. The words became more distinct as they climbed up on the porch, at least Ned's voice could be heard. "I told you not to bring her into this house. How many times did I tell you there was something wrong with the child? You're a vile, willful woman. I won't have it! Not in my house." There was an interlude, Bertie's words indistinct, but pleading in tone. Pádraig knocked loudly and sharply before Ned could return the volley. He made sure to make himself visible through the kitchen window when Ned looked out to see who was there. Ned stomped to the front door and flung it open.

Ned was flush red, disheveled, his shirt open to the middle of his chest, which heaved with his excited breathing. His eyes were still wide and protruded from the yelling. His jaw tightened when he saw Pádraig had brought company. Still, when his mouth open, his words were more or less civil.

"I'm afraid it's a bit of an inconvenient time for a pastoral visit, Father. We're having a conversation, the missus and I, about the girl. It's put a terrible worry on her, as you can imagine, Father. Perhaps you and your friend could come back tomorrow."

Pádraig took a step inside the house to prevent Ned from closing the door. Stephen took a step backwards, away from whatever was about to happen. "I'm afraid this won't keep until then. We have some news."

Bertie had been lingering in the kitchen, giving Ned his distance to talk to Pádraig, grateful for the respite from the bile. She edged out into the hallway. "Have you found her, Father? Is she safe?" Bertie seemed to smile and weep at the same time. Pádraig hated to disappoint her, so he delivered the news quickly.

"No, not yet. But Ned's boat is missing from the quay." He turned to Ned. "Do you know anything about that Ned? Did you take the boat out today?"

Ned slammed his fist on the hallway table. "Ah, Christ Almighty. This, and now they've stolen my boat!" He retrieved his glass from the kitchen, and Pádraig saw him drain it.

Pádraig called after him as Ned refilled his glass. "So you didn't take it out today, I gather. When was the last time you used it?"

"Yesterday," Ned shouted. I went fishing, caught nothing. Rode it up on the sand, pulled the motor up and knotted it to the concrete block as I usually do. Brought it up above the tide line since I had no need for it until at least as long as Tuesday afternoon's high tide. Then it practically floats itself."

Pádraig thought for a moment and Stephen dared to take a step into the hallway. "Bertie," Pádraig whispered, "this is very important. Is it true he's not been near the boat today?"

Bertie answered in a whisper, not sure why, but always a good idea when Ned was drinking in the afternoon. "It's true, Father. He's not been out of the house since I got back here, when you were with me after we went to the garda. Been in the house and at the bottle all afternoon."

"Wait a damn minute," Ned bellowed from the kitchen, he step quickening toward the three of them in the hallway. "What are you about here? The girl is missing, so's the boat and you're here asking me did I take the boat out. You're saying I killed the girl, aren't you now." Ned had refilled his glass, and the whiskey sloshed over its edges as he gesticulated.

Pádraig appeared stunned, lost for words that would defuse Ned. Stephen stepped forward. "Now, sir. Please don't take offense. This is just the logic of a process of elimination. Of course no one would think you'd do such harm to your own daughter, but..." Ned's left arm moved quickly, and Stephen recoiled from the shock of whiskey stinging his eyes and nostrils as Ned flung his drink at him.

"The devil take you, you queer little man. What do you mean coming into my house accusing me? And the both of you spent the afternoon, no doubt, down at the pub spreading gossip about me. Get out, both of you!" Stephen and Pádraig made a hasty retreat down the steps of the porch, looking over their shoulders as the door slammed behind them.

"Is it safe leaving Bertie there with him?" Stephen asked. "Not entirely, but I don't know what else we can do. He'll tire himself out soon; she'll open another bottle for him and he'll be asleep by sundown if it goes as best it can." They walked on a few paces and Pádraig stopped short and slapped his forehead. "Sundown! I almost forgot. I have an errand to run out to my mother's house. Come with me and I'll drop you at home after. It won't take long," he said as he handed a clean handkerchief to Stephen, "but use this to wipe the whiskey off your face. My mother doesn't like the smell of drink."

12.

Pádraig stopped at his mother's home long enough to
dispense communion to his mother, his aunt and her friend,
arrived from Dublin earlier that day. Stephen had begged to be
left alone in the car, claiming that the social engagement so far
in the day was enough to last him a week. But Pádraig had
pried him out of the car and into the house for a brief visit,
during which Pádraig's mother was apparently charmed to
meet him and complimented him with sincerity on his
"pleasant aftershave cologne." She really is getting on, Pádraig
thought. She's forgotten absolutely everything she used to
dislike.

Pádraig had intended the visit to be brief, but they didn't
get away until after a pot of tea. The moon was rising by the
time they were back on the road and Stephen was reminding
Pádraig of how to get to his uncle's house up on the hill past
the horse farm.

"Come in for a bit. Have a drink. You can even meet my
mother if she's still up. She almost certainly is. Even at my
age, I've got to be under the roof before she'll go to bed."

Pádraig followed Stephen across the porch and through
the unlocked front door. Mrs. Attergood sat in the parlor
reading, leaning toward the dim light of the electric lamp on

the table next to her chair. "Hello, mother," Stephen said warmly as he leaned over to kiss her on the cheek. "Look who I've reeled in as a visitor. Meet Father Hart." Mrs. Attergood started to push herself up from the chair. "No, no please don't get up," Pádraig said reaching out his hands to embrace hers. "It's late, and I only wanted to say hello to the mother of the man who's been so helpful to the parish today." Mrs. Attergood beamed at Stephen. "He's more than clever, this one. He went to university and has his philosophy doctorate, but I bet he didn't tell you that. Too modest. I keep telling him it's not prideful to say what's true about yourself." She snagged Stephen's hand in hers and squeezed it. Pádraig looked at Stephen. "Well, as you know, Mrs. Attergood, 'he who exalts himself shall be humbled, and he who humbles himself shall be exalted.'" Mrs. Attergood nodded thoughtfully, "From Matthew, I believe, and who would argue with that, but there's no point hiding your light under a bushel, now, is there Father." Pádraig chuckled, "You know your gospels, Mrs. Attergood. And at this late hour, I'll concede you've outgunned me on pertinent quotes." He turned to Stephen, "I should run along. Thank you for all of your help." Mrs. Attergood pushed herself up to standing. "Father, please stay a bit and visit with Stephen. He's made a great sacrifice moving away from England to be with me here, and he's got no friends to keep up with him in conversation. I'm going up to bed, but please visit as long as you like."

She started up the stairs. "Good night, mother," Stephen called after her. He motioned Stephen to a room across the entry hallway from the parlor. "I've set up a library of sorts over here." He slid open the double doors into their pockets inside the wall. "It's how Uncle Randall used the room, so the shelves were already installed." Two-thirds of the shelves, Pádraig judged, carried full loads of books. "I could only take a fraction of what I'd accumulated at university," Stephen explained. "The rest are on consignment or given away to friends," he said wistfully. "It's quite a collection," Pádraig said, stepping closer to examine the spines of some of the books. "You even have a few Jesuits in here. My late brother Pierre

Teilhard de Chardin, for example."

"You're a Jesuit?" Stephen asked.

"Yes, I'm one of the Jesuits, the know-it-alls of the priestly profession, as the other orders call us behind our backs."

"I thought you were all university professors or off starting boys' schools in the jungle somewhere. What are you doing here?" Stephen said.

"I've done both, as a matter of fact. Why I'm here is a long story. Perhaps another time. What about you? I gather you're here to be with your mother. You're a good son to her."

"Try to be," Stephen said holding up a bottle of scotch in one hand and two glasses in another. Pádraig nodded yes and Stephen started pouring. "But that's only half of a long story meant for another time." They sipped their drinks. "Your mother said you had a Ph.D. What's your field?"

"Oh, it's kind of hard to describe. I think you could call it philosophy of spirituality."

"Spirituality as distinct from religion?"

"No, intertwined with it, but more than it, too."

"Still not sure I'm grasping it. What was your dissertation about?"

Stephen put down his drink and boosted himself on a step stool to one of the mid-height shelves. He pulled down a volume in a dust jacket in almost mint condition and handed it to Pádraig. Pádraig read the title aloud. "Knowledge and Belief, Faith and Doubt. An intriguing title." He flipped the pages. "Perhaps I can borrow it, if you can spare it for a week or so. I'm a quick reader."

"Well, I don't know," Stephen said, "seeing as the publisher only has about five thousand unsold copies they'd like me to take off their hands. Not only can I spare it for a week, but why don't you keep that copy."

"Thank you. I look forward to reading it. Mine never came out as a book."

"Ah, I should have expected you're a man of high letters. What was your field and dissertation?"

"My degree was awarded from the history and religion

faculties at the National University. My field was the history of Irish Christianity."

"I'd think that was a crowded field, hard to plow new territory impressively enough for a dissertation committee."

"You're right about that. It was a foolish choice for me, but it was always a topic of fascination for me, how a deeply pagan island was overtaken by Christianity. It seemed to me almost like a laboratory experiment, and I thought if I could understand it, it would help me in the missionary part of my work. By the time I realized how difficult it was going to be to find fresh material for a good research question, I was already many years into the time that my province had allotted for my Ph.D. I had to plow ahead or watch all the time I'd devoted up until that point go down the drain. You don't get a second chance, generally, to go back and finish. You get moved on to wherever you're needed."

"So what did you write about?"

"St. Patrick, my namesake."

"St. Patrick? That seems like the most written about topic of all. Why did you go down that path?"

"Well, as much as has been written about him, there's still a lot of mystery surrounding him because he wrote so little himself. Take a saint like Augustine. He was prolific. You could hardly shut him up. His Confessions alone run [xx] pages and that's only one of his books. Patrick, on the other hand doesn't have Confessions -- he has Confession. Just one. That and a rather passionate letter bordering on whiny that he wrote to Coroticus, a British general, protesting the slaughter of converts who had recently professed Christianity. He was a talker, not a writer. Judging from what was written about him, he was a brilliant, persuasive orator which made him a good preacher."

"So where's the mystery if there's a fair amount written about him, even if not by him?"

"Some of the accounts written about him appear to be reasonably contemporaneous, so they're tentatively reliable. For example, he had a secretary, a monk who travelled with him for part of his mission, making notes about things he said and did. But that was only in the later part of his life when he had mostly secured Ireland as a Christian stronghold. Regarding the rest of his life, most of what was written about him can't be relied upon because it was written years or even decades or centuries after he died, often based on hearsay by people who never met him or heard him speak. That means that there's a giant potential for mythologizing his actual deeds and words. It means that if you're a scholar of Irish Christianity, you can never really know the most important figure in Irish Christianity."

"That's a frustrating puzzle. Unless you can introduce new original sources, you're stuck not understanding the most famous Irishman in the world."

"You're starting to illustrate the conundrum of how little known he really is. For example, Patrick wasn't an Irishman. Not by birth, anyway. He was British. The son of a Christian minister of some sort. He was kidnapped by slave traders trawling along the coast of what's now Scotland. You might not know that, either. This part of Ireland was farmed and shepherded by foreign-born slaves owned by petty kings. Patrick became a reluctant shepherd at age fifteen to a man named Miliu who was a king in Antrim. He writes in his Confession that he was frightened, lonely, homesick and miserable. He was hungry, unclothed and unsheltered. He slept naked, in the open fields with the animals he tended. He did what a lot of people do in those circumstances. He prayed. He prayed at all hours and in all weather."

"How did he get himself out of that situation?"

"He didn't. God did. God answered his prayers, and spoke to him one night by telling him. 'Your ship is ready. You are going home.' He walked four hundred miles to a port on the west coast, we don't know which one, and we don't know how he got there with no money and no food."

"And no clothes," Stephen added, sipping his drink. "Seems a bit fantastic already. But you say this is the part documented in his own writing."

"Yes, and it's the fact that it's hard to believe that's said to make it a miracle. But there's more. When he gets to the port and finds the ship that God spoke to him about, the one that's going back to Scotland, the crew won't let him on. They can tell, perhaps, that he's on the run, and they don't want the authorities coming after them. He slinks away to figure out what to do, when one of the crew members comes running after him to say they've changed their minds, and he can come along if he hurries."

"That's a lucky thing."

"It's considered part of the miracle. Anyway, things get odd for a bit when he gets on the ship. There's apparently an old pagan custom where as a sign of friendship and apology, one man offers his nipples to another for licking."

"Are you having me on? That can't be true."

"No, it is. It's part of his account. And he records that he declined the offer because it seemed at odds with his Christian beliefs, though he doesn't say how."

"Well, if they were just trying to be nice, did his refusal put them off or make them change their minds again?"

"No, another part of the miracle. You might think this would confirm their concerns that he was nothing but trouble. But they just shrugged and said, 'you can make friends with us however you want.' So they sail away but have many travails on their voyage including a shipwreck. They stagger inland for days without food, and when things are especially dire, they taunt Patrick along the lines of 'if your God is so great, why don't you pray to him for us to get some food?' So he kneels down and beckons them to join him. And behold, here comes a herd of swine stampeding down the hillside. Dinner on hooves."

"Wow."

"Wow, indeed. So he finally makes it home, where he's tearfully welcomed by his family and enjoined never to leave again. Not that his first departure was a matter of choice. But his second one was. He heard the voice of God again, in the form of a dream. In the dream, an Irishman was God's emissary, bringing Patrick a sheaf of letters from the people of Ireland. He handed the one on the top of the stack to Patrick, who began to read it, in the dream. It had a title: 'The Voice of the Irish' and without finishing his reading of the letter, Patrick wrote in his Confession, he could hear the voices of the Irish clamoring for him to come back to them. He left almost immediately to obtain the education that he needed for ordination so that he could be an effective missionary to Ireland."

"So what did you do to break new ground for your dissertation?"

"I did what you suggested was necessary a few minutes ago. I found new original source material."

"From fifteen hundred years ago? Sounds suspect, it you'll forgive my skepticism."

"Completely understandable. I heard a lot of that from my dissertation committee. But I was eventually able to persuade them of its reliability."

"What was it that you found?"

"It was more like the source material found me. I was at National University, spending almost all of my time in the humanities library. It was thinly populated, that particular library. History was out of favor during that period as a doctoral field. I don't know why."

"How long ago was this?"

"More than twenty years. It was 1958 when I finished the work and took my degree. Anyway, since there were so few patrons in the humanities library, I struck up a friendship with the librarian. He was an elderly man named Rory Corcoran, one of the keenest scholars I've ever met. He had a doctorate himself in Irish history. Being a little past the age where he ought to be climbing ladders and shelving folios, he was glad to have a fellow my size hanging about to reach things for him and push the heavier books up where they belonged.

"So I was up there in the library one Friday afternoon, no one else about, and he whispers from behind the desk, 'Pádraig, come over here a minute. I need some help up in accessions.' It wasn't unusual for him to ask me for help; I didn't mind the interruptions and he knew that. But it was odd for him to ask me to come into the accessions area with him. That was forbidden territory in his library, even to a friend."

"Understandable. If you have too much foot traffic going in and out of accessions, you might have things disappearing between the time they come into the library and when they get catalogued into the collection."

"Exactly. When we got to the accessions area, he took me to the carrel where he handled the accessions work for the humanities library. He looked around to make sure no one was paying particular attention.   And then he did the most remarkable thing."

"What was that?"

"He handed me a package, brown paper wrapped, torn open on one side, which made me realize that he'd already looked it over. It was a book, a leather bound volume, an old one, the kind with the edges rubbed off, the grit comes off in your hands if you touch it carelessly. You know the kind of book I'm talking about." Pádraig drew deeply on his scotch.

"Sure. Handled plenty of those at Oxford. They turn your hands orange for a day until you can rub it off. Never really washes out; you just have to let it leave of its own pace. So what was it, the book?"

"Well, you're not going to believe this. I could hardly believe it at the time, and still shake my head over it." Pádraig paused to drain his drink. "When I fished my hand inside the package, what I pulled out was a volume titled, 'The Years of Pádraig, Missionary to Hibernia.' It was stiff with age, and I was a little afraid to open it wide. I thought I might crack its spine. But Rory showed me how to place it on a reader that supported the spine and let the pages fall wide open."

Stephen poured them both another generous drink. "So what was it, the book? What did it cover?"

"It was marvelous. It covered the most interesting and hermetic parts of Pádraig's life that no one thought would be illuminated, especially his time on the mountain, now known as Croagh Patrick when he fasted for forty days and saw God, and his time at Station Island, when he took his legendary tour of Purgatory through its very own front door."

"What?   He claimed to have seen all that?"   Stephen paused for a moment. "Wait a second. Who wrote all this?

64

You started out saying that he'd written next to nothing. Makes me wonder whether he was mostly illiterate or just very busy. Then you say that you've found a volume cataloguing all these experiences attributed to him in legend and history. Did he write it?"

"It was written in the first person, as though he'd written it. But I came to believe, for the reasons you've stated about doubting his advanced literacy, and the comparative complexity of these texts compared to those that are generally acknowledged to be his by pen, that they were the transcriptions of another earlier secretary who was with him in the early and middle years of his work. They read more like a journal, not kept every day, but periodically updated, recounting significant episodes in Patrick's life. The language is dressier and better transitioned than what you read in his Confession and his letter to Coroticus. It sounds like him, is what I'm trying to say. Only better."

"What was the provenance of the book? You must have thought it credible, I assume."

"Yes. I was determined not to fall in love with the source. It did seem a bit too good to be true, turning up just when I needed it, flailing dead in the water on my dissertation. But I trusted Rory. I still do. Well, he's passed on now. But if he were alive, I'd still trust him like a brother."

"But where did it come from?"

"From America. Someone who's grandfather had studied at National University found it in his library when he wound up his estate. The letter had some kind of confession implying that the grandfather had nicked it from the library, according to family lore. The grandson felt he was making a reparation by returning it. His letter said he'd had it examined by antiquarians in the States who were able to authenticate it back a fair ways, not all the way back to the saint himself, of course, but far enough back for me to treat it as an important secondary source, at the least, and to make an argument that it should be treated as an authentic original source."

"How can it be an original source if you can't prove St. Patrick wrote it?"

65

"Here's the irony, if you're a truly strict scholar. In my discipline, an observer of the events at issue is considered an original source. Even if the account isn't written by the central actor, it can still be an original source. That's why the gospels stand up as they do. Not written by Jesus Christ, not a word of them. They just quote him extensively and annotate what he did. Nonetheless, these are original sources in my profession. Add to that the reality that these are not even eyewitness accounts."

"Are they not? I thought the apostles for whom the gospels were named wrote them. Seems that's what I learned in catechism. But maybe I wasn't paying proper attention," Stephen said, his voice trailing off a bit.

"No, each of the gospels was written many years after Christ's death. Some of them were written by groups of people across several generations. Each of the gospels has a voice that characterizes them and a writing style that makes it a coherent read. But Matthew the apostle, that particular man, didn't write the gospel that bears his name."

"Well, that ought to be pretty shocking to your parishioners when you tell them next Sunday."

Pádraig smirked at Stephen's sarcasm. "It's not really necessary to the faith. It's not a secret, of course, anyone can read up on early Christianity and learn all about this. It's just simpler to keep the picture, well, simpler. But let me get back to my main story about the book, The Years of Patrick."

"Yes, please do, but the detours are so attractive. We'll have to come back to them."

"In time, perhaps. I was able to use the letter accompanying the book to contact the sender, the guilt-ridden grandson in Virginia. I sent him a letter, then called him long distance, by appointment. The telephone bill was a fortune to me, after the fact. We talked for a long time. I squeezed out of him every detail, even ones he was surprised he remembered when pressed, about the book. It turns out that the grandfather had stolen it not from the library stacks, but from the office of a professor he visited about a rather poor mark he'd been given. He was piqued about the grade on an exam he'd written. At the time his father was giving him a good deal of trouble about his overall devotion to his studies, so this particular mark fell rather hard on him. Feeling sorry for himself and angry with the professor, this young man waited until the professor excused himself to confer with his secretary to obtain the name of a suitable tutor for the unhappy student. Then he grabbed this book randomly off the nearest shelf and stuffed it into his briefcase, feathering some other papers over it to hide it. He took the name and number of the tutor and left.

"He kept it among his possessions for years, moving with it from place to place, and didn't spend any time with it until he'd almost forgotten he had it. He had recently retired from his practice of law – when he left Ireland, he regained his academic zeal and become an attorney in America. He started picking up things to read, and Years of St. Patrick was among them. He began to understand what it was and the great gaps it purported to fill in about St. Patrick. It became a hobby and a pursuit for him to try to authenticate the book, by documenting its provenance as far back as he could."

"But he faced an immediate problem, of course, because he couldn't exactly call up the professor from whom he'd thieved it to ask where he got it."

"Worse than that. The professor was dead by then, long since past. But the publisher's name was available to him, and that gave him a good start. He was trying to authenticate the text, remember, not the book itself, which was old by perhaps a century, but certainly not an original manuscript.

"At any rate, he spent the last twelve years of his life in active pursuit of authentication. And he kept good notes, which the grandson agreed to send to me. I think he was pleased for his grandfather that someone else cared about the book and its story as much as he had."

"So how good were the notes?"

"Very good. I'll get to that. I'm getting ahead of myself. Rory had the book in his hands and now had placed it into mine. But the book isn't officially part of the library's collection yet because it hasn't gone through the accession process and put into the catalogue. Very often, an important book, such as this one was presumed to be, would be passed through the department with jurisdiction over the subject matter. Rory knew that if this book took such a tour, it would be impossible to pry the senior lecturers' hands off of it for months, perhaps years. It would be too late for me."

"What did he do?"

"He said, just loudly enough for everyone to hear, 'Pádraig, I think that reading stand has a screw loose in it. See, it wobbles when you try to turn it. Take it back to my desk, could you? I've some small tools in the long drawer. See if you can adjust it.' And he smiled and turned his back. Just like that, I had custody of the book.

"You can imagine that I lived night and day with that book and the provenance evidence. Suddenly, I was flooded with new and interesting source materials about St. Patrick. It was an embarrassment of riches."

Stephen had just tippled a thin stream of whiskey into each of their glasses. "So how did it come out? What new ground did you break based on what you found?"

A thud echoed from upstairs. Stephen slammed his glass down on the table and sprinted up the stairs. Pádraig followed him as far as the hallway, then hung back, unsure of whether he was wanted upstairs. Momentarily, Stephen came trudging back down the staircase. "False alarm. Mother turned over in bed and sent the cat flying."

"Late enough for us to stop, I think," Pádraig said, fishing in his pocket for his car keys. Out with the keys came a small piece of red sea glass, which Pádraig polished with his thumb as he stood near the front door. "You're a good listener, Stephen. Thank you."

"And you're a good storyteller. I'm on pins and needles to find out what happened with your work. Are you busy tomorrow?"

"I plan to look in on the search again, get everyone fired up to go back out there and give the head a good scouring. Fianna may yet be right here under our noses."

Stephen thought for a moment about disagreeing, but

instead said, "See you tomorrow, Father.

13.

Pádraig mustered out promptly after the seven o'clock mass on Monday morning, over to the post office rather than his usual visit to the pub to rally another round of search. The chatter died as he ducked into the shop and suddenly the assembly was on their feet. He waved them back to their seats.

"Any news about the girl? Claire McGettigan asked.

"No, nothing new. She hasn't turned up. We need to keep looking, and I'd appreciate some help from all of you doing a more thorough house to house inquiry. I think we gave up a bit too easily yesterday when we learned about the boat." The group shifted uncomfortably. Martin O'Flaherty spoke up. "Do you not think that it's really a family matter at this point, Father? I mean, mightn't we be taken as meddlers for insisting on another search?"

Pádraig recognized the beginnings of an argument for the group's staying put. "No, not at all, Martin. I know the family would be grateful for any help in finding her safely. Let me suggest that we go out in pairs and divide up the street names. If we all participate, we can be done by mid-day. Martin, you and I could..."

"Begging your pardon for interrupting, Father, but it's a

small village after all. Everyone knows she's missing. Who wouldn't already have checked their sheds for her hiding there?" Martin smiled indulgently. "And even respecting the family's wishes for continued help, I might inquire whether a search is what they'd really want."

"What do you mean by that, Martin?" Pádraig asked, barely keeping his temper in check.

"Well, were we to do a search that rules out she's still on the head somewhere, mightn't they be concerned that it will focus attention, shall we say, on Ned's behavior and his involvement in all this?"

Pádraig could feel the back of his neck growing warm, one of his reliable signs that an explosion was imminent. He forced himself to speak quietly and slowly. "Martin, we've spoken on previous occasions about how distasteful it is to spread rumors and gossip. Ned told me last night that he had nothing to do with the boat going out, and I believe him. Fianna is here somewhere, or nearby, and we need a methodical search to narrow the possibilities."

Martin sniffed at the reprimand. "Not wishing to seem obstinate, Father, but the wisdom of a further search is a moot point for me anyway. I can't just close up An Post and go traipsing over fences and fields on a Monday morning." Pádraig eyed the rest of the group as they listened to the exchange. One by one, they volunteered their own reasons that they couldn't help this morning, much as they professed they'd like to. Pádraig left the post office and slammed the door behind him.

He thought for a moment about heading over to the pub for a visit with Willie and his long pours, then changed his mind. It's a day to keep my tools sharp, he thought. He headed up the hill toward the overlook of the Red Islands.

As he reached the crest that turned into the curve, he saw Stephen approaching from the opposite direction. They stopped in the middle of the road. "You look wretched," Stephen said cheerily. "Rough night?"

"Rough morning. I can't get a soul to come out looking for Fianna. They've given up when they ought not to. I'd go

71

myself, but it will take a full day at least for one person to make the rounds."

Stephen shifted his rucksack over his left shoulder. "It may not be the best use of your time."

"Why do you say so?"

"I assume at this point that we're looking for a live girl, not a corpse. Forgive me for being blunt, but it's meant to start with the optimistic hypothesis. If she is alive and hiding somewhere, it's likely that it's in an unconventional place, not in someone's milking house or whatever you call those rickety sheds everyone seems to have out in back of their houses."

"You mean to say that it's a small village, everyone knows she's missing and has probably been in and out of those outbuildings a time or two since learning that we're looking for her, so she can't be holed up in the sheds."

"That's a succinct way of putting it. You've already run this path of logic, then."

"Someone ran it for me, let's say. If you're right that she's hiding in an unconventional place, how do we run that down?"

"We need someone who can think unconventionally. Who's the most eccentric person in the village?"

"What do you mean, eccentric?"

"You know, the person who enters the room and everyone snickers because he's dressed funny, or got a dead flower in his lapel, bursts out with odd things to say and so forth. Ringing any bells?"

Pádraig thought for a moment, "I think I know who we should talk to. We'll need the car." Pádraig headed down the hill and back to the rectory with Stephen following. "And it's a she, not a he," he called over his shoulder.

14.

"Where are we going?" Stephen asked, clutching the seat belt strap. "Is it far?"

"Not so far in miles," Pádraig said, as the car bumped along a poorly paved road that forked off the Castle Road northward toward Bundoran. "We'll still be technically on the head, but it's a world away from the village. You'll see."

"The sooner the better we get there," Stephen muttered under his breath.

Pádraig turned off the road onto an even narrower lane and eased the car down past the woods. To Stephen's eye, it looked like a dead end, but then Pádraig steered the car sharply left, and a caravan camp came into view. Stephen looked up the hill and counted rows and rows of trailer, some shaded by trees and some in full sun. There must be people here somewhere, he thought, but no one made himself visible.

"What is this place?" Stephen asked. "Who lives here?"

"This, my friend, is Murphy Town. Have you never heard of the Travellers?"

"Sure, I have. I thought they were gypsies and lived in Hungary or Romania or somewhere over there."

"That may be their origins, but they've evolved. They are everywhere. And they abound in Ireland, especially in the west, where they've found that they're mostly left alone if they keep to themselves."

"Kind of hard to keep to yourself when your trade is thievery. It's sort of inherently sociable work, isn't it?"

"Oh, it's much more nuanced than that. They're not just thieves any more. They're con men specializing in the trades. Plumbing, painting, machinery repairs. This is their winter base. They head out from here just a few weeks from now, after Easter, to Dublin area, up north, England and the continent where they find naive homeowners who aren't on to them yet. Good luck and best wishes to those people. None better than the Murphys to charm, cajole and lie their way to pocketing gullible money in exchange for badly performed work."

Pádraig spent a few minutes giving Stephen a lesson in the ways of the Travellers. It was art more than a science, doing a job just well enough to cover their retreat without threats or complaints, and poor enough to require redoing next season by different, less familiar looking members of their extended family. They'd been at it long enough, generations, to have it as carefully planned as a farmer's rotation of crops, with never the same part of the family visiting the same route closer than six years apart, yet all the same territory blanketed every year.

"Of course, there's no money to be made for them here, where they're well known, every man, woman, child and hound, to each and every. Some say they'd sooner tear down a shed that have a Murphy repair it. Others say that even their dogs are thieves, trained to pull tins of potted meat off the lower shelves in the shops. They know the local dogs, and will give them a treat, but any Traveller dog who visits the shop gets the boot, and not too kindly."

Pádraig explained that the residents of Mullaghmore and the Murphys had reached a cautious truce over the years. The Murphys mostly kept to themselves and sent a few of the women into the village for provisions once a week or so. They didn't drink, at least not in the pubs of Mullaghmore or Cliffoney, but some suspected they might have their own still hidden deep in their camp somewhere, probably disguised as a baby's pram. If the wind was quiet on a night when the fog was low, you could hear fiddle music and whooping from the general direction of the camp. It was a bit eerie, but the sound was distant and somehow comforting for that. "If I can hear them," Martin used to say, "I know where they are. And their being that far away is a good thing."

Pádraig and Stephen walked up what passed for the main lane in the camp. They had only passed a few of the caravans when a screen door creaked open and a woman waddled down the improvised wooden steps, her arms raised in greeting.

"Father Hart! What are you doing here on a Monday? And who's your friend? Come in and have a cup of tea, both of you."

"No, no, Mary. Very kind of you. But I'm afraid we're a bit pressed today. Do you know, is Liddy Duncan about?"

"I'm sure she is," said Mary. "She's not much for going out." She lowered her voice. "Probably for the best, I'd say. I'll call and see if she's here."

Stephen whispered to Pádraig, "They have telephones out here?"

"Not exactly," Pádraig said, giving Stephen a look of amusement. "Listen."

Stephen gave a start as Mary turned her formidable frame up the hill and raised her voice. "Orla, see is Liddy in." Pádraig and Stephen watched as a woman, presumably Orla, trundled out of her trailer and turned up the hill to repeat the shouted message. The voices got more faint, but it seemed as though there were two more links in the chain carrying the message. There was a pause, and then the message cascaded back down the hill. "She's coming," Mary told them with a polite smile. "Are you sure you won't have some tea? It may be a little while."

"No, thank you Mary. We'll be fine waiting here."

Mary approached a little closer. "Father, it may be a little while since you've seen her. Her dress has gotten a bit colorful, let's say, and combing out her hair has gone by the wayside. Oh, and she prefers to be called Seth nowadays."

"Seth, as in the man's name?" Stephen asked.

"Yes, the same," Mary said with a shrug.

"Listen, Mary, I'll be happy to call her Queen Liz if only she'll come out and help us, truth be told." Pádraig said with a nervous laugh.

"She'd probably like that," Mary laughed. "But you probably should start out with Seth."

Just then, Liddy Duncan came walking at the pace of a tumble down the hill. She charged past Pádraig and Stephen toward the car, without a word of hello. "We'd best be getting on with it," she yelled over her shoulder. "I'll sit in the back, if you don't mind." She folded the passenger seat forward and squeezed herself behind Stephen's seat. "Pull up the seat, you.

You're short enough to spare the legroom. Who are you anyway?"

Stephen turned halfway around to be polite. "Stephen Ramsey Attergood. Defenestrated scholar, late of Oxford. Pleased to meet you, Seth."

Pádraig looked sideways at Stephen. "That was a lot of information in a short sentence."

"Sentence fragment, actually."

"We'll discuss it later?"

"I doubt I can avoid it," Stephen said gloomily. "I suggest we fill Seth in on the basic chronology, then take her to Fianna's hideaway. Just the basic facts, now Father. We don't want to cloud her perceptions with out theories and suppositions. Agreed?"

"Agreed. Why don't you take the lead so I can concentrate on the road. It's a bit tricky in places out here."

"An excellent idea."

15.

On the way to Fianna's hideaway, Stephen gave Seth a crisp factual summary of what had happened since Sunday afternoon.   He covered the discovery of Fianna's disappearance, the half-hearted search of the villagers, the discovery of the missing boat and the foray he and Pádraig had made to the area near the grounds of Cassiebawn.   He explained that they had stumbled upon a subterranean space that Fianna apparently had occupied.

"How do you know she went in there?" Seth asked sharply.

"We found some notebooks of hers in there, and..."

Seth shrieked.   Pádraig slammed on the brakes and Stephen smashed his shoulder against the dashboard. "Christ!" Stephen screamed. "What's the matter with you, Seth? You can't scream like that when a man's driving. Especially this one."

Seth was pushing against the back of Stephen's seat and reaching forward to try to grab the door handle. "You idiots, the both of you, begging your pardon for saying so, Father.   I held out hope for a moment that you didn't go in, but you did, didn't you?" Stephen forced his seat back to keep her in the car. "What the devil are you talking about? Go in where?"

"Into the fairy rath, you moron! Do you not know one when you see it?"

"Apparently not," Pádraig said as calmly as he could manage. "Please tell us about it."

"I'll tell you nothing til I see what it is. I've said too much already." With that she slammed Stephen's seat forward grabbed the door handle and slid out of the car behind him. She marched with certainly toward the fence surrounding Cassiebawn. Stephen stood up outside the car and called over the roof, "It's straightaway ahead of you."

"I know, shite-for-brains," Seth called back at them. Pádraig was already far enough off the travel lane to park where he was. He pocketed the key and he and Stephen hurried to catch up with Seth.

They were only a short distance behind Seth when she came upon the mouth of the hideaway. She was crouched and peering in. "Aye, just as I thought. It's a fairy rath. You've probably already done a great deal of damage going in there to the cause of getting her back. You're lucky to have come out. Probably more the lucky because of the priest being part of the intrusion."

Pádraig blinked and looked back and forth between Stephen and Seth. "Can one of you please tell me what's going on here?" Seth continued to peer into the cavity. Stephen handed her his torch, which seemed to baffle her at first, but then she managed to turn it on and put it to use in her exploration.

Stephen breathed out a long sigh. "Okay, I'm not saying I actually believe any of this. But here goes. I've been reading about this, the book you saw me looking at in Beach Club yesterday afternoon."

"Yes," said Pádraig. "The one you handed me yesterday when I was writing the note to Fianna. An old Yeats book I'd never heard of."

"Right. "Writings on Irish Legends, Folklore and Myth.' It's a compendium, rather well edited, in my opinion, of his writings between 1887 and 1904 published in various periodicals. These writings are an early form of ethnography before the field was even recognized. The idea is to explain popular culture by talking to people to collect stories and experiences that comprise popular culture. The problem with history as an academic discipline is that what becomes recorded as history is determined by elites -- people who can read and write and contribute to politics, arts and other forms of high culture. Yeats was ahead of his time in recognizing that there was another deeper layer to history that would vanish unless contemporaneously documented by someone who could listen and write."

"I always thought of Yeats as a poet. A rather dense one, at that," Pádraig said.

"Right, we can save the literary critique for later. There's a lot more I want to tell you about what I've been learning about him, but here's what's important for now. Yeats records dozens of stories told by people in the west, including the parts of Sligo near Ben Bulben, about fairy raths, or forts. According to the lore, these are magical places, dangerous ones, where people and animals disappear. Yeats records the story of a man who said his dog wandered into one near Rosses Strand and never came out, for example. That's what's got Seth all frenzied up."

"Um, okay then. Who's responsible for the disappearances?"

Seth stepped away from the entrance and stomped over to where Pádraig and Stephen were talking. "Don't say it," she warned Stephen, her face only inches from his and red as a beet.

"Okay, okay, I won't say it. Not a peep." He raised his hands in surrender. Seth paced in a circle. She glanced up at the sky, streaked with the bright colors that announced sunset. "It's close enough to end of day to do it, and less dangerous before it really gets dark." She sat down on the ground suddenly. "Give me something belonging to the girl. Or at least something she touched." Pádraig and Stephen looked at each other. Stephen dug into his bag. "Her notebooks. Those should work, right?" He extended them to Seth, who snatched them out of his hand. "They'll have to, since the two of you came up to this so unprepared. Unbelievable." She closed her eyes and held the notebooks in her upturned palms, concentrating silently for many minutes. Pádraig felt his patience beginning to fray. He started to whisper to Stephen about giving up the effort in a short while, and Seth shushed him angrily. They stayed on in silence past sunset and as the first stars began to appear. Seth opened her eyes and stood up, working out the kinks in her hips and knees.

"Well, they have her," she sighed. "Not a word from you, mister," she said pointedly at Stephen. "Not here." She looked around the mound near the entrance. "I guess we'll have to burn her out." She began gathering up a sheaf of burnable things, dry grass, fallen branches. Stephen and Pádraig looked on until it dawned on them that she was serious. Pádraig grabbed the kindling from her. "No, no, we're not going to start a fire here. That's very dangerous, and not our land to be doing that on." He felt as though he was lecturing a small child on the dangers of playing with matches.

Seth was indignant. "Listen you, stick to your preaching, if you're any good at it, and I'll stick to my doctoring, which I happen to be very good at. I've asked them nicely, and it's well known that if that doesn't work, you have to light a fire and brandish it about the place. You don't burn anything down, but they're afraid of fire, and even the smell of it will get them to doing the right thing."

"Nonetheless, Seth, we appreciate all you've done here, but we can't be party to a brush fire of any size or purpose." He took her by the arm and led her back to the car. Stephen gathered up the notebooks from the ground and followed along.

16.

The drive back to the Travellers' camp seemed to Stephen much longer than the first out and back. Seth seethed and muttered in the back seat and Pádraig and Stephen rode with eyes straight ahead. For the first time since meeting Pádraig, Stephen wished he'd drive a little faster.

Pádraig slowed the Escort into the same nook he'd used earlier to get the car out of the way back at the camp. Before the car had even come to a full stop, Seth had shoved her way out of the car, flattening Stephen against the glove box in the process. She stood, hands on hips, staring at Padriag and Stephen as they got out of the car. Stephen wondered whether it might be wiser to keep the car rolling and head straight back to the village, but felt too guilty to leave Pádraig alone to deal with the situation.

"Well, you've made a mess of it, that's clear. And it's too far gone for me to help you if you won't let me do what's needed. So I'll be taking leave of you now." She remained standing before them, now tapping her toe. "I'm sure you didn't think I was doing that for my own pleasure, did you now?" She held out her palm. Pádraig retrieved his wallet, flipped through it with a frown and found a five punt note, which he gave her. She snorted. "That's all for my trouble?" She looked at Stephen, who now wanted, more than anything else, never to see her again. He parted with a ten punt note, and she pounded her way up the hill, arms pumping, leaving a trail of indistinct curses in her wake.

Mary came out of her caravan. "Didn't go so well as

planned, Father?"

"No, Mary, not well at all. We learned nothing useful and I'm afraid we upset her a great deal."

"I should have told you a bit more about her, maybe, Father. I thought you were aware of her background."

"Only that she's lived here since she was a tiny girl, came here with her father, I think, after her mother had passed."

"That much is true, but you don't know, it seems, how the two of them ended up in this particular neighborhood of nowhere."

"I'll admit that I don't, Mary. What do they say about that?"

Mary stepped in close to the two of them. "You'll notice her accent is a bit off. Not pure west of Ireland like the rest of us," she said with an air of superiority. "Her family is from Scotland, I mean her father and his father going all the way back. And a long line of witch doctors they were."

"Witch doctors? I'm at a loss, I'm afraid. What do you mean by that?" Pádraig said, struggling to listen to the story with a straight face. "You can't be serious about this, Mary. Are you?"

Mary eyed him warily. "Perhaps it's not a story for telling to a priest after all. Begging you pardon, Father, I should go back in." She turned to go. Stephen stepped forward. "I'd love to hear the story, Mary, if you'd be willing to tell me. I've read some about the witch doctors, but don't know any of the stories firsthand." Mary turned back to the pair, glad again to have a willing ear.

"I'm serious as the blight about this, what I say here. The witch doctors can talk to the others." She paused for a moment. "Bless them, it's Monday," she added lifting her voice to the trees.

Stephen and Pádraig looked at each other. "Mary, why did you add that last part, the part where you said 'bless them, it's Monday'?", Stephen asked.

She looked back and forth between the two as though they were idiots. "They don't like to be talked about, not at all. But if you mention them, then you must bless them to make it plain that you mean them no harm."

"But why 'it's Monday', that part as well?" Stephen asked.

Mary regarded him incredulously. "Well, it's not as though they keep careful track of the calendar on their own, so you must tell them which day it is that you bless them, so they don't get confused that maybe it was yesterday you blessed them, and then again today you mentioned them but forgot to bless them!"

"So it needs to be date stamped?" Pádraig was struggling not to laugh as he asked this, and poured a pretended coughing fit into his fist to cover his mirth.

"I remember this from the Yeats book. It's an old tradition to keep the others calm and happy and dissuade them from inflicting any mischief." Stephen said. Mary stared at him. "Bless them, it's Monday," Stephen mumbled hastily.

"Oh, all right then, me too, bless them it's Monday, and let's agree that now we've all said it we're covered for the full twenty-four hour period known as Monday. Can we please get on with the story?" Pádraig said in exasperation. Mary nodded hesitantly in acknowledgement of the arrangement.

"Well, the Duncans lived on the other side of the sea on the Isle of Islay. Innkeepers there. It's a spirited place, that island. You can't do a thing without running into something that annoys the others, and they put the people to all sorts of tests, all the time, to see what they're made of.

"For instance, there's the story of the poor family, on Islay, I think, but it could have been Jura, who sent the children out every day to cut peat for the fire. It's a hard job, though I don't think you might know it, Father, out on the bog, no break from the wind, cutting out bricks from the bog. This family sent their two boys and their young sister, barely old enough to walk on her own, out to cut the turf. Every day, the girl would come home with her basket overflowing. But the boys came home, just as exhausted, with barely an armload between them. The father was quite cross with the boys while he ladled praise on the girl and fed her all the milk while the boys went to bed hungry.

"After a week of this, the boys were determined to follow

their sister close as could be to find out how she did so much better than they at gathering peat. They watched her carefully that next day, circling ahead of her to look back at what she was doing exactly. Once she had gotten a certain distance out on to the bog, she stooped down and then, as they watched, a hand emerged from the surface of the peat and handed the girl a small poniard, sharp as an axe. She took it carefully by the hilt and began cutting away. The peat yielded like butter and shortly her basket began filling up. When it was as heavy as she could manage to carry -- she had no thought of asking her brothers for help in case they might steal some of her work -- she stooped down again and handed the knife back to the hand, which knew exactly when and where to meet her outstretched hand.

"That evening passed as usual with the girl rewarded and the boys punished. The next day, the boys rushed ahead to the place where they'd seen the hand emerge and waited. Soon the hand popped up above the surface and offered the poniard. One of the boys grabbed the knife and the other held the hand while the first boy slashed hard at the hand and severed it. They leapt for joy that they now had the magic knife and never had to give it back.

"The little girl cast about the bog looking for the friendly hand, and cried when it didn't emerge as it always had. She looked ahead and saw the gleam of the blade working between her two brothers. But instead of rejoicing at the yield it produced, the brothers were cursing the knife, which had broken, blade from hilt, on the surface of the bog. The girl stood and tried pushing the heel of her shoe into the peat and found it strangely solid. The three of them realized just then that the cruelty of the boys to the helping hand had turned the bog rock hard, a curse to them all. That winter, without the peat fire, they froze to death, the boys, the girl and their parents."

"That's a dark tale," Stephen said after a moment of silence had passed among them.

"And what is it supposed to mean, Mary, along the lines of the point you were making?" Pádraig asked politely.

"Don't you see, Father? It was them that put up a test. Would the girl be their friend and let them help her and her family? Exist peaceably, side by side with the others. Or would they strike a blow to take more than was offered them? Here, they did, and my point is there's the Scots for you. They couldn't leave well enough alone. Never could. Always at war with the others as though they meant to drive them out. A goose's chance at Christmas of that happening, I'd say! And dangerous to try, that's the point of the story." She stopped, crossed her arms and leaned back to let them absorb the lesson.

"Same thing it was with the Duncans. The Scots can't help it. They're always at war with the others. Liddy's father, Camron, he was the one that brung the curse down on the family. The grandfather was Alistair, and he was an exception to the rule, as I heard it. He got on well with the others, always offered them some cool water and a place to sleep when they passed by. Mind you, he offered them the barn, not a soft bed in the inn. He was running a business, after all, and couldn't give the rooms away. But he had a reputation among them as being hospitable and not afraid, so they let him in on some of their secrets, little by little, and he was allowed to share these with his sons."

"What sort of secrets were they, do you know?" Stephen was listening intently, taking notes in his mind.

"All sorts of important things. Like where is it safe to build a cottage or a shed so it won't be on the fairy highway that they travel when the go about at night. Build it in the wrong place, and it will never work for the purpose intended. People living in the house won't get a wink of sleep, with the doors and windows slamming at all hours. Milk stored in the shed will sour before the dairyman comes to pick it up in the morning. Also, when is it best to plant the potatoes or the grains so that you won't be planting the field just at the time when the fairy troops are planning one of their night battles. They have contests four times a year among the troops that belong to different parts of the land, and you can imagine the awful trample they'd leave in a field if you planted at the wrong time. So all sorts of valuable things like that is what the others shared with Alistair, and he with his sons."

"The others and the fairies are one in the same?" Stephen asked.

"More or less, that's so. But they don't like to be called fairies, because it sounds as though they're tiny ones. They're not like that at all. They're tall and grand and handsome as can be. The women among them are as beautiful as ladies at court. I've no idea why anyone ever thought to call them fairies. What they really are is the other name they go by: the gentry. They like that name because it lends them proper respect for their wisdom and how they're always helping people."

"It sounds as though the Duncans were on their good side. What went wrong that caused what you say is the curse?" Pádraig asked, finally intrigued enough to play along.

"Camron was the younger brother to Colin. Colin was thrifty and industrious, and admired by his father. Camron lacked the same resolve and lazed about the inn most of the day, and spent a good part of the evening hiding in the wine cellar, taking his fill. When it came time for the running of the inn to pass to a new owner, Alistair entrusted it one hundred percent to Colin, leaving Camron in the lurch. Camron was furious, blind to his very own shortcomings that undid his share of the succession. He knew his brother would never tolerate his freeloading when he undertook management of the inn, and so the night that the father laid down his decision was a roundly bad one for Camron. He stormed out of the inn and stumbled down the road. He hadn't gone a quarter mile when he encountered a tall man with a sack over his shoulder. 'Pardon me,' says the man, 'but I'm told there's an inn nearby with a kindly keeper who makes bed and board for strangers passing through these parts. Do you know of it?' Camron told him, 'There's an inn, but as for the character of its keeper, I cannot endorse what you say. Follow on this road, and you'll come to it.' They went in opposite directions, Camron straight to the pub in the village where he drank until his pockets were empty.

"Past midnight, Camron tripped his way back to the inn.

Seeing the lights out in the inn, he decided not to go inside. He didn't want to wake the family and the guests because he wasn't eager to see his father in his present condition. He decided to sleep in the barn instead. He was full of drink, his head spun and he couldn't fall asleep. So he took out his pipe and lit it and smoked for a bit, which calmed him enough to doze off."

"I think I see where this is going," Stephen said. "There was a fire?"

"A blaze that lit the sky for miles around. Camron woke up when it was just in the barn, but burning hotly. He knew in a moment that if he were deemed responsible for the blaze, his father would have him arrested and thrown into the workhouse. As he cast about for an answer to his problems, he realized he wasn't alone in the barn. There, across in the stalls, was the man he'd encountered the night before, lying still, probably overcome by the smoke.

"The plan formed quickly from then. Rather than pull the man out into the fresh night air, he ran out alone and met his family and the guests pouring out of the inn, not just to see about the barn fire, but to rescue themselves from the flames already lapping at the eaves of the house. Camron played the hero for them, 'Look, I'm just coming home from a long walk tonight, and what do I see but the barn ablaze.' The barn was coming apart at this point, from the way I've heard the story told. 'Did you take on a guest last night, father, to sleep in the barn? I met someone on the road asking about a place to sleep. Did you take him in?' Alistair was slowly registering the gravity of what was happening, his entire life's work going up in the flames. 'Yes, I did take him in. And now he's done me in.' He wrapped a quilt around himself and sat down in the road and cried for his loss.

"That night, the family moved to lodgings in the village. Camron was relieved that he'd slipped the noose on blame for the fire, and secretly pleased that he'd defeated his father's plan to pass the inn to Colin. It troubled him some that the stranger had died in the fire, but he let his relief and pleasure stifle the thought.

"While his father and brother assessed the family finances, Camron slipped out to walk back to the scene of the fire and to relish the joyful result that chance had produced. He was just a quarter mile from the site of the inn, when he saw a stranger approaching with a sack over his shoulder. Camron was startled when he realized that this was the very same man he had come upon the night before. 'Are you quite content now, Camron?' the man asked. 'We'll be seeing each other again, and quite frequently as long as you're in these parts. I'll be reminding you of what you did. It's a rupture, you know, of the treaty between your family and us. You'll see us, you'll know we're nearby, but no help from us will you ever get again.'

"The next day, Camron tricked the bank teller into giving him what was left of his father's account, and he took the ferry across the sea. He ended up here. The remoteness of the head suited him. He took to what we do, providing services here and there during the summer. He married, had a daughter, Liddy. She calls Seth the part of her that can speak to the others, but that's just it. She can speak to them, she knows when they're about, which can be useful by itself, but they don't talk back to her the way they did to her grandfather. It's the curse. That and the fact that she takes money for it. The gentry don't like that. The services are to be freely given."

"Wish I'd known that part a few minutes ago," Pádraig muttered. "Mary, thank you, this is fascinating. But if she can't help us, is there anyone else you know of who might be able to?"

"No one else up here in the camp, I'm sure of that. Sorry, Father."

Stephen thought for a moment. "This is a long shot, but here goes. This book I've been reading by Yeats – the reason he's so devoted to collecting Irish folklore is because he wanted to use it to build a national identity for the Irish so that they could face the future. His point was that sometimes the way to move forward is to look at the past. Who's the oldest person in the village

17.

"So who are we going to see?" Stephen asked on the drive back to the village.

"We're looking for Easmon Walsh, easily the oldest man in the village if not the whole county."

"How old is he?"

"Ninety-three in January just passed. I always visit him with communion on his birthday. He doesn't get out much. Except to the pub. He lives across the street from Beach Club."

"So ninety-three means he was born in…1887, right?"

"About that. I think so."

"Fascinating. That means he lived here when Yeats was tramping about collecting stories. I wonder if he met him."

"If we can get to him before he goes to bed, you can ask him tonight."

Pádraig pulled the Escort into the yard behind the rectory, cutting off the engine and rolling the car the last hundred feet. "The sisters, some of them are asleep already at this hour, the ones getting on in age." He waved to a white-haired woman in the sitting room overlooking the waterfront, and she returned the greeting. "Except Sister Alex. She seems to be up at all hours." He popped out of the car and led Stephen along the waterfront to a small house diagonally across from Beach Club.

He knocked lightly on the door. A red-haired man

answered the door and smiled when he realized Pádraig was visiting.

"It's himself!" he exclaimed. "Uncle Easmon will be tickled to see you, Father." Pádraig briefly introduced Stephen to Ricky Walsh and the three went inside the house together.

"Uncle Easmon, look who's here to say hello and how are you," Ricky said leading the way to the back of the house where Easmon sat in the kitchen, finishing his stew. He grinned with mostly gums when he saw Pádraig and pushed on his cane to try to stand up. Pádraig put his hand over Easmon's and said. "There's no need, Easmon. Stay where you are."

"Easmon, my friend Stephen and I are here to talk to you about the old times," Pádraig began exploratorily.

"Love to talk about the old times, Father. What do you want to know?"

Pádraig glanced at Stephen. "Well, I'm really the curious one, Mr. Walsh. I'm a student of W.B. Yeats. I've been reading his work on stories about the others..."

"Bless them, it's...Ricky, what day is it?"

"Monday, Uncle."

"Then bless them, it's Monday. If it's that you want to talk about, I'll do a lot better with something that will keep me from getting thirsty while I'm telling what I know." He paused for a moment and waited. Finally, Pádraig caught on. "Oh, you wouldn't like to go across to the pub and have a small something, would you, Easmon?"

"I think I might enjoy that, Father. Of course, Ricky will have to come along to make sure I get home all right. If you don't mind, of course."

In a few minutes, Ricky had gotten Easmon on his feet and organized to go across the street to Beach Club. Stephen carried Easmon's walking stick at Ricky's request in case Easmon wanted it later.

Easmon's entrance into the pub brought a few hellos, but mostly quiet stares. Easmon surveyed the place and pointed to the corner. "Let's sit over there on the carmody."

"Did he say 'carmody'?" Stephen asked Ricky.

"Yes," Ricky smiled. "It's either an old-timey word for banquette, or something he completely made up. I'll try to help you keep up during the evening with which is which, but I've got my limits, too."

With Easmon settled, Pádraig asked, "What will you have, Easmon. A pint of stout? A short whiskey?"

"I'll have both, if you don't mind. That's just what I want. Only make the whiskey not too short." He eyed Stephen. "No offense, now."

"None taken. I'd love to ask you a few questions, if you're willing," Stephen said, taking a pen and notebook out of his rucksack. Easmon looked at the implements suspiciously. "You don't have to be writing things down, do you?" he asked.

"Not if it makes you uncomfortable, no." Stephen put the notebook on his knees, under the table, but kept the pen at hand. He capped his pen and laid it on the table, a tentative promise to leave the conversation undocumented. Pádraig returned with Easmon's drinks; the barman followed in tow with a tray carrying the others' pint glasses. Easmon took a sip of whiskey then a draught of stout that cleared the top three inches of the glass.

"Why is it people come around here to talk and they feel the need to write everything down? Can't a person just listen to a story with his two ears, enjoy it, learn from it and remember it? I'm not cross with you, but you remind me of that fellow who tramped around here when I was a boy, always pestering my father and his friends for a story from the old days. Not just that, not just the story, but where did you first hear that, do you know it to be true, did anyone else see anything like that, did you ever hear a similar story, and so on. He was a pain in the arse, that one." Easmon repeated the process with his two drinks and Stephen began adding up in his mind how many pints the contents of his wallet could buy. This was not an evening that should end early.

"By 'that one', Easmon, I don't know if you could possibly mean the writer William Butler Yeats, could you?"

Easmon smacked his palm on the edge of the table.

"That's the one! We called him Willy to his face and Silly Willy to his back." Stephen's fingers itched to start using his pen.

"What do you remember about him and the work he was doing here?"

"Work? Is that what you call it? I never saw himself lift a shovel or dig for peat. That's what I call work. What he did, Willy, that is, was tramp about the village and down to the houses off the road by Ben Bulben, knocking at the door of whomever he pleased to intrude upon, and ask to be told a story. Can you believe the gall of him?" Easmon shook his head. "Some of the men had him on, though. Not like they planned it, exactly, it just came together, as if they'd all had the same dream almost." Easmon laughed. "Three of them, in the space of a fortnight, told him the story about a rich lad driven mad by the gentry, when they made him to run all around the county with a corpse on his back, the dead man's arms draped about the boy's back, the corpse telling him at each churchyard he came to that this was not the right one for the corpse to be buried in. The lad was the cousin of the priest who left the parish a dozen years earlier, they told Willy as a way of giving it the varnish of truth.

"On the first two tellings, each of the men insisted he not write a thing down. 'Best not to court trouble,' they told him. But on the third time, the man giving him the story put up a fuss, but backed down after a while and said, yes, Willy could write it down. And that's how it ended in his book." Easmon finished his whiskey and looked at the empty glass with disappointment. Stephen didn't take his eyes of Easmon.

"Father, I'm happy to foot the bill, but would you mind claiming another whiskey for our friend. I don't want to interrupt our conversation." He handed his wallet to Pádraig.

"But there was never really any authentic story about a man carrying a corpse?"

"Nah!"

"And I suppose it goes without saying that there never really was a man carrying a corpse on his back?"

Pádraig deposited the whiskey in front of Easmon who took a sip and swished it around his mouth for a moment.

"Well, now. I wouldn't say *that*."

18.

Pádraig smiled into his stout as he watched Stephen's reaction to Easmon's matter of fact acknowledgement of the possibility of a talking corpse. "Shall we talk about something else for a bit?" Pádraig asked.

"Not on your life," Stephen replied. "Easmon, what do you mean, you're not saying that a man went about with a corpse around his shoulders? You're joking, right? You're having one on me like they did back then with Yeats, aren't you?"

"No, no, young man. About these things I am very serious. And I'm saying that you can't rule out that it happened when the gentry are about. There's no profit in saying too much about what the gentry do, but it's even more dangerous to deny it." He leaned in toward Stephen. "I know about these things. Always have."

Stephen looked over at Ricky, who shrugged. "He's said that forever, I can stamp the truth to that. When I was a boy, he'd tell us, me and my cousins, about his commerce with the fairies." He glanced over at Easmon, who glowered at him. "Sorry, Uncle. I mean the gentry." Ricky looked around at the pub's tables to see who was closest by. "Not everyone likes to hear him talk about this, or me talk about it either. Some think it's crazy talk and wish he'd stop up. Others think it's true and wish he'd stop up. Either way, not a popular topic around here.

"I can tell you that he always seemed to know things like which plants make good teas for medicines for goiters and sour stomachs and such. When to plant various things to avoid damage from hail storms, for instance. When to bring the cows back from the farthest meadows just before the worst weather comes in. He saved my grandfather a dozen milking cows one summer the very day that two or three families had milkers taken away by a freakish flood. No one saw it coming, except Easmon. My mother said that after he'd told their father to hurry and bring the cows in, he wanted to run down the road and tell the neighbors, but my grandmother would have none of it. 'If a storm's coming that bad, it's right here you'll stay,' she said. My mother made the mistake, next day, of telling the kids from the families that had lost the cows that Easmon had known. The parents were none too pleased that they'd not gotten the warning. And you can guess how they categorized what happened."

"The evil touch?" Stephen ventured.

"Exactly. The belief was, back then, that the only way you could get such power was from some contact with the others. They might touch you, or breathe upon you, and give you that kind of ability."

"It sounds as though it would be useful to have some friends among the others, then."

"Sure, it could be, but there was also a lot of superstition and fear about the others. The taking away of people, for example, was a source of fright. Everyone had a story in their back pocket about this one or that one who was taken away, a pale and silent replica put in his place. They especially liked to take newborn babies, happy brides, nursing mothers and good dancers and athletes."

"Yes, I've read some of those stories in the Yeats book I'm getting through." Stephen said.

Easmon was by this time on his third whiskey and his second pint. "They took me once, you know," he said, loudly enough for a few heads to swing in the direction of the carmody. As people realized who was talking, they chuckled and turned back to their own conversations. Stephen noticed

Ellen, the owner of the pub, staring intently at Easmon from her place behind the till.

Stephen looked at Ricky. "Is that true?" Ricky smiled and shrugged. "I couldn't say. Part of me wants to say how could it possibly be true? It's all just a legend. And yet…my mother tells me that he did disappear for a month and a half when he was twelve and she was fourteen."

"A month and a half?" Stephen asked. "It was six weeks, was it?"

"No," Ricky said slowly, "as a matter of fact, she told me it was seven weeks, forty-nine days from disappearance until he turned up again. The family was terrified of what might have happened, but she said she felt confident for no reason she could put her finger on that he'd be back. So she counted the days off on the calendar she'd gotten for Christmas the year before. Forty-nine days. Is that important?"

"Not sure. Perhaps." Stephen reached instinctively for his pen, but put it down when Easmon raised his eyebrow at the gesture. "What did he say when he came home?"

"Ask him yourself," Ricky said, nodding toward his uncle.

"So Easmon. What was it like, your time away with them?" Easmon took on a faraway look. "A lot of dancing, as I recall. Food like I'd never seen, let alone be allowed to eat. Everyone happy, all the time. No shortage of drink, either, I remember that," he said nodding obliquely toward his empty pint glass. Stephen looked at Pádraig, who rose to fulfill the unspoken request. "At least I had my toes when I came back," he said.

"Pardon me. Had your toes?" Stephen asked. Ricky smirked as though he knew what was coming.

"Of course, glad I kept them. Lady from Rosses Pointe, she came back from being away with them, and she had no toes. She'd danced them off!" Easmon said. "That's what it's like being away with them. And you've no sense of time, it just seems always a ceili-party!"

"Do we need to cut him off?" Stephen whispered to Ricky. Ricky raised his palm. "It doesn't matter. He talks like this when he's sober. Anyway, he can hear you, don't discount it." Stephen glanced over to see Easmon's sour look.

"Listen, I appreciate the refreshment," Easmon said, in a voice keener than Stephen would have guessed he had left in him at this point in the evening. "But I'm serious about what I'm telling you, and you'd better listen if you're dabbling around in what Silly Willy wrote.

"I have come to know them, over the years. The others. They like that name, that and the gentry, they like to be called. Not the other names, which are disrespectful. I won't mention them out loud, but you'll guess what they are."

"Fairies," Ricky mouthed, cupping his hand against his cheek to avoid upsetting Easmon again.

"It's late," Pádraig said. "We've had a wonderful time talking with you, Easmon, but we should get you home before too long." He pushed back his empty glass. Easmon turned his face to Pádraig. His eyes were glassy, but still bright in spite of the drink.

"I knew your grandfather on your mother's side. Peter Murran. Knew him like a brother, practically." he said. "Well before he began visiting the merrow."

Pádraig sat up straight. "What?"

"The merrow. Did you not hear me, Father? I'm sitting right next to you. And they say I'm the one who needs the aids in my ears," Easmon muttered. "The merrow and the mermaids, over there by the Red Islands."

Pádraig regarded Easmon warily. His grandfather's stories about visiting below the waves with mermaids and the merrows were confined so far as he knew to his closest family, and even met there with embarrassed and indulgent laughter. He'd heard them often during his grandfather's later years, repeated under cloud of confusion watered with drink. But here was a man entirely outside the tightly bound circle of the Harts and Murrans going on about his grandfather's claims.

"You know, of course, about his cap, do you not, Father?"

He hadn't thought of it in years, but his grandfather had been known around the village by his red cap, a sort of beret he wore pushed back on his head. He was never seen without it. The bright color was his trademark.

"Mister Red, they called him," Easmon said.

"And you say he visited with the mermaids and the merrow?" Stephen asked.

"Oh, yes, quite regularly to hear him tell it. I believed him. That's where he got the red cap. A merrow-man named Coomarra gave it to him so he could visit as often as he liked. Only if you wear the red cap can you go under the waves without drowning."

"How did he come by such a friendship, do you know?"

"He loved to walk the road up there where it looks out over the Red Islands. Spent hours and hours up there watching the waves come in. One day, he'd been up there most of the afternoon when he looks out and sees something, a man, but green and scaly with a pig-nose, push up out of the water and sit on the rocks in the sun, facing out to sea. He rubbed his eyes and squinted a bit. He thought maybe the light was playing tricks on him. But he looked closer and was sure of what he saw. Just than the merrow-man turned toward the shore and saw him staring. He quick, quick dove under the surface and disappeared. He jumped in so fast that his little red hat fell off and he had to pop back up to grab it and put it on. Peter thought this was curious, and wondered what was so special about the red hat.

"Of course, then he couldn't keep himself away from the place. He was there from morning til night, hoping to see the merrow-man again. He even started climbing down the face of the cliff, using ropes and such to get down there. It didn't occur to him until much later that he could just sneak across the back of Randall Ramsey's meadow and get down there more easily. He'd get down there and huddle in one of the little indentations in the cliff, hiding himself to encourage the merrow-man to show himself again.

"One day, his luck returned and the merrow-man swam right up to the shore. Peter hadn't hidden himself all that well, it turns out, because the merrow-man called right out to him. 'You've come here forty-nine days in a row. You seem genuine in your curiosity, and there's far too little intercourse between our peoples. I'll take a chance that you're friend not foe. Say which you are.' 'Friend!' Peter calls out. 'Then you are welcome in my home if you'd like to visit.' 'Yes, I would,' says Peter. 'Come along then, but be sure to hold this red cap tight to your head when you dive in, otherwise you'll drown like the others.'

"Peter wasn't sure he liked this last mention of others drowning, but he was too excited to hesitate. He took a big breath and plunged in. They swam along for a while, then came to a place where the merrow-man signaled him to descend. Peter followed him down, and then all of a sudden they were on a beach, standing on dry sand, looking up at the ocean surging above them."

"So the merrow live under the waves, not in the water?"

"Correct. Lots of people think they swim around like fishesThat's not true at all. Everything on the land has its twin in the sea. Horses and waterhorses, for example. The merrow live like we do, only under the water. That's what Peter said. And the bit about them having fish tails instead of legs – pure nonsense, according to Peter."

"And they got on during that visit, so he kept the hat and got to visit whenever he wanted?"

"Yes, that's about right. They were fast friends, to hear Peter tell it, and I believed him. It didn't last, though."

"What happened?" Pádraig asked. Stephen couldn't tell whether Pádraig was playing along or suddenly drawn into the story.

"As I recall, it was right about the time you left to start seminary, Father. I'm not disrespecting your grandfather, I hope you know, to say that he wasn't a religious man, not much of a churchgoer. But when you left to study for the priesthood, it got him to thinking.

"One of the things he saw when he visited Coomarra disturbed him, but only a little at first. The merrow are great scavengers. Anything that ends up in the sea is likely to become a decoration in their houses. They wear beautiful jewelry that slips from ladies' wrists and fingers when they bathe in the ocean. When a ship goes down, they swarm all over it, taking mirrors, fastenings, ropes – anything they can lay hands on. And if the crew is lost in the wreck, they gather up their souls."

Stephen looked over at Pádraig, expecting him to start laughing at any moment, but Pádraig sat straight-faced and rapt.

"What do they do with the souls?" Pádraig asked.

"When Peter first went down there, he saw some things in Coo's yard that looked like fish traps. Sort of a metal box with netting all around. Something that a fish could swim into but not find its way out of. Each one of them had a shiny bright speck of light in it. Coo told Peter, 'If any a soul is spilled in the sea, it's ours to keep. These are soul cages, and each of us has a few.' 'But why do you keep the souls?' Peter asked. 'Look at them,' said Coo. 'They're beautiful and they sparkle with a light that we never see here under the ocean. Why shouldn't we keep them?'

"At first, Peter let this pass. But it didn't seem right to him that just because a man happened to lose his life at sea he should be prevented from presenting himself to St. Peter for judgment. The issue gnawed at him. He finally decided to do something about it.

"He invited Coo to dinner at his house one night when his wife, your grandmother Veronica, was away visiting her sister in Galway. He got him drunk, and while he was sleeping at the kitchen table, Peter stole away under the waves to Coo's house, tip-toed through the yard so as not to wake Coo's wife and family. He quickly went from cage to cage and cut the netting so that the souls could float up through the ocean above and beyond. He hurried back to his house to be there when Coo woke up as though nothing out of the ordinary had happened.

"Time came, of course, when Coomarra stumbled back to the shore and through the waves to go home. He discovered that the souls had escaped and knew from the cuts in the netting that they'd had help. He was furious. He couldn't say for sure that Peter had done the deed, but he was suspicious. He confronted Peter when next he saw him, but Peter denied everything, saying that he'd never left the house and spent the night watching over Coo since he seemed unaccustomed to strong drink. Coo cursed Peter and swam away. Peter never saw Coo again."

Pádraig sighed. "That's quite a story, Easmon. Thank you for sharing it. I must ask my mother all about it when I see her." He stood and extended his hand to Easmon. "And now we really do need to get you home because even if you're not tired, I am." Pádraig helped Easmon to his feet, waved to the crowd still lingering in the pub and moved Easmon gently toward the door.

Stephen remained behind with Ricky. Between the two of them, they settled the bar bill.

"Damn it, I forgot to ask him the most important question of all," Stephen said as they gathered up their things.

"What's that?"

"When he was taken away, how did his family get him back?"

"Well, I'm not sure they got him back exactly. He just came back."

"You're not aware that they did anything special?"

Ricky sighed. "Let's see. It's a long time since I talked to my mother about this. Her mind is fading, sad to say. But last year at Christmas, she did go on a bit about this. There were some superstitions involved, I think. Gifts laid in a special spot, red threads laced on a blackthorn tree, things like that. But the main thing she said, what made the difference in his coming back was just this, she said: 'We loved him more than they did.'"

They walked out into the night and Stephen thought, *if that's the key, she may never come back.*

19.

Stephen and Ricky caught up with Pádraig and Easmon at the front door of the house.   Ricky opened the door and Pádraig turned Easmon over to him.

Pádraig slid his hands into his pockets. "Care for a night cap?"

"No, not another drink. I'm exhausted. I'm dying to talk with you about what he said about your grandfather, but that will have to wait. Good night. See you tomorrow."

"I have a bottle of Lagavulin in my study," Pádraig called after him. Stephen spun about face. "I'll have mine neat."

Pádraig pulled the bottle out from his lower desk drawer and poured generous doses for both of them.

"So what about it?   Did your grandfather consort with fish people?"

Pádraig snorted. "Look, my grandfather said all manner of things, especially as he got on in years and became a bit addled. I never took it seriously. I figured that at best he was passing on a few stories, the kind you tell children late at night to give them a fright."

"What about the red hat? Is that accurate?"

"Yes, he did have a red hat that he was fond of. Wore it all the time.   But that doesn't mean that he got it from a merrow."

"Were you aware that he was friendly with Easmon and had shared all those stories with him?"

"That, I didn't know. I was surprised by that."

"I'm not sure what to make of all this, but it seems pretty clear that your grandfather believed he had these experiences. The red hat and his attachment to it are one tangible part of it, and the fact that he told his story to others, or at least Easmon, suggests that he was willing to subject himself to scrutiny or even ridicule. The experience was that important to him. That name, by the way, Easmon, isn't it usually pronounced Eamon?"

"It was meant to be Eamon, but the mother made a spelling error on the baptismal certificate. Or the vicar of the parish at the time did. More likely the mother. But once it's on the baptismal certificate and in the parish register, it's official and you're bound to use the name as it's been given to you."

"I was hoping to learn something useful tonight about what happened to Fianna and how we might find her. But there was really nothing particularly helpful. Maybe we didn't ask the right questions, though. Maybe I should have asked him straight out would he tell us how to find her, asked for him to intercede or something," Stephen mused.

"Please," said Pádraig. "I emptied your wallet and mine during that one conversation. If it's my turn to strike up another conversation with him, it will have to wait until after the collection on Sunday. Anyway, you're not lending any credence to this idea that she's been taken away, are you? You're not turning mad so soon after arriving in our barmy little village, I hope. It's rubbish."

Stephen put his glass down slowly. "Father, what was it that the search party found in Ned's boat out by the Red Islands? Wasn't it a red hat?"

"It was a hat. I didn't see it clearly myself. But you're right – one of the divers called out to Bertie, 'was she wearing a red hat?'"

" That's quite a coincidence, don't you think, given everything we've heard tonight?"

"Sure, it's a coincidence, but if you asked me how many red hats are there in Ireland, I'd guess it's hundreds of them at least. Listen, why are you so rattled by all of this?"

"I'm not saying we should give up the basics of a good search, not saying we shouldn't go back to the garda on Wednesday. I'm just saying that we shouldn't dismiss out of hand that there may be other approaches to this." Stephen paused. Pádraig stared.

"I've heard thousands of confessions since I was ordained. I can tell when someone has more to say, or they're just getting to the good part. Go on."

Stephen sat in one of the overstuffed chairs next to the fireplace. He was silent for a moment, then looked back at Pádraig. "I'm not in Mullaghmore entirely for the purpose of taking care of my mother. That's part of it. But the whole truth is that I was more or less booted out of Oxford. I suffered what they called a nervous breakdown. Not a very manly thing, is it."

"Sorry to hear. What happened?"

"A lot of things happened. But it started with this. I was with some friends one evening, a Friday night. This was during the period when I was finishing my dissertation, but it was putting up quite a fight. We had a few pints back at one fellow's apartment, Twomey, his name was, which was in the top floor, the attic of an old house about half a mile from the main quad. Twomey's first name was Russell. He was a nice looking man with bright red hair and loads of curls all over his head. The other fellow was Darnigan, first name Edward, called Teddy by his parents, though none of us knew that at the time.

"We all got a bit pissed, then bored. Bored and pissed is a bad combination because it leads to lots of mischief and bad judgment. We all three were in philosophy together, but Twomey had an anthropological bent, and Darnigan had an idea about going to seminary one day. We started talking about belief systems, and I must say, for a bunch of would-be humanists who should be open to all hypotheses until each is disproved, we were a closed-minded bigoted lot. The conversation pretty much ran on about how could this culture believe this or that.

"We came around to theosophy, and the whole voodoo

around the Theosophical Society. The idea of being able to communicate with the dead, or see things thousands of miles away or receive telepathic messages from people at such distances -- none of that was new. But Helena Blavatsky, the founder of the Society, took it to a whole new level. Madame Blavatsky, as she insisted on being called, wrote extensively about her experiences and purported to document the experiences of others. Soon she was in demand all over Europe and America to hold seances. She had flocks and flocks of people who were desperate to believe that they could talk to their dead spouses and siblings to make sure they were all right, whatever that means to a dead person.

"Years later, of course, she was proved a fraud, at least with respect to the telepathy part of her scam. Her rise to popularity had come at an interesting time in the battle between science and spirituality. Frederic Myers and others, who really were scientists, had their own dearly departed whom they missed terribly and wanted to check up on. So they were predisposed to believe that this kind of communication was possible. But like good scientists, they wanted proof that it really worked. So they established the Psychical Research Society in London to do a methodical investigation of reported phenomena. Over several decades, they deployed volunteer investigators to collect anecdotes from people claiming to have had messages or conversations with dead relatives. They were also interested in telepathy, which they regarded as a close cousin of empathy. They started with the observable phenomenon of empathy -- everyone has had the experience of understanding how someone else is feeling, or what they're about to say, without a word spoken. They reasoned from there that if empathy worked between two living individuals, then telepathy wasn't that much of a stretch because the only variable was distance. From there they reasoned that mediumship, or direct communication from a person's dead wife to the widower, wasn't a big leap because the empathy that exists between living individuals is a function of human personality. The key to that bit of reasoning, obviously, is that human personality survives death. Myers wrote a whole book about that, I discovered later.

"Anyway, as part of their detective work, the Psychical Research Society sent an investigator to India, a man named Robert Hogsdon, where Madame Blavatsky was then holding forth. Her practice at that time, meant to dazzle the gullible, was to separate herself from the audience -- sometimes as small as one well heeled client. An assistant would remain in the room with the client, and gently question the client about the deceased person the client wanted to contact. The questioning, even though gentle, extracted probing emotional reactions. Blavatsky and her assistants referred to this room as a shrine. After the questioning, all of which Blavatsky could hear from her bedroom on the other side of the wall, the assistant would encourage the client to sit quietly and meditate on the best qualities of the deceased. Then, miraculously, a handwritten message would appear to come out of one of several slots in the wall. The message always assured the client that the loved one was safe and happy and contained a few details gleaned during the earlier interview. The message was passed, Blavatsky's organization said, by an ancient Hindu master who had become a medium in the spirit world. His name was Coot Hoomi. I know, right? The name alone should have gotten people giggling.

"Hogsdon was serious about his mission, and he travelled all the way to India to inspect the shrine. And what did he discover? The slots were not just emanating from the wall, they went all the way through into Madame Blavatsky's bedroom. It was a fraud all the way through. Here's the best part: the day after Hogsdon's visit, the whole building burned down. Nothing left but ashes. So, of course, Hogsdon couldn't bring in a fellow investigator to verify his observations. But he wrote a two hundred page report on his work tearing the life work of Madame Blavatsky limb from limb.

"You probably think that this would be enough to shake Blavatsky's supporters away from her. But no. Even the ones who were willing to accept that she had been a fraud on the messages from Coot Hoomi -- she eventually admitted it herself -- maintained that on the whole, she'd done a lot for the world. She'd opened people's minds to eastern practices, and on and on. And the Theosophical Society lived on spreading the principles of theosophy. Unfortunately, these included the belief that mankind had descended from a handful of prior races with the Aryans at the top of the line. Blavatsky maintained that intermarriage with Jews had brought the Aryans into decline. You can guess who found that idea convenient to exploit.

"Anyway, with that history behind it, with theosophy totally debunked by observational science and common sense, we laughed the hardest that night when we came to talking about it in the catalogue of crazy things people believe. We had quite a few good side splitting laughs about how stupid the main of humanity was. That was when Twomey turned on us to play devil's advocate.

"He pulled this all the time, taking the odd side of an argument. That night he was saying, 'Sure, that particular woman was a fraud, but in Myers' book, there are legions of examples of people who convinced the SPR that they were genuine mediums.' We said that if Hogsdon had time, he certainly could have debunked them all. We went back and forth, more and more amazed at how attached Twomey was to the idea that mediums could be legitimate. Finally, we challenged him to give us one iota of evidence that it could be real.

"Twomey had an old Ouija board, which he hauled out from the back of a closet. He lit up a few candles and switched off the light. We sat around the coffee table in his tiny living room, an old scarred cherry thing that his parents had cast off in a recent move. He made us promise not to laugh during the experiment.

"'There's some curiosities I've heard about in connection with this old house, he said. The old lady Darnigan and I rent from doesn't seem to want to talk about it, but I've got the idea that something bad happened to someone somewhere in this house. I say we ring up the afterlife and ask about it. What motive have they got to pull punches?' he asked cheerily.

"So we started off as solemnly as three drunken twenty-two year olds can pretend to be. We poised our fingers lightly on the Ouija speller.

"Twomey asked, 'Is there a spirit who would like to tell us something about this house?' We waited a few minutes. Nothing. Darnigan and I lifted our hands off the speller after a few minutes. Twomey stayed with it, and after about another thirty seconds, his eyes got big and he said, 'I think it's starting to move!' Darnigan and I laughed out loud and Twomey shushed us. The speller moved slowly under Twomey's hands to spell 'Who'.

"'What the hell does that mean?', I asked. By this time, Darnigan's face was looking something past surprised and on the way to frightened. 'I think it's asking who we are. Don't tell it!' Darnigan said sharply. 'We should never have done this on a Friday night. The devil's Sabbath. Stupid, stupid, stupid!'

"He was really working himself into a lather, so I told him, 'crank the lights back on and let's go down the pub before it closes.' He ran for the switch, almost fell on his face in the dim light, and when he snapped the tripper, nothing happened. 'It won't come back on. What does that tell you?' He was practically screaming by now.

"Twomey couldn't have been less empathetic. 'It tells me that the fuse is blown again and you're a sack of shite. Sit down. This is just getting interesting.'

"I had to admit that it was getting a lot more interesting than when we had first started. I said, 'tell it who we are, but leave Darnigan out of it.' Twomey quickly spelled out our names, family and given.

"Twomey moved on after a brief pause. 'I'm asking who this is we're speaking to.' He glided the speller across the board. But instead of an answer, we got another question: 'Want what'.

"This completely unnerved Darnigan, who was now standing up on the divan, as if something might grab his ankles from under the furniture. He shouted, 'Twomey is definitely fucking with us. He's driving the speller wherever he damn well pleases. This is shite.' He started toward the door, then

108

came back and crouched on the sofa. 'I'm not going down those dark stairs by myself without the lights on.'

"Twomey shrugged and threw his hands in the air. 'You think I'm making this up? Fine. Let's see if it can drive itself.' He sat back against the sofa, and I'll be damned if the little speller didn't shimmy across the board to spell 'too slow'.

"At this point, all we could do is say 'fuck' quite a few times and stare at the board. Darnigan was coming quite undone. And then the most unusual thing happened.

The old coffee table had drop leaves on either side, ones that you cold pull out and prop up with sliders from under the table. The leaves began to flap. First the one facing the sofa would go up and down with a few taps, then a pause, then the one facing out into the room would do the same, but not necessarily with the same number of taps. It went on and on. We sat there with our mouths open.

"It occurred to one of us at some point that we should write down the number of taps on each side and make a symbol for the pauses when they occurred. We did this over the period of half an hour while the tapping continued. And then it stopped.

"Well, I can tell you that we were well and truly sobered up by this time. It was unspoken among us that none of us would talk with anyone about what happened until we had some idea of what had in fact happened. We sat silent as stones for a full hour after this. All of a sudden, Twomey leapt up and grabbed the notebook from my hands. He rushed over to his pantry and grabbed a box of cereal.

"Darnigan rolled his eyes. 'Really, Twomey, can't you put the present matter ahead of your stomach for a few more minutes?'

"'Shut up, idiot,' says Twomey. 'It's an American cereal, Captain Crunch. I fell in love with it when I was visiting my cousins in Brooklyn. They sent me a dozen boxes for Christmas.' He turned the box to look at the back. 'There's a game on the box. It's a simple code. Look.' He brought the box over to the table.

"What he had there on the box was a code key. The

alphabet was arranged in five columns and five rows, with 'z' by itself in a sixth row in the first column. Can you picture that or should I draw it out?"

"I'm with you," Pádraig said. "I can picture it."

"The game that the cereal company invited kids to play was to tap out words by giving the location of the letters of the word. The first set of taps was the row number, followed by a pause, then a series of taps to designate the column number. So 'A' would be tap, pause, tap. 'B' would be tap pause tap tap."

"Sounds laborious," Pádraig said.

"It is that. But it's useful when you aren't in a position to speak. I looked into it afterwards and found out that some of the war prisoners in Viet Nam used it to communicate between their cells. Trying to speak out loud to another prisoner was harshly punished.

"So you probably can guess where this is headed. We used the code key to translate the taps of the coffee table. I know this sounds insane already. But it gets more so." Stephen took a gulp of his drink and held it out for more.

"Ah, not that I'd refuse you another pour, but scotch of this quality is more for sipping than drinking," Pádraig said as he filled Stephen's glass with another inch of liquor.

"You may want to take a stiff one yourself before I put this on you. We used the key code, and found that it spelled out a message."

"Which was?"

"I memorized it, I read it over so many times. It was this: 'Do not care to talk about myself. Message from another: 'Hello, Teddy, I'll always love you. Be good.' Well, you can be sure that Darnigan pissed his pants. Literally. We didn't know what had driven him so berserk until he finally told us that his family nickname was Teddy. 'No one calls me that, no one, outside my parents, my brother and my sister.' I was about to ask him couldn't it be a grandparent saying a friendly hello, when I remembered that when the spirit had asked us to identify ourselves, we didn't say that Darnigan was in the room.

"That is pretty unnerving. You're sure you didn't just

110

make out a message in the taps because you wanted to see one?"

"Absolutely sure. We checked it and checked it. Once we figured out that we were watching a pattern of taps, we took pretty good notes. As we applied the key, we saw that we had missed the first part of the message the first time around, but picked it up when it began to repeat. Whoever was sending the message was persistent and wanted to make sure that we three dunces had ample opportunity to catch on to it." Stephen sat silently for a minute.

"That's it?"

"No, there's more." Stephen hunched forward and cupped the glass between his hands. "After a while, the lights came back on. Darnigan still didn't want to go downstairs to his own apartment, so Twomey gave him some dry clothes. We fell asleep, finally, all three there in Twomey's living room. At some point after dawn, there was a loud banging on Twomey's door. It had to be the landlady so early in the morning, and I assumed she was there to pass on a noise complaint. But instead I heard her shout through the door, 'Mr. Twomey, Mr. Twomey, do you know where Mr. Darnigan is?' Twomey opened the door and told her he was inside. 'There's a long distance call for him in the office for you.'

"So Darnigan goes downstairs to the office, and a few seconds later, we hear him shrieking. Twomey and I almost knocked the landlady over the railing running downstairs to get to him. We get to the office, and he's in a heap on the floor. He looks up and tells us, 'My sister was in a car crash yesterday. She died last night.'

"I could feel the hair standing up on my neck, my arms, even my beard stubble tingled. I mean, I was sorry as could be for poor Darnigan. He was very close to his sister, talked about her all the time. But the implications of what had just happened were as exciting as they were alarming. The way the whole evening had unfolded, this seemed like the real deal, the genuine article that Frederic Myers spent years trying to authenticate in his research and his experiments.

"I was enthralled with the possibilities of further

experiments that I could design and conduct as follow on research to my dissertation. I spent the rest of the weekend thinking about it, that and helping Darnigan get ready to go home for the funeral. I sketched out pages and pages of bibliographic research that needed to be done and experiments to isolate and test the elements of what we had seen. How did the spirit know that Darnigan was in the room even though we withheld that piece of information? Did the presence of the spirit disrupt the power and make the lights go out, or was that a separate phenomenon? What exactly had we done to get the spirit to make its presence known? Was it our initial skepticism that softened into receptivity? Was it the physical space we were in? Who was that spirit anyway? Hundreds of spin-off questions from those.

"And then I made a mistake. A huge mistake."

"Which was what," Pádraig inquired gently. The stress of retelling the story was taxing Stephen's energy.

"By that time, I had almost finished my dissertation. It was time for me to look for a job teaching at university. I was not quite a shoo-in for a job at one of the better colleges at Oxford, but a solid candidate, well thought of by the dons. Then, stupidly, stupidly, I told the don of my own college about my post-doctoral research plans, which, of course, included telling him about what happened that Friday night."

"Oh no, you didn't really, did you?"

"Oh yes, I did. This was a problem for many reasons. First and foremost, the don immediately recategorized me from promising scholar to nutters. I think my dissertation defense was so smooth because they just wanted to get me out of there and that body of work I'd already done they couldn't legitimately criticize. Of course, that meant no job in Oxford. The dons all talk, and once I was stamped barmy by one of them, the rest came in line. I could feel their contempt and amusement as I walked through the town.

"Second, it was a breach of the implicit promise I'd made to Twomey and Darnigan, that we three made to each other. We agreed we wouldn't talk to anyone about what happened until we understood it better. In my mind, that promise was released when Darnigan got his phone call. The call, to me, put a name to what we had experienced. It erased any doubt about that, though it launched a fleet of other questions. Plus, I figured that Darnigan was going to be telling plenty of people about it, starting with his parents and the rest of the family.

"But what I did by bragging about my research plan, in hopes of securing an appointment, implicated Twomey. I never named him when talking to my don, but it was known that we went about together, and people readily assumed that he was one of the people in the room with me. I'd had to tell the don that I was not alone in the room both to give credence to the story and to explain about another in the party getting the phone call the next morning, the validation of the experience. So the opprobrium fell on him, too, people laughing behind his back just as he'd pass by a shop, people knocking on tables and asking him to translate the message. He was humiliated. He wasn't as far along on his dissertation as I was.

"Eventually, he'd had enough, and dropped out. Gave up on his dissertation and left Oxford. There was an ugly good-bye where he told me he'd never forgive me for what I'd done. Everything he said about me, I deserved. I've never seen him since."

"What about Darnigan?"

"He eventually came back to university. But he was different. No life in his face. I hadn't named him in my story, either, but if anyone figured out or supposed that he was there, he didn't get the same treatment as Twomey did. I think somehow people gave him the benefit of the doubt in view of his sister's death. He avoided me, though. We never spoke about what happened after that night. I could tell he didn't want to."

"Well, that's quite a story. I can see how it might unravel a man, having his career side-butted by events like that. Your nervous breakdown occurred when, last year?"

"Yes, end of term in the spring. I went to ground at my mother's house in Dublin for the summer. Never left the house. Had a beard down to my chest by September. I came out of it slowly. At least I think I'm out of it. There are still some bad days."

"There's a lot to talk about in what you've said. Should we put a comma here, and talk some more tomorrow? It's...three in the morning," Pádraig said squinting at his wristwatch.

Stephen sat quietly for a minute. "It needs a comma, yes. But not right here. I haven't been fully honest with you yet."

Pádraig put his glass down on the desk. "Is this the part where you tell me you're a homosexual?"

Stephen sat up, startled. "Yes, but how did you know? I mean, I really try not to let on. It's so distressing to most people, I just keep it to myself. What gave me away?"

"Relax, it's nothing about your appearance or mannerisms. It's the way you talked about Twomey. He was your man friend, am I right?" Stephen nodded. "You are obviously pained about how you hurt him. And you miss him."

"Terribly."

"You punish yourself every day for what you did, don't you?"

"It's never out of my mind. Not for a moment I'm awake. I dream about it sometimes. Nightmares, really, reliving that day he left and what he said."

Pádraig walked across the room and put his hand on Stephen's shoulder. "I've never seen a more contrite penitent, Stephen. If this were confession, this would be the part where I absolve you. But it's not confession, and so my advice to you is that you do something even more important than obtaining absolution: forgive yourself."

"I'm not sure that's possible," Stephen shrugged. "But I've got to go home and get some sleep. I hope to God that my mother hasn't stayed up waiting," he groaned. "I'm sure I'll run into you in the morning, Father. We don't seem to be able to avoid one another."

"Well, it's a small village. I'll look forward to it." Pádraig said, showing Stephen out through the kitchen door. "And by the by, it would be all right to call me by my first name, at least when we're talking privately."

Stephen walked through the door.   "All right, Pádraig. And thank you for listening. You're a very kind person."

"Sometimes I am.   But mostly I'm just good at my job," Pádraig said, gently closing the door.

20.

Tuesday was Mrs. O'Flannelly's day off, so Pádraig rummaged around the kitchen for bread and preserves to make breakfast after morning Mass. It had taken some persistence to get the housekeeper to take a regular day off during the week. It had never occurred to Padriag's predecessor, Monsignor Hardagon to offer her a day off. Even after Pádraig had suggested it soon after he took over as pastor, she ignored him for months until he finally put his foot down and insisted she choose a day off. When they finally settled on Tuesday, it was still many more months before he persuaded her to stop cooking for him on her day off and bringing over two meals a day from her kitchen. She resorted for a time to sending her sister instead, but Pádraig had a talk with Myrna, and asked her to please, please tell her sister that he'd be just fine on Tuesdays, living on the leftovers from Sunday and Monday or popping over to the village's Chinese restaurant, Luck Boat.

He stretched his legs walking over to the Gunnings' place. The dogs greeted him, but no one came to the door. He walked around back, and saw Ned in the milking barn. He had really only wanted to talk to Bertie, to see how she was holding up. He wasn't concerned that anything eventful had happened; he knew he'd hear right away if Fianna came home. He stood in the yard for a moment debating the merits of engaging with Ned, then walked away without saying hello.

He paused at the top of the Hill leading back into town. There was a spot he liked that he could get to by stepping over the guard rail and edging toward the top of the cliff. It was a grand overlook of the Red Islands, three rocky outcroppings of red granite jutting up out of the water a quarter-mile or so from the shore. He hadn't realized it until last night, but this must be the place that his grandfather frequented, the place he first saw Coomarra, if anything like that really happened. Pádraig laughed to himself. Gone all these years, and still pulling my leg from the grave, he thought.

He liked this view of the waves crashing in on the Islands, the bigger ones making towers of water as they came in against the rocks. He often spent hours here, standing in the breeze, watching one wave after another, predicting where it would first touch the Island, then another and just one more until most of a morning was gone. He rationalized it as meditation, or homily preparation and never felt guilty enough to give it up or cut back.

He was just climbing back onto the roadway when Stephen turned the curve, walking toward the village.

"Here we are again, as predicted," Stephen said as he approached Pádraig.

"Yes, as predicted. I was up knocking on Bertie's door, but she wasn't there. Ned was out in the barn, I saw him, but I had no interest in talking to him."

"Understandable. It won't be Wednesday until it's Wednesday. What do you think we should do in the meantime?"

"I don't know, really. I'm getting more and more worried. Do you ever think that once something's lost, it gets somehow more lost the longer it's missing?"

"I have noticed that. If you don't find something in the first few days of missing it, it's less and less likely it will turn up. I think it's that if you've lost it in a usual place, close at hand, you're likely to come across it again in your routine. But if you've lost it in an unusual place, somewhere you hardly every go, you can't reconstruct the moment you lost it. Something like that." They walked along together for a few moments.

"Say, this is probably silly to bring up, but when I was little and lost a toy or a book, my mother used to say I should stop looking and say a prayer to St. Anthony. It always seemed to work. I don't believe in prayer; I always thought it was just stopping for a moment to clear your head was what made it work. Is there any precedent for doing the same thing for a lost person? I mean, at this point, I think there's no idea too crazy to try. What do you think?"

"Um, well I understand your point of view, having heard you out last night. Do you really believe it happened? The message from Darnigan's sister?"

"I never did the follow up research that I mapped out, of course. But on its face, yes, those events really did happen while I observed them. Two other people saw the same thing and came to the same conclusion."

"I don't know about praying to St. Anthony. You're right, the main reason that works is that you pause and reflect on where you probably last saw the thing you're missing. Pausing allows you to mentally retrace your steps. But overall, you may be on to an idea about putting prayers on the problem."

"I've never really understood what people think prayer is all about. Do they really think that an omniscient God doesn't already know what you're petitioning about? That God was withholding the recovery of a sick child until someone got down on his knees and asked for it with a few Our Fathers? And that He'll still withhold it unless you say enough Our Fathers? How many is enough? It goes on and on, and it's just sad how some people hang their lives on it."

Pádraig glanced at him sideways. "Your burst of candor last night seems to be running all over everywhere, Stephen. Most people are a little shy of telling a priest that the main tool of his profession is a sack of shite."

"I'm sorry if I've gone too far. Sometimes I can be too blunt. But I've really always wondered what people think prayer accomplishes and why it's necessary. Any thoughts by way of clarification on the subject?"

"Look, there's a juvenile view of prayer that's all about 'I lost my doll, please return it to me.' Some people take that into adulthood. A lot of people, actually. They pray for results like good health, success at work, winning a football match. It causes a lot of snarls in public relations for God. If they get what they want, he's a hero. He might even get a prayer of thanks after the fact. If they don't get what they want, well, He's all kinds of things including nonexistent. How's that for deflating?

"The Jesuits have a different, more mature approach to prayer, and when we can reach people, we can teach people. But it's hard to overcome those engrained, juvenile expectations of how prayer works."

"I'm not surprised to hear that prayer is another thing that Jesuits are better at than other people. What's the Jesuit approach?" Stephen asked.

"We look at prayer as a relationship with God. You don't have to recite a formula to be engaged in prayer. Prayer is just an opening of the self to a friendship with God. You talk to God the way you would a good friend. You share your dreams and fears. You're candid about your problems and shortcomings. You replay the triumphs and defeats of the day.

"It's a two-way relationship, too, just like with a friend, but a very wise and patient one. God, as a friend, talks back. Not in a booming, instructional voice, but in insights, some small and some large, that come to you during or after prayer."

Stephen frowned. "But isn't that just like the mechanism that makes a prayer to the patron saint of lost things work? If you just give yourself a break from clenching your mind around a problem, an idea may come to you. Not from God, but from inside yourself."

Pádraig shook his head. "Listen, I see the logic of that. But there have been enough times when I know I've been completely devoid of the resources to solve a problem. And the answer came to me through prayer. Here's an example. My sister was in some trouble a few years ago. The details don't matter at the moment. My mother and I were desperate to console her and help her, but she just kept herself beyond reach. I prayed a lot over what to do. This was when I was away at National University working on my dissertation. I got home as often as I could to support my mother, but the situation seemed intractable.

"I got into the habit, during my novitiate, of setting aside an hour each day for prayer, and I devoted all my time during my sister's troubles to praying for an insight on this thorny matter. I was immersed in prayer one day, when it suddenly came to me, a voice inside me, not my own, saying, 'She will be taken care of. No need to worry.'

"It was too late to call home at that hour, but the next day, I did reach my mother. She was brighter and happier sounding than I'd heard in months, She said, 'Pádraig, you'll never believe this. Your sister came around yesterday.' My sister was not living at home at this point. 'She's getting married!' my mother told me. I was speechless. Depending on the details, this could be very good news. An answer to my prayers. 'In fact,' my mother continued, 'She's already married! They eloped to London a while ago.' Now, that surprised me, but still, to know she'd be taken care of and stop putting the fret on my mother the way she'd been doing -- that was important progress, and responsive to my prayers." Pádraig smiled.

"But isn't that the kind of petitionary prayer that you were just criticizing? 'Give my sister a good husband?'"

"No, it's a little different. I wasn't praying for an outcome. I was praying for an insight as to what to do to help my mother and my sister, though she was fairly resistant to help in those days."

"And the answer was, 'you don't need to do anything, it will all work out'?" Stephen asked.

"Yes. The way we look at prayer, it worked. I had a conversation with my friend, God, and he gave me good advice."

"Okay, if you say so. I still say that the answer could have come from your own intelligence. Maybe you just realized that there was nothing more you could do than you'd already done. Maybe you wanted a reason to let yourself off the hook."

Pádraig shrugged. "You may think so. But I'm just telling you that that was not my voice that delivered that message. It was someone else's voice. And since God was the only being I was talking to at the time, I choose to believe, I am confident believing, that it was an answer to my prayers."

Stephen sighed. "Choose to believe? If that's the best you can do....Well, there must be more to the Jesuit approach to prayer. What else have you got?"

"Oh, there's loads more we've got. The founder of our order, St. Ignatius Loyola, created a whole regimen of prayer. It's captured in his book Spiritual Exercises. After all these centuries, it's still the best single text on how to develop a spiritual, prayerful life. You don't even need to be Catholic to benefit from it."

"But you probably do need to believe in God, I'd guess," Stephen scoffed.

"Actually, while that's what Ignatius presupposed, it doesn't seem to be necessary. I've instructed from the Exercises to a lot of people who don't believe in God, or at least the Christian God. Buddhists in Hong Kong, Hindus in India. They seemed to get a lot out of it, which may surprise you."

Stephen shrugged, "I believe you if you say so."

"Anyway, the most basic prayer, the one that all novitiates habituate themselves to incorporate into the evening hours, is called the Examen. It's just like it sounds: it's a mental review of what happened during the day. But it's not just a chronological review. You examine your interactions with other people. You look for Christ's presence in those interactions. Did you engage fully? Respectfully? Did you meet Christ in that person? Did that person meet Christ in you?"

"Sounds like a recipe for perpetual guilt and second-guessing," Stephen said.

"Obviously, if you approach it with that mindset, you can turn it into that. But if you look at it as a laboratory for self-improvement, it is fabulously positive. As in all prayer, the Examen can yield up insights. You get ideas about how to do your job better, how to be a better friend, how to be a better son or brother. And you get to forgive yourself for any things you've done wrong or inadequately." He looked at Stephen. "Some things require more than one Examen to truly forgive yourself."

Stephen kept his gaze on the road leading down to the village. "I can see that. Listen, you were very copacetic about my big revelation last night. You barely blinked when I told you. In fact, you more or less beat me to the punch."

"Stephen, I've seen a lot of things over many years. There isn't much left to shock me. There aren't too many people who'll be that honest with a priest, and I respect you for it." He paused. "Also, don't forget that my job is to live celibate in a society of men who are also theoretically celibate."

"So, are you...."

"No, not I. I'm just saying that I've seen a lot of things. I pass no judgments where consenting adults are involved. In other circumstances, I have views....but that's for another day, perhaps."

They walked on without speaking for a bit. They grew close enough to the quay to hear the seagulls keening.

"Say, you wouldn't like to join me for lunch, would you, Stephen? I generally take lunch on Tuesdays at the Chinese place, Luck Boat. Have you been there?"

"No, but count me a yes on your invitation. I've been dying to try the place."

"Wow, that's more enthusiasm than I usually hear about Luck Boat."

Stephen rolled his eyes. "It's the only faintly exotic thing about Mullaghmore. On that score alone, I owe it my patronage, that's how I see it. Let's go."

21.

"Joe Poon, meet my new friend Stephen Attergood," The two shook hands. "Stephen recently moved here from Oxford," Pádraig explained.

"Oh, welcome, then. I'm from Hong Kong. In case you thought I was from here," Joe deadpanned.

"Your English is flawless, so it wouldn't have given you away. In fact, you have a slight west of Ireland accent. Is that just bending to the local winds?"

"No, not exactly." He gestured toward Pádraig. "Meet my teacher."

Pádraig smiled. "You did all the hard work, Joe. I was just your sparring partner in conversation practice. If only I'd learned as much Cantonese as you did English."

Joe dealt out placemats and silverware, with a pair of chopsticks at Pádraig's setting. "You're a good student. And not so old. There's hope for you yet. Should I give you menus or just tell you what to have?" Joe looked back and forth between the two men.

"I always eat what he tells me to, and I haven't gone wrong yet," Pádraig said.

"Fine, then, I'll do the same."

Joe's wife, Yin, arrived with a pot of jasmine tea. Joe introduced her. "She's studying English, but still has a way to go before she's fluent. She's a little shy about speaking to new people, but that'll change if you're around for a while," he told

Stephen.

Pádraig and Stephen made their way through the meal slowly, in no hurry to do anything else until there was a plan in place. "So any other tricks in the bag when it comes to prayer?" Stephen asked.

"I'm trying hard not to get annoyed with your attitude toward all this. It's not like I haven't been praying up a storm over Fianna's disappearance already."

"I'm sure you have, but it hasn't worked yet, by any measure. I'm just trying to find out if there's another approach available to us. Or to you. I'm not likely to fall on my knees just now."

Pádraig returned Stephen's smirk. "It's not all about wearing out your knees, Stephen. I'm sure you already know that. Especially if you're going to be at it for an hour, you need to make yourself comfortable. Otherwise, sooner or later, you'll get distracted.

"Here's one of my favorite ways to pray. It comes right out of Exercises. You summon up a passage from the Bible, or re-read something you haven't looked at for a while. The New Testament tends to work a little better for this, because as you'll see, the central character is Jesus. It's a little easier to do with Jesus than an incarnate God. So let's say you pick the passage where Jesus raises Lazarus up from the dead."

"Okay, I'm reasonably familiar with that one."

"Right. So in this form of prayer, you let God touch your imagination. You imagine the scene as it is in the Bible. But you put yourself into the scene. You make yourself a present observer. You take note of what you see, what you touch, what you smell, what emotions are going on around you. You turn yourself around in the scene and experience it as if you're there."

"And then what happens?"

"Well, you never know. When you enter the story, you change it, of course, because it wasn't written with you in it. So it unfolds around you in unexpected ways sometimes."

"The observer effect. Fascinating."

"Meaning what?"

"It's a principle in physics, anthropology, sociology -- lots of fields of physical, natural and social science. You can't observe some things, or study them, without changing the thing you're trying to observe. In anthropology, for example. How can someone like Margaret Mead know whether she's seeing authentic native behavior, or some self-conscious shadow of what the natives would be doing if she weren't there? From what Easmon said, it sounds as though Yeats fell into the trap himself. By trying so hard to extract authentic stories from people around here, he annoyed them enough for them to put out a fake one. And he took the bait."

"Right. I never heard it compared to that, but that's the general idea. You just never know how it might unfold as an experience for you. One of the first times I did this was after my ordination at a retreat that was part of my formation. Becoming a Jesuit doesn't stop with ordination. There are years of formation after that. How long it takes depends on how hard you work at it, how it fits with your other duties and how ready you are for each stage at a particular time. If you're on assignment in Africa, for example, it might be hard to break off and go to Philadelphia for a thirty-day silent retreat."

"You? Thirty days of silence. That must have nearly killed you."

"I thought it would, going into it. But it's surprising how comfortable you get with it after a short time. Anyway, it was during that retreat that I practiced this prayer technique, which we call Ignatian Contemplation, reflecting on the passage about Jesus raising Lazarus from the dead.

"I remember putting myself into the scene from the viewpoint of one of the disciples with Jesus walking up to the village of Bethany where Lazarus had lived with his sisters, Mary and Martha. The family had befriended Jesus, and believed in his divinity and his ability to perform miracles, so they sent word to him in Jerusalem when Lazarus fell mortally ill. No one knows exactly what his ailment was, but it was clear to the sisters that his condition was dire, so they sent for the one person that they knew could heal him and prevent him from dying.

"Jesus got the message, but deliberately decided not to go right away. In fact, it wasn't until four days after Lazarus had died that Jesus traveled the two miles -- only two miles -- back to Bethany to see about Lazarus. He foreshadowed to the disciples who were with him that he had something big in store and was actually glad that Lazarus was going to furnish a proof case for his power to work miracles.

"Mary and Martha didn't know any of this. So when word came that Jesus was on his way and entering the village, Mary was so mad at him that she stayed home. Martha went out to greet him, mostly with recriminations about why he had waited so long; that if he had been there, Lazarus would still be alive. Jesus reassured her that Lazarus would rise again; she replies that she knows that he'll be resurrected in the final judgment. Jesus corrects her with a belief challenge: 'I am the resurrection and the life: he who believes in me, though he be dead shall live: and everyone who lives and believes in me shall not die forever. Do you believe this?' Martha says she does and secretly goes off to tell Mary to come see what happens next.

"Now, as I mentioned, my viewpoint upon entering the scene was that of someone accompanying Jesus, walking into Bethany with him and hearing the recriminations of Martha. But at the moment that Martha went off to get Mary, my viewpoint switched mentally to Mary. I mean to being Mary, of being the one so angry that Jesus had not shown up when he could have prevented death and suffering that she wouldn't even come out to greet him.

"And I realized that I was angry with Jesus, with God, over being absent at times, or a particular time, in fact, when his presence could have prevented great harm to people who deserved none of what happened to them. I had the experience of Mary, coming out to greet Jesus reluctantly, only when pressed by news that he might be ready to do something to make up for his lapse. But unlike the Mary in John's gospel, whose recriminations melted when it was clear that Jesus was about to raise Lazarus up, in my experience of this passage, the recriminations continued.

126

"Now, as John writes it, Mary goes down to the tomb with Martha and some other Jews from Bethany and confronts Jesus, sobbing, with the same rebuke that Martha started out with. Jesus listens and accepts the rebuke. He asks the two sisters to point out the tomb of Lazarus. His reaction upon seeing it is captured in the shortest verse anywhere in the Bible: 'And Jesus wept.' The fact that it's so short makes it even more powerful. Seeing what happened to his friend Lazarus was the event that so struck Jesus through, that he wept."

Pádraig paused for a moment. "Up to this point, I was John's character, Mary. But in that moment, in my contemplation of the verse, suddenly, I was myself again, standing in that scene at the tomb. Jesus was staring at the tomb, weeping. And then, the most amazing thing happened: in his weeping, he turned to me.

"I was deeply into the contemplation at this point. I don't know whether it was officially a trance or a lucid dream. But the experience was so vivid. And the effect on me was so...profound. It was like the arm of Jesus on my shoulder, not an apology, but an acknowledgement that something had happened in my life that his presence could have prevented.

"I didn't wake up or come out of it, whatever the right terminology would be. But I could feel warm tears on my face. I was so grateful for what was happening, it was such a relief."

"Wow." Stephen said. "I don't know what actually happened, but the way you tell it, something extremely moving happened to you."

Pádraig nodded and took a deep breath. "Yes. But there's more." He paused again. "In John's gospel, at this point, Jesus tells the crowd to roll away the tombstone that closed up the cave where Lazarus was lying. When they do that, he makes a short prayer to God and calls Lazarus out of the tomb."

"Right, and Lazarus comes walking out of the tomb. The whole point of the story, isn't it?"

"Yes. But for me, in the contemplation, the viewpoint character switched again. It was me, as myself, who walked out of the cave."

Stephen sat silently for a moment. "What does it mean? To you?"

"Well, that's given me a lot to think about over the years. Some comfort, some pain. I think it means, to me, that bad things can happen when God isn't where you'd like him to be. But you can rise above the damage that happens. You can move on, even with the guilt that comes with feeling as though you didn't try hard enough, didn't do enough to bring God into the places where he could protect people who need protecting."

"Hmm. All this is very abstract. I have a feeling there's an actual story behind all this that fills in the part about what you were overcoming and feeling guilty about."

Pádraig smiled distantly. "There is. But this isn't the time for it. Another evening perhaps."

"What do you have on your schedule for tonight?"

"Nothing, really. I should start thinking about the homilies for the Triduum. It's coming right up. I'm little too distracted to give it its due." Pádraig looked out the window, squinting. "There's Bertie. I've got to catch up with her." He pushed back from the table and called a quick thank you to Joe, with apologies for the quick departure. Stephen lingered near the table for a moment, unsure whether to ask for a bill. Joe smiled and waved. "Never any bill for Pádraig and his friends. See you again soon, I hope." Stephen mustered out of the restaurant to catch up with Pádraig.

Pádraig was in earnest conversation with Bertie, holding both his hands in hers. "You poor woman," Stephen heard him saying. "You've been walking all the way over to the Cliffoney bus terminal on your own?"

Bertie was crying, "It's all I can think to do, Father. Maybe she's just gone off on a lark and will be back any day now. I just go down in the morning to wait and come back in the afternoon, before it gets dark."

Pádraig tried to console her. "The good news, Bertie, is that tomorrow is Wednesday, and we can go back to the garda and they'll have to help us then. It's their own policy. Meanwhile, Stephen and I have been continuing to look. She'll turn up soon, Bertie, right as rain and no harm but the worry she caused you. And Ned."

"It still puts a fret on me, Father, what conclusions the garda might jump to when they talk to Ned. And he hasn't many friends on the head who'd speak up for him." She looked down at the ground for a moment. "Father, I know you see him for what he is. He's no saint. But if you could explain to them, please, that he's got a good heart, and he loves Fianna in his own way. Could you do that when they come?"

Pádraig let out a long breath. "Bertie, I'll try to make sure they understand the context, the whole situation. But I couldn't say anything to put them off a legitimate investigation if they had good reason to think he'd caused her disappearance. You understand that, don't you?"

"Yes, Father."

Pádraig cast about for a transition from the awkwardness of the conversation. "Listen, Bertie. I have an idea. It's Tuesday, and the prayer group is meeting in the social hall tonight. I usually leave it to their own administration. But tonight, I think I'll go and ask for some special prayers for Fianna. Why don't you come? I can come around and collect you."

"Oh, I couldn't ask you to do that, Father. Besides, they don't like us much, the women who go. Will it upset them?"

"They'll be fine. I'll see to it."

Stephen stepped forward. "I'd like come to. And I can pick you up and bring you around, Bertie. I mean, if you don't mind terribly coming down the lane to the road."

"No, not at all, Mr. Attergood. It's very kind of you. I'd walk from home to get there, except that I don't see as well in the dark."

"You are very welcome. I'll be there at...." He looked at Pádraig.

"Starts at seven, so quarter til should do it."

"Right then, see you in a few hours, Bertie." Bertie smiled wearily, and marched off toward home. Stephen and Pádraig walked toward the rectory.

"You have a car?" Pádraig asked.

"Uncle Randall's old one. It still runs. It's out behind the house. I started it up a couple of times to make sure it was in good order in case my mother needed something."

"Well, then. You're such an uneasy passenger, it never occurred to me that you drove a vehicle at all."

"Only in an emergency," Stephen sighed. "This is starting to qualify."

22.

Pádraig was working at his desk, sketching out notes for his Maundy Thursday homily when he heard the screech of tires on the street in front of the rectory. He rushed to the window in time to see a red Citroen, engine off, cruising toward the curb in front of the sisters' retirement home adjacent to the rectory. He winced as saw the car's front tires bump off the edge of the walk and come to a stop. Stephen emerged from the driver's side, then dove back in as the car began to roll. He set the hand brake and stood by the car, collecting himself.

Pádraig met him, arms crossed at the front door of the rectory. He shook his head.

"I didn't say I was good at driving. Just that I knew how."

"Ah, yes. This is one area, though, where theoretical knowledge is a lot less valuable than practical experience. Are you sure you're okay to pick up Bertie? I'm not sure I should let you...."

"I'll be fine. This was just a practice run. I wanted to talk with you before I go meet her."

They went into Pádraig's study together. "I'd offer you a drink, but..."

"Of course. A priest with drink on his breath is unlikely to command much respect at prayer group. "

"Right. Especially because they're not expecting me. I usually let them run the show themselves." He glanced at his watch. "What did you want to talk about? It's almost time for you to go to the Gunnings'."

"I was thinking about the contemplation you were talking about today. Entering the setting of the story, the insights it yielded."

"Yes."

"I wondered, why wouldn't it work in other settings? "

"What do you mean?"

"As I understand it, the contemplation works because you believe – not saying I do – you believe that God touches your imagination."

"Right, that's the idea."

"What if you imagined entering a different scene? One that's not from the gospels, that doesn't even involve Jesus as the main character. Why wouldn't the same principle of illumination and insight work? Assuming you entered the scene with the same attitude. I mean a prayerful attitude, seeking an insight?"

"I've never heard of it in the Ignatian tradition. What do you have in mind?"

"What if you entered an imagined scene where Fianna is the main character?"

"That's pretty abstract. It would be totally imagined. None of the anchor points of a gospel story."

"You have Mullaghmore as an anchor. And the places where she was recently seen. What if you imagined the continuation of the rest of the day Sunday, after she was last seen by you and Bertie? Or any part of Monday or today?"

"That sounds pretty far-fetched. How would we know whether we were making up the rest of the story?"

"Um, far-fetched? You were just telling me about walking with Jesus into Bethany and taking Lazarus' place coming out of the tomb, Pádraig."

"That's different."

"Why? Because back then you used your imagination on a story written years after the event, if it ever really happened, by someone who never met Jesus? As opposed to a girl you saw on Sunday and what happened to her after? Which one is far-fetched?"

"Where do you come up with these ideas anyway? I understand that our talking about Ignatian contemplation gave you a point of departure. But what on earth makes you think that someone in prayer group has the skills, talent, whatever you might call it, to give us anything useful about Fianna? In all events, Ignatian contemplation is not a group event, so I'm not even sure how you think it could work with a group practicing it."

Stephen pulled a book out from under the flap of his bag. "This is what makes me thing it could work." He held the cover up and read the title aloud. "Ideas of Good and Evil, another work by our friend Yeats. Do you know this title?"

"No, never heard of it. I never knew Yeats wrote in these mystical genres at all. In fact, I was happier when I thought he was just a treacly poet."

"The most lionized poet of nineteenth century Ireland, dismissed by you as syrupy. Wonderful. I can't believe you didn't make it as a scholar. "

"Keep your sarcasm to yourself, if you don't mind. We don't have time for this detour. "

"Just give me a minute. The most famous essay in Ideas of Good and Evil is Yeats' chapter on magic. Famous, I mean, among a certain kind of seeker." Stephen flipped through the pages of the book. "In this chapter, he recounts visionary experiences that he and a friend had through a seer, a woman, so that makes her a seeress, if that's really a word. They're long passages, but the gist of it is that this little group of four, including the seeress's husband, sitting together had two shared visions.

"The first vision kicked off with the husband brandishing a wooden mace and picking out symbols from a set of colored tiles imprinted with various shapes. There was an incantation, of course. Then, Yeats writes, 'Almost at once my imagination began to move of itself and to bring before me vivid images that…I could not change or shape.' During the whole thing, the participants are talking to each other and describing what they're seeing. Yeats sees an image of the friend he came with in a crowd of white clad figures in the vision. Someone else comes into focus, and the seeress says that's the friend as he was in a past life. A whole story ensues, and they talk their way through it. Yeats says, 'The story unfolded chiefly in the mind's eye of the seeress, but sometimes I saw what she described before I heard her description.'

"It gets a bit gory after that part. The friend was a physician in a past life, evidently, who experimented with creating life and had some sort of primitive success. For this he was punished with infirmity and forced to kill the life he created. He never regained full health and was sickly for the rest of his life. Lonely, too, since when the story got out, his pupils left him and his friends shunned him.

"Apparently, the rules of engagement for this sort of session say that if you're the subject of the vision, you yourself won't be able to see it, but you can hear the other participants' descriptions. So when the story is finished and the lights came up, Yeats says that his friend was 'white and awestruck.' The friend says that he has always, since childhood, been fascinated with the idea of 'making a man' and thinking of 'contrivances for galvanizing a corpse into life.' Then he says, the friend does, 'Perhaps my bad health in this life comes from that experiment.'"

"Sounds like someone took Frankenstein a little too much to heart, that's all."

"Interesting you should mention that, because it occurred to Yeats, too. He asked his friend and the others in the room if they'd ever read Frankenstein. The only one who had read it was his friend."

"So?"

"He's also the only one who couldn't see the vision, remember? He was the subject, so he just sat there and listened, apparently in shock and horror at how close to home it all was, to what the others said they saw. So he couldn't have generated the vision, and the others, even if they were vaguely aware of the plot of Frankenstein, didn't have the detailed imagery to drive what Yeats said he saw.

"Then they go a second round, and summon up an epic story that involved armored knights and giant stone crosses. It's all very interesting, but the detail isn't important. Some of how Yeats writes about it is fascinating, though. In these visions, time passes in a way that allows it to speed up to let the viewers see the important parts without having to sit through every minute of a story that may span years. Here, he writes 'Many years seemed to pass, making the vision flutter like a drift of leaves before our eyes'. It's a bridge between parts of the story.

"Does Yeats have an intelligible explanation for what happened?" Pádraig asked.

"He tries to form one. Listen to this: 'Who was it that made the story, if it were but a story? I did not, and the seeress did not, and the evoker of spirits' – that's the husband – 'did not and could not. It arose in three minds, for I cannot remember my acquaintance taking any part, and it rose without confusion, and without labour except the labour of keeping the mind's eye awake, and more swiftly than any pen could have written it out.'

"He goes on a little later: 'At the time these two visions meant little more to me, if I can remember my feeling at the time, than a proof of the supremacy of imagination, of the power of many minds to become one, overpowering one another by spoken words and by unspoken thought till they have become a single intense, unhesitating energy.'"

"So he thinks it's something to do with a group mind?"

"Exactly," Stephen said, flipping back several pages. "In fact, he starts the essay with a declaration of his belief in magic and the underlying principles. Listen to this: 'I believe in the practice and philosophy of what we have agreed to call magic, in what I must call the evocation of spirits, though I do not know what they are....' He says he believes in three doctrines that have been handed down through the generations. Here they are:

"'(1) That the borders of our minds are ever shifting, and

135

that many minds can flow into one another, as it were, and create of reveal a single mind, a single energy.

(2) That the borders of our memories are as shifting, and that our memories are a part of one great memory, the memory of Nature herself.

(3) That this great mind and great memory can be evoked by symbols."

"Wow," Pádraig said. "He really was crazy. Articulate, of course. And crazy."

"Maybe. But I'd say he was more a man who was behind his time, as opposed to ahead of it as they usually say about genius. Here's how he concludes the introduction to the essay: 'I often think I would put this belief in magic from me if I could, for I have come to see or to imagine, in men and women, in houses, in handicrafts, in nearly all sights and sounds, a certain evil, a certain ugliness, that comes from the slow perishing through the centuries of a quality of mind that made this belief and its evidences common over the world.' In other words, he'd rather not invest belief in it at all if he had a choice, but he feels as though he has a responsibility as one of the last keepers of the knowledge. It's as if the whole world believed in magic and spirits at one time, but that world fell away and left him holding the gold."

"More like dross than gold, I'd say. What is it you want me to do with all of this ridiculousness?"

Stephen closed the book and put it on Pádraig's desk. "I know you'll think of something. Bring the group together in a prayer for Fianna, and take it from there. Use a little guided imagery as if you're helping someone through one of your contemplations." Pádraig sat impassively on the edge of his desk, shaking his head. "This is daft. And they'll think I'm daft."

Stephen fished his car key out of his pocket. "Not if you propose it cleverly. I mean reverently, and all like that. " He stood silently, waiting for an answer. Pádraig studied the floor, still shaking his head.

"You are the most maddening....listen, we don't have

time for this. You have to go get Bertie, and I've got to get over to the parish hall to make sure they're all civil to her when she arrives."

"We said this morning that nothing was too crazy to try," Stephen reminded him.

"All right, all right. We'll try it. Now go. " *Let's see if this gets me run out of the country a second time,* he thought as he organized himself to leave.

23.

Pádraig entered the parish hall a few minutes before seven o'clock. The chairs had been drawn into a circle, but the women hadn't taken their seats yet. Pádraig greeted them warmly, postponing his explanation for his unusual appearance as long as possible. He was vaguely aware of who regularly attended the group, but was surprised to see Sister Alex milling about the tea table.

"Sister Alex," Pádraig said, sidling up to her, "I didn't know you came to these gatherings. I thought your prayer life was mostly inside the Order."

"Oh, mostly, yes. But where else can I get a cup of tea at seven in the evening without boiling it up myself?" She winked at Pádraig. "Besides that, I think my being here prevents them from praying for truly silly things. Keeps them in line a bit."

"Well, I could use some moral support from you tonight, Sister. I'm here to ask for prayers for Fianna Gunning."

Sister Alex blew gently on the surface of her tea. "I see. . . I understand she's gone missing. Very sad, very trying for the parents, no doubt. I've lifted a few prayers up for her on my own. She's had a hard enough life as it is, given her circumstances." Sister Alex looked around to see who was nearby.

Pádraig nodded gravely. "You more than most know how deserving she is of help and prayers. Not everyone here will agree, given the low regard they give the family. Bertie will be here."

"Is that wise, Father?"

"I think it's necessary. If they see her here, it'll be harder for them to refuse to include Fianna in their intentions. Besides, she needs something concrete to do. She's been walking all the way to Cliffoney every day to sit at the bus terminal in case Fianna comes back. We need to occupy her with something productive. Most of all, what I need from this group is that they behave civilly toward her and that they give what I'm going to propose a sincere try."

"Count on me, Father. I'll do what I can."

Sister Alex made her way to the chair nearest the tea table. She refused to allow her arthritis to cabin her, but saving a few steps now and then didn't count against her resolve, she decided. Others stepped around the folding chairs to take their seats in the circle.

"Well," said Claire Kennedy. "Father, it's a welcome surprise to see you here. Usually, we just start right out with a rosary. But perhaps you have something special in mind?"

The door at the rear of the parish hall opened, and Bertie walked through clutching her handbag. Pádraig looked for Stephen coming in right behind her, but was surprised to see Easmon come in, leaning on his stick, with Ricky just behind him. The four stood for a moment at the back of the hall looking as lost as castaways. Sister Alex stood, smiling and waved them in. "Come, all of you! Join us here. When it comes to a prayer circle, the more of us there are, the stronger our prayers." The four made their way to the closest chairs. Stephen held Bertie's chair, and then stepped back to find a seat along the wall.

"You too, young man. I don't believe I know you. What's your name?" Sister Alex asked.

"It's Stephen, ma'am. I mean, sister. I'm just here to observe. Father asked me to bring Bertie."

"Oh. Well, do join us. It"ll be good for you."

"Thank you, sister. I'm really just here in an assistive capacity. I'm not from here, I've just arrived from Oxford."

"And they don't pray there?" Sister Alex asked, just a touch of reprimand in her voice.

"No, I don't pray there. I mean I don't pray here. I mean I don't pray."

"Oh, I see," Sister Alex said curtly. She sat down and shrugged in Pádraig's direction. "Well, I suppose there are enough of us here to do it for you. Sorry for the diversion, Father."

"No, it's quite all right. It's wonderful to see all of you here tonight, including a few outside the regular attendees, myself included in that lot!" He laughed nervously. Already, he could feel Ellen glowering at him, and Claire's pretended delight at his showing up was turning to puzzlement.

"As you all know, Bertie's daughter Fianna has been missing. She was last seen by Bertie and me on Sunday after Mass. I'm sure you're all aware that there's been a search by the men of the parish?" A few heads nodded. "We've been over to see the garda in Cliffoney, but they won't start their official search until tomorrow. As I'm sure you can imagine, the waiting has been agony for the parents, and I thought that the good we might do while we're waiting for the authorities to take action would be to pray for her safe and swift return."

The women looked at one another and back at Pádraig. If anyone resented going to an effort for the Gunnings, no one spoke the thought. But the diversion from routine was unsettling to them, Pádraig could see. Claire finally spoke up. "How many rosaries would that be, Father?" She was fingering the first decade of her rosary. "We usually pray just one at the beginning and the end of the meeting, but we could...."

" No, no Claire, saying the rosary is a fine thing to do. But I have something different in mind here. I'd like to teach you a way of praying that I learned in seminary. It's called contemplation."

Myrna Whalen, Tom's wife, looked up in puzzlement. "Father, if you learned it in seminary, it sounds as though it would be rather difficult for lay people like ourselves, more something for the professional ranks, wouldn't it be?"

"I think you're all up to it, Myrna, I really do. I'll guide you along. First, I recommend we join hands and close our eyes." He sensed the discomfort in the room. "Is that part really necessary, Father?" Ellen asked with annoyance.

"Which part, the joining hands or the closing of the eyes?"

"Well, both."

"No, Ellen. It's just a recommendation. It will work just as well if you do neither. As long as your intention is sincere," he added correctively. Meanwhile, Easmon and Ricky had linked hands with each other and with Bertie on one side and with Sister Alex on the other. Myrna and Claire joined the chain. Ellen kept to herself. Pádraig reached over and took Bertie's hand gently in his. He took care not to squeeze too hard; Willie had recently told him, with great embarrassment, that some of the parishioners had complained about his vise-like grip during the exchange of the sign of the peace at Mass.

He turned his mind back to the task before him. "Imagine yourself standing outside St. Molaise's this past Sunday after Mass. Most of you don't have to imagine it, since you were there, I grant you that. Now imagine that you see Fianna and Bertie talking with me after Mass, outside the church. Notice what Fianna is wearing. She's wearing a blue skirt, white blouse and her school jumper. She has a blessing from me, and starts toward home while Bertie and I continue to talk. Let your mind follow her along the way that she walks. Follow her as far as you can until the vision fades away." He was silent for a full minute. "Now that you can no longer see her, let your mind imagine where she is now. Let your senses help you understand where she is. What do you see with your mind? What do you sense? Is it warm or is it cool where your mind finds her? Are there any fragrances about? Are there any familiar landmarks you notice?" He paused between each question and the next.

"As you see things, or feel them, tell us what you become aware of," he urged the group. Silence prevailed for several minutes. Ellen cleared her throat. "I beg your pardon, Father. But I don't see that this has the least bit to do with prayer." Pádraig opened his eyes and saw that everyone had done the same, except for Easmon who seemed to have fallen asleep.

"Prayer is a conversation with God, Ellen. That's what we're undertaking here."

"I didn't hear a single invocation, Father. I don't know what this is, but it's not prayer as I know it."

"Perhaps a little deference to Father is in order, don't you agree, dear?" Sister Alex said sweetly.

"With great respect, Father, Sister, this is all too odd for me. Call me old fashioned, but this just seems....well, occult! I must be going." She ran out the door. Easmon opened one eye, then the other. "That's a first. Me in the room, and someone else calling themselves old fashioned!" The group laughed a little.

"I didn't mean to cause anyone any discomfort," Pádraig said, standing to stretch his legs. The others in the room stood with him. Easmon pushed himself up on his stick with Ricky's help. Pádraig turned to Stephen. "I didn't think this would be productive, Stephen. I told you that in advance. I'm sorry, everyone, for the disruption and for taking your time. If anyone would like to stay for a quarter hour, we could say the rosary."

"Father, I'll stay. But before Ellen got so upset, you were saying we should speak about anything we felt or saw?" Claire asked.

"Yes?" Pádraig stood still. Stephen put his rucksack back on the chair behind him.

"Well, I couldn't say what the place was where I felt she was. But it was brightly lit and music everywhere ringing out. A fiddler, I think, and the elbow pipe were playing. It was very gay. She seemed happy. Not that she was dancing about or singing herself, but she was watching others and seemed happy."

"Anything else?"

"No, not really. Just a feeling like that."

Bertie began sobbing. "What does it mean, Father? Is she in heaven already? Is she dead?" Pádraig put his arm around her shoulder. "No, no, not at all Bertie. We're not privileged to see heaven during our lifetimes, so Claire can't have seen that." He looked over Bertie's head at Stephen, who was shrugging to ask how he could rule out a vision of heaven. Pádraig looked away.

" I think I saw something, too, Father." Myrna stepped forward. "This may be silly. I don't know if it means anything at all."

"Please tell us, Myrna. It can't hurt to have all the information out in the sunshine."

"While we were....what did you call it? Contemplating. While we were contemplating, I kept seeing a picture of a mountain in my mind. It was a grand picture, like a calendar photo or something. And there was a small figure walking towards it. Do you think that could be Fianna I was seeing?"

"I don't know. Did you see anything about the figure's appearance? Was it a girl? How was she dressed?"

"I couldn't see anything about what the figure was wearing. I couldn't see the face at all. But I had the feeling that it was feminine the way it moved. Female. I thought this was all a distraction from what we were supposed to be doing. Do you think it was helpful, what I saw?"

"Ricky, get me over to the window," Easmon said. He led Ricky there, leaning on his arm. He raised his stick and pushed the curtain away from the window. Ben Bulben, the summit that hulked over the north of Sligo County came into view in the twilight. "Myrna, did your mountain look like this?"

"Yes, that's it."

24.

Stephen took two quick steps toward Myrna. "Let me make sure I understand what you're saying. In your mind's eye, you saw a figure, maybe Fianna, walking toward Ben Bulben?"

"That's what it looked like in what I was seeing," Myrna said. "And that's exactly why I thought I was off the track. I see Ben Bulben every day from my kitchen window. How can it mean anything to do with Fianna?"

"Aw, Christ!" exclaimed Easmon. "Sorry, Father," he mumbled. He turned to Bertie. "Listen, Bertie, awful sorry for what you're going through. But tell me a little about your daughter."

Bertie hadn't stopped sobbing since Claire had first spoken. "She's a good girl. A bit withdrawn and has...a hard time seeing herself as I see her for the beautiful girl she is." Bertie's tears overtook her. Easmon continued his gentle questioning. "Would you say she hasn't been herself lately? A bit melancholy, short of words? Maybe a bit pale? Paler than usual, would you say?" Bertie nodded yes to all of his questions. Easmon was silent in his assessment. He hobbled over to Pádraig.

"Listen, Father. I hate to say it, but it's all too typical of these situations."

"What's that, Easmon? Typical of what?" Stephen stepped in closer to hear the conversation.

"It's plain, Father. She's been taken."

"Taken by whom? Where?" Stephen asked.

Easmon huddled in closer to the two of them. "Taken by the others," he said in a whisper. "It's what they do. Take a joyful one, and put a sullen one in her place. Or his place as the case may be. They take the best of us. Mothers, new mothers, they take from their infants because they need a wet nurse in their own world. They have children, like we do, but they can't nurse them. Dancers, good ones, are a magnet for them. And athletes. Anyone who excels at what they do."

"Whoa, whoa!" Stephen shook his head like a dog coming out of a lake. "You're saying that the girl who disappeared on Sunday wasn't really Fianna, just a factotum resembling her?"

Easmon rested both of his gnarled hands on the knot at the top of his stick. "Aye, it's very likely."

Pádraig looked at Easmon, then at the remnants of the prayer group who were consoling Bertie. "Easmon, I mean no disrespect to you, but someone has got to say it: this is insane."

"Father, if you're not open-minded to it, I can't persuade you to be. But if you haven't the imagination to consider the possibility, you're just not very Irish, I'd say." He shrugged, "And no disrespect to you, Father, but I stopped coming to Mass ages ago because I couldn't talk myself into believing that the consecration turns the wafer into the body of Christ. And don't get me started on what you claim to do to a perfectly good goblet of wine." He smiled to mitigate the brashness of what he'd said, touched his forehead in salute, and began his way to the door. Ricky put down his teacup and started after him.

"But wait, what does all this mean?" Claire asked. "Did we really see something, Myrna and I? And what about what Ellen said about all this being occult? Did we do something dark and dangerous here tonight?"

Easmon stopped in the doorway and turned around. "Tell me," he said to Claire "I'm sure I should remember, but what's your maiden name?"

"It's McGettigan. Same as Myrna's. We're cousins."

"Your fathers were brothers, Hugh and Henry?"

"That's right."

"Ha!" Easmon yelled. "I should have guessed it! It runs in families. You just didn't know it 'til now, it seems. The McGettigans are all famous gazers. Father, I know you don't believe it, but if these McGettigan cousins saw her doing what they say, you can take it to the bank."

"Wait, Easmon," Pádraig said across the room. "If anyone were to see something here tonight, I'd have thought it would be you. Did you see nothing at all to add to the picture? I'm not saying I believe any of this, but we might as know everything we can," Pádraig added, hedging his bets.

"Nah, not a thing. It's not my talent. I'm more of a communicator, an explainer of things. Besides, truth be told, I was dozing a bit while you were speaking, Your voice is very soothing, Father. Almost made me want to come back and hear your sermons. But not quite."

"Why did you come, then?"

"Your man Stephen there promised me a drink afterwards." He looked at Ricky. "Though I think I wasn't supposed to mention that, come to think of it." He turned to Stephen. "You're good for it anyway, right, young man?"

"Absolutely, Easmon. You go over there now and order up. Get a pint for me, too. I'll just bring Bertie back up the road and I'll join you as soon as I can." Stephen collected his bag and hoisted the strap over his shoulder.

"You're eager to get along away from me, it seems," Pádraig said to Stephen. "I think you realize you've put us down a road to mischief here."

"Not at all. I think we have our first concrete clue about what to do next to get her back. Why don't you come to Beach Club with us? I have a few more questions for Easmon. You might like to hear the answers. Could be important."

"No, I've had enough for one night. The only concrete thing to do, as you put it, is to wake up early tomorrow and get over to Cliffoney to put the garda to their promise to start looking." He touched Bertie's shoulder lightly. "Good night, Bertie. Try to give yourself a rest from worrying. Tomorrow we start a new plan for looking for Fianna, and getting her back home."

25.

Pádraig went back to the rectory and thought about an early bedtime. But the consideration was momentary. Soon, he was on his feet and on the way to Luck Boat. Beach Club was out of the question for tonight with Easmon holding court and Stephen egging him on.

The supper crowd was long gone when Pádraig let himself in. The light jingle of the bells attached to the transom brought Joe out from the kitchen just as Pádraig entered. "Hungry again?" Joe asked. "Must be true what they say about Chinese food." Pádraig smiled. "No, Joe. Just looking for some company." They went to the back of the restaurant to the booth furthest from the door and closest to the kitchen and service door where Joe had spread out his invoices and other paperwork.

Joe reached into the kitchen from where he sat and retrieved a bottle of Cutty Sark. "This is the kind you like?" Pádraig nodded. "These days, there aren't any kinds I don't like, Joe." They clinked glasses and sipped.

"Joe, why don't you get a proper liquor license so I can come over here instead of Beach Club. Drink in peace for a change."

Joe paused for a moment. "Oh, I guess I never told you. I thought you'd just get mad when you heard the story."

"What story?"

"About when I tried to get a liquor license. It was about a

year ago. Business was good, lots of take away, pretty good lunch business. Supper was slow. Still is." He gestured toward the empty dining room. "I thought a liquor license would bring in some customers. So I made all the applications. I was getting a pretty good feeling that the license for on premises sales was going to come through. I started calling a few distributors to line up buying relationships. Not being cocky, just trying to be ready. The calls I made -- that's how Ellen found out."

"What happened?"

"It wasn't more than a day after I'd made the calls that I was out back emptying the rubbish when she came out the back door of Beach Club, screaming at me. Right up in my face. 'You don't know your place!' she said. 'My family have been the publicans in this village for four generations. Who do you think you are coming in to our business?' She said a few other things, too, about my heritage and appearance. Not too nice at all. At one point she said, 'How would you like it if I started serving up Chinese food?' Here, I admit, I made a mistake."

"Why? What did you say?"

"That's the mistake. I started laughing so hard that I couldn't say anything. It was just so absurd that she might do that in the first place or that I would consider it competition if she did."

"It is pretty funny. But I'll bet she didn't like that."

"Apparently not. She went back inside in a huff. I was thinking of going over and apologizing for laughing, try to patch things up between neighbors."

"Did that help?"

"I never got to do it. I went outside to go over there and what do I see but the little lorry I use to haul supplies with four slashed tires, cut right down to the rims."

"That's terrible, Joe!   And obviously she did it, you suppose, or had it done."

"Pretty sure about that."

"So what did you do."

Joe shrugged.   "That afternoon, I withdrew the

application. Sorry. I was looking forward to having you as my number one customer."

"I'm so sorry for all that, Joe. Here I thought your transition was going so well. I didn't know that Ellen could be so vicious. Difficult, yes, but not up to property damage. In fact, I saw a flash of how difficult she can be tonight just a little while ago." Pádraig gave Joe a brief rundown of what happened at the parish hall, finishing with an explanation of why he had no inclination to go anywhere near Beach Club tonight.

Joe topped off their glasses. "Wow. That's some pretty wild stuff." He swirled the scotch around the bottom of his glass. "One thing has me puzzled," he said.

"Just one thing?" Pádraig snorted. "I've got a list as long as my arm."

"I'm puzzled why they'd take Fianna. If they -- whoever they are -- are prone to take people who excel at something, what is it that Fianna excels at? Easmon says they're a discriminating lot. They don't go about dragooning just anyone at all off the street. What was it that they admired in her? Or envied? From what you've said about her, she's a bit...ordinary. Not a stand out at school, or socially. Why did they want her?"

"Joe, you're giving this more credence than I do, that's for sure. The whole idea of taking brides, new mothers, talented dancers and athletes -- don't you see the pattern there? Not a a single elderly person on the list. I think the legend of people being taken away was to help people cope with tragic early deaths. You know, 'Seamus isn't dead -- he can't be, he was just a few days ago playing at hurling like a champion. No, no, he was carried away by jealous faeries who wanted him among them.'" Pádraig cupped his ear and mimed listening to faraway music. He thickened his west of Ireland accent. "'Can you not hear them now? He's dancing and dancing with them. He'll be back again one day, perhaps.'"

"What about the part where they bury the corpse? Wouldn't that be pretty convincing to them? Burst the bubble?"

"From what Easmon says, apparently they'd explain that away as burying the substitute put in place of poor Seamus. Here's the bonus: it's a good explanation of melancholy, isn't it, which we have in legendary ample amounts out here in the west. If your husband or son, wife or daughter mopes about, or won't get out of bed, it's the fault of the faeries. They've kidnapped the real person, and put a pale shadow in his place. It's probably saved the government a fortune in counseling and institutional costs, hasn't it?"

Joe was quiet for a moment. "You're really worked up about this, obviously. Why is that?"

"Well, it's just a matter of reason, isn't it? There's not a shred of proof that faeries exist or that they like to kidnap teenagers like Fianna. It's pure fantasy. And a grave distraction from what we should be doing, marching over there to Cliffoney and demanding that the garda do their job!"

"Oh, good! This is like the old days, back in Hong Kong, when I'd ask you how you know that God exists, and you'd say that you know because there are too many things you can't explain. We haven't had a talk like that in...."

Pádraig stood up. "All right, all right. You win this round. But only because I'm too tired to argue. Thanks for the drink." He drained his glass and started toward the door. "You know, Joe, no matter how frustrated I sound, I'm glad you're here."

Joe leaned on the table in the booth. "Me too. I'm glad I'm here. Thanks for rescuing me."

"You're welcome, if that's what I did. But I've come to think that you were the one who rescued me. Thanks for that." He waved good-bye over his shoulder as the door closed behind him.

26.

Pádraig was looking for his car keys, getting ready to collect Bertie for the trip into Cliffoney when the telephone rang.

"Hello?"

"Yes, this is Finney from the garda in Cliffoney. Have I reached the rectory over in Mullaghmore?"

"Yes, you have. Father Hart speaking." He held his breath for a moment. "Do you have any news for us about Fianna Gunning?"

"Well, no. Nothing definitive, really. I'm ringing you up because I can't find the Gunning household in the directory."

"That's right. They haven't a telephone. At present," he added. Somehow making the absence of the telephone, which the Gunning had never had, seem a temporary inconvenience seemed a way of defending their honor.

"I told you when you and Mrs. Gunning were here on...what day was that? It was Sunday, I think, no one here but me."

"Yes, it was Sunday, though it seems ages ago."

"What? Yes, right, I'm sure it seems like a very long time to wait. But as I explained, we have a policy --"

"Of waiting three days before bothering to look, yes, yes,

I remember, and I'm sure Mrs. Gunning does, too."

"Right, well I did say that we'd start looking on Wednesday, which is today, and that I'd drive out to Mullaghmore with one of my men to take a statement."

"I was just preparing to pick up Mrs. Gunning and bring her to the garda station, which was her preference to your coming here.

"I think neither will be necessary, actually, Father."

"Have you found her?"

"No, Father."

Pádraig raised his voice. "Will you kindly come out with it and tell me why you're calling then?"

"Yes, of course. No need to shout. Though I couldn't commit resources to a search, I did think it would be appreciated by the family if I made some preliminary inquiries. We have a regular patrol that goes through the bus terminal. There are a lot of hangers about down there, mostly harmless, but a few drug addicts and vagabonds we need to keep an eye on. We chase them out from time to time, but they're always back in a few days.

"We did a sweep through there on Sunday just before you were here -- we have a couple of plain-clothes officers rotate through there. They know the regulars and vice versa. One of the usual hangers about, Roddy, was back on Tuesday. I asked the officers who were on patrol yesterday to ask Roddy and a few others about Fianna. Roddy said he saw her get on the bus to Bundoran Sunday mid-day."

Pádraig stood still. "I don't understand, Mr. Finney. We gave you no description of Fianna. You wouldn't take the report. How did your man Roddy know it was Fianna?"

"Well, surely you remember showing me her photograph. I gave them a description based on that to use in asking around for her."

"You only glanced at it for a moment. How could you possibly form a description, a useful one, based on that?"

Finney laughed indulgently. "Well, Father, in my line of work, I've had to develop certain faculties for investigative work. I happen to have a mind like a mimeo machine. I never

153

forget the details of a face. They're all captured and recorded up here." Pádraig conjured up a picture of Finney tapping the side of his tiny head.

"This is not satisfactory at all, Mr. Finney. Please wait for us at the garda station. Mrs. Gunning and I will be right over."

"But that's why I'm calling. Since we have the eyewitness report from our source at the bus terminal that she got on the bus by herself and without coercion, we have to classify the disappearance as voluntary."

Pádraig pulled the receiver away from his ear and stared at it for a moment. He visualized a violent encounter of the receiver meeting the desk, hoping it might compromise Finney's hearing for life. But a broken telephone was of no use to him. He took a deep breath.

"Hello? Hello?" Finney was saying.

"Yes, I'm here, I'm here. So what are the next steps, Mr. Finney?"

"Well, now that we know she went to Bundoran, we can pick up the trail from there, if you wish. It's not strictly protocol in the case of a voluntary disappearance, the girl being of a reasoned age and all, but in deference to your office, Father, we'd be willing to contact the garda in Bundoran and ask them to keep an eye out for her."

"I would appreciate that, and I know the family will, too. I reserve my opinion about whether your investigative work really supports the conclusion that she's gone to Bundoran. This fellow Roddy, by the way. What makes him reliable?"

"He's a good chap, on the whole. He's given us good information in the past."

"Is he in the vagabond category or is he just a drug addict?" Pádraig asked.

"Oh, just a drug addict," Finney responded, missing Pádraig's sarcasm. "Has a bit of a problem with the drink, too."

"I must keep his number close at hand in case I ever need a character witness, then," Pádraig growled. "Listen, at least let us get you a proper picture of Fianna to work with. I assume you'll accept that from us."

"Yes, of course."

"We'll get it to you this morning. Mr. Finney, I don't want to say anything to put you off the limited search you've agreed to --"

"It's not a search, Father. I could get in a lot of trouble if you go about calling it that. We're simply making inquiries."

"Yes, as you wish, we'll call it inquiries. I don't want to discourage your doing that, but I must tell you I reserve the option of escalating this with your superiors. The theory you're proceeding on is so tenuous...."

"You may do as you think best, Father. It's a republic, after all," Finney said stiffly. "But I generally think it's best for people to do their own jobs and not start directing operations outside their own expertise."

"Understood, Mr. Finney. I'll get the photograph to you right away."

Pádraig walked to the school office adjacent to the church and had a copy of Fianna's latest class picture within minutes of hanging up the phone. He was walking over to Luck Boat to ask for Joe's help in delivering it, when Joe rolled up in his white lorry.

"You're on your way to see me, Father?"

"Yes, I need your help." He tersely explained the situation with the garda and a minute later, Joe was on his way to Cliffoney. Pádraig walked to the Gunnings' house and relayed an explanation of what was going on to Bertie, making Finney's lackadaisical plan sound a little better than he thought of it.

Pádraig trudged back into the center of the village. Following my own advice from time to time might be a wise thing, he thought and turned his steps to St. Molaise.

He'd expected to find the church empty this late in the morning. He'd concluded the morning mass hours ago, and even the few women who lingered afterwards to say the rosary would be gone. But as he entered the church he saw Sister Alex and Stephen in the entryway.

"Is this a first for you, Stephen, coming inside St. Molaise?" Pádraig asked.

"Technically, I'm not inside, I think.   Does this part count?"

"I'm not sure. What do you say, Sister Alex?"

"I'd say it's close enough," Alex responded.   Stephen shuffled a few steps closer to the exterior door.   "I'd better ease into it, I think.   Anyway, I was looking for you, Pádraig, and met Sister Alex.   Which is a good thing, because I wanted to apologize to you, Sister."

"Whatever for, dear?" Sister Alex asked.

"I was a bit flustered last night when you invited me to sit in the prayer circle.   I may have seemed rude, and if I did, I'm sorry for it."

"Oh, not at all.   I'm worldly enough to know that there are people who haven't yet realized the importance of prayer. The comfort of it, too.   There's time yet for you to wake up to it. I'll pray for you.   You can't stop me from doing that, can you?"

"I admit I'm a little curious about that. You pray quite a lot, I gather."

"Yes. It's more or less my job, you might say."

"Do you ever run out of things to pray for?"

Sister Alex laughed.   "No, hasn't happened yet anyway. The way we pray in my order, the Sisters of Continuous Adoration, it isn't just a series of petitions.   It's a conversation that we keep up with God.   You might think of it as keeping a phone line continuously open to God. But less expensive. Like a local call, not cross-country."

"So you pray continuously, is that why the order's called that?"

"We had a tradition, going back to the founding of the Order in Bundoran in the 1880's, of keeping a continuous vigil in our chapel, praying in adoration of the eucharist.   It was 'round the clock in four hour shifts, two per shift to make sure no one dozed off.   Of course, the novitiates got the least convenient shifts, which is how I ended up with the midnight to four in the morning tour of duty.   I could have traded it off over the years, but I got used to it.   Sometimes my prayer partner didn't show up, but I never said anything. I preferred the solitude. Very comforting.

"We don't do that any more," she sighed. "We got a new superior from America who decided that it was more useful for us to lead lives of action rather than lives of contemplation. Stopped wearing habits about that time, too. I'd say it's not to my liking, but that would be insubordinate. And I take my vow of obedience seriously." She smiled, and Stephen assessed her as anything but obedient.

"And your name? It's short for Alexandra, I assume?"

"No, a lot of people do think that, but my baptismal name has no resemblance to the name I took in holy orders. When we profess our vows, the superior gives us the name of a saint, could be male or female, that has something to teach us. I'm named for St. Alexander or Alexandria, who's famous for his arguments against a heretic named Arius. He was a gifted polemicist, who beat back the Arian heresy with zeal."

"And why did the superior choose that name for you, do you know?"

"Oh, yes. I had a reputation for being disputacious, to put it politely, in my studies. You couldn't just tell me something, you had to tell me the why behind the something. And do a good job of it too to make me stop asking questions. I just couldn't help it, really. So the point of being named after St. Alexander was to teach me to put my skills of argument to good use, in defense of the faith."

"Fascinating."

"Fascinating, yes. But it's been a frustrating morning for me, if you'll excuse me, I need a little time in the pews to put my head straight. I'll be back in a bit. We needn't go into Cliffoney, by the way, Stephen. Finney is still refusing to do anything."

"What?" Stephen said. "He promised he'd start on Wednesday, didn't he?"

Pádraig sighed. "He's doing something, I'll grant him that, but it's nothing worthwhile and probably badly aimed." Pádraig crossed his arms. "He's decided, having had only the merest glance at Fianna's confirmation class picture, that he's had her spotted getting on the bus to Bundoran."

"That's ridiculous!" Stephen said. Sister Alex raised her eyebrows. "Perhaps not, actually. She's been there a few times that I'm aware of."

"Really?" Pádraig asked. "When? Where did she go in Bundoran?"

Sister Alex looked at Pádraig intently and started slowly. "Well, as you know, she was born in Bundoran. The order has a small house there, with a few sisters in residence. They helped care for her as an infant, and as you might expect, attachments formed. I'm aware she's visited there a few times in the past two or three years. They've even let her stay in the residence when the bus schedule prevented her from coming home."

"Does Bertie know she's been up there?"

"I don't know. But since she's been up there before, it's not so implausible that she may be there now. I didn't think of it until just now, I'm sorry. At my age, a few of the connectors get a little loose." She patted the top of her head. "Father, if I can use the phone in the rectory, I'll call up there right away and see if the sisters have heard from her."

"Yes, of course."

Stephen stepped away from the door and held it open for her. "Sister Alex, I know you have to run, but could I ask, if it's not too familiar of me, what is your age. Do you mind my asking?"

"Well, she said, a lady never tells. But a nun doesn't care. I'm eighty-three years old. Spent most of them right here in Mullaghmore."

"Wait, does that mean you were here when Yeats was working in this part of the country?"

"Oh, yes, I was here."

"Did you ever meet him?"

Sister Alex laughed as made her way down the steps, leaning on the railing. "'Meet him', my dear? He proposed to me once!"

Pádraig chuckled, "That's a good story. You'd better walk with her and hear her out." Pádraig pushed through the interior doors and into the sanctuary. Stephen dove through the door to catch up with Sister Alex.

"He proposed to you? What happened? What did you say?"

"I said no, of course. I was only sixteen at the time, so it was out of the question. I'm not sure he was serious. Just infatuated. He was lovesick all the time with the ups and downs with the woman he thought he truly loved, Maude Gonne. He kept proposing to her, three times, here and all over the continent. She kept saying no. I think he proposed to me because he was tired of hearing no and thought I'd be delighted."

"Still, to be that close to genius, it must have been intoxicating."

Sister Alex stopped on the sidewalk for a moment and looked at him. "He was a genius, I agree with you on that. But he had a dark side that's hard to reconcile."

"Well, I know that he was a collector of tales about the gentry in this part of the country. Collecting them seems harmless. In fact, it's to his credit to preserve the culture, I think."

"You don't understand. He didn't just collect them. He started to believe them."

"No, not really. Surely he was too intelligent for that."

"Have you read about the time he and some unnamed friends went up Ben Bulben and conjured up the faeries?"

"No, I haven't gotten to that one yet, but I'll look for it. Maybe he was just having the reader on, winding us up."

"You might think so. But I was here when it happened, or he said it happened. The unnamed friends were not unnamed to me. I knew everyone in the party. He believed that he had witnessed a faery parade and had interviewed some in the troop."

"All right, I'll grant you that's a bit odd. But what's a little idiosyncratic behavior up against a lifetime of unmatched eloquence in print?"

"That's not the least of it, young man. If you're going to be an admirer of Yeats, be aware of the full measure of him."

"Well taken, Sister, but I'm not sure what you're getting

at."

"Look, when I told William that I wouldn't marry him, I was gentle and respectful. That made him think I might change my mind. So he kept asking me from time to time. It was during this time that I was beginning to discern my calling to religious orders. On one occasion when he repeated his proposal, I told him that my life path was not defined yet, but I suspected I might have a vocation in the church. He recoiled in horror. He apparently was not aware that I was more than a casual Catholic. He never asked me again. He'd cross the street to avoid me. We never spoke again."

"That's too bad. He doesn't seem to have been a very tolerant man, then."

"No, he detested religion, especially Catholicism. Had to do with his nationalist views, in part. But even though he rejected religion as a way of making sense of the world, he was still human, and still craved an explanation of life and the afterlife. So he invented one. He invented his own religion."

"What? Yeats invented a religion?"

They had arrived at the door to the rectory. "I have to go in now to make the call I promised Father. But I'm serious about his dark side, and you should make yourself aware of it before you make him your hero. Find a copy of his work A Vision. You'll see how your man goes off the rails." She slipped into the rectory and closed the door behind her.

27.

Stephen was sitting on the steps of the church reading when Pádraig emerged, blinking to adjust to the bright sun.

" Did Sister Alex make the call?"

"Yes, no joy in the immediate response, but the sisters in Bundoran said they'd keep an eye out. I'm given to understand by colleagues who studied in primary and secondary school under nuns that they're difficult to hide from. Maybe she'll turn up after all, if she did go to Bundoran."

"What are you up to at present?" Pádraig asked. "Care to have some lunch?"

"Back at Luck Boat? Sure, I liked that place. And the proprietor."

"Not today. He's closed on Wednesdays so he can pick up supplies and be ready to work both days of the weekend. We'll have to eat at Beach Club. I'd love to have you over to the rectory. Mrs. O'Flannelly's a wonderful cook, but I don't like to surprise her with guests she didn't expect. Another time for that, then." He tapped a boy running through the yard on the shoulder and asked him to run over to the rectory to inform Mrs. O'Flannelly that he'd be out at lunch hour. The boy nodded and smiled, happy to be of help to the priest, and made off to his mission.

They ensconced themselves in the pub, in a corner far from the bar. No sign of Willie, Pádraig noted. Another man, much younger and taller than Willie stood behind the bar and shortly came over to wait the table.

"I don't believe we've met. I'm Father Hart, priest of the parish, and this is my friend Stephen Attergood." The man stood silently for a moment, as if deciding whether disclosure of his name was required for the present transaction. He shifted right to left on the balls of his feet. "I'm Leonard Gilconnell. Nephew to Ellen, the proprietor, recently moved up from Galway to help out. Most people call me Deacon."

"I see. Are you in fact ordained as a deacon?"

"No, Father, it's just the way I dress, particularly in the winter. I wear the longest, darkest coat I can afford. Can't stand the cold. It's more of a nickname."

"Ah. Well, I hope you won't mind if I call you Leonard? My calling you Deacon could be confusing to the flock, if you see what I mean."

"Makes no difference to me at all, either way," he shrugged. No smile accompanied the exchange. "What'll you have today?"

"I'll have the fish and chips, and my friend will have...."

"Do you have some sort of chef's salad, anything with some vegetables in it would be brilliant." Leonard eyed Stephen as if he'd ordered something unimaginably exotic. "I'll see what we can find in the kitchen," he said, his voice dripping with disapproval. "Drinks?"

"Pint of stout for me," Pádraig said.

"Ah, do you have any white wine?" Stephen asked. Leonard coughed into his hand to cover his smirk. "I'm sure I can find something for you. I'll go check."

"That's odd, Willie not being here. He's worked here for twenty years that I know of. Probably longer than that." Pádraig scowled. "I'll have to find a polite way to inquire what happened. We're friends after a fashion, and he said nothing to me about changing his schedule or quitting altogether, for that matter, if that's what happened."

When Leonard had moved away from the table, Stephen looked around the room. "That's quite a portrait gallery," he said, nodding toward the two rows of photographs against the far wall. "An earnest lot. Who are they?" Pádraig answered without turning to look. "They're the O'Rourkes, the publicans of the village going back all the generations depicted there. The ones at the far right on the bottom row are Bernard and Lorraine, Ellen's parents, next to the left are Daniel and Ellen, her grandparents, and so on back in time." "All named O'Rourke?" Stephen asked. "Yes, every one of them by that name, the place handed down father to son over all these years, until Ellen took it over." "She's no brothers, then?" "Did have. He died some years back as a teenager. The circumstances were unclear, but he turned up floating face downward just past the end of the dock. He'd been gone for a few weeks, unaccounted for, then turned up dead. Very sad." "And I take it Ellen's never married since she still has the family name?" "Correct, never married."

Stephen paused for a moment, looking for a transition to the more serious topic he wanted to raise. He leaned in toward Pádraig. "I know you won't like it, but we have to talk about what happened last night."

"I'd really rather not, if you don't mind, Stephen." Pádraig stared out at the quay, avoiding Stephen's gaze.

"I realize it's odd and uncomfortable, but we really do need to talk about what they saw. It could be the first real clue as to where to find Fianna."

"What we saw and heard last night," Pádraig whispered fiercely, "was a bunch of suggestible middle aged women trying to please an equally suggestible priest who should never have embroiled himself in such a crazy, unholy scheme. Now let that be the end of it. Please, Stephen, please."

Stephen was silent for a while as their drinks arrived, then the food. When he judged Pádraig had cooled off enough to continue, he asked, "Have you ever heard of an author named Emanuel Swedenborg?"

"No. Not another addled Irish poet, I hope?"

"No, obviously not. He's Swedish. He started out as a scientist, then took a spiritual turn, rather suddenly, when he had a vision of Jesus Christ appear to him in a tavern in London, and later the same night in his dreams."

"I'd guess that the great majority of reported apparitions of the Savior occur in or near taverns," Pádraig commented as he bit into a cluster of chips.

"That part doesn't matter, whether it's true or not. Here's the point. Yeats was a great fan of Swedenborg. Look, here's an essay he wrote in If I Were Four and Twenty Years called Swedenborg, Mediums and the Desolate Places." He passed the open book over to Pádraig, who wiped his fingers on a napkin before accepting it. "Where are you getting these books, by the way?"

"A few were in Uncle Randall's library. But I've made friends with Terence over at Open Books, and he's got quite a Yeats collection. I've bought a few, and taken a few home on examination. May buy them later."

Pádraig turned the pages and read a paragraph here and there. "So what's this got to do with Fianna?" He handed the book back across the table.

"Swedenborg was famous for his remote viewing skills, among other forms of psychic abilities attributed to him. In 1759, he was at a dinner party over two hundred miles away from his home in Stockholm. At six o'clock, he told his companions with alarm that there was a fire raging in Stockholm on the street where he lived, and that his neighbor's house down the street had just been destroyed. His own house was threatened. There was no point trying to get back to Stockholm to prevent any damage -- it was days away by carriage. So he stayed at the dinner table. Two hours later, he sighed with relief and reported that the fire had stopped three houses away from his, and there was no longer any risk to his own house. It took a couple of days for information of any sort, including the particulars of the fire, to arrive from Stockholm to Gothenburg, where Swedenborg was. But when the news arrived, it confirmed the detail and timing of what Swedenborg had said, right down to the minute."

"If it's true, that's a pretty remarkable story. But who's to say whether something that happened over two hundred years ago is true?"

Stephen looked at Pádraig for a moment. "I'll pass on the

cheap shot about verifying written accounts that are even older, say, going on two thousand years. Sticking with the current topic, how about the five people he was dining with? And countless biographers and contemporaries of Swedenborg who heard the story while he was alive. He was rather a big deal back then. The queen of Sweden made him a nobleman. He was offered high ranking university appointments. He was also persecuted as a heretic, which makes him a respectable fellow in my book."

"All right then, assuming that the story was verified, as you say, and couldn't be explained in a thousand different ways as a trick or a coincidence, still, what does this have to do with Fianna?"

"I think what we saw last night was a genuine remote viewing experience. I think that the two women saw what Fianna was seeing. And is seeing."

Pádraig dropped the piece battered cod that he was about to bite into back onto his plate. "Now that is daft, Stephen. Listen to yourself."

"Pádraig, this is all new to me, too. But I'm asking 'why not' and trying to keep an open mind. Nothing else is on offer at the moment to find the girl." He poked at the greens in his salad. "Stephen, please. Be reasonable. How could something like that even work?"

Stephen put down his fork and leaned toward the middle of the table. "There are two theories. One has to do with the idea that empathy can shade into telepathy. We talked about that one before, you'll remember. Credit for that one goes to Frederic Myers, the Brit who founded the Psychical Research Society I was talking to you about yesterday. I found out that Yeats was a member, by the way."

Pádraig rolled his eyes. "Of course, he was. How could he have sat out that kind of thing?"

"Anyway, the telepathy theory should be pretty obvious, that anyone can reach out to the mind of another they care deeply about and gain access to their thoughts. That would include thoughts about whether they're happy or sad and their surroundings."

"Sure, but there's no particular love between the McGettigan cousins and Fianna. Or anyone in the Gunning family, for that matter."

"That brings us to theory number two. It's right out of Yeats's essay on magic we were talking about. One of his principles is that there is a joint consciousness or shared mind that embraces everyone, living or dead. It's always present and available to us. It's just that some of us are more adept at accessing it."

"It sounds like it'd be a crowded mess in there. Noisy, too. If that's the theory that's supposed to explain how the McGettigan women saw Fianna and found her well, how on earth would they find her in there, in the joint mind or whatever you call it?"

"I don't know exactly how, that's the part where being adept at it helps. If Easmon's right, it runs in families, which suggests that there must be some innate ability that gets coached in families with that kind of talent. But from what I've read, it seems as though Myers thought that everyone had the talent at one time."

"And so the people who are good at it just remember better how to do it?"

"Not exactly. They've forgotten to forget what we all once knew. Myers was enraptured by Plato, particularly his Phaedo, who called this anamnesis. It's kind of the opposite of amnesia, but in a more cosmic way. Myers believed that all great ideas pre-existed humanity as ideals, like the good Platonist that he was. He believed that ideas come into human knowledge when carried here by great souls born into the world. So Euclides brought us geometry, for example. Ptolemy brought us the early principles of astronomy. And people like the McGettigan cousins bring us telepathic capabilities. Only that kind of knowledge doesn't have a scientific or mathematical pedigree like geometry and astronomy have. So it's not only difficult to teach in classrooms, it's regarded as embarrassing to try."

Stephen looked over at his empty wine glass. "I'd better not have another, I'll be nodding off this afternoon. I need a glass of water." He looked over at the bar, but Leonard was nowhere in sight. "Excuse me, won't you, just a minute." Stephen walked over to the bar and peered over the top and down the length of it to see if Leonard was on duty but just out of sight. Two men sat at the bar huddled over pint glasses. "Looking for the new barkeep?" the grayer of the two men asked.

"Yes, I was. He'll be back soon, do you know?"

"Oh, I expect so. I just met the young man, but he seems responsible. Not likely to be wandering off in the middle of his shift, in my preliminary opinion."

"He mentioned that he's the proprietor's nephew," Stephen volunteered.

The man clapped his hand on the bar. "Ah, all the more reputation to him, then. But no need for you to wait on him," the man said, sliding off his barstool. "Ellen's known me longer than I've known myself. She wouldn't mind a bit if I were to serve you something. To be put on your bill, of course, and paid properly." He slid behind the bar. "Now, what'll you be having. A pint of something, I'd reckon?" He had a pint glass in his hand.

"Well, yes, thank you, a big glass of water is what I was looking for." The man's face fell. "Plain water? You want plain water?" He looked at his companion, who was now also staring at Stephen. "Gerald, have you ever heard of that? Someone drinking plain water?" Gerald shook his head. "No, never. No one drinks plain water. It's not healthy for you. Could be full of germs and such. That's why we mix it with whiskey or something else to take the bad out of it." He glanced over his shoulder at Pádraig. "Unless, of course, it's holy water. The blessing takes the bad out of it. Just as surely as the whiskey does. Then you can drink it, I think."

"You don't drink holy water, Gerald," Pádraig said from across the room.

"I'm only saying that you could, Father," Gerald answered.

"I hope that's what you mean. I've been noticing that it disappears from the baptismal font a little faster than it should."

Gerald clutched his cap to his chest. "I've nothing to do with it, Father. On my mother's grave, I say it."

The gray man behind the bar was fussing with the cold water tap. He managed to fill the glass for Stephen and passed it over the bar to him. "Up to you, young man, but passing strange if you ask me." He started shuffling back to his seat. "Even your own grandfather, Father, had the sense to drink salt water, not plain, when he wanted something other than a Guinness or a Bushmill."

Stephen made his way back to the table. "Your grandfather drank salt water? Isn't that terrible for you?"

Pádraig chuckled. "There are some things you can't stop a man of a certain age from doing. He took it as a laxative."

The gray man called from across the room. "That's not it at all, Father, begging your pardon. I suppose he might have told you that, but that's not the real reason he took it." Pádraig peered back at the two at the bar. "Then what was it, Connor?"

"I guess he never told you, then. It was that merrow-man friend of his, told him to do it. That's what your grandfather said. 'Take a quart of salt water every morning, finish it by noon. That will make you ready when it's time for you to join us.'" Connor nodded to the stool next to him. "Himself was sitting right there when he told me that's what the merrow-man told him to do. Sometimes he carried his little salt water milk bottle right in here to finish up before having a pint with us, middle of the day."

Pádraig was poking at the remains of his lunch and shaking his head. "Well, that's awfully interesting, isn't it?" Stephen said. Pádraig shot him a look. He raised his voice to conclude the conversation with Connor. "Whatever you say, Connor. Any memory of my grandfather is a happy one, and I'm glad to hear your stories about him." He lowered his voice to address Stephen. "Are you about ready to take the bill and get out of here?"

"Well, no. Not just yet. There's a thing or two more I want to go over with you."

"We can talk back at the rectory."

"I'd rather do it here."

"Why?"

"Because....I'm not sure how you're going to react, and I want you to hear me out before you throw me out. I think you'll be a bit calmer with even a small audience nearby." He nodded at Connor and Gerald and noticed that Leonard had returned to his post.

Pádraig gave a long sigh. "All right, then. Let's have it." He slumped back in his chair in resignation. Stephen dug into his bag and pulled out a book. "I've shown you this book before." He handed Pádraig his copy of Yeats' Writings on Irish Folklore, Legend and Myth. "Open to the page where the bookmark is."

"'Regina, Regina Pigmeoreum, Veni'."

"Yes, that's the one I want to talk about. You understand the Latin?"

"Of course, I do. It means, 'Queen, Queen of the something, Come', as in a command. I don't recognize that word 'pigmeorum', though. Doesn't sound liturgical."

"It's not." Stephen said, staring at him. "It means 'faeries'." He waited for Pádraig's reaction.

"It's about someone summoning the faeries?"

"Not someone. Yeats himself."

Pádraig was pushing himself up out of his chair. "Please stay. You promised you'd hear me out." Pádraig paused for a moment and reseated himself. He crossed his arms and leaned back. "It's a short piece, let me summarize it and just read out some of the important parts," Stephen said as he turned the pages.

"He starts out explaining who's along on the hike to call out the Dinny Math, which is what they call the faeries. It's not exactly Gaelic, it's just Yeats' phoneticization of the Irish name in use back then, which means 'the good people'. He says it's himself plus a middle-aged man, most people think that's his uncle, George Pollexfen, who lived in Sligo, and a young girl who had a reputation as a seer. That was probably a cousin named Lucy Middleton, according to the notes in the back of the book. The notes also say she had a local reputation as a witch. He says that she's seen now and then 'a glimpse of unaccountable lights moving over the fields among the cattle.'

"He says they came to a place known to be frequented by faeries, and that she passed into a 'waking trance' and became indifferent to the cold breeze and the sound of the sea in the distance. Then Yeats writes that he 'called aloud the names of the great faeries, and in a moment or two she said that she could hear music far inside the rocks, and then a sound of confused talking, and of people stamping their feet as if to applaud some unseen performer.'

" Then George tells Yeats that they were about to be interrupted, because he could hear children laughing nearby. But, Yeats writes, 'We were, however, quite alone.' He concludes that George is falling into the enchantment of the place, just like the girl. Then the girl confirms that she can hear laughter, too, amid the music and the stamping. Next, she saw 'a bright light streaming out of the cave, which seemed to have grown much deeper, and a quantity of little people, in various coloured dresses, red predominating, dancing to a tune which she did not recognize.'

"Then Yeats himself calls out the queen of the troop who turns out to be a 'very beautiful tall woman'. He and the girl then get the queen to 'marshal her followers according to their natural divisions.' Then Yeats writes that the creatures came out of the cave and formed four groups. 'One of these bands carried golden boughs, and another had necklaces made apparently of serpents' scales.

"He starts asking the faerie queen questions about her people. She begins answering him, but all he can see is that her lips are moving. He can't hear her speech. So 'I bade the seer to lay her hand upon the breast of the queen' and after that they can hear every word distinctly.

"So here's the key part. Listen to this. 'I then asked her whether it was true that she and her people carried away mortals, and if so, whether they put another soul in the place of the one they had taken. 'We change the bodies,' was her answer. 'Are any of you ever born into mortal life' 'Yes.' ' Do

I know any who were among the Dinny Math before birth?' 'You do.' 'Who are they?' 'It would not be lawful for you to know.'

"Then he starts peppering her with all sorts of questions, mostly about abstract matters like the meaning of life, things she can't or won't answer. Finally, she tells him 'Be careful and do not seek to know too much about us.'"

"So you think he really believed he'd visited with the faeries?"

"Definitely. He definitely believed he had. And it wasn't even the first time he'd done it. The Regina essay was written in 1893, and the footnotes in this anthology date the actual occurrence to 1892. He wrote a letter to a friend about it in October of that year." Stephen flipped forward in the Yeats book. "Here's an essay from 1890 in which he is so casual about invoking the faeries with a seer friend of his, a different woman, who's just put on a kettle for tea for his visit, that he can conjure them up and 'there is time for them to come and go before the water is boiled.'

"His description is more detailed in this earlier essay." He handed the book over to Pádraig, who read it aloud in a whisper.

"So the queen comes first, like in the other account. 'We commanded this woman to show us the fairies of Ireland marshalled in order. Immediately a great multitude of little creatures appeared, with green hair like sea-weed and after them another multitude dragging a car containing an enormous bubble. The white woman, who appeared to be their queen, said the first were the water fairies and the second the fairies of the air. The first were called the Gelki and the second the Gieri....They passed on and a troop who were like living flames followed and after them a singular multitude whose bodies were like the stems of flowers and their dresses the petals. These latter fairies, after a while, stood still under a green bush from which dropped honey like dew and thrust out their tongues, which were so long that they were able to lick the honey-covered ground without stooping, These two troops were the fairies of the fire and the fairies of the earth.'

"And then they see the evil fairies. The king of that group appears to be a serpent with heavy scales." Pádraig ran his finger over the lines on the page. "'The name of this serpent was Grew-grew....About him moved quantities of things like pigs, only with shorter legs, and above him in the air flew vast flocks of cherubs and bats.' This is wild stuff." Pádraig read on. "Then, of course, there's a big fight between the two hosts. Doesn't say how it ended. Or whether Yeats and his hostess got back to their tea as quickly as he predicted." Pádraig handed the book back. "Well, I guess that's how Yeats knew which groups of fairies to call out when he got to the cave in the later essay. It's not that obscure, actually: water, air, fire, earth." Pádraig looked off into the distance and seemed lost for a moment. The door opened and Martin O'Flaherty tumbled in.

"Hello, Father," he waved his newspaper in Pádraig's direction by way of greeting. He regarded Stephen curiously, but offered no salutation. He took a seat at the far end of the bar, away from Gerald and Connor. Leonard served him his black and tan right away, as if he'd anticipated Martin's order. Stephen began packing up his books and papers, and Pádraig walked over to the bar to settle the bill. He was counting out the notes and coins when Martin spoke up.

"Say, Father. It's a shame about the Gunning girl gone missing, isn't it?"

"Yes, it is that, Martin. But we haven't given up on finding her even though the help in looking has been scarce."

"So you're still looking, after a fashion?"

"More than that, Martin. We're turning over every stone looking for leads about where to look." He watched Martin sip his beer. "Right, of course." He paused. "But isn't it time to leave well enough alone?" Pádraig jolted upright. "What do you mean, Martin? Just give up looking? Declare her dead and gone and get on with life?"

Martin slid off his barstool to face Pádraig. "No, no, Father, I'm not suggesting that we give up on her as dead. It's just that...she seems to want to stay disappeared from here. Maybe she's happier wherever she is." He smiled in a way that made Pádraig shiver. A cold thought formed in his mind. "Martin, you don't have anything to do with the disappearance, do you?"

"No, not I, Father!"

"But you do know something about it, don't you?" He used his best inquisitorial manner, his voice dropping in volume so that only Martin could hear him. "I want to know what you know about this matter."

Martin shook his head vigorously. "Oh, no, Father, I'm sure I don't know a thing that'd be relevant. I shouldn't even have inquired about the status. I see I've upset you." He climbed back up on the barstool and took a long gulp of his beer. Leonard looked on silently, polishing glasses and putting them up for later use.

Pádraig leaned in on the bar inches from Martin's face. "To the contrary, Martin, I think I've upset you. You've said something you feel you shouldn't have, isn't that right? Tell me what it is, Martin. Now."

Martin was trembling and looking away from Pádraig. "Oh, no, Father. I'm sure I couldn't tell you. Not I." Pádraig stepped back. "We're not finished talking about this, Martin." He walked back the table where Stephen was waiting for him. "What was that all about?" Stephen asked. "Too strange to talk about here. Let's go."

They walked out the front door and across the plaza toward the rectory. Pádraig had just started to recount the conversation to Stephen, when he heard steps running up behind him. He turned and saw Leonard approaching. "Hey, Father, Stephen. I'm bring a message to you. My aunt invites you to come back to the pub after closing tonight. She said to tell you she might have some information of interest to you. Will you come? I'm to tell her your response."

Pádraig and Stephen looked back at Beach Club, and at the window where they'd been seated. He saw that the blind had been lowered, but one edge was tilted up. Pádraig imagined he saw Ellen looking out at them. He stared back a few seconds, then turned to Leonard.

"Yes, Leonard. Tell her we'll be there."

28.

Once away from the plaza in front of Beach Club, Stephen insisted on an account of what had happened. Pádraig gave him a staccato blow-by-blow of the conversation. Stephen jogged along side of Pádraig on the way back to the rectory.

"So what do you think it all means, Pádraig? Are we on to something with the Yeats material?"

"I can't say yet. And won't say until I feel I can. We need more information. An inductive process. That's what'll work here." Pádraig was walking quickly enough to induce his own fast breathing, and Stephen was struggling to keep up. He made a note to himself to be thankful for how close the rectory and Beach Club were relative to each other.

Back in the rectory, he deflected Mrs. O'Flannelly's disapproving look occasioned by the missed lunch. He asked her to send tea into his study and retreated there with Stephen.

"What do we do now, do you think?" Stephen asked once the tea tray had been settled on the side table and he was alone again with Pádraig.

"We wait until closing time and go back there to hear whatever Ellen has to say. There's no point crashing in there before then. She was very definite about the time. And she's a stubborn woman, as you saw last night."

"I wouldn't have said stubborn, based on what I saw. Just

closed-minded. Opinionated."

"Closed-minded is a good description." Pádraig snorted. "Runs in the family."

Stephen set his cup down. "What does that mean? Did you have a problem with her parents or grandparents or something?"

"Both." Pádraig walked to the window. "I haven't told you the whole story of why my dissertation never got published." Pádraig walked back to his desk and pulled out the long drawer in the middle. He retrieved a yellowed, folded sheet of onionskin and handed it to Stephen.

Your Eminence,

We write as the Executive Committee of the Society of St. Patrick on an urgent matter in defense of the Faith. As you no doubt are aware, we are a lay society chartered by His Holiness Pope Urban VIII in 1650 to serve the Holy See by assisting the clergy here in Ireland in assuring the integrity of the teaching of the Faith. We have functioned continuously since receiving our charge to service, sometimes secretly when the climate was not hospitable to the open practice of the Roman rite. We have never abandoned the mission, even in the face of grave danger. Among our hundreds of members are some whose families have been in service to the Society for generations going back to its inception.

Having sheltered the flame of the Faith from outside threats for nearly two centuries, the Society was doubly surprised to hear of a threat of incomparable magnitude not only from within Ireland, but from within the clergy. The Society has become aware of a book called "The Visions of St. Patrick" by one Father Pádraig Hart, and we should be very surprised if Your Eminence may not already be aware of its blasphemy.

The perfidy of this outrageous book may be

summed up in three sentences from the author's own introduction:

An analysis of the contemporaneous writings of the ascetic later canonized as St. Patrick supports a modern conclusion different from that recommended by legend. The visions that Patrick experienced in his forty day exile on the mountain in County Mayo now named for him may have been genuine, divinely generated mystical experiences. But it is just as likely that they were a physical and mental reaction to lengthy abstinence from food, liquid and sleep."

It can do no good to cast doubt on the divinity of St. Patrick's experience, particularly as mere academic sport. Fr. Hart's cavalier speculation harms the integrity of the teaching of the Faith, and opens the door on a darker agenda that must be nipped in the bud by Your Eminence.

St. Patrick's call to exile on Croagh Patrick was no doubt a divine one, beckoning the young monk to experience the sacrifice and privation to which our Lord and Savior Jesus Christ submitted himself on his path to the acts that ensured our eternal salvation from sin.

In short, the Society urges you to consider that Fr. Hart's attack on the divinity of St. Patrick's experience is nothing short of an impertinent and blasphemous attack on the One he sought to emulate and the divinity of His exile in the desert. The miracles of Jesus in the desert are foundational to the Faith, and undermining them is intolerable.

We urge Fr. Hart's immediate defrocking, and should Your Eminence judge it proper, the commencement of an inquiry into his excommunication. The Society shall be happy to provide witnesses and other supporting testimony in connection with such an inquiry. At the very least, Fr. Hart must be decried as a disparager of the Faith and punished accordingly.

The Society anxiously awaits the favour of Your
Eminence's earliest reply to this entreaty.
Your Humble Servants in Christ,

Mr. & Mrs. Bernard O'Rourke
Mr. & Mrs. Daniel O'Rourke
Mr. Joseph Martin O'Flaherty
Mrs. Geraldine O'Neill
Mr. & Mrs. Cormac O'Conor

"The O'Rourkes and these other people tried to have you defrocked?"

"Yes, but as you see in the letter, they'd have been happier with excommunication. They thought me a heretic, after all."

"Obviously, neither happened. How did you weather it?"

"My superior solved the problem for me. He decided I was needed in Hong Kong. I told him I'd rather stay and reason it out with the people I'd offended. I felt that leaving was abandoning the truth of my research.

"So he gave me a choice. I could leave quietly and obediently -- obedience is one of the vows we take -- or I could stay, but I'd have to disown the dissertation and recant the things that people found offensive."

"A scholar can't abandon his work that way, didn't the Jesuits understand that?"

"In principle, yes. But they didn't think that what I'd written was such a fundamental truth that it was worth the fallout of the controversy it created. My superior said to me, 'We succeed in our missions by teaching within the indigent culture, not by replacing it entirely, and certainly not by insulting it.' Everything we do, including parish work and teaching right here in Ireland is regarded as a mission. And he was convinced I'd insulted the culture and broken that fundamental rule that undergirds all the successes Jesuits have had over the centuries."

"Well, that's a lot to lay on you. It must have been hard to leave and go halfway around the globe, so far from here."

"It was. It was hard for my mother. Mind you, I wasn't

even living in Mullaghmore at the time. I was still in Dublin, just preparing to come back here. No one in the Jesuits wanted such a remote assignment, so it was easy for me to snatch the post when I saw it open." Stephen handed the letter back to him, and he put it back in the drawer. "This letter had the effect of preventing me from coming home."

"They certainly went to a lot of trouble to derail you. Why such spite, do you know?"

"I don't really know. I want to say it's in their nature."

"This Society of St. Patrick, is it legitimate? What sort of group is it?"

"I had never heard of it before this letter. Maybe I should be embarrassed to call myself a St. Patrick scholar and admit that, but it's true. My superior certainly acted as though they had the clout to get the bishop's attention. It's not totally out of the question that it's on the up and up. The Church sometimes recognizes lay religious groups. People who can't take vows because they're already married, for instance, but want to make a deeper commitment to religious practices in daily life. There's a group formed in Spain that Pope Pius authorized that operates like that. Opus Dei."

"But did you ever look into the Society of St. Patrick?"

"In a minor way, yes. After I'd been back in the parish a while, I asked Martin – that's his father, Joseph among the signers of the letter – about the Society. He told me it had died out with his father's generation. No one cared to carry it forward, he said. The ideas were for a different time. He did say that his father had been secretive about it. Apart from knowing that his father was involved, he said he knew nothing else. I let it drop after that."

"But you kept that carbon of the letter all these years, close at hand. Why? I think I'd have torn it to tatters and burned the shreds by now."

"I'm not sure exactly why. Even though it's painful to think back on, I keep it. I think it's important to me because it was a crossroads in my life. I could have given up on what I believed to stay comfortably here, but I decided not to. I think I'm a bit pleased with myself for sticking to my guns, even though that meant leaving for a time. After all, I did get to come back eventually. And going to Hong Kong allowed me to meet Joe." He nodded in the direction of Luck Boat.

Stephen sat quietly for a moment. "The signers of the letter, are they all local families?"

"Well, yes. The family names are common ones. There are O'Neill's scattered all over the country. All over the world. But the family's origins are here and it's an especially common name in County Sligo. The same goes for the other three families. Those particular family names are of some renown, come to think of it. The O'Neills, O'Rourkes, O'Conors and O'Flahertys are all descended from the kings of Connaught Province, of which Sligo is a major county. Major in terms of land mass, I mean. The population has been declining for nearly a century."

"Do you think it's odd that they claim to have hundreds of members and the entire leadership is from right here in Mullaghmore?"

Pádraig opened the drawer and looked back at the paper. "I never focused on that before. But you're right, it 's quite a coincidence. Ellen's an O'Rourke, Martin an O'Flaherty. You haven't met them yet, maybe, but there still an O'Neill woman in the village, Mary, and then there's Darren O'Conor. You met his uncle just a little while ago, Conor."

"He's Conor O'Conor?" Stephen giggled with the discovery.

"I'm afraid so. Parents were a bit fixated on the family name. Or had a bad sense of humor. Not sure which."

Stephen looked at his watch. "So we have a little time to kill. I'll be hungry again in a little bit. Is it out of bounds to ask Mrs. O'Flannelly for some sandwiches?"

"Not at all. I'll ask her." He stepped out for a moment and came back. "Half an hour, is that soon enough?"

"Brilliant, thanks. I must say I'm anxious about what Ellen will have to say and why she's so hugger-mugger about it."

"I feel the same way. I'm half torn about telling Bertie about it ahead of time. I know she's just sick about the whole

179

thing, but I don't want to get her hopes up with a false lead. I think it's better if we wait and hear what Ellen has to say, then go on from there."

"I agree." Mrs. O'Flannelly knocked softly on the door and Pádraig opened it wide to accommodate the oversized tray, arrayed with more sandwiches than the two of them could eat. Pádraig thanked her profusely and ushered her out, closing the door quietly behind her. He gestured at the tray. "Mrs. O'Flannelly lives by the maxim that what's worth doing well is worth overdoing."

"Well said. I wouldn't mind something to drink with this, but I think we finished your bottle the other night."

"I make it a point not to run out," Pádraig said. "Open the door under the dictionary stand." Stephen retrieved a half-empty bottle of Cutty Sark. He squinted at the label. "Isn't this a blend?"

"Yes, but it's not bad. I lived in New York for a while and acquired a taste for it. They order it for me over at the bottle shop on the road to Sligo."

"You go all the way over there to buy scotch? Aren't there places a lot closer?"

Pádraig poured out two portions of the drink. He shook his head. "Not such a good idea to be buying scotch by the bottle too close to the parish." Stephen accepted the glass and sipped it while he worked on a roast beef sandwich.

"Let me ask you something, Pádraig. Seem like you have kind of a mixed relationship with this place. At times you seem quite at home here. But others, you seem like you'd like to be anywhere else."

"So what's your question? Seems like you've already reached your conclusion about my innermost thoughts."

"My question is, what keeps you here? You're obviously intelligent and talented. Aren't the Jesuits wasting you by posting you here?"

"It's my choice. We have to go where we're told for the most part, at least during the advancing parts of a career in the order. But I think they've mostly forgotten me out here. It's just as well. I never wanted one of those high-flying careers, postings to Rome and that sort of thing."

"But what about a university teaching position? I suppose you might be put off from that Or running a seminary? You're perfectly well qualified for that. You'd be good at either one of those."

Pádraig shook his head. "It's like any job market. The good jobs are very competitive. You need a mentor, someone to put your name forward and push your candidacy. You almost have to make a little campaign of it. That's not for me."

Stephen was quiet for a few moments. "Forgive me, Pádraig, but it's my nature to press when something doesn't make sense."

"What's that?"

"Why you're here. It doesn't make sense that you should have given up on yourself the way you're saying."

"I haven't given up on myself! You are quite presumptuous, Stephen, having made my acquaintance less than a week ago." Pádraig stood and walked across the room to the window.

"Well, I certainly didn't mean to upset you. I've been rather candid with you about my own circumstances. Not that you're expected to return in kind. But I did think we had the beginnings of a frank friendship here."

Pádraig sighed and put his hands in his pockets as he turned back to Stephen. "I could never run a seminary. Or teach in most of the religious institutions. Not based on what I've seen. I don't deserve the trust that responsibility entails." He looked at the floor.

"Why do you say that? What happened?"

Pádraig stared at the harbor as if steeling himself. "It was a long time ago. It was 1958, and I was finishing up my dissertation. I had already been ordained a few years earlier, but I was living in the seminary at Milltown near Dublin. Funny you should say what you did about running a seminary because that's what I was being groomed to do. I wasn't even thirty years old yet, but I'd been pegged in the Society as someone who might be good at it. I was an assistant rector of the college helping with spiritual formation. The thought was that by age and disposition, I'd be approachable by the new seminarians. Some of them were so young, still teenagers. Some had never been away from home for a single night when they came to us.

"There was one young man, Kevin McCarran was his name. Nineteen when he decided firmly enough that he had a vocation, or wanted to have one that he applied to seminary. He was bright and earnest and not the least bit worldly. Well read, but unsophisticated. I helped him with his reading list. I told him I'd help him with food for his mind, but he'd have to see to food for his bodily strength. He was a slight boy, and I encouraged him to take bigger helpings at meals. He was getting thin enough to slip under a door, I told him.

"He was coming along in his formation, but my rapport with him seemed to be getting more and more distant. I thought I'd put him off somehow, or that he was just homesick. He was from out here, Ballindoon in County Leitrim. He was one of the boys who'd never been away from home before.

"I prayed on what to do, how to do a better job for him. He was promising and I didn't want him to get discouraged and drop out. Back then, we had weekly meetings of the senior administrators of the seminary, and we'd go through the ranks and talk about who was doing well, who was not and what to do. I brought Kevin's name up at the meeting one Friday morning.

"There was another priest, senior to me by twenty years, who was part of the committee. I'll not mention his name for reasons you'll see. When I said to the group that I was worried about Kevin, this priest was quick to dismiss my concern. 'Och, another farm boy missing his mum and da. He'll be fine. Just leave him to me. I've got an eye on him.'

"Now, right away his choice of words and his eagerness that we pass on to the next seminarian struck me as odd."

"Ugh. I think I know where this is headed," Stephen said, putting his half-eaten sandwich down to listen more carefully.

"Right you are. That night, I was checking the

easternmost wing of the dormitory. Making sure that nothing was amiss. I heard yelling behind one door, and a sort of thrashing about. I stopped and listened for a moment, then knocked. The noise stopped. I checked the room number and realized that this was Kevin's door. I knocked again and called his name. No response.

"I had a passkey, which I made a point of using very rarely. For the most part, I didn't even need it. Few of the seminarians bothered to lock their doors. In fact, we issued keys only upon request. I should have sensed something wasn't right when Kevin asked for a key near the beginning of the term.

"When I opened the door with my master key that night, everything went sideways.
There was himself, the priest, astraddle of Kevin with his hand on Kevin's mouth shutting him up. Neither was fully clothed. It was Kevin's voice I'd been hearing, of course. It was plain that this encounter was not his idea." Pádraig's face bore the signs of reliving the scene as he recounted it.

"What did you do?"

"I'm ashamed to admit that for just a second, I thought of closing the door and doing nothing until the morning. But I knew that was wrong. I stepped into the room and shoved the priest off the bed. He landed on his arse and actually growled at me. 'Get out and mind your own business, Fr. Hart,' he said. I ignored him, which was a risky thing for me to do with such a senior member of the Society. But I'd made my mind up. I grabbed Kevin's bathrobe off the back of the door, threw it around his shoulders and cinched him up. I took him to my rooms. I didn't try to get him to talk to me that night. He'd already been through so much for one day. He cried until he fell asleep, exhausted.

"Did you go back to deal with the priest?"

"Not that night. I felt I needed a plan and some allies. I needed a night to sleep on it, and I intended to go to the rector of the seminary first thing in the morning."

"What happened when you told him? They must have run this priest off into the hills."

Pádraig sat on the edge of his desk, his hands on his knees as if he were suddenly lightheaded. "No, that's not what happened."

"What? You were on the right track, turning him in. What happened?"

"On my way to the administrative offices, this unnamed priest accosted me. He grabbed my arm outside the Blessed Sacrament Chapel and pushed me inside. Caught me completely off guard, which was apparently his hallmark. Once we were inside he said, 'I need to make my confession.' I told him 'I'm not your regular confessor, and it's just not done someone as junior as I hearing the confession of someone so senior as you. I haven't the wisdom, or the experience." I paddled as hard as I could against hearing his confession. I was pretty damn sure what was coming, and I didn't want to hear it.

"'Nonsense,' says he. 'I've an urge to confess, and you'll do just fine. Now, bless me Father, for I have sinned,' Once he invoked the rite of the sacrament , he pretty much had me, there wasn't much going back, but I really did not want to hear his confession. I told him, 'I protest. This is highly irregular, and if I understand where you're headed with this, I shan't be part of it.'

"I had started to leave, and he pushed me back down in the pew. 'Sit down, young man. You are an agent of God in the confessional, and have no business denying a penitent the sacrament.'

"'I'm not denying anyone the sacrament,' I told him. 'I'm only saying that I'm not the right one to administer it, to you, at this moment.'

"'I say you are,' he said 'Sit down. And keep your voice low and calm when you speak to me. Others may hear not what we say but remark upon how it is said.' He lowered his eyes, pretending contrition, and went on. "It has been five days since my last confession. These are my sins. I have transgressed my vow of chastity by intimate involvement with another person.'

"I told him, 'Father, please stop. I can't hear this. He's

my friend and I don't want to know this.'

"He was vociferous. Poked me in the chest and said 'You listen, Pádraig. You listen to me. At this moment, you are not his friend. You are my confessor and God's agent. A sincere confession requires a detailed accounting of the sins committed, offered with humility. And you will hear it. I had sexual relations with a novitiate named Kevin McCarran. There were repeated encounters, perhaps three dozen of them. Our dealings were consensual, though I can't discount the possibility that he may not be so candid on this point, accepting his own mutual culpability for what went on, and say that our contact was not consented to on his part.' He paused for a moment, and added the rest of the formula of the rite, 'For these and all the sins of my past life I am truly sorry and ask forgiveness.'

"I was so angry. I couldn't speak for a full minute or more. I was as surprised by the vastness of his sin as I was by the casualness of how he laid it on the table. Finally, I managed to say 'You forced yourself on a nineteen year old boy, that's your confession?'

"He actually smirked at me, pleased with himself for entrapping me. 'Ah, well,' he says, 'my confession is that there was sex, and I was part of it. There may be a dispute about modality, and I can't help that. But it happened.' He shrugged as if this were no big deal.

"I rolled out the only weapon I had left. I told him. 'You don't sound at all contrite, I must say, Father. It will be impossible for me to grant absolution in these circumstances.'

"That really set him off. He grabbed my lapel and pulled me within inches of his face. I could feel the shower of his spit on my face. He said, 'listen, you smug little prick, I've been hearing confessions since you were an altar boy. This is nothing, nothing compared to what I've heard and absolved. So you take your righteous tone and turn it into a few Hail Marys for me to say and we'll call it all done.'

"I looked up at him. He was on the verge of true rage. I realized in that moment that he could have me dismissed on a whim and end my career before it started. And what happened next makes me truly sick, even when I remind myself that it was twenty-one years ago."

"What happened?" Stephen asked softly.

Pádraig took a deep breath and let out a long sigh. "I absolved him. I told him, 'You'll say three rosaries and fifteen Hail Marys and stay away from Kevin. And anyone else in the class who looks at all vulnerable or attractive to you.' So he makes the sign of the cross and tells me 'Thank you, Father, and God bless you.' Then he finally left. I sat there for a few minutes. I thought if I moved I might be sick. I was collecting myself to move on, when I felt his hand on my shoulder again. I looked up and saw him wearing an ugly smile. He said, 'I probably needn't remind you, but will out of an abundance of caution, that what I've confessed to here is sealed in the confidence of the confessional and may be discussed with no one else. Not a soul.' I told him that I understood canon law on penance. Then I ran to the gents, and threw up until my sides hurt.

"Wait a minute. That can't be right. The priest confessed to a crime, the rape of a minor. There must be some exception that allowed you to tell the garda, or at least the rector of the seminary."

Pádraig reached for a volume on the shelf behind his desk. "No, actually not. Canon law is very explicit on this point." He turned the pages. "Here's what it says: 'The sacramental seal is inviolable; therefore it is absolutely forbidden for a confessor to betray in any way a penitent in words or in any manner and for any reason.' I read this a thousand times that day after the confession, looking between the words for a way out."

"Couldn't you go to the rector and...I don't know... strongly hint that something was wrong in regards to Fr. Connor?"

"No. Any intentional act that leads to the discovery of the penitent's identity and the sin violates canon law."

"Well, what about a more general warning that something was...wrong. And there should be...inquiries made. If the rector asked around based on that suggestion and found out for himself what was going on, what would be wrong with that?"

"That didn't work either. Here's the next section of the code: 'A confessor is prohibited completely from using knowledge acquired from confession to the detriment of the penitent even when any danger of revelation is excluded.' I might have been able to minimize the danger of revelation if I just encouraged a general inquiry, but I couldn't eliminate it. And if the inquiry did what it needed to do, it would certainly be to the detriment of the priest involved."

Stephen's jaw dropped. "This is unbelievable. You have to imagine that this was neither Connor's first infraction nor his last. Couldn't you treat it as a warning of a future infraction and act on that?"

"No. Listen, believe me, I explored every angle you've mentioned and a few you haven't. I was desperate to see the priest punished and end any opportunity he had for future malice."

"So what did you do?"

"After I'd collected myself, I talked to Kevin. I persuaded him that the rector had to be informed, though it wasn't very hard. He'd had enough of it. I went to the rector without him, though.

"I got to see him almost right away, which was unusual. I told him I was there to talk about a transgression by one of the persons of authority in the seminary. He asked me who it was, and I told him. Before I could say anything to stop him, he'd opened the door to the adjacent office, and summoned the priest in question. Suddenly I had the feeling that I wasn't the first to raise this issue. It was almost as if he'd been expecting me."

"It must have been awkward, having the bad priest right there in the room with you."

"Terribly awkward. For a moment, I thought I should just retreat. The bad priest, as you call him, pretty well strutted into the room. He didn't seem at all concerned. When I started speaking, he interrupted me. 'Fr. Hart, you're familiar, no doubt, with the consequences of breaking the seal of confession?' 'Who said anything about a confession?' the rector asked. 'Let's just say that I happen to know that this story he's about to tell involves what he's learned in a confession,' the priest said archly. 'Is it your own confession, Father?' the rector asked him. 'How could it be, Rector? He's not my regular confessor.' The bastard was playing with me, quoting back my own words to him right before his confession. Trying to scare me off track.

"I knew I had to choose my words very carefully. Clearly, the priest thought he'd immunized himself with his confession. But he didn't fully protect himself. When I opened that door, I saw firsthand evidence of one transgression, and I thought that might be enough to get him what he deserved. But still, what I saw was interlinked with what he confessed. I had to proceed carefully."

Stephen was up and pacing. "What's exactly was the risk? What could they do to you?"

"They don't have to do anything. A priest who breaks the seal of the confession is automatically excommunicated at the moment he breaks the seal. It's called latae sententiae."

"A career-ending move in your line of work." He lowered his voice. "I guess it's that important to you, your religion and your vocation. That you'd be worried about getting kicked out for doing the right thing. You'd actually balance one against the other. So what happened? And by the way, aren't you breaking the seal by talking to me about this now?"

"No, the seal is broken by identifying the penitent and linking him with the sins confessed. I've withheld his name. Besides, he's dead. And in hell, I hope. Not around to turn me in. Anyway, I told the rector what I'd heard and seen. I held back nothing, no detail of what I saw, sticking strictly to my firsthand knowledge."

"What did the rector say when you were finished?"

"It was astonishing. He didn't even look to the priest for an explanation. He just said, 'Thank you, Fr. Hart, for bringing these allegations to my attention. I'll handle it from here.' I said to him, 'But canon law requires you to make inquiries, Monsignor.' He got cross with me. 'I'm aware of your high marks in canon law, Father, but you needn't educate me on the point. You may assume that I shall make appropriate inquiries.' He went back to his desk. 'Listen, it's not the first time a boy has led one of us astray. I'll have a talk with this novitiate. It's always tears and apologies. We'll sort it out from there.' I was flabbergasted by now. 'But Monsignor,' I said, 'how can you assume it's the novitiate's fault? Or that he participated willingly?'"

"'Do you have information to the contrary?' he asked me. I couldn't say that I did, because that was under the seal. I couldn't say I didn't, because that would be a lie to a superior, and it would have me covering for the priest. So I did what a priest is supposed to do under canon law in these circumstances. I told him I didn't know."

"That's sort of a nonsense answer, isn't it? Saying you don't know if you have information to the contrary?"

"Yes, you're right. I was rather hoping that the rector would piece together the different parts of the conversation… that the bad priest alleged that information from a confession was involved, that I'd given a non sequitur answer to his question, and that what I'd said, 'I don't know', is the standard fall back when a priest can't answer a question without breaking the seal."

"Did he put it together?"

"I couldn't tell for sure. He said he'd speak to Kevin and dismissed me. The way he looked at me, though, it seemed as though he'd added it up."

"And the bad priest was just standing there the whole time?"

"Yes. Hadn't said anything since the beginning of the conversation when he tried to shut me up. But he didn't look at all worried.

"I found Kevin and told him that I'd reported what I saw to the rector, and that the rector would be sending for him. I advised him to pray for calmness and to be direct and thorough in explaining everything that happened. I went off to teach my classes. But I was worried about Kevin. He'd been so quiet during my time with him, almost unable to speak.

I wasn't sure he could acquit himself in front of the rector."

Pádraig sat in his desk chair, slumped back as if suddenly exhausted. "It wasn't until the end of the day that I next saw Kevin." Pádraig covered his eyes. His hands were trembling. "He was in the reception room of the seminary. With his suitcase."

"His suitcase?" Stephen exclaimed.

Pádraig nodded. "He said he'd talked to the rector, told him everything, and the rector counseled him that it would be best if he went home to remove temptation from himself and others. He said he'd pleaded for another chance, but the rector was firm. He started explaining the matter had not been at his initiative, and the rector cut him off, saying that he would not entertain a truth contest between a novitiate and a respected member of the faculty."

"Unbelievable. So that was it?"

"No, I couldn't leave it at that. I stormed over to the rector's office, barged in past his assistant. I told him he was being unjust, that he had put the blame on the wrong person. I told him it was ridiculous to think that a nineteen year old was the guilty party. That the priest's position of authority made any supposed consent null and void. That the responsibility to avoid compromise rested with the priest, not the teenager. 'Careful, Father.' He's wagging his finger at me at this point. 'Remember the seal of penance.' I said to him, 'Didn't Kevin tell you what happened?' 'Yes,' he said, 'but I don't believe him and his version of events. Besides,' says he, turning back to his papers, 'we can always replace a novice. Others are not so easy to replace.' He could tell I wasn't being quick to leave his office, but he sat there saying nothing for almost a full minute. Then he said, 'Well, perhaps Father X could spend a short time away from the seminary. I'll think about it.' I said to him, 'Monsignor, am I to understand that this isn't the first allegation against him?' He looked at me with indignation. 'That's no business of yours, Father.' I thought that pretty well confirmed it. Then he dismissed me."

"And that was it?"

"No, he saved the best for last. As I'm going out of his

office, he says 'By the way, your provincial superior wants you to call him about a matter. I believe it may entail your reassignment. Nothing related to today's events, of course. But it may be best for all if you move to new duties.'"

"And that's when you found out about the Society of St. Patrick's letter?"

"Exactly, that's when that began to play out."

"So the priest got away with it in the end?"

"A lot of people got away with a lot of things."

"Doesn't it infuriate you? Or disgust you? Why do you stay in the priesthood?"

Pádraig looked down at his hands then up at Stephen. "It's all I have."

29.

"Should we head over to Beach Club now?"

Pádraig nodded. "In that direction, yes. But we can wait out in the fresh air. I need to clear my head."

Pádraig and Stephen sat on the bench overlooking the harbor and within view of the Beach Club's front door. The moon was sheathed in clouds, but cast enough light for them to make out faintly the line where the waves came to shore. "It's a little past closing time. Should we head over there now?" Stephen asked, glancing at his pocket watch. "We should allow a little time for the stragglers to make their way out." Pádraig replied. They saw the pub's door open and close a few times as the last customers tumbled out into the street buoyed by the extra rounds they'd ordered at last call.

At half past eleven, Pádraig pushed himself upright. "I guess we might as well go find out what there is to know." The two made their way over to the pub.

The front door was locked, but Leonard answered Pádraig's knock. "Good evening to you both. Come right in." He held a broom in one hand. "It's after closing, obviously, but I haven't locked up the bottles yet. Will you have something?"

"No, thanks just the same. We're eager to speak with your aunt since she more or less summoned us here."

"Yes, of course. I'll tell her you're here."

Pádraig and Stephen watched as Leonard went around to the left of the bar and through a door. Pádraig wrinkled his brow. "That's strange. I thought Ellen's office and room were around to the right. I thought that was just a closet over on that side." Leonard emerged from the same door. "Right this way, gentlemen," he said holding the door open. Pádraig and Stephen followed him. A dim light bulb illuminated the space which contained mops, brooms and cleaning supplies. "Leonard, what the devil is this? Is this a joke?" Stephen looked around as Leonard pulled the door to the pub closed behind them. "Sweet Jesus," Stephen muttered. "I don't do well in enclosed places, Pádraig, let's go back...."

"Gentlemen, gentlemen, please be patient. The discomfort is strictly temporary." Leonard tapped the wall that defined the right side of the closet, and it hinged open into another larger space. "Your eyes will adjust in a moment to the lighting. Mind the steps here," Leonard cautioned. "There's three of them, going up."

Pádraig and Stephen followed closely behind Leonard up the steps into a cavernous room illuminated by dozens of white candles. At the far end of the room was a large wooden table. As his eyes absorbed the candlelight, Pádraig saw familiar faces around the table: Martin O'Flaherty, Darren O'Conor, Mary O'Neill. Ellen rose from her seat and greeted them. "Welcome, Father, Mr. Attergood."

"Um, we haven't met," Stephen said, "yet you know..."

"I know who you are, Mr. Attergood," Ellen responded imperiously. "I am a resourceful woman." She crossed her arms and offered a smug smile.

"More owing to it being such a very small village, actually," Pádraig said curtly. "Let's get on with this, whatever it is. You're the one who asked us here. What is going on here anyway?" He looked around at the candles. "If you're having a séance, you'd best move it along before this place goes up in flames."

"No, Father, no séance. Not tonight," Ellen said.

"Well, what then? Tomorrow's Maundy Thursday, busy day, beginning of the Triduum. I don't have all night."

"Please, Father," Mary pleaded. "We asked you here for your own good."

Pádraig was growing more and more agitated. "For my own good, you say? I'll be the judge of that!"

Stephen shifted toward Pádraig slightly. "Pádraig, let's just listen a bit," he whispered. "We're already here. We might as well invest a few more minutes, as bizarre as this is turning out to be."

"Fine, fine. What did you want to tell me? Tell us?" He gestured at Stephen.

"The message is more especially directed to you, Father," Ellen said. "But seeing as Mr. Attergood has become your... partner in crime, shall we say..."

"Partner in crime! How dare you, Ellen?" Stephen grabbed Pádraig's arm to prevent him from charging the table. "It's a figure of speech. Let it go," Stephen whispered fiercely.

Ellen looked pleased at her success in inciting Pádraig. "The message is for both you."

"And the message would be from whom, may I ask?" Pádraig reddened and struggled to contain his irritation.

Ellen gestured around the table. "It's from us."

"A message from you four?" Pádraig asked. "Delivered in the middle of the night, in a secret attic? Who do you think you are?"

Martin looked up from his black and tan. "We're The Four, Father," he said somberly.

Pádraig clenched his fists to his sides. "Oh, bloody hell. The four what for the love of Christ?"

Martin sat up sharply and looked around at the others. "Well, no one ever asked me that before. Do you not know?"

Ellen swatted Martin's arm. "Idiot. We're the Four Síolta, that's what we are. Among ourselves, we are known as The Four."

"What's a....what's that word?" Stephen asked, turning to Pádraig.

"Síolta," Pádraig said. He exaggerated his mouthing of the word. "It's SHAWL-ta, is how you say it. It's plural of síol, which means seed."

Stephen scowled in thought. "So your group is the Four Seeds?"

"That's the literal meaning, yes," Ellen sniffed. "But it carries a lot more import that just that."

"Well, it can carry more import." He turned to Stephen to explain. "It's used to describe lines of ancestry sometimes. Dates way back to when Ireland was ruled by kings, bunches of them, in different corners of the country. There were half a dozen or so important ones just here in what's now Province Connaught. So the descendants of the famous king Aed Uí Briún would be 'Síol Aed Uí Briún' or 'progeny of Aed O'Brien'."

"Oh. Why isn't it Siolta Aed O'Brien?"

"Collective noun. This lot has probably been using it wrong all this time."

"We didn't make it up ourselves. It's a name and a sacred responsibility handed down through many, many generations," Ellen huffed, hands on hips.

Padriag crossed his arms. "I rather thought I had a monopoly on legitimate sacred responsibilities in Mullaghmore. What are you talking about?"

Ellen paced behind the seats of the others. She sighed in exasperation. "Martin, Darren, one of you explain to him. He's clearly not inclined to listen to me." Martin and Darren looked at each other for a moment. "All right then," Darren finally said, breaking the silence. "I'll start out. Each of us has part of the knowledge. Others will add to what I say." He stood and paced out to the middle of the room where Pádraig and Stephen stood. He took a deep breath.

"The story goes back a long, long way. Back past the time of St. Patrick. Cattle roamed freely back then and there was more land than anyone could cultivate. Wealth was counted by the size of a clan's herd. Land was plentiful, so no one really bothered to establish who owned it.

"Tending the cattle was a migratory career, driving them to the north in the summer and back to the south in the colder months. But eventually, people spread out to the western coast, the area where we are right now. The land wasn't as arable, but you could graze cattle all year round without driving them too far north or south or away from the coast. That was because of the temperate climate owing to the sea." He gestured out to the harbor.

"The people who figured this out were descendants of the famous King Conn."

"Conn of the Hundred Battles," Pádraig interjected. "'Hundred' is probably a little low. He was High King of Ireland, the Tara King, for more than a quarter century. He was trying to keep the country under his consolidated control, but he fought constantly with another lesser king from what's now Munster. He ended up conceding half the country to him."

"But this was part of what he kept, called 'Conn's Half', and his descendants, the Connachta settled down here. That's what the name of the province means: 'descendants of Conn'." Darren paused for a moment and looked at the floorboards. His voice trembling, he added, "It's a noble, noble heritage."

Pádraig rolled his eyes. "Save the drama and let's get on with it, can't we?"

Darren ignored the barb. "We come down from a brave and earnest people. They understood that living here conferred a sacred stewardship."

"Which entailed what, exactly?" Stephen asked. Mary rose from her seat behind the table and assumed the speaker's position facing Pádraig and Stephen in the middle of the room. Darren receded to his chair.

"Our ancestors appreciated that they were not the first to live here. Centuries of inhabitants preceded them, they knew that. And not all human people such as ourselves." She lowered her voice. "Different races of people lived here before us, sometimes fighting among themselves, sometimes overlapping in peace." She looked toward Pádraig and Stephen, but past them. "First were the Fomorians, who came up from under the murragh, the sea, after the Great Flood."

Stephen whispered to Pádraig, "Does she mean the one with Noah and the ark?"

196

"Aye, I believe so," Pádraig said quietly. Mary was oblivious to the exchange.

"They were a fierce people, built sturdy as goats, who loved this land. They defended Ireland against invaders who wanted to claim it, the followers of Partholon, who subjugated the Fomorians. But the land land itself rose up against this injustice and put a plague on the people of Partholon that claimed all but one of them. Then the people of Nemed invaded, and put the Fomorians under the yoke."

"If these are the people who are supposed to be defending the land, they don't seem to be very good at it," Stephen whispered to Pádraig. Pádraig suppressed a smile.

"But the sea itself rose up against such ignominy and flooded the strongholds of the Nemedians. The survivors were cast to the four corners of the world.

"Two hundred years later, one band of these survivors yearned to return to Ireland. These were the Fír Bolg, 'men of the bag', a people so attached to this land that they had passed down among the generations bags of earth gathered up from this place by their ancestors. These soils were carried with them wherever they went as precious relics, reminders of their rootedness, their connection to this place. They sailed thousands of miles to return here, to their ancestral home.

"But their hold on the land was brief. They were challenged by invaders, also descendants of the surviving Nemedians, from the northern seas. They were a tall and beautiful people, fair of complexion. They called themselves the Tuatha de Danaan. So committed they were to remaking their lives in Ireland that when they landed, they burned their ships. They proposed a peaceful co-regnum with the Fír Bolg, but the Fír spurned them and terrible battles ensued.

"A contest between champions was finally to decide the outcome. The champion of the Fír was a formidable warrior named Bres. The king of the Tuatha, Nuada, insisted on championing his own people. Bres slashed away at him, and cut off his sword hand. But that wasn't the end of the war. The Tuatha had learned secret wisdom while pining away in the northern lands for their return to Ireland. One among

197

them inflicted a magic that hid all sources of drinking water on the Fir and at the same time gave them a terrible thirst. None among them could fight and so they were vanquished.

"The Thuatha had gotten what they came for, the whole of Ireland. But they admired the valor of the Fir and offered them a safe retreat and possession of one-fifth of the country, left up to their choice. They chose Connacht. They have never left.

Stephen spoke up. "But what does that mean? Do they live among you? Is this one of the lineages you were talking about?" Mary didn't answer him. She walked trance-like back to her seat. Martin took the floor.

"It's not the end of the story. The Tuatha lived here and ruled Ireland for a century and a half. But the charms and allures of Ireland were no secret to adventurers from the continent. The Tuatha beat back one throne-seeker from Spain and soon after his nephews arrived with a fleet to demand the high kingship. These were the family of Mil Espaine, who called themselves Milesians. The Tuatha pretended they wanted to counsel among themselves about the demand and possible compromises, so the Milesians agreed to withdraw from the shores to the distance of nine waves. The Tuatha deceived them, though, using this retreat to give their druids time to conjure up a great storm, fierce enough to capsize the fleet. But the Milesian druids were even more powerful, and the chief druid, Amergin, drew up a counter-magic in the form of a poem to calm the seas. It was Ireland's first glimpse of how powerful poetry could be."

"What happened to the Tuatha then?"

Martin pushed his hands into his pockets and looked at the floor. "This is the part that lots of people have trouble with. The Tuatha were defeated by the Milesians. But just as the Tuatha had done with the Fir, they made a truce that allowed the Tuatha to retreat. But remember, they had burned their ships upon arrival, and the Milesians were in no mood to have them stay around long enough to see them rebuild the vessels or help them do so."

Pádraig shook his head. "It makes no sense. They

couldn't leave, then. Where did they go?"

Martin paced in front of the table. "This is the hard part. They left, but at the same time they stayed, in a fashion." He turned back to the others at the table. Mary nodded slightly. "They're here, in a separate world, a separate kingdom." He stamped his heel on the floor and locked eyes with Pádraig. "They live beneath us."

30.

"Hah!" Pádraig exhaled a laugh that bent him over at the waist. The Four looked back and forth among one another. Stephen stood still, following the scene with his eyes and no turn of his head.

"Father, see here!" Martin said, hands on his hips. "This is a very serious matter we're discussing, and it will pay for you to please treat it as such." He sounded hurt, Stephen noticed.

Pádraig retrieved himself from another gale of laughter and wiped his eyes with his handkerchief. "Really, the four of you had me going for a bit there." He folded his square and replaced it in his pocket. He patted Stephen on the shoulder. "Well, it's clear they've had their turn at scaring us with ghost stories." He turned to leave. "But it's also clear they've nothing useful to share about the girl's disappearance." He jumped at the sound of Ellen's fist slammed to the wooden table. "You're not going anywhere, Father, until we're finished here." Her voice was a low growl.

"Um, Pádraig," Stephen said quietly, "I know it's unappealing to you to follow orders from....well, anyone, but especially her." He thrust his chin in Ellen's direction. "But I think we should stay and hear them out." Pádraig rolled his eyes and groaned. Stephen showed no signs of moving, so Pádraig snatched two wooden spindle-backed chairs from along the wall and dragged them into the area where he and

Stephen had been standing. "Might as well be a bit more comfortable." He scowled and lowered himself into the chair. He gave Ellen a dismissive wave. "Carry on, then. I haven't got all night."

Ellen remained seated, fuming at Pádraig and Stephen. "You've bumbled into something that's none of your affair. You need to bugger out of it." Pádraig stood and took a quick step toward the table. "See here, Ellen, you've no cause to use such vulgar language with me. I'm still the priest of this parish whether you care for me or not." A moment of silence hung between them.

"This won't make you feel better," Stephen said quietly, "but I think the bugger comment was directed toward me." Ellen laughed and smiled cruelly at Stephen. "You're an astute little man. And yes. We know what you are." She spat on the floor. Pádraig turned to Stephen. "Still wanting to stay to hear this gentlelady out?" he asked sarcastically. Stephen sighed. "I think we've no choice, sorry to say." Pádraig shook his head and walked back to his chair.

"What you've stumbled into is something much larger than yourselves, and much more important than a little girl gone missing. The Four have a sacred, centuries long responsibility."

"Bloody hell! We've been dancing around this sacred work all night. Just out with it, say what it is for the love of heaven." Pádraig remained seated but turned red with his shouting."

Martin took over the narrative. "It's the treaty, Father. it goes way back. Way back to the earliest times when there was no trade and no career to follow that didn't require living off the land. Even those who tinkered or blacksmithed grew their own food. If there was any marketing or trading at all, it was primitive and occasional. A bad year on the family plot meant you didn't eat unless your neighbors had enough to share and a charitable impulse.

"The Gentry have no such problems. We don't know why, but they never run out of food. When we're slack in the larders, theirs are bulging. He stroked his chin pensively. Of course, it may have a bit to do with the fact that they don't eat much of the kind of food that keeps us alive. Only pure water and a dab of honey now and then. No bread, no porridge, nothing like that. And so in lean times, they are good friends to have, I'm sure you see. They're right generous with what they have when we're in need."

"But there's no such thing as a free meal, is there." Stephen interjected. "What's the catch?"

"Well, now, it's not so much of a catch, you see, not like they've deceived us or anything." Martin shrugged, palms up as if explaining the most reasonable thing in the world. "It's an honest bargain, that's all."

Pádraig paused for a moment before pressing on. He felt a surge of nausea as he resisted the realization that was coming over him. "I see. You say we get food when we need it. What do they get when they're in need. Not food, I'd say, as you indicate they eat nothing much we could give them. What do they get?"

Martin walked around the table, his glasses perched low so that he could look over the tops of the lenses. He spoke slowly, as if explaining something difficult but obvious to a child.

"Now, Father, we've every reason to believe that they are spiritual creatures, beings with souls, just like we folk here and the angels themselves. They get curious now and then about how we live. They're different from us. They have wild merriment in their world, and they never do a lick of work. They wonder at how we folk can work as hard as we do and still be happy. They don't age, few of them have children, and them that do can't feed them by the mother's pap. They wonder what that's like."

"And so?" Pádraig asked, alarm rising in his voice.

"Well, they make off with the odd girl or fellow now and then. To satisfy their curiosity and advance their learning about us."

"And the lot of you and your fathers and grandpas have gone along with this? The kidnapping of children from Mullaghmore all these years?"

"Well, not everyone has. Some tried refusing their bounty, even in hard times. Reilly, the old one who lived over the hill past the Green Street, wouldn't eat a thing they gave him, even were it one of us who passed it on as if a gift from our own hearth. He knew somehow where it came from.

"Reilly was adamant. 'I'll take not a morsel of their food,' he said. He stuck to his guns. But meanwhile, his wife and daughter were getting awful, awful thin. The mother wasn't concerned for herself, but was afraid for the daughter's health. She had caught a bad cough and had begun to lay about the house most of the days as she felt to weak to go out at all. At length, the mother came to us and begged us to find a way to put some food in their pantry. We talked to the Gentry, and they were very sympathetic and understanding.

"At the full moon, what should have been the harvest moon, but there were no crops to pull out of the ground, the good people came by his lot and put an enchantment on the soil to make it grow like it should in a good year. Within a week, Reilly had beans wandering up trellises and potato tops popping out of the ground. I've never seen anything like it! It was an abundance for him just in the knick of time.

"But Reilly was never one to believe his own luck. He was suspicious right away about how his land produced when everyone else had a black thumb that year. It was practically overnight, though, when his pumpkins came in. I guess the Gentry were a little overzealous in their generosity. It was too good to be true.

"So he stayed up late one night soon after this. He'd refused to let his wife and daughter take a single thing out of the garden. He tilled in soil and acid from the chemist shop, fixing to kill every last sprout that'd come up. When he'd done that, he dragged an old sail tossed out on the quay clear down to his property and oiled it to weight it down. He stretched it across the patch, thinking to block out the sun from raising anything else up from that plot.

"What he didn't know was that for the first time in their marriage, his wife had defied him. She couldn't stand her daughter's desolation another moment longer. So she'd stolen out into the garden the night before and rolled the biggest pumpkin she could find in through the back door and hid it behind the boots and coats in the mudroom. When Reilly went out to salt the garden, she made a soup of the pumpkin, quick as she ever had, throwing in old onions made of almost nothing but their own papery skins and some carrot tops she'd otherwise have thrown to the goats. By the time Reilly caught waft of the simmering pot, it was too late; she'd already poured a steaming ladle of the concoction into her daughter's bowl, who sipped it up as quickly as it cooled off enough not to scald her lips on the way in.

"Reilly wandered back to the house at the smell and saw all this, and into his field of vision slipped a figure he'd never seen before but well enough recognized by instinct and description: Tan Mithy, King of the Gentry.

"What are you here for, then, coming into my home uninvited," he shouted at Tan Mithy. "Out with you, and don't be coming back!"

Tan Mithy took off his cap and gave a little bow. He had no need, mind you, bowing to Reilly, he being royalty of his kind and all, but he was a polite and respectful type. Then clear as my voice is to you now, he said "But, sir, you are mistaken. When your daughter accepted the gift of our food, she invited us into your home, and a good deal more."

"She did no such thing!" Reilly shouted and stamped his foot. "Out, now or I'll be calling the garda and they'll put you out, and not too kindly."

Tan Mithy gave him just a little smile, sort of sad and polite. "There's no need for that, Mr. Reilly, nor any point to it either. The chief of garda is a good friend who understands our ways and our rules. Our families have been taking care of one another for many years."

And then Tan Mithy explained, very gentle and softly-like that in times of need, the Gentry provide food to the villagers out of their magicked stores. "The last of the villagers to accept the food in the harvest moon is ours to carry away, Mr. Reilly, by tradition and treaty," Tan Mithy concluded. "They are shown by their resistance to be the stronger ones, the ones with fighting spirit, and we want them for our own, as brides if they be girls and as fighting men if boys."

Reilly stamped and cried and cursed first Tan Mithy then his wife for her double-crossing of him, but there was no way around it but that the daughter had to go along with Tan Mithy. She had by then fallen into a trance, enthralled at the voice of Tan Mithy, which was part of the magic worked upon her by eating the soup, and it was no hard thing at all to get her to stand up and follow him out of the house.

Reilly followed him, still ranting and cursing, and calling his neighbors to come out of their houses and help detain his daughter from that one who was a-thieving her, but none did any more than look our their windows and doorways, then rush inside to close their houses up tight against such a visitor.

And so you have it, Father, that not all have gone along with the pact, but then again none has succeeded outside it, either.

Ellen resumed her place at center stage. "So you see, Father, there is much more at play that you can possibly understand. It's our four families, descendants of the four high kings of Connacht, that have protected this land for all these centuries. The land was well and truly fought over, what with being so beautiful and coveted on its own, and so exposed to the sea on the west. Someone had to step in and take up the burden." Ellen paced across the floor, the length of the table and stopped in front of Pádraig. "Really, Father, we've all done our part to find the girl. But it's time to stop. It's clear at this point that the Gentry want to keep her, and we must abide by their wishes."

Pádraig sat silently for moment. "So that's it then? You expect me to give up the ghost on the search for Fianna because of a fireside story about failed harvests? Because of your self-important family yarns? You lot truly are barking mad." He stood and glared at The Four. "You must know that I'll do no such thing. There's a thousand places we haven't looked yet, more than that even." He shook his finger at Ellen. "You mark my words. I will never give up." He glanced at Stephen. "This time, I really am leaving, like it or not. Come

205

along unless you fancy some private time with your new friends." Stephen quickly collected his sack and made sure nothing had spilled out. "No thanks, not just now." He started toward the door. "But one question: I don't suppose we could see a copy of the Treaty, could we? Perhaps there's some exception or something in the text that would help us in this particular case."

Ellen leapt to her feet. "Get out! Get out of my establishment right now!" Pádraig had already accelerated his exit after Ellen's first exclamation. But Stephen stood his ground. He cocked his head as if listening to a distant voice that made a piece of the puzzle snap into place. "Does that mean we're not allowed to see it?" He took a step backward toward the short staircase. "Or that it doesn't exist?" He ducked out the door just in time to miss the pint glass Ellen hurled toward his head.

31.

The front door of the pub had already jingled closed behind Padriag by the time Stephen hustled himself through the front of the house. He hit the door running, twisted the bolt and burst out onto the sidewalk. He flipped up the collar of his jacket and jogged to catch up with Pádraig.

"Well, that was interesting, don't you think?" His breath steamed out into the night air.

Pádraig stopped and looked at him. "Interesting?" he shouted. "I've just learned that my parish includes a delusional sect of fairy worshippers!"

"Shhh, shhh," Stephen said, tapping Pádraig's forearm. "I think we ought to handle the information a little more discreetly than all that." He looked around. No one had emerged from the pub, and the park in front of the quay was empty at such a late hour.

"Oh, I've got the opposite idea. I'm going to tell every soul I see in this village that their lives are held in the balance by a crazy group that fancies itself lineal keepers of an imaginary treaty with the fairies. Why not start now?" He filled his lungs and tilted his head back to start a proper bellowing. Stephen punched his arm. "Ow, that hurt, you little shite." Pádraig rubbed his arm. Stephen was unapologetic. "I had to get your attention to prevent you from making a terrible mistake. The answer to your question, why not start now, is this: do you not remember a single word of the story I told you two days ago about the sudden death of my academic career?"

"Well, of course I do. That was a very moving story. But this is completely different."

"How?"

Pádraig looked at Stephen for a moment, then sighed. He glanced at his pocket watch. "Obviously, we've got a lot to go over. One more drink, okay, but then that's really it or I'll be incoherent for Holy Thursday."

"Absolutely. Not a drop more than just one more drink," Stephen nodded solemnly and followed Pádraig into the rectory.

Pádraig led the way into his study and turned up the lights. A cat, curled up in the chair that was usually Stephen's blinked at the sudden brightness and stood to stretch its back. The cat accepted a stroke from Stephen's hand and purred. "I didn't know you had a cat. Mother's down to just the one cat you heard making a ruckus the other night. I rather like cats."

"And apparently they like you, or at least this one does. Not a full time resident, this one. Comes and goes, weeks at a time."

Stephen squinted in the light and turned the cat's fur up. "What color would you call the coat on this one?"

"I'd say tan."

"Yes, I guess that's about right. What's its name?"

"Tancat."

"I'd ask if you were joking, but I'm absolutely sure you're not."

Pádraig shrugged. "It's easy to remember. The little ones at the school find it amusing. They play with him at recess."

"So it's a male?"

"I've actually no idea. I work on the assumption that no female would care to live with me. Must be male.

"Do you want me to check?"

"No, not really. I prefer to stick with the assumption."

"That won't be much comfort when you're trying to find

homes for a dozen kittens. I mean, in case you're wrong."

Pádraig fell into the chair behind his desk and put his hand to his forehead. "This has been the longest day I remember in more than a dozen years." He looked up at Stephen. "So what is it you think we should do with that bunch?"

"Nothing directly with them. Think about it. If you go about talking about what they said and who they claim to be, people will think you're crazy. Unless some of them are in on it, too. Maybe half the village thinks the Four are doing a great service. Or maybe they don't have the specifics, they just have family stories handed down from generation to generation about the vague idea that someone protects them from the gauzy unknown."

"Well, I've certainly never heard of it. And my family's been here a long time, going back quite a ways."

"Could you ask your mother, do you think? Ask her if she remembers anything like that? Oh, and we should definitely ask Easmon. I mean, not tonight with respect to either of them."

"Certainly not. My mother's asleep, as I should be, and there's no talking to Easmon when the pub's not open," Pádraig grumbled. "You really think we should keep this quiet? It's just so ludicrous, I think putting a little sunshine on it…"

"Would accomplish what? Listen, either they're self-deluded, in which case they're irrelevant to finding Fianna, or…."

"What? You're not about to say that they're genuinely telling the truth, I hope."

Stephen positioned himself in front of the desk. "Well, let's not rule that out as a possibility," he held up his hand to stem Pádraig's incipient protest. "Remote though it might be, I'll grant you that. There's another way of thinking about it. What if they genuinely believe they're telling the truth?"

"If they're wrong, who cares if they believe they're right?" Pádraig rubbed the top of his head vigorously, a stay-awake technique he'd relied on in seminary near end of term when the work piled up.

Stephen rolled his eyes. "Jesus, for such a smart man, you sure missed a lot in your epistemological formation. It matters hugely." He snatched up the copy of his book that he'd given Pádraig and pointed to the title. "This is what I'm talking about in my book. 'Knowledge and Belief, Faith and Doubt.' It's a circle. Listen, what is knowledge?"

"It's things you know. Things that are known to be true. Unless I'm very tired and those basics have changed."

"Right. And how are they known?"

"They can be observed. Measured and verified by scientific method or by experience."

"Correct. And what happens when you get to the outer edge of things that are known, in the way you just described, but you need to rely on the information anyway? Or you want to. Even though you can't prove it well enough to qualify it as knowledge."

Pádraig drew two glasses and a bottle from his bottom desk drawer. "My brain isn't working. Maybe this will help. Meanwhile, please do just spell it out."

"It's like this. Let's say you come to the edge of a frozen pond. The easiest and best way for you to get to the other side is to walk across the middle of it. You take a few steps away from the bank of the pond, and you're okay because the ice is solid. The further you go toward the center, the more uncertain you become because you don't know that the ice is solid and will support your weight. What do you do?" Stephen paused and Pádraig looked at him, his eyes drooping. "Oh, never mind. I guess this just became a lecture. What you do is go back and collect some rocks from the edge of the pond, go back to where you left off in your progress and throw some rocks toward the center of the pond. You try to establish the knowledge that the stretch in front of you is safe."

"Myself, I'd just walk around the pond. Or on the solid edges of it if I wanted to save a little bit of time without the risk."

Stephen wriggled in frustration. "Just, please accept my

premise that you dearly want to go straight across the pond because you desperately need to get across the quickest possible way. Pretend it's a giant pond."

"Well, then it would be a lake."

"Okay! Okay! It's a fucking lake!" Stephen took a deep breath to calm himself. "My point is that you keep testing the limits of what you know – that at least some parts of the lake are solid enough to rely upon. Why do you keep going on beyond the point where you can know for sure that it's safe to walk on?"

"Because you want to get to the other side," Pádraig said obediently.

"Well, yes, but why do you keep going when you can't know it's safe?" Pádraig sat dumbly and sipped his drink. "Oh, you really are going to make me do all the work, aren't you? You keep going because it's useful, since you're so eager for the most direct way across the lake, for you to believe that there's safe passage across the lake even if you can't know it. Even if it's not true, it's useful."

Pádraig handed a short glass of scotch across the desk to Stephen. "That's a terrible analogy! No one would take a risk like that of falling through the ice and drowning or freezing to death based on a belief. The instant the ice breaks, the belief that it was safe to go that way is useless, not useful."

"That's the risk of relying on belief instead of knowledge. But if you don't like that analogy, I can offer you another. Though it may strike a bit close to home."

"I think I know where this is going. Give it your best shot."

"Catholicism, the basic hermeneutics of it, the divine messages and revelations. You can't know any of it's true, can you? Even the most vivid accounts of say, John baptizing Jesus, had no eyewitnesses. They were written up centuries after the fact based on oral accounts."

Pádraig sighed. "This really is old ground, you know. No, I can't personally know that the skies opened up after the baptism and that the voice of God came down to earth. But we've put our best people on it over the ages, and it's been declared as authentic as anyone can say."

"Still, it can't qualify as knowledge, you'd have to agree. But you believe it nonetheless."

"That and a lot more."

"So you don't know it to be true, but you believe it to be true. Why is that?"

"Look, don't imagine that I never entertain a single doubt about my beliefs from time to time. I'm a Jesuit, after all. It's in our nature. But yes, I do generally believe it to be true. It's who I am," he shrugged.

Stephen walked over to the window. The Four were saying their good-byes to one another in the plaza near the strand, parting ways some on foot and some by car. Leonard came out last and jiggled the door handle behind him to check that it was securely locked. "It's who you are," he repeated. "It's the way you live and work. It's the way you organize your life, it guides your behavior and your decisions. Why not rely on something else? A different religion or just a purely humanist approach to life?"

"Well, because I believe Catholicism is true and it's a better way than any of the others I might consider.

"Which is to say that it's more useful," Stephen said, crossing his arms.

"I suppose that's fair. But anyway, what has this got to do with the Four?"

"I'm just getting back to that. Even if what they painted out to us today isn't true, they seem to believe it. I postulate that they do this because they find it useful for some reason. And if it's useful to them, it may be that others find it useful, too. After all, that's what fills the pews every Sunday, isn't it?"

"Maybe. Though I think a lot more people than you realize regard the Church as true, not just useful."

"Granted, but my point with respect to the Four is that even if they merely believe that what they said is true, even if it isn't, they're doing that because relying on that belief is useful to them. And if it's useful to them, we should be able to make it useful to us."

"How do we do that?"

Stephen gathered up his jacket and bag. "I need to sleep on it. But we may be in for a little fieldwork tomorrow. You should get some rest."

"Yes, you needn't encourage me much in that direction. I'll see you out."

Stephen raised his hand. "No need for that. You go put yourself to bed. I'll find my way."

"Wait," Pádraig said when Stephen had just crossed into the hallway outside the study. "We never got to talk about the other part of your book, Faith and Doubt. I don't want you to think I'm not interested."

Stephen smiled, "You're kind to say it. If you're a willing listener, we'll do it. But it will have to be another night or I'll fall asleep on your doorstep rather than making it all the way home. What will people think?" he added jokingly.

"We can't have that kind of talk going about!" Pádraig agreed, laughing and yawning at the same time.

32.

Pádraig found himself wide-awake at five in the morning, his usual rising time. But today there was no morning Mass at seven; it was cancelled, as it was every year, in consideration of the duties he'd have later in the evening. He groaned and rolled over, willing himself back to sleep. Ten minutes later, he'd given up and thrown himself out of bed.

He dressed and went down to the kitchen in shirtsleeves to make tea. He took his mug to the parlor window and stared out at the quay before taking a first sip. Then he noticed Stephen, sitting on the wooden bench facing the sea.

"Stephen," he called from the front steps. He motioned an invitation to come inside. Stephen trotted across the street and up the steps. "What are you doing, out so early?" Pádraig asked.

"I couldn't sleep. I've been walking and thinking all night. I thought I'd wait a little while before knocking. We need to talk about our plan."

"Our plan?" Pádraig said, leading the way into his study. "Can I least hear a run-through before I adopt it as mine?"
"Sure, sure, of course." He looked at Pádraig for a moment. "Do you need to finish dressing?" Pádraig looked down at his shirtfront. "No, it's fine. I'll put on the rabat and the collar before Mrs. O'Flannelly arrives at half seven."

"I've never seen you in anything but jacket and collar," Stephen noted. "It's a bit weird, even for me. Your parishioners would probably faint."

"That is why we must never speak of this moment," Pádraig said with mock earnestness. "Now what's the plan?"

Stephen unpacked some books from his sack. He laid Yeats' Irish Myths and Legends of Western Ireland on the top of the stack. "I propose that we do something that's both outrageous and obvious. I propose that we ask the Gentry to give Fianna back."

Pádraig sipped his tea. "It's certainly outrageous. But what makes it obvious? Just for argument's sake, I'm asking. It's still not my plan."

"What's obvious about it is that it's a direct approach. If I'm right about this, we don't need anyone's help. It's obvious, too, because it's one category of what can be done to get Fianna back that we haven't tried yet. And finally, it's obvious because it's the one way we can make what we heard last night useful to us even if we don't believe it."

"You mean even though we don't believe it."

"Right, right, have it your way. But you believe in the power of prayer, correct?"

"Of course, I do."

"You don't need someone's permission to pray for him, do you?"

"No."

"So if you, on your own, prayed for someone who didn't believe in the power of prayer or believe in God, more fundamentally, it could still work, right? It could still help that person."

"Yes. I think there are lots of documented cases confirming that. Even a few academic studies where people prayed for patients in hospital without their knowing about it. The ones who were prayed for seemed to get better quicker from comparable ailments and surgeries than the ones who had no prayers. They interviewed the prayed-for patients after the experiment about their beliefs, and it didn't seem to matter whether they were religious."

"See, that's how what someone else believes can be useful not only to the believer, but to non-believers. Even if – I mean though – we think the Four were talking a lot of rubbish, it can't hurt to try things in their canon. What do you say?"

Pádraig set his mug down on the windowsill. He crossed his arms and leaned back against the sash. "I don't know about this, but I'm willing to try just about anything at this point. I didn't even go see Bertie at all yesterday. I'm so ashamed of how little the town has turned out to help. I'm embarrassed I can't do more." His voice broke momentarily. He collected himself and raised the mug to his mouth, his hand shaking. "I simply can't believe how unconcerned the garda are! And can you imagine, people around here cloak themselves in fairy myths to excuse their hardheartedness!" He was shouting and pacing around the furniture in the study. Stephen walked over and closed the door. "We need to talk about this. If we lose track of time, I don't want Mrs. O'Flannelly walking in on an unguarded moment." He eased himself into an armchair and waited until Pádraig's pacing stopped.

"What is it that hits you so hard about this girl's disappearance? Why are you so drawn into it?"

"Obviously, someone has to step in. No one else is doing a thing. I'm the parish priest, after all." He threw his hands up in the air.

"But you're overwrought about all this. You've lost all detachment, which makes you less alert, less effective. And sure, you're the parish priest, but there are tragedies unfolding all around you, some large and some small. You don't get drawn into each of them, do you?" Pádraig said nothing. "What is it about this girl, Pádraig?"

"I'm...I'm fond of her. She was in the confirmation class last year, as I told you. I had to tutor her to pull her through. I got to know her and..."

"It's not just that, though, is it? It goes back longer than that, doesn't it? I mean, you don't carry a picture of every confirmation class around in your wallet. What's special about her?"

"Stop badgering me! It doesn't make a lick of difference why I'm doing what little I can.   She needs help.   And someone has to do it."

Stephen picked up the Yeats book on the top of the pile he'd made.   "Listen, Pádraig, we're about to go on a limb together.   What I'm suggesting we do is rather extraordinary, and I want to understand what's going on here before we go off together."

Pádraig shook his head and kept his arms crossed.   He said nothing.

"You could kick me out of here at any moment, but you haven't yet.   Something tells me you want to discuss this, but don't know how to start.   I'm not sure I do either."   He fell silent for a moment, thinking.   He cast his gaze around the room and his eyes fell upon a framed picture on the bookshelf behind Pádraig's desk.   "Who's that in the picture?"

"My mother.   A bit younger than now."

"I've met your mother, remember?   I'm asking about the other woman."

Pádraig glanced quickly at the picture, then turned away.   "That's my sister, my younger sister, Eileen."   Stephen walked to the bookcase and picked up the frame to look more closely.   "Yes, I see the family resemblance."   He carefully replaced the photograph.

"You never mentioned having a sister."

"Forgive me, then for not laying out the whole family tree in the four days since we met," Pádraig said mockingly.   He walked to the bookshelf with his hands in his pockets and bent a bit to bring himself eye level with the photograph.   He'd been careful as to where he placed it, keeping it visible on a daily basis, but out of the sun to avoid its fading.   He gently adjusted the position of the frame.

"Where does she live?"

"I don't know."

"She's your sister, your only sibling, can I assume?"   Pádraig nodded impatiently.   "And you don't know where she lives?"

"No one does." Pádraig hung his head.

"What happened?" Stephen asked gently.

"She disappeared one day. Never came back."

"What?" Stephen bolted to standing attention in astonishment. "From here? When? Don't you think mentioning that might have been relevant? Or helpful?" Pádraig made a calming gesture with both hands. "It was entirely different circumstances, I assure you." He walked to the reading stand and absently spun the globe positioned next to it.

"It was years ago, the late sixties. She was living here, yes. But the place had no hold on her. She had the fever to go places. Anywhere. But no means to do it, of course."
He leaned back against the reading stand. "We were very close when we were younger. She was born five years after me. My mother loved having a daughter to bring up, teaching her all the things she'd learned from her mother and grandmother. "I looked out for her in her early years, made sure no one gave her difficulty, or teased her too hard."

"What did they tease her about?"

"Oh, nothing of substance, just picking on her the way children do for anything that's a little bit different from the crowd."

"How was she different did they think?"

"She was...imaginative. A story teller. She had vivid imaginary friends, for example, who told her all sorts of things about the olden days, as she used to put it. When we'd hunt for treasure -- really we were stumbling among other people's trash and discards, but it was treasure to us -- she'd always have a magical story behind the ordinary things we found."

"Like what, for example? Do you remember?"

Pádraig chuckled. "Well, it wasn't really funny, just the memory of it brings me back. She came home one day -- I hadn't gone along because I was immersed in my books, as I increasingly was in those days -- with her hair in tangles and her jumper torn to holes. I intercepted her before my mother could get a look at her. I knew how upset she'd be. I took her up the front staircase avoiding Mum in the kitchen. I helped her change her clothes and brush out her hair. Once she was a

218

little more presentable, she began to calm down. I asked her, 'Were you in a fight?' "Yes, I was,' says she, not the least bit regretful. 'Over what?' I asked. She reaches down to the inside of her Wellies, the right boot, and pulls out a little bottle, like the ones from an apothecary. 'Over this,' she says, triumphantly. Now, to me, the bottle looks like an absolutely ordinary piece of glass that you'd throw out once you'd finished whatever was in it. So I said, 'Over that? Eileen, darling, it's not worth two pence. And not worth a tussle and a ruined jumper.' She got very cross-looking and says to me, 'You don't know anything. This is a sprite prison. It's very special and I'll be brought good luck for it. Sean Brady wanted to use it for target practice with his slingshot, but I told him that was stupid. He fought me for it.' She showed me the lip of the bottle up close. 'See here, there's a dot of wax and the end of a red thread.' I could barely see them, but up close both the wax and the red thread were there. 'It had a cork in it when I found it, and the thread was sealed across the top of the cork with wax. I opened it up and let the sprite out.' 'Was that wise, to let the sprite out?' 'Oh, yes,' says Eileen. 'She'll be very grateful to me and you and Mum. We'll get lots of favors from her.'

"Now, I had set my sites on the priesthood by this time. I was fourteen, she was nine. I suppose I should have been more shocked that she was trafficking in sprite prisons, but that was Eileen. She had that kind of imagination. And she was stubborn, as that story illustrates. Once she saw something a certain way, there was no talking her out of it into a more ordinary explanation."

Stephen sat thinking for a moment, then lunged for the stack of books, knocking Yeats to the floor as he grabbed up the book below it. He paddled past the first hundred pages, then put his finger on a passage. "I knew I'd heard a story like that before. It's right here in Katherine Briggs' book A Dictionary of Fairies." He passed the book over to Pádraig who scanned it silently. "Only you see there," Stephen pointed out, "it's called a sprite trap. A witch might set it either because the sprite is interfering with his or her work, casting spells, giving cures and such. Or the witch might do it at the request of a householder to rid the home of the sprite's mischief. There's a lot in there about how to set the trap properly. I wonder, was the dab of wax you remember seeing red, like the thread?"

"I don't remember, might have been. It was a long time ago. But what's the point anyway?"

"Do you think your sister would have had any access to a book like this back in the -- how long ago was this?"

"Middle of the fifties, I'd say. And no, I'd never seen a book like that around our house, and the nun's wouldn't have one around the school, that's for certain. Anyway, my sister wasn't much of a reader."

"Then either she heard the story some other way from a relative or someone else in the village. Or she had some intuitive way of knowing the story behind what Briggs wrote down. And that would make her different in the ways that got her teased. Maybe it made her special, too in ways relevant to the problem at hand."

"Now, why in God's name would you think that?" Pádraig shouted. He hurled the book against the wall, cracking its spine. Stephen jumped in surprise. He stared at Pádraig for a long moment while Pádraig bent and tried to put the broken book back in order.

"Pádraig," he said gently, "I can see that this is terribly upsetting to you. But I'm not sure I understand why. It seems as though there's something important here left unspoken." Pádraig said nothing. Stephen paused half a minute before taking a deep breath to steel himself for the reaction to his next question.

"Pádraig," he said cautiously, "is Fianna your daughter?"

Pádraig lunged across the room at Stephen before catching himself. "No!" he roared, dissipating the energy originally aimed at Stephen by swiping his forearm across his desk, clearing it of lamps, paperweights, papers, books and framed pictures, which clattered to the floor at the foot of the bookcase nearest the window. He paused, winded, red in the face and hugged his arms around himself.

"No. She's not my daughter," he said quietly. "She's my niece."

33.

"What? Your niece?" Stephen asked shrilly. "Don't you think that might have been significant enough to mention?" He paced about the office, hands in the air. "I mean really, it's only been four days' acquaintance as you say, but still!"

"I'm sorry, I'm sorry. Of course, I should have told you. But it's been a secret a very long time. Almost no one knows. I can't risk it getting about. I didn't know you'd become so trustworthy to me."

"Well, thanks for saying so, but among other things, don't you think you'd have gotten an upgraded kind of help from the villagers if they understood the relationship?"
Pádraig shook his head vigorously. "No, no, quite the opposite, I assure you." He sat down in one of the wing chairs, exhausted from emotion already, so early in the day. "It's a long story, Stephen."

"It happens that I have time just now for a long story."

Pádraig sat for a while longer, then heaved himself up from the chair and carefully retrieved a framed photograph to show to Stephen. It captured Pádraig as a young priest standing next to another priest, older than he by perhaps a decade, and clad in a long cassock. Stephen recognize the vestibule of St. Molaise as the backdrop.

"Who's this next to you?"

"It all begins with him, this story. That's Roger Hargadon, former pastor of St. Molaise, served just before me. He was in charge when I arrived, finally, after managing to get here via halfway around the world. It was after my assignment in Hong Kong, when the Society finally judged things to have cooled off enough for me to come back here.

"Roger was born and bred here in Mullaghmore. His family was wealthy and went back generations in this part of the country. Cassiebawn, the castle that looms over this place, that was their family estate." Pádraig snorted. "An estate, such as it was. Tim Larkin, a fellow I went to school with here, his family going back to his great grandfather, at least, has always been caretaker to the castle. He told me that the place was damp and cold all winter long, but the Hargadons pretended to love living there just to put on appearances." A small smile of satisfaction flashed across Pádraig's face then vanished. "But that's just gossip. I'm sure they found ways to make apartments in the estate comfortable. With that much money, they could live anywhere they wanted, I'm sure.

"Anyway, Roger was older than I, ten or twelve years senior to me, so I didn't know him growing up. He was an only child, so there were no younger siblings in my forms, either. My family knew his to say hello to in church, but nothing more, and since they lived way up there on the hill, it wasn't as if we'd be running into them all the time. Roger's father, Edgar, I'm told, was sociable enough in the pub on the odd occasion, but not a regular.

"Now Edgar was the only surviving brother of his generation, so that meant that the considerable money that came with the Hargadon name was all his after his parents passed. And Roger, being the only child of Edgar's only marriage, was set to inherit it all. And he acted the part, according to the reputation he made for himself. He had no job after he graduated and had no inclination to university where he'd heard the required studies were dreadfully laborious. With all the free time that having nothing to rise early for gave him, he became quite a hellion.

"He put himself up to a lot of odd sorts of fun, mostly at

223

night after he'd helped close the pub, first here in Mullaghmore, then later over in Cliffoney after Ellen asked him to stop coming to her establishment. I think she more told him than asked him, in fact. It was after the third or so time that Roger drove his car through the cemetery in Bundoran that Edgar began muttering over his pint that he needed something to soak up Roger's time in a mandatory kind of way. And then he had a stroke of luck.

"There must have been something to what Larkin said about the place being a kind of white elephant, difficult to keep livable, even with the Hargadons' resources. Because what happened next was a stroke of luck that Edgar leapt upon: The Royal Family expressed an interest in buying the place."

"You're kidding. The Royal Family? The Windsors?"

"The Mountbatten branch, cousins to the Windsors. Lord Louis Mountbatten specifically. There was some ancient claim that they already actually owned the place, but he decided not to prosecute the title and buy it from the Hargadons even though it was a tremendous additional expense that they might have avoided."

"He was either extremely gracious or extremely foolish. How likely was it that they'd lose if they went to court? I'd say the Royals probably have a pretty good scorecard at bar and bench."

"He was gracious. Is gracious, I should say. He vacations here. A real sportsman, loves deep sea fishing and lobster potting. I've met him a few times. He bought the place for some real money even though it needed urgent repairs and remodeling.

"Now even this good fortune presented a problem for Edgar. The tax on transfer, the stamp tax, would be a grand sum. Crushing, confiscatory in Edgar's view. Edgar had a career in law and banking, and he thought there must be a way to forgive the tax, especially in a transaction with the Royals. In the end, and don't ask me for the details on why the law allowed this, they struck a deal: As long as Roger, Edgar's sole heir remained affiliated with a charitable institution, the tax was postponed and the sum passed to the Hargadons on closing was theirs to enjoy unencumbered by the tax-gatherers.

"This condition struck lots of people as very odd. Most people thought the Hargadons had plenty of money even before the sale of Cassiebawn, but apparently not Edgar. But agreeing to the condition solved two problems for Edgar. First, he avoided the tax for the duration of his lifetime and tapped into all that additional money from the sale without subtraction of the tax. Second, it gave him a reason to rein in Roger with a built-in incentive for Roger to comply. If Roger wanted to inherit the money, and have access to it during his own lifetime, he had to go along with it."

"So they packed him off to seminary?"

"Exactly. He was off and back in record time, less than it takes to train a busman, it seems. Quick as all that, here he is in a Roman collar back in the village, taking over a parish from a priest in his eighties and long overdue for retirement."

"So did it take, his ordination?"

"On the surface, yes. He gave up the rabble rousing, did his drinking in private. I don't think he ever became truly pious, but he did like the trappings of the profession. And he could afford the best, believe me. Even his vestments for Sundays in Ordinary Time, the green ones, had gold-thread decorations in the detail. You should have seen what he wore on feast days! Blinding red, those vestments. His ciborium -- the container for the consecrated eucharist; no reason that should be a familiar word to you -- twenty-four karat gold. The furniture you see around here," he gestured at the desk and the side tables, "mostly genuine French antiques, purchased by Roger or his father."

"He just left them here? Where did he go anyway?"

"I'll get to that part of the story about how he came to leave these treasures behind. But to answer your second question, he's in Dublin. He's been in Dublin and 'on his way to the Vatican' according to himself, for over fifteen years." Pádraig snorted and shook his head. "Bloody prig."

"So back to Eileen for a moment. We grew up, we grew apart. Starting when I was about fifteen, I figured out that the priesthood was calling me. At least I think that's what it was. It could also be, I can say after thinking it over for about thirty years, that I may just have seen it as a way to get out of here, get an education and do some good while seeing the world. The Jesuits seemed just the right path. They were the elite of the priestly profession as far as I could tell. The vows of poverty, obedience -- all that seemed like a fair trade off for getting to hang about with such a smart group."

"How about the vow of chastity?"

"That's for a different conversation." Pádraig looked into the distance for a moment. "Anyway," he said abruptly, "I had my nose in the books every moment of every day from then on, and I didn't pay as much attention to Eileen. None at all, really. She'd knock on my bedroom door late in the evening, wanting to talk, and I'd put her off. Continually. I just kept putting her off. When I finally left for seminary, she didn't even come to say good-bye.

"I barely paid any mind at all to home while I was at seminary. My mother and I exchanged letters. Mine got briefer and briefer. Usually, I'd ask after Eileen and ask Mum to give her a hug for me, but eventually I forgot even to do that."

"Aren't priests supposed to be a little less self-involved than that? Just my impression of the requirements of the profession, maybe I'm wrong."

"No, you're right, absolutely right. I was full of myself in those days, I hope a little less so now. After all, I was 'in seminary', studying to become a Jesuit, a soldier of God in an order with a direct mandate from the Pope to spread and protect the faith. I even justified my indifference to my family and whatever might have been going back here by telling myself that I was doing what the Gospels said about leaving your mother and father behind to follow Jesus.

"At one point, just after my ordination -- Mum had come to Dublin for it; Eileen had not -- I got a telephone call from my mother. She'd wanted me to come back to Mullaghmore with her, mostly so she could show me off in the new collar to her friends, but I insisted on staying in Dublin to get ready for the beginning of my doctoral program. I hadn't even started the program and was already feeling behind on the reading list for new entrants. Getting a phone call from her was startling in itself. We didn't have a phone in the house in those days; she'd come down to the village to use Martin's phone -- for a fee, of course.

"She was crying; I could barely understand her. Eileen hadn't come home in three days, she said. The garda had turned out to help -- they were not so lazy and full of excuses in those days -- but had found no trace of her. She begged me to come home to help find her.

"Of course, I had to say yes. And as it happened, I had a pretty good idea of where to look. And it wasn't a place where the garda were likely to have any success even if I told them where to go.

"The one thing I had noticed about Eileen's doings when I tore myself away from the books was that she always seemed to be coming home from the direction of the Travellers Camp. A few times when I'd walked down to the quay to stretch my legs or run an errand for my mother, I'd noticed her off to the far side of the green, where the road to the camp comes into the village, talking with, playing with some of the Traveller children. Most were her age, but there was one fellow a little older than she, younger than I who was often hanging about the edges of the group she spent time with. I recognized him because, a bit unusual for the Travellers, he would come to Sunday Mass every now and then. He'd introduced himself as Terry Johnson on the way out of church one morning. I wasn't right behind him in the greeting line, but the priest, Father Loiselle, the one Roger replaced, was already advanced in age and quite deaf, so Terry had to repeat his name several times, each louder than the last.

"Eventually, what I noticed was that Eileen had forsaken the group of children her own age, and sat and talked with Terry instead. I suppose another big brother might have intruded out of concern or jealousy. But it seemed harmless to me. And while no one thought well of the Travellers, Terry seemed decent to me, or at least potentially so since he bothered to come to Mass.

"So the short of it is that I had an inkling that if she wasn't coming home -- she was eighteen years old at this point, considered a mature young woman in those days -- she hadn't gone far and might be with Terry in the Travellers Camp. I knew that if I sent the garda to look for her there, the Travellers would close ranks and the garda would never find her and she might take steps to hide herself more permanently. So I went myself."

"What happened? Did you find her?"

"Yes, I did. I dropped my bag off at the house and went straight over there. Stella, Mum's sister, had come to stay with her since she was so upset about Eileen. I borrowed Stella's car and made the same drive you and I made a couple of days ago. Parked in the drive up and asked after Terry and Eileen, politely at first. When that didn't work, I escalated things until I was stamping around the lot and screaming things that they probably didn't expect to hear from a newly minted priest. Finally, finally, after half an hour of this, just when I was going to have to give up out of exhaustion, Terry and Eileen came out of one of the caravans up the hill and made their way down to the drive up.

"Everyone else in the camp had come out to see the commotion I'd started and now that I had my sister and her beau in front of me, no one moved. I'd hoped to have a quiet, persuasive and decisive conversation with Eileen. To take her home with me in Stella's car. But that's not what happened."

"She wouldn't leave?"

"No, wouldn't leave. I begged her for our mother's sake to come home. She refused and begged me not to tell my mother where I'd found her. 'I'll be happy here, Paddy, you know I will. They don't mind here that I'm different. And they'll help me get away from here from time to time. Terry says he'll take me to England and France come summertime. He loves me, and I him.'

"Well, that's all I needed to hear, that Terry was taking my little sister far and away with him. I grabbed her arm and tried to pull her along with me."

"Ooh, I bet that didn't go well with the horde assembled around you."

"Terry stepped in and removed my hand from her arm. I think if he hadn't done it so gently, or if I'd given him any real resistance, there'd have been mayhem with me on the wrong end of it. He just looked at me and said, 'She's with me now, Father.' I think wearing the collar saved me from being torn limb to limb in the lead up to that moment.

"I was utterly defeated. All I was left with was to ask her, 'What shall I tell Mum?' 'You'll think of something,' she said, 'You're clever and good with words. Tell her I've joined a convent, that's the answer! Tell her I've joined one that has a vow of silence. And the sisters are not allowed to write letters or see visitors. Tell her that!' I said to her, 'That's nonsense. I don't think any such orders exist anymore. She'll never believe it.' Eileen says, 'Of course, she'll believe it. She's got a blind spot when it comes to vocations. How do you think you get away with ignoring her, and she still thinking you're a wonderful son? Better even than her daughter close at hand.' She might as well have slapped me across the face as said that. I was stunned. Stunned because she was right and I knew it.

"My protest was pretty feeble after that about how it was wrong to ask me to lie to our mother. She quite unexpectedly had taken the high ground in the exchange and there was no going back. 'It's up to you,' she said. 'Tell her a lie that will please her or the truth that will kill her.' So I drove back to the house and told my mother and Stella that I'd made inquiries and found that Eileen had run away to take vows. My mother had a million questions about why would she do that without saying a word. 'She was afraid you'd try to talk her out of it, with one child already in holy orders. She worried you'd be sad for having no grandchildren.' 'Well, I'm a bit sad for that, but overjoyed that God's called both of my children to service. That's never happened to anyone else in the parish that I know of. Or in the whole county, for that matter. He couldn't have answered my prayers more abundantly!'

"Of course, I was sick, sick to my stomach lying and then embellishing on the lies. She wanted to know when would the final vows be taken, and could she go to the Mass. And I had to tell her no, these were cloistered sisters, and on and on, locking down the path to her finding out what Eileen was really up to. I was disgusted with myself."

"But she believed you and was happy with the little Potemkin village you built for her?"

"Evidently so. She told everyone in the parish about it, and if any of them knew otherwise, they went along with it. I don't think anyone outside the camp besides me knew, really. The Travellers started especially keeping to themselves around that time, not one of them even coming to Mass anymore."

"So no one was the wiser, and you got away with the cover up?"

"Almost no one. As I was leaving the house, I passed Stella, sitting on the porch smoking. It was dark by now, and I almost walked by her completely, lost in my own shame, when she took an inhale and the tip of the cigarette put out a bright red glow. I told her good night and was headed back into the house to put myself to bed and end this awful day when she stopped me. 'Just a minute, Pádraig,' she says. 'I didn't hear you mention the name of the order Eileen joined. What was it again?'

"Well, she completely had me. The name of the order should have been the first thing out of my mouth if my story were real. After all, what was the most important thing about my priesthood? That I'm a Jesuit, of course. You can't talk about a priest being a priest or a nun being a nun without saying, or having someone immediately ask the equivalent of 'what kind?' by asking 'which order?' I was an idiot for not having thought this through. I was very lucky that my mother was too overwhelmed by what she took as good news about Eileen to ask very specifically. But Stella had no illusions. She was a natural born skeptic. Since I didn't have a ready answer to her question, the hesitation in my voice was a dead giveaway, and my answer was even worse."

"What did you say? Which order did you pretend-assign her to?"

"I said 'The Sisters of Sequestered Silence'."

"Wow. That sounds implausible even to me, and I don't know anything about religious orders. Except a little bit about Jesuits by now. What was your aunt's reaction?"

"She was silent. Took another puff of her cigarette, then said, 'When your mother comes around to asking, I'll tell her to say to people that it's a small cloistered order they've never heard of.' And Stella and I have never spoken about that conversation on the porch since that night."

"So is your sister still out there with the Travellers, out in the camp or on the road with them somewhere?"

"No," Pádraig sighed, "neither there nor on the lam with them. She did go with Terry that first summer, I came to learn later. Most of the scams they put over on people are by teams of two or three men. But every once in a while they cook something up that only works if there's a woman involved. I heard about this one: the couple drives up to a machine shop or auto repair shop. The man says that he works for a wealthy manufacturer in -- pick your own faraway country, preferably one with a language foreign to the locale you're in at the time. He says he took his wife on a sales trip, and their hotel room was burglarized. Everything was taken from them. The wife starts weeping at this point. The trip was supposed to be a bit of a vacation for them, the man says, now he doesn't even have enough money to get home. His sister was looking after the baby, but she'll be impatient soon, and they have to get home. Could the repair shop owner possibly help them out? They're not asking for charity, the man says emphatically. He has something of value that the shop owner might need and like: a lathe or parts stamper or engraver, whatever is likely to sound most appealing at the moment. He can have it for a steal, of course, merely hundreds of pounds when it usually sells for thousands or what have you. The wife cries some more, the shop owner agrees to take a look at the chunk of metal in the back of the van, and eventually agrees to buy it. For cash, of course. The man embraces the shop owner and the wife tearfully kisses him on the cheek and promises to send him a picture of their baby, which he is by now very eager to see, so far bought into the story he is.

"I'm sure I needn't tell you that the first time the shop owner uses the machinery, it splinters into useless pieces. And unbeknownst to him, the man and his wife have gone back to the barn where additional copies of the same piece of junk are stored to reload their van and repeat the same routine one county away. That's the romantic, nomadic life that my sister aspired to, and then embraced. Wonderful, isn't it?"

"You sound very angry with her."

"No, not angry. Just very, very sad. And sorry. Very sorry. If I'd been paying more attention, I might have prevented it."

"What? Her running away with Terry? She sounds pretty unshakeable from what you said. Determined to go away with him."

Pádraig sat quietly for a moment. "No, not that. Not preventing that. It's what happened next that I should have prevented." Mrs. O'Flannelly knocked softly at the door. "Father, it's half noon. Will you have some lunch?" Stephen, seated closer to the door, opened it. Mrs. O'Flannelly stepped back quickly, almost in recoil, Stephen thought. He smiled to cover his reaction. "I think that would be lovely, Mrs. O'Flannelly. I don't think Father had his breakfast, either. Did you?" he asked turning into the room to address Pádraig. "No," he answered. "That would be fine, Mrs. O'Flannelly. Whatever's handy to fix as a sandwich would be wonderful." Mrs. O'Flannelly peered into the room past Stephen as if verifying that Pádraig was really within. Satisfied, she retreated to the kitchen.

"Well, that was odd," Stephen said to Pádraig after closing the door.

"What's that?"

"She seemed very surprised, even disturbed to find me here. Does she not like me for some reason I'm unaware of?

Pádraig frowned. "I haven't a clue as to what she thinks of you, but you've given her no reason to treat you in any way but cheerfully. I can have a word with her if it makes you uncomfortable. She can be a bit possessive sometimes. She has a protective instinct towards me, I think."

Stephen swatted away the offer. "No, no need to speak to her. I'm probably over-reading her demeanor. I don't know her well at all. I'm probably wrong. Anyway, you were saying about you wished you could have prevented what happened next?"

Pádraig put his hands on his knees and let out a long breath. "It all started from an idea I had when I arrived back in the parish. Things had gotten very tense between the villagers and the Travellers. The garda had been cracking down on the summer adventures of the Travellers, and that meant they were all over the place around here. It annoyed the villagers and made them wish more than ever that the Travellers would keep to themselves and stay away from the town center altogether. The ones who wanted to come to Mass, the few of them, stopped coming because it was so clear that the parishioners didn't want them here. So I had the idea of bringing the church to them: a mission church. I was young and energetic, eager to spread the faith, and this seemed poised to till fertile ground. I also had the vague hope that Eileen was in the camp somewhere, and I could reestablish a relationship with her.

"So I went out there, hat in hand, so to speak, and suggested the idea to a few of the leaders, the senior Johnsons, who spoke to their wives. It was the wives that put the idea over the top. They were the ones who missed church the most and wanted some sort of formation for their children. I'll say one thing for the Johnsons: once the idea was approved, they put their shoulders to the wheel and started building a place to hold Mass the next day. Within a month, we had a decent sanctuary with a sturdy altar. The last thing you want is some flimsy table put up to serve as an altar that'll collapse during the consecration and scatter the Eucharist all over the floor.

There was a knock at the door and the muffled voice of Mrs. O'Flannelly offering sandwiches. Stephen opened the door. He made the extra effort of displaying his best smile. "I'll take the tray in, Mrs. O'Flannelly. Thank you very much." She resisted handing the tray over. "It's my job to take it in, Mr. Ramsey, thank you all the same." Stephen remained firm.

"Yes, but only not today." He continued smiling as he pulled the tray from her grasp. She huffed and walked away.

"Why so insistent about taking in the sandwiches? Or are you just trying to antagonize her now?"

"No, not at all," Stephen said weaving a path around the furniture to set the tray down on an end table. "It's just best for her not to see the room in this shambolic state. We'll clean it up later."

Pádraig took a few bites out of a lamb and mint jelly sandwich, normally one of his favorite combinations. He wasn't sure, but he thought he might have invented it as far as Mullaghmore went. Today, though, it seemed chewy and tasteless. He put down the uneaten remains. "You asked me a while ago whether Roger's ordination took root in the sense of whether it truly changed him. There was one front on which absolutely nothing changed. And that was the matter of celibacy.

"The mission church was my idea, and I was pleasantly surprised how supportive Roger was of it right from the start. It wasn't until later that he'd come to regard the whole project as a godsend. Ugh. Wrong word. Let's just say that the project presented him with certain opportunities. Up until then, and I must say I was so naïve about this, he'd have an abundance of overnight out-of-town trips to Donegal or Galway. He always had a story about what he was doing, and I never questioned him on any of it.

"When I suggested the project, I assumed that as the junior clergy, the commuting would fall to me. It was like that for a while, but then he started insisting that he should go. Not just the Sunday Masses, but the Wednesday evening prayer group, which met after a short Mass. I started realizing that he was spending a good deal of time out there. There was something about it that bothered me, but I couldn't put my finger on it, not exactly. There was just something a little off about the whole thing, especially his seeming devotion to this mission church for a group that his family surely regarded as a band of thieves and cheats. I'm not judging; that sounds a bit harsh, but it's how they were viewed, how they are viewed by the village.

"It all came to a head one Sunday, late in the afternoon. He always said the sinners Mass, that's the slang for it, at half five in the evening. No matter how hard you've partied on Saturday, you ought to be able to make a Mass that late in the day, and the Church aims to accommodate every soul's attendance. He left the rectory earlier than he usually did, nearer to four than five. I thought that a bit curious, but not worth remarking upon.

"It was my habit every Sunday evening when I was to say Mass on Monday morning to visit the sacristy to double check that the altar boys had put everything back in place after the Sunday Masses. It was then that I realized that Roger had left without any hosts to consecrate for the Mass he was about to celebrate. His ciborium was still in the sacristy. It was unthinkable that he'd celebrate Mass without his ciborium, and impossible without any hosts. He might have improvised with some bread to make up for not having the hosts, though he objected to that practice as too casual. But mostly I think he objected that it was indecorous to pile bits of bread instead of hosts into his precious ciborium. It was his signature piece. He took it with him when he travelled. Wherever he was, the ciborium was close at hand. A fair chunk of the family's cash must have been invested in the ciborium. It was an ornate piece, gold of course, the real thing, not just gilded, and dotted with rubies here and about. I was hesitant about it, but then sure I should take it to him, save him the embarrassment of having to cancel the Mass. So I wrapped it up in the protective purple velvet cloth he always used when he travelled, got into the car and drove out to the camp.

"I didn't find him in the sanctuary, and not in the sacristy either, which was odd because it was after five o'clock by the time I got out there. Roger's pre-celebration ritual was pretty elaborate, a lot of primping in front of the mirror in the sacristy after the vestments went on, did the collar line up right with the alb, could you see the Roman collar properly, on and on. It took a fair amount of time, so he should have been in there already.

"The only other possibility was that he was in the little camper caravan that the Johnsons had set aside as a kind of rectory outpost. The thought was that there might be the odd night where the road flooded, as it sometimes still does, and a priest couldn't get back to the village until it receded. Or if a parishioner of the mission church was ill, and the priest decided to stay close at hand. I'd only been inside it myself once, and then only to look it over so that I could say a proper and specific thank you to the Johnsons for providing it. As far as I knew, it was completely unused up until that point.

"So I walked over to the caravan, just a little distance from the church and knocked on the door. There was no answer, so I tried to open the screen door so I could give a louder knock on the inner door. But it was locked from the inside. I jiggled it a few times to make sure it wasn't stuck, but it didn't budge. Obviously, someone was inside with the screen door locked that way. I knocked again; no answer. I might have walked away at that point, but I was really puzzled by the situation, so I stood there for a moment. That's when I saw Roger move the little lace curtain on the window and peek out. He saw me looking at him, so now he had to open the door.

"He opened the door, but he didn't invite me in. He was in shirtsleeves and rabat, but his shirt was not tucked in all the way around his waist. He laughed a bit when he saw me noticing this. 'Ha! You've caught me taking a nap before Mass. What brings you out here?' he says. 'You forgot this,' I tell him and hand him the wrapped-up ciborium. 'Oh, this,' he says, taking it from me. 'Thanks for bringing it, but I'd decided not to use it at the Masses out here.' He looked around and lowered his voice, 'Too much of a temptation to these people to be displaying treasures like this. You can take it back with you, please. I've got an older one with a few dings on it to use out here.'

"Now, I didn't like this bigoted remark, but I held my tongue and nodded as plain faced as I could and began to back away when I heard more noise inside, another person moving about. Roger brought the door up close behind him, he now leaning out of the caravan to talk to me, clearly concealing something or someone inside he didn't care to have me see.

"But it was unnecessary, the seeing. His swinging the door forward to obstruct my view pushed a little air out of the camper, and that's all it took. The fragrance, White Shoulders, the very same I'd given her when I came back from New York, wafted out to me. In that moment, I knew Eileen had been with him. I almost tripped backwards disentangling myself from Roger at that point. My face, my discomposure must have told him that I knew. He broke away from my stare, looked down at the ground for a moment. And then, do you know what he did? That bastard smiled and winked at me."

"Jesus Christ," Stephen whispered. "Oops. Sorry. It's reflex, not disrespect."

"It's okay. I've let out more than a few of those myself over the sixteen years that this story's been unfolding."

"What did you do next?"

"I got out of the camp as fast as I could and back here to think. I walked the length of the rampart and back a thousand times that night, thinking about what holy hell I'd give Roger when he came back. But he didn't come back that night. I finally exhausted myself around four in the morning and went to sleep. He came in sometime that night, though, because there he was at breakfast the next day, asking could he have some strong black coffee, not tea, that day, and downing oceans of it. When I saw him in the dining room, I told Mrs. O'Flannelly I wasn't hungry and could I please have tea in my study, but Roger nixed that, 'No, no, nonsense Mrs. O'Flannelly, Fr. Hart will breakfast with me as usual this morning. I know he'll get his appetite back when he takes a bite of one of your scones.' It was disgusting, all too much, his playing the knave, as if all were normal. As soon as I sat down across from him and Mrs. O'Flannelly had left the room, he leaned in and said, 'Now Paddy, I'll have no pouting, and no letting on to anyone else that you've been upset. And with absolutely no cause!' I raised my hand in protest, but he shook his head and said, 'Eileen is a grown woman, and can make her own choices. I'm kind and generous to her, after all. You have no grounds to interfere. I expect you to carry on as normal.'

237

"What an arrogant creep. To expect you to stand by and do nothing in those circumstances. What was he thinking?"

"Of himself, as usual. Here's the shame of it. I did as he asked. God forgive me, I did as he asked. Not willingly; I just couldn't think of another way out of the situation that didn't betray Eileen and her insistence that I not tell my mother where she was and what she was doing."

"What about reporting him up the chain, to the bishop or whatever?"

"I thought about that, and it's eventually what I did. But at first, it seemed futile. Here was a priest that had brought great wealth and prestige with him into the Church, willingly serving out here in the middle of nowhere. Without Eileen's corroboration, which I couldn't provide, he could lie his way out of it, and I'd come out the worse for it. If I couldn't prove an allegation involving my sister, you see, I'd end up looking as though I had suspect motives."

"Like what?"

"Like moving him aside so I could become pastor."

"What? As if this spit of land is such a prize?" Pádraig glowered at Stephen. "I'm sorry, I don't mean to run the place down, but it seems silly that they'd suppose you'd mount a false allegation just to step over the man."

"On the contrary, it would be altogether plausible to them, because it happens all the time. We priests are a den of snakes when it comes to internal advancement. After all, we're in a profession where you can't really get a rise in your pay unless you move up in rank and title. But it isn't even the money that clergy care about. With a higher title, comes more respect from the flock. Psychic income, you've heard of that? The non-monetary benefits that your job gives you. The whole economy of the Church depends upon the clergy clutching to that psychic income."

"How long did this go on?"

"For a few months after I discovered him. I found out later that it had been going on for quite some time before I knew. It was sometime in August when I caught him. That November, all of a sudden he was all afflutter about a trip to

Dublin. I didn't listen too carefully to what he was going on about, I was just happy he'd be gone for a while. Turns out, had I listened more closely, I'd have heard him talking about a promotion in the works for him. I wasn't listening carefully to much of anything or anyone in those days. I'd been sick to my stomach every minute of every day since I caught him. I kept going over it again and again in my mind, praying on it every waking hour, what to do about what I'd learned."

"Did you try talking to Eileen, to help extricate her?"

"I tried, I did. I should mention that even before I learned Roger's secret, I had been able to speak civilly with her on a couple of occasions. I even gave her union with Terry a blessing, not nuptials, but a handfasting in the old Celtic way, like a brethrothal; she asked me to do it, and I was happy to be asked. But I never gave up my begging her to let me bring her and Mum together. She was adamant that I not do it. And the last time I remember talking to her before that day I caught out Roger, I raised it, and she exploded. She said if I didn't leave off of it, she'd disappear for good, and then I'd be well and truly sorry. She was right about that. I was terrified she'd go off with Terry or even without Terry and end up in even more horrific circumstances than where she was, and with me having no clue as to where.

"After that day with Roger, I went out to the camp every day, or nearly that, sometimes twice a day, and every time, her neighbors told me I'd just missed her. She was already unhappy with me, just to begin with for may having raised the reunion one too many times, and now she had shame as an additional reason to avoid me. I think she slipped into the woods whenever she heard my car, or maybe she had friendly look outs who knew or didn't know about Roger, but knew she didn't like talking to me. She'd vanish into the woods behind the bog every time I went out there. She had an uncanny knack for avoiding me when she wanted to. But finally it was she who came to me."

"How did that happen?"

Pádraig shut his eyes tightly and rubbed his temples. "Roger had been gone two days, I think, maybe three to

Dublin when the roof fell in. I was here by myself on a Wednesday; I'd insisted that Mrs. O'Flannelly take a day off while Roger was away. I was alone at the small table in the kitchen when there was a soft knock at the kitchen door. I almost convinced myself it hadn't happened, and even when I realized it really had, my first instinct was to ignore it and keep a little quiet time to myself. I thought it might be the breadman or the milkman, but nothing that required me to bother myself. But then I felt a little guilty and had to go see who it was."

"It was Eileen?" Stephen asked.

Pádraig lowered his gaze. "It was herself. I couldn't believe it. There she was, stooped against the trash bin, crying oceans, arms tight around her middle. I gathered her up, she still half struggling against my help, but when I assured here there was no one inside, she let me bundle her inside to the kitchen. We sat down at the little table in the kitchen. I managed to boil some water, and over a shaky cup of tea, she spilled out the truth.

"It had started out the previous autumn. There had been a wave of enthusiasm in the Travellers camp over St. Molaise's commitment to the mission church. There was a surge of pride among them that they were being taken seriously and earning some respect, that's how they saw the church coming to them. Eileen had volunteered to lead the committee organizing the altar linens. A few of the families had dug up some old but well cared for table clothes, and they not being used for some time in the life of the Travellers, Eileen persuaded the women that they'd be put to the greater glory in the sanctuary. So she was in the sanctuary a good deal, with Roger close in contact with her work. And there, as they say, began the slippery slope. Next, she was invited to the sacristy to make sure he had the proper inventory of linens, Roger chastely insisting on propping the door open making comments about proper appearances. Next, of course, the door was closed and his praise wasn't limited to his words; his hands were involved. She was reluctant, of course, Eileen was, and tried to rebuff him, politely of course, he being who he was and she seeing no premium in rocking the boat against the only clergyman in a quarter century who had the affection of the Travellers. She protested, of course, that she was a married woman; he laughed and said it wasn't a proper marriage, wasn't official and that the blessing I'd conferred was just a quaint accommodation. His performance was classic predation. He was patient and persistent, telling her when she objected outright to his touches that no one would believe her over him.

"So all those months as I had seen him spending more and more time at the mission church, telling me to stay in the village and visit the sick, say the daily Masses, he was waging his campaign on Eileen. It was in the fall of that year, just as the men in the Traveller's camp were filtering back in from their travails abroad, that Roger lowered the boom on her. He offered what he called counseling, saying he could intervene to unite her with our mother. This was the one thing, of course, that she adamantly didn't want. I'd accepted this for the time being, hoping she'd change her mind one day, and judging that as I knew where she was, and she was close by, it was still possible before it was too late to matter. but glad that she'd made contact with me and I knew where she was and that she was as safe as I could make her within her rules. I knew it would do more harm than good to force the issue before she was ready. But for Roger, that tender spot was exactly the vulnerability he needed to complete his evil plan.

"He told her that her behavior toward her mother, and her refusal to reconcile with her was a mortal sin, no less, a violation of the commandment to honor thy mother and thy father. While it was unresolved, he said, she couldn't receive absolution in confession and with a mortal sin on her soul, she could not receive communion. But, he offered, if she'd continue to take counseling with him, he could see his way clear to letting her receive communion."

"But what's the big deal about that? Loads of folks must stick in the pews and take a pass on communion every week."

"No, you're wrong on that, not in the Catholic church, and not in a small parish like St. Molaise or the mission church. If you're not able to receive communion, not worthy by your own measure after examining your conscience, you can't receive. There's a reason that all those who come to church knowing they won't receive communion sit in the very back pew, the sinners' pew, hoping to draw the least amount of attention to themselves as being absent from the file to the communion rail. When you sit back there, or wherever you do, and don't rise to take communion, it's a self-judgment of grave guilt for all the world to see. The only thing worse than that is to approach the communion rail unsure of whether the priest might refuse you communion. That's the threat he laid on her. That's how he got her to have relations with him, and keep her in his control."

"Did he know that he had gotten her pregnant?"

"Oh, he couldn't have failed to notice that even with both eyes shut. Eileen wouldn't tell me if they'd discussed that, but my guess is that if she did talk with him about it, he'd make it clear that he'd have nothing to do with the child and would make sure she took the blame for sleeping around with other men. Which was not true, by the way. That much I do know. Apart from what Roger got her to do, Eileen assured me that she was completely faithful to Terry."

"So did Terry rise to the occasion? I'm gathering not since Fianna's living with Bertie and Ned."

"Correct. After we'd arranged for Eileen to go away for a bit to have the baby, I asked Terry to come visit me here. It was all too inflammatory to try to talk about it over in the camp. He came as I asked, stood right by the window over there, then took a step away into the middle of the room. I gathered he didn't want anyone to see him from the street and start asking what occasioned his first-ever visit to the rectory. He stood there clutching his cap, sweating, looking like he might faint. I asked him to sit down, but he wouldn't.

"There was no way of putting him at ease, so I just asked him flat out, would he welcome the baby into his home and treat the child as his own. 'Father,' he says, 'it pains me to tell you no, I know she's your sister, your only sister. What you're asking wouldn't be so unreasonable, except....' 'What?' I asked him. 'Except for what?' 'Well,' says he, 'not everyone over there knows, best I can tell, that she's even expecting. She's

242

done a good job of hiding it. I don't know how she did that, but she did. If she turns up now with a new baby, they'll all know.' I felt that I was being rather dense here; of course, they'd know she was pregnant. That's where babies come from. So I pressed him. 'Know what, Terry?' He's grimacing and twisting his hat as if he'd like to wring someone's neck at this point. Then he starts sobbing. 'They'll know the child isn't mine, Father. They'll all know. They're simple out there, but not stupid. We've all been away together, Father, the whole working season. Think about it! A baby born in December would've been made after Easter. When I wasn't here, Father!' He was a wreck by now, and I finally got him to sit down. I told him babies don't come on an exact schedule; there'd be room for making the timing work. But he was stubborn. So afraid of his own embarrassment that he just couldn't see past it. I'd like to say that I didn't think less of him for that, but I can't, not honestly."

"I guess even thieves have values, then, is that it?"

"Well put. They're mens' men out there. Clannish. Loyal. Disloyalty is punished. Who knows whether they would even have let Eileen stay. Maybe they'd have thrown the two of them out. Maybe that's what he was afraid of. When you grow up among the Johnsons as blood family, you know nothing else. Anyway, he wasn't wiling to live among them with the risk that they'd be smirking at him behind his back as a cuckhold, And he certainly wasn't willing to get kicked out of his tribe and lose his career for an outsider woman who got pregnant by another man. That's my reading of it, not that he spelled any of that out, exactly. After the sobbing quieted down, I patted him on the back and sent him off. I didn't have the heart to be too hard on him, not at that moment. But I was bitterly disappointed at his failing."

"So you eventually placed Fianna with Ned and Bertie, I follow that, but what happened to Eileen?"

"Well, there was really only one thing to do: Find her a safe place to go away and have the baby. No other alternative for her or for me."

"I suppose that a trip to England was out of the question

at that point?"

"At any point, really. So we sent her up to the convent in Bundoran, to the nuns up there. Same order as Sister Alex. They run a little home up there, next to the hospital, also run by sisters of a different order, for girls in that way."

"Who do you mean by 'we'?"

Pádraig looked out the window at the waves for a long moment. "I've never told anyone this. Sister Alex helped us."

"Aha! I knew there was a seditious side to her. She took her up to Bundoran, then?"

"Yes. I drove them up there late one night. Sister Alex stayed up there with her until Fianna was born. It was just three days after that...Eileen disappeared again."

"Well, I guess it's evident that she wasn't in the picture after a certain point. But I rather thought she was more involved in the adoption, that she hadn't just dropped out of sight."

"No, she'd gotten wind, I don't know how, that Terry was none too pleased with her having gotten herself into the situation. Or maybe she didn't know specifically that, what Terry thought; I've no reason on my own or through Sister Alex to suppose that they spoke after she went up to Bundoran. But maybe she sensed having lived among the Travellers for long enough that she'd be shunned and gossiped about and Terry along with her. She might even have thought she was doing him a favor by going away.

"When Sister Alex called and told me Eileen had disappeared, I half expected it. Sister Alex asked me if I wanted to have the child put up for adoption through the Bundoran house. But I'd thought ahead a little bit on this and told her to bring the child back to Mullaghmore, but to give me a couple of days to get things set up.

"I'd been hearing from Bertie for years about how she wanted a child but hadn't been able to conceive. She and Ned had been married perhaps twenty years by then, and the prospect that she'd have a child of her own was getting more and more remote. So I went out to the house, the same place they live now, and put the question to them, did they want to adopt an orphan girl from Bundoran."

"So you didn't tell them who she was, that she was your niece and the father was Roger Hargadon?"

"No, not a word on any of that. When they asked if she was a healthy baby, I said yes."

"What did you tell them about the parents?"

"I said that the father was very religious."

"That's it?"

"Look, Bertie didn't take much convincing. She was thrilled at this unexpected blessing. It was Ned who started in with reservations. 'We're too old for a baby, Bertie.' he said. 'We've been on our own together for too long. I'm too old to change to make room for a baby.'"

"It sounds as though that all played out as he predicted then. He seems to have little affection for the child. Maybe you should have taken 'no' for his answer."

Pádraig shook his head. "No, it's more complicated than that. He was very tender towards Bertie back then. When he saw how much she wanted to adopt the baby, he relented. I was there. He practically melted when she explained how much it would mean to her. And he was very tender with Fianna, too. At first, any way."

"What happened to make him change?" Stephen asked.

"Nothing happened. He just figured it out. Or at least part of it. And it infuriated him." Pádraig walked to the window. "He was a churchgoer back then, fairly regularly. They'd bring the baby to Mass every Sunday, the second Mass at quarter past eight. That one was rather lightly attended; even more lightly nowadays, sad to say. I had a little more time to say good-bye to people as they passed out the door.

"This one morning, probably a year after the adoption, it was a beautiful spring day, I remember that, Bertie and Ned came out of the church and into the little courtyard into the bright light. Usually, I said my greetings just inside the doorway, in the shade of the vestibule. But it was such a fresh, beautiful day that I moved the process outside. Bertie and Ned came out, Bertie carrying Fianna, everyone all smiles. 'Will you take the baby, Father, give her a blessing?' Bertie asked me. She hands over the child. I was delighted to hold her, of course, but was always reserved about asking too readily. It might look odd, I thought. But here was Bertie offering me a chance to give her a cuddle and a blessing and I leapt at it.

"I took little Fianna in my arms and held her up in the air. She giggled, and I laughed. I swung her around to hold her in the crook of my right arm and looked back at the parents. Bertie smiled as much as I've ever seen her do. But Ned. He had a look of horror. He looked stricken. And in that moment, as I glanced down at Fianna, I understood what he was seeing. There we were, niece and uncle, smiling and squinting in the sunshine. He'd just figured out the family resemblance."

"But what did he conclude? Did he think you were the father?"

"I'm sure he did, but he didn't say anything. He just stayed away from church from then on. I don't know what he told Bertie about not going to church, but I'm sure he kept his suspicions about Fianna to himself."

"So did you ever straighten him out? I mean, it might have improved his attitude toward Fianna, don't you think?"

"I didn't think I could safely say anything without unraveling things for a lot of people. But it didn't matter. He arrived at the truth without me. At least the part about Eileen being the mother, I'm sure of that."

"How do you know that?"

"Well, I continued to visit the house. Even though Ned wasn't coming to church, Bertie did, and the both of them still counted as parishioners. My practice is to visit everyone until they ask me not to. So I was out there at least twice a month. And I could see Ned watching Fianna. I could see what he saw."

"What was that?"

"Fianna was exactly like Eileen. Not nearly like or very much like. She was exactly like Eileen. In every way. Her expressions, her laughter. But beyond that. The things that amused her, the things that held her attention. You could give her a doll to play with, for example, and a dress to change her in and out of. Most little girls would play at changing the dresses back and forth. But Fianna, she'd undress the doll, make a chair out of stones for it and adorn it with moss and blackthorn twigs. That's just the sort of thing that Eileen did when she was little.

"And singing to herself. When Eileen was little, and even when she passed ten years, she'd spend hours on the porch, rocking in the chair by the peat pile, singing rhymes to herself. Some of them were quite pleasant in melody, though the words were hard to follow. Fianna, the same thing. I'd be out there having tea in the kitchen with Bertie, Ned sitting next to the radio in the parlor, looking out at Fianna on the porch, scowling."

"So granted, that kind of play may seem a little bizarre to a parent. But your mother didn't have a fit over it, did she? Don't you just say in these cases that the child has a vivid imagination or something like that?"

"That's how my mother looked at it. That, and the idea that she'd grow out of it, find a nice husband, et cetera. But for Ned it was more than that."

"What d'you mean?"

"Ned knew Eileen growing up. He's a bit younger than I am, two years closer in age to Eileen than I am. Apart from Terry Johnson, the only boy who ever showed any appreciation of Eileen's uniqueness, any affection toward her at all was Ned. I now believe that he was in love with her."

"Oh, no! So for him, having Fianna around is a constant reminder of someone he couldn't have, right?"

"I think so. That and an infuriating reminder that the woman he would have liked to marry went off and had a child with someone else, out of wedlock. And now he's had to change his settled life, with a wife taking care of him full-time now to make room to take care of this unwanted child."

"Well, that makes a lot of things clearer. In a sense, who can blame him for being angry all the time? Having a secret like that, one that makes you fume all the time, not being able to tell anyone without destroying a bunch of lives all around you. No wonder he drinks."

Pádraig laid his forehead down on the desk for a moment. "So now you know it all. What do we do next?"

Stephen surveyed the glass and ceramic remains still piled between Pádraig's desk and the bookshelf.

"Next I fill you in on the plan and what we'll need to make ready for tonight. But before that, we clean this mess up."

"I could ask Mrs. O'Flannelly to do it.

Stephen shook his head. "No, I'll do it. She's reeling enough just from finding me here this morning. No need to give her cause to wonder about what went on in here." He turned a dustbin on its side and used yesterday's newspaper to sweep in the larger pieces of debris inside. "Besides," he said, "my people are a tidy bunch. Can't help it. We see something askew and we just have to put in in order." He shrugged as he swept and made his explanation. "I guess we're just born that way."

34.

Pádraig went through the rest of the morning and afternoon in a daze. He'd hoped that Mrs. O'Flannelly would leave a little early to get ready for the Maundy Thursday service, but she kept at her scrubbing and dusting until nearly five o'clock. Pádraig had promised himself a short nap if she left early, but lying down in the middle of the day wasn't something he felt he could do with her in the house without claiming to be ill. He soldiered on, zombie-like, fueled by dark brewed tea and frequent visits to the open window in his study for a lungful of fresh air.

At six o'clock, he dragged himself over to the sanctuary to make sure that it was in proper preparation for the Maundy Thursday Mass. This was the beginning of the Triduum, the three most sacred days of the liturgical year that carried the whole point of the Christian faith: the death, burial and resurrection of Jesus Christ. He looked around the stripped down church, the candles before the statues of the Blessed Virgin and St. Molaise extinguished, and the racks adorned with tiny polite signs reminding the faithful that no votives could be ignited until after Easter. The crucifix was covered in purple flannel. Pádraig took one last glance, pronounced everything in order to himself and went to the sacristy.

"Stephen!" he said, upon rounding the corner to the short staircase leading to the sacristy. "What are you doing here?"

"I thought I'd come and watch, if it's all right with you."

"Yes, yes, of course. Everyone's welcome, especially you. Come up into the sacristy while I dress and get ready. You can help me from dozing off and missing my cue to get out on the altar." Stephen followed close behind as Pádraig unlocked the sacristy. "You keep it locked? Is that necessary?"

"Probably not, but it's standard procedure. We have consecrated hosts in there and that's the holy grail, the whole deal as far as the Church is concerned. We can't have the chance of someone coming in and making away with them." Stephen wandered around the sacristy, looking the chalices and pattens. Pádraig opened the door of his armoire, and Stephen smiled in surprise at the splendor of the vestments. "The red one is beautiful. When do you get to wear that one? Tonight maybe?"

"No, that's for feast days. Tonight is a solemn occasion. I can wear white or violet."

"I vote for violet, for what it's worth."

"Violet it is, then."

Stephen leaned against a counter, then stood upright. "Is this okay, if I just lean over here?"

"Yes, yes. Make yourself comfortable. Ther're a couple of chairs over there under the table. Pull one of those out for yourself, why don't you?"

"They're so small, these chairs. Just my size. But why?"

"For the altar boys. They seem to get younger every year. We brought those seats over from the primary school."

Stephen sat and looked around some more. He returned his focus to Pádraig. "You must be dead tired. I got a little sleep on the bench out there by the water while I was waiting for a decent hour to knock. But you, dId you sleep at all?"

Pádraig slipped the alb over his head and fought its cling to bring it to hang properly about his body. "A little. Though it seems like I can't remember doing it. I think I floated in and out. Or just floated below the surface. No dreams I can remember." He went over to the armoire and took out the violet vestment on its hangar. "Help me with this, will you? I can do it on my own, but it's a struggle. Here, just take this part by the shoulders, stand up on the chair while I put my head under it." He pushed his head through the opening toward Stephen. "Thanks much, my friend," he said and turned around to see two astonished altar boys standing in the doorway. "Terence, Timothy, come, come, you're nearly late, but thanks for agreeing to help out. I know tomorrow's a day off from school, but a big day nonetheless. So thanks for helping out." The two stood still in the doorway. "Ah, you've never seen a…" Pádraig turned to Stephen looking for guidance.

"Do not say midget. And I'm not terribly fond of 'dwarf' either."

"…Little person before," Pádraig improvised. "This is my friend Dr. Attergood, a very learned man, recently arrived here from Cambridge, England."

"Oxford, actually," Stephen whispered. "I hate to quibble."

"Oxford, then. Even more learned than advertised, young gentlemen. In any event, hurry up now and get into your cassocks and albs. And don't forget the special arrangements for tonight, the foot washing basin we discussed last week. It's all organized over there in the cupboard. Just remember to bring it out before the Mass and have it ready when I tell you."

"Yes, Fa'her," the two answered in unison and dove into the armoire of the sacristy to start their routine.

"Foot washing?"

"Yes, part of the ritual of Holy Thursday. Replicates how Jesus humbled himself before his Apostles, representing all of mankind."

"Whose feet get washed?"

"Why? Are you wanting to get in line?"

"No, no. Not me."

"We have a couple of the male parishioners fill in the role. There's no scriptural reason it couldn't be a woman, but apparently the bishops think it could be misinterpreted as an erotic event, I guess. They've vivid if misguided imaginations running their brains."

"Well, it is sort of intimate. Anyway, do you know who's up for the role, or is it a surprise to you too?"

"I don't bother with it. I let the parish council decide. If I'm really supposed to be imitating Jesus, it shouldn't matter to me whom they pick. That's the theory anyway." He glanced at his watch. "Showtime. See you out there." Pádraig summoned Terence and Timothy and processed out of the sacristy to the altar.

Stephen walked as discreetly as possible out of the sacristy and down the right-side aisle of the church. He sat down quietly on the outermost edge of a pew a few behind the most tightly packed ones. None of his discretion prevented the turning of heads to note his unusual attendance at the Mass. He gazed off above their heads, pretending fascination with the every move of Terence and Timothy on the altar.

Pádraig desperately wanted to rush through the Mass, but he forced himself to keep an even pace as he worked his way through the liturgy. He read John's gospel giving an account of the Last Supper and gave a passable sermon on the drama of Jesus' last meal on earth. He lingered on the foot washing scene in the account as a lead in to his upcoming reenactment.

"Many people are uncomfortable with the ritual of foot washing. If you are one of those people, let me ask you to reflect on what John is saying to us about Jesus' role when he was here among us. Think of the verse from Matthew, 'He who exalts himself shall be humbled, and he who humbles himself shall be exalted.' Here is Jesus humbling himself before his followers, the teacher humbling himself before his students. His actions are not a one time lecture from the front of the classroom. They are a field demonstration to us of the principal lesson that his life and death were meant to convey: We are meant to serve one another, humbly and with love." Pádraig made the sign of the cross and dismissed himself from the lectern. He signaled the altar boys; Terence walked slowly across the altar with Timothy, one carrying the white linen towels and the other nervously balancing the cruet of water in the washing bowl. They stood with Pádraig next to the two chairs that had been set on the altar for the ritual. Pádraig turned to the congregation to invite the volunteers to the altar. Two men rose from a pew in the middle of the church and made their way down the center aisle.

"Oh, no," Stephen said softly to himself as he recognized the backs of the heads of the two men and realized that Pádraig was about to wash the feet of Martin and Darren. That's some bad luck, Stephen thought, then realized that the humiliation had to have been intentional.

Pádraig accomplished the ritual without showing his irritation at the Parish Council's selection, he hoped. He rebuked himself for not paying more attention to the details of this Mass which unlike others required a special performance on his part. Ellen still had great sway over the Council though she hadn't served officially since the end of her term two years prior. She might just as well still be president of the Council, he thought.

Finally, the Mass was ended, and Pádraig completed the Holy Thursday offices by removing the Eucharist from the sanctuary to the tabernacle in the sacristy. When Terence and Timothy made their exit, Stephen slipped into the room and closed the door.

"Wow. That was really something. No coincidence that, don't you agree? The Four were sending you a message."

Pádraig unwrapped the stole from his shoulders and threw it violently onto the credenza. "Blast them! It's one thing to be humbled and something altogether different to be humiliated, which is what they were after."

"I agree," Stephen said, crossing his arms. "They mean to show you who's in charge around here. Subtle but effective."

Pádraig continued returning the elements of his garb to their proper places. "Well if they think this sort of thing is going to get me to stand down, they've got another thing coming."

"So we're on with the plan? I wasn't sure. I thought you might find it a bit scary."

"Scary? Which part? It all just seems bizarre to me, but I'll give anything a try at this point. But let's go before I calm down and have another chance to change my mind about it.

I'll drive."

"For me, that's the scary part," Stephen muttered as he followed Pádraig to the car.

35.

Pádraig nudged the Escort up the winding road leading to the car park for hikers intending to assault Ben Bulben. He drove more cautiously than usual, careful not to drive beyond the light cast by his headlights. He couldn't afford a tumble down the side of the mountain.

They dismounted the car at the car park and mustered out. Stephen unfurled a map from his rucksack and put it under the light of his torch. "This way," he nodded, gesturing to the vague beginnings of a path up the side of the hill. Pádraig followed a short distance behind. He had pulled on two sweaters over his shirt and rabat, but had already begun wishing for one more and a pair of gloves, too.

"I haven't been up here in probably thirty years, maybe more," he said as he huffed up the pathway, "but I don't remember there being particularly well marked trails."

"You're right about that," Stephen called over his shoulder, "especially where we're going, over to the east face. Most people want to get up to the summit as directly as possible, up over the south face. Enjoy the splendid views. The foolhardy ones go up the north face, from what I've read. They get the double challenge of climbing a sheer rock face that could crumble out of their hands at any moment and the excitement of high winds and squalls coming in off the ocean."

"What fun," grumbled Pádraig, hoisting his weight, step

by step against the incline. "So where are we headed exactly?"

"The east face, the one that looks back against the inland. We'll have to go around the south face somehow and then up a bit on the east side. That's likely to be the hard part -- as far as I can tell, there are no good footpaths marked over there. We'll have to wing it."

Pádraig shook his head but held his tongue as he followed along behind.

Within ninety minutes, Stephen had gotten them onto the east face of the mountain. The stars were bright and distinct at this altitude and Pádraig was almost dazzled enough to forget the discomfort that the lather of sweat he'd worked up was causing him under his sweaters. But standing about for even a few minutes in the cold air while Stephen consulted the map reminded him he'd rather be home in bed.

"Are we there yet, or at least nearly so?" he asked, looking over Stephen's shoulder as if the map might make sense if he frowned enough over it.

"Almost, I think." Stephen cast the beam of the torch around himself in an arc. "There. I think that's it." They walked together to the spot illuminated by Stephen's beam. Stephen dropped his rucksack and went on his hands and knees, sweeping dead vegetation and dust off a spot on the ground. Pádraig held the torch for him, and as he watched, a slab of dark stone emerged into sight.

"So that's it, then. What they call in these parts the Fairy Door."

"The Fairy Door? Are you.... Never mind, I was going to ask if you were mad, but here I am with you, so what's the point? What do your books tell you about the Fairy Door?"

"It's partly from books and partly from a little further conversation with Easmon. This is the portal to the world of the others. Easmon says that farmers used to come out on the full moon nights to see would it swing open. Depending on what kind of shadow it cast, they could risk a prediction about the weather and the best days to plant which crops. Sort of like a self-declaring almanac."

"So let's pop it open and get this done with."

"Um, I'm not sure that's the right thing to do, or a wise one, either. Anyway, if you see a handle, we can give it a try, but I don't see anything to lay leverage on. It's well and good recessed into the mountain, and flush with its frame. I'd guess that it only opens from the inside."

"'Opens from the inside?' You have gone around the bend. So if we can't open it, what do we do?"

"I think we take a page from Yeats and try calling them forth. I mean, what he and his friends did, that happened over in Rosses Strand, which I gather is sort of the back door to this one. This is reputed to be the front door. But there's no reason to think that the incantation wouldn't work just as well here."

Pádraig rolled his eyes, a gesture lost on Stephen, who was digging through his pack to find the Yeats book. "Here it is. Are you ready? I think you should say it."

"Me? Why me?"

"You'll be more...convincing. First of all, you're a priest and that kind of authority has got be worth something. Second, Latin is practically your native tongue!" Pádraig looked at Stephen for a moment. "If I thought I was really performing an incantation, I'd be troubled by this. But since I regard it as a harmless waste of time at best, here goes." He took the book from Stephen, who held the torch over the page for him. Pádraig filled his chest and turned to the black slab. Raising his voice into the night, he shouted, 'Veni, Veni Regni Pigmeorum!" He looked back at Stephen. A moment passed silently. "Say it again," Stephen whispered. Pádraig stood tall and called out, "Veni, Veni, Regni Pigmeorum!" They stood listening. Stephen turned to the south and stood still. "Listen," he said quietly. "Listen, do you hear that? It's music! Pipes and fiddles. Don't you hear that, Pádraig?" Pádraig took a few steps to the south and listened intently. "I do hear it. I think I even recognize the tune they're playing. It's a reel; forget the name of it at the moment." He stood listening for a few more seconds and took another few steps descending down the face to the south.

"Ah, Christ!" he cursed, turning back toward Stephen and

stomping back up towards him. "There's a guest house half way down the hill on this side. It's McSlarry's place. The lights are still on -- they have a residents' bar for after hours. That's where the music's coming from."

"Are you sure?" Stephen asked, his disappointment palpable. "Doesn't it sound closer than that?"

"Pretty damn sure it's coming from there, Stephen, unless you see a fairy orchestra around here."

"Let's give it a few more minutes. It took us a long time to get up here."

"Oh, bloody hell!" Pádraig yelled. "I just stepped in a stream over here. I'm soaked halfway up to my knees."

"Sorry, I should have warned you that the trail books say it can be boggy up here. Listen, why don't you just...I don't know, say a prayer or a petition or something for Fianna's return?" Pádraig glared at Stephen, then relented. "Okay, fine." He raised his palms upwards and said, "Heavenly Father, we seek your help and guidance in the matter of Fianna's return. All the peoples of the earth are your children, and we ask your commune with our...brothers and sisters, even those unseen by us, to work cooperatively for her safe return. We ask this in the name of your son and our redeemer, Jesus, with whom all things are possible."

"Amen," Stephen murmured. Pádraig thrust his hands into his trouser pockets and stared down at the distant lights along the coast, some of them emanating from Mullaghmore. "I'm giving this fool errand another five minutes, then going down with or without you. And I'm looking at my watch. Not another second more." They passed the time in silence, then picked their way down the trail.

It was past three in the morning when they got back to the car. Not a word had passed between them since they'd left the Fairy Door. Pádraig sulked in resentment over the wasted time and the crushing fatigue that had been building over the past days. Stephen broke the silence. "You know, I'm more disappointed than I thought I'd be that this didn't work. I'm even a little surprised it didn't work. Maybe I have gone around the bend. I'll have to think more about this. In the spirit of self-reflection and science, of course."

"Of course," Pádraig said absently. He was hunched forward toward the windscreen, focused as intently as he could on the winding road as he eased the car down the mountain. Suddenly, the front tire on Pádraig's side caught on a rut and lurched to the right pulling the tire into a slurry running along the side of the road. "Fuck!" screamed Pádraig. Stephen jumped, then looked at Pádraig in amazement. "Wow. First time I've heard that from you. We must be in real trouble." Pádraig glowered at him and opened the door to step out and examine the damage. "Fuck!" he yelled again. "Twice in one night? Now what?" Stephen asked. "There's a damned creek running along the road here and I've just stepped in it. The water's freezing cold."

Pádraig hoisted himself back into the car and slammed the door closed. "We are well and truly stuck, my friend. The front tire is hanging over the edge of the ditch. We're going nowhere unless we put it in neutral and get out and push."

"I'll do what I can," Stephen said pushing open his door, "but brute force is not my strong suit. I mean, I don't have a lot of mass to contribute."

"Good point," Pádraig acknowledged. "You get behind the wheel, put it in reverse and we'll see if we get any traction from the other wheels. I'll push it backwards."

With twenty minutes of effort, the car hadn't moved, and Pádraig was covered in the mud and gravel that the other front wheel had kicked up. He climbed back into the passenger seat. "I think the choices are to wait for someone to come along in the daylight, or start walking back toward the farms on the south side of the mountain to ask for help."

"Walking will at least keep us warm," Stephen said. He reached into the backseat for his sack and pulled out his torch. He flicked it on and after an encouraging spurt of light it faded to yellow and then out altogether. "Hmm. That won't work. We can't very well walk in the dark. We're too good at finding roadside hazards for that to be safe."

"Very funny," Pádraig said. "I guess we'll stay put until daylight, then." He pushed back the passenger seat as far as it would go and slouched in resignation. He closed his eyes.

"So you're just going to sleep?"

"Aye, I am," Pádraig said without opening his eyes.

Stephen sighed, realizing that he'd have no company during the last hours of the night. He was no good at sleeping in unfamiliar places, and he counted this among the strangest to challenge him. He tried to occupy himself by calling to mind every book he'd read since a year ago April, then alphabetizing them in his head. He was up to the letter "h" when he heard an odd animal sound. He held his breath and listened closely. He shook Pádraig's shoulder. "Pádraig, wake up. There's something out there. Some animal." Pádraig opened his eyes. "What does it sound like?"

"Listen! There it is again! It's kind of a heavy breathing and a lowing sound. What do you think it is? I don't want to get out and look. What is it?

Pádraig shifted forward in his seat ad rubbed his face. "Probably not a lion, we can rule that out."

"If you're just going to make fun of me..."

"All right, all right. It's an ox."

"I tell you it's heavy breathing and a lowing sound and you come up certain that it's an ox? Do you have a lot of farm experience I haven't yet heard about?"

"No, I can see in the side mirror. It's an ox, with two men walking it down the road. Maybe they can help us." Pádraig launched himself from the car, taking care to hop over the watery ditch then back on to the road behind the immobilized car. Stephen warily let himself out on the driver's side.

"*Dia duit,*" Pádraig called out, the old-fashioned Irish greeting, God be with you. At the very least, using the greeting identified him as a harmless and friendly local. In the dim light, he saw the two men exchange a glance before one of them called back, "Dia is Muire duit " raising his hand in greeting. God and Mary be with you.

"I wonder if you can help us," Pádraig said walking toward the men. "Our car is stuck. We haven't been able to move it."

"Is it damaged?" the taller of the two asked.

"No, I don't think so. If we can just get it back on the road, I think we'll be fine and on our way."

"We're on our way down to near McSlarry's place." He nodded at the ox. "Sally's due to plow out the potato field. But we've time to lend a hand. Sally won't mind, will you, dear?" He rubbed her neck, tenderly, Pádraig thought, and she moaned out a gentle low in seeming assent.

The men, both of them, were tall enough to be remarked upon in a village like Mullghmore. They stooped down in front of the car and laced Sally's traces to the underside of the bumper. "We'll drive her out slowly. Don't want to tear the front of the car off." The two of them spoke softly to Sally and walked her forward a few steps. Stephen held the wheel steady with the car in neutral. Gradually, the car moved forward and sideways back onto the road.

"Brilliant!" Pádraig declared. "Thank you so much for stopping to help. We're very grateful."

The men smiled a little. "You're very welcome," the shorter one said. "You'll do the same for someone else one day. That's the way the world works."

"I agree with that. Thanks a million."

"What brings you out here in the middle of the night, may I ask?" the taller one ventured.

Pádraig chuckled, thinking back on the antics of the night. "The long story made short is that we're looking for a girl who's disappeared from our village, over there on the other side of the N15." He pointed in the general direction of Mullaghmore."

"And you thought she might be up here?" the taller one asked.

"Yes," Pádraig said hesitantly, realizing how implausible their adventure would seem if he tried to explain it. "A remote possibility that didn't prove out, unfortunately."

"That's a shame," said the shorter man. "What's her name?"

"It's Fianna Gunning."

The two men glanced at each other.

"I see," said the taller man. "Is it spelled the usual way, her first name?"

"No," Pádraig answered, pushing back the thought of why such a detail could be of interest at the moment. "As a matter of fact not. It has two 'n's'. Between the parents and the parish clerk, there was a misspelling on the baptismal certificate when it was enrolled in the parish register. After that, it's more trouble to change than it is to live with it. I'd already baptized her with the double 'n' version of the name."

The men's head swiveled toward one another, then back to meet Pádraig's gaze.

"So you're a priest, then?"

Pádraig fingered his collar. It was dappled with mud and the white notch was invisible because of the dirt and the poor light. "Aye, I am. Father Hart from St. Molaise over in Mullaghmore."

"I see," said the less-tall of the two. "We must be going, but we'll keep an eye out for her." They turned and nudged Sally back up the road. Their abrupt departure left no time for reiteration of thanks or further good-byes.

Stephen had watched the exchange silently. "Now that's odd."

"What's odd? Apart from the whole encounter, I mean. Move over, I'll drive."

"Yes, quite a coincidence that they should turn up with towing capability just when we needed it. But there's something more. They said they were on the way to a plowing job down the road in the direction we're headed. But they turned around and went back the way they came. Almost as if they changed their mind about something. And did they not seem preternaturally tall to you?"

Pádraig rolled down the window for a dose of fresh air. "Pardon my saying so, Stephen, but doesn't everyone seem tall to you?"

"You're probably right about that," Stephen said yawning and leaning his head back against the seat. In a moment, he'd lost his discomfort about sleeping in strange places and was fast asleep as the car sliced through the dark towards Mullaghmore.

36.

Pádraig was grateful that Good Friday required no morning mass. Decorum required, however, that he present himself on time for breakfast no matter how difficult it was to unstick his head from the pillow. He couldn't have Mrs. O'Flannelly wondering to herself or out loud about the parish priest sleeping in.

"I assume it's just tea this morning, Father?" Mrs. O'Flannelly asked, a bit louder than Pádraig's cottony brain could tolerate. He flinched a bit then remembered his fasting obligation. He quietly cursed himself for not having filled up a bit more the evening before. In fact, he couldn't remember supper, then realized he'd skipped it to go up the mountain with Stephen right after evening Mass. He groaned inwardly, then said as cheerfully as he could, "Yes, Mrs. O'Flannelly. Just tea this morning." He sipped slowly and tried to keep his eyes open.

He spent the morning studying his breviary and preparing a short homily for the afternoon Mass. The length of the service required brevity, but as usual, he found a short talk more difficult to compose than a longer one. He struggled to express himself and had so many hash marks on the pad by the time he'd finished that he had to recopy the text to a clean page to make out his own words.

Late in the morning, he dragged himself off to Luck Boat. He was surprised to see Stephen, the only other customer, talking with Joe. Joe's wife was included in the conversation through Joe's periodic translations summarizing the conversation with Stephen. Pádraig took a seat in the booth with Stephen.

"You're looking pretty rough, if you don't mind my saying so," Stephen said.

"I certainly do mind, you being the cause of it. It's not like I can sleep in, which I suppose you did until just a quarter hour ago."

"More or less right. And now I'm famished. I didn't eat a thing last night. I'm certainly not going into Beach Club nowadays. Anyway, the food here is more interesting. And better," he said smiling at Joe's wife. Joe translated and she smiled and bowed.

"Go ahead, rub it in. I'll be back in a minute from the loo."

"What's he so grouchy about?" Stephen asked Joe.

"Good Friday. A day of fasting. It always makes him irritable. He's like a car without gas when he doesn't eat."

Pádraig came back from the toilet and threw himself back into the booth. "Bowl of rice, then, Father?" Joe asked. "Sure, yes, thanks Joe. Make sure it's a small bowl. Don't coddle me, now."

"Dr. Attergood, you'll have something more substantial? Sub gum chow mein is good today."

"Absolutely, I'll go with your recommendation. But to be completely frank with you Joe, the taste on that one is a bit tame for me. Is there anyway to crank it up a bit?"

"Funny you should ask. Father has been asking me about that for years, especially on these days when he's fasting. I've been working on it, and I've come up with something I think you'll like." He hustled off to the kitchen with his wife.

"Um, Pádraig, if you're eating a bowl of rice, how is that fasting? I understood fasting to be rather binary as in not eating when you'd like to be eating."

"As usual, it's a little more complicated the way the Church sees it. I can eat twice today as long as on each occasion what I eat is less than a full meal. I take it a little further and eat just one small meal on a fast day. There used to be more of them, but now it's down to Ash Wednesday and Good Friday, which is today. So it's not much of a burden."

"Okay, good for you, but I can hear your stomach growling from over here. If you eat something more, I won't tell."

"Appreciated, but not my style. It's about the observance, not about getting away with something."

The fragrance of the chow mein and steamed rice wafted in from the kitchen, and the dishes they ordered arrived shortly thereafter. Pádraig looked enviously at Stephen's mounded plate, then down at his meager bowl of white grains.

"Here's something to spice it up, for both of you," Joe said, putting a tiny bowl, the size of a tablespoon in the space between them. Pádraig picked it up and brought it close to sniff it. Joe's wife gasped; Pádraig froze. "You really don't want to put that near your nose. And if you get some on your fingers, do not rub your eyes. Or touch anything else that's... sensitive."

Pádraig tipped a little of the powder onto his rice with a chopstick and poked it into the grains. He tasted the rice. "Sweet Mary!" he shouted. "That is the hottest pepper powder you've ever tried out on me." He chased a gob of rice that hadn't been treated with the pepper and leveraged it into his mouth to tamp down the burn.

"You like it?" Joe asked.

"I love it!" he said. Joe's wife smiled broadly. "What is it?"

"Ghost chili. Wendy's father used to grow them back in Hong Kong. He got the seeds on a trip to India. Wendy just started a window box growing a few plants. This is the first production. I expect demand will be slim, but I thought you'd like it. How about you, Dr. Attergood? Care to give it a try?"

"Sure, how could I not with that back story and the affirmation from himself over there?" Stephen carefully pushed a quarter-gram of the powder over his chow mein with his fork and took a small bite. His eyes popped wide and he swallowed quickly. "Oh my God, how can food hurt that much?" He took a gulp of water. "But I do like it, I'll give you that. Put me on the slim demand list. I'll eat my share as long as you're serving this."

A few minutes after half eleven, Pádraig and Stephen settled their bill and walked out into the bright sunshine. Pádraig put a hand up as a visor over his eyes while they adjusted. "It's a beautiful day, but I've got to go right back inside, I'm afraid. Time for the Passion service."

"You mean Mass. Service is for Protestants, isn't it?"

"No, it's a service today. No Mass on Good Friday. The tradition is that there's no consecration of the host from Holy Thursday until Easter Sunday, which actually begins the night before with the Vigil Mass."

"So Saturday is Sunday. As well as Sunday being Sunday. Or is it actually Monday?"

"Ha, ha, very funny. But there's a logic to it. In the daily prayer cycle, vespers are observed at sundown. We've regularized it now to five in the afternoon; we can't have people wondering what time the vespers Mass is this week or that. If you're a medieval monk in a monastery up on a mountain somewhere, you can't get a lot done after dark, so you might as well call it a day. Which is what they did.

"Anyway, you've made me go off on a tangent again. I've got to get ready."

"I'll go along for the spectacle," Stephen said, hustling across the plaza with Pádraig. "I do hope it's the purple vestments again."

"No, it's black today. Or red."

"Oh, definitely red, then," Stephen said as they rounded the side of the church to enter the sacristy from the side door.

37.

Pádraig was pacing the small floor area of the sacristy a few minutes before three o'clock, checking his pocket watch every half-minute.

"This makes no sense," he told Stephen. "Timothy and Terence knew to come here at half two to get ready. They should have been here before we got here. And Willie, he's always here on Good Friday to read Jesus."

"I thought you said he was an no-show for last Sunday, too."

"Yes, but that was an anomaly. I think Ellen detained him with make-work just to irk me. She knows how I depend on him for Holy Week. I haven't seen him since Sunday afternoon, when I first met you over in the pub. Listen, Stephen, do me a favor. Just go out there and take a peek, see if the twins are out there with their mum. May have been a misunderstanding. And see if there's any able-bodied gent out there I can impress to service to read Jesus."

Stephen was gone for moment, then back. "Not a single male of the species out there, Father, of any age. The place is packed with girls and women."

"Och." Pádraig threw up his hands. "Well, then. There's no alternative. You'll have to help me."

"Me?" Stephen said, startling himself as he realized he's raised his voice just a little too loudly. "Me?" he whispered.

"You've got to be kidding. I can't go out there on the altar with you."

"Why not? You'd be doing me a big favor, and I'd be very grateful."

"But, but I don't believe in....anything!" Stephen sputtered. "Not God for starters, and certainly not Jesus, for Chrissakes."

"It doesn't matter. I'm not asking for a profession of faith. Just a little stage help. I'll tell you what to do and when to do it. It will be seamless, I promise, and not the least opportunity to embarrass yourself." Stephen crossed his arms defiantly. Pádraig softened his tone. "Please, Stephen. This service can't be done solo." Stephen remained impassive.

"Listen, I hate to put it to you this way, but just think of all the nutty things I've done this week just because you asked me to. Can you please just do me this one favor, Stephen?"

Stephen uncrossed his arms and shook his head slowly. "All right, all right, you've got me by the guilt muscle, right here around my neck." Stephen mimed a tight collar around his throat. "Am I dressed all right?"

"Yes, you look fine under the circumstances."

"What do I do when you say the prayers and I don't know them? Or don't agree with them?"

"Keep your eyes down, your hands clasped in front of you, and move your mouth and mumble. No one will notice you're not actually saying anything. Try to blend in with the 'amens' if you can."

"Okay, I guess I can do that." Pádraig positioned Stephen in front of him for the processional and handed him the lectionary. "Here, hold this out in front of you like a steering wheel. A little higher. Look solemn. And remember to speak up clearly and project when you read Jesus."

"Read Jesus? What does that mean anyway?"

"We're reciting the Passion today. You're standing in for Jesus, reading his part."

Stephen turned, wide-eyed to confront Pádraig, but before he could object, Pádraig spun him to face forward and gave him a shove between the shoulder blades propelling

268

him into the sanctuary with the lectionary in the lead.

38.

"I thought that went rather well, Stephen. Thank you very much for your help." Pádraig flipped the red vestment over the back of his head and caught it in mid-air to give it the proper fold to tuck it away in the drawer.

"Do you think so?" Stephen asked, scowling. "I'm not so sure. I felt bathed in dirty looks out there. I mean, shock and surprise at first, you know, 'what the devil is that one doing up there with Father?' But then at least a few of them seemed a little angry. To me, at least."

Pádraig shrugged. "Don't take it too personally. They're used to the same people doing the same thing year in and year out. Change is hard in a small place like this."

"Well, you'd know better than I. But did you not notice a few in the back leaving during the reading of the Passion? "

"It's just a bit longish for some of them. Happens every year. They like to say they came to church on Good Friday but they'd rather not stay for the whole thing."

"Okay, well it's your place of employment," Stephen shrugged. "I still think casting an atheist to play Jesus must have been a little offensive to some of them."

Pádraig moved about the sacristy putting things in their places, checking to see that the drawers and cabinets were closed up. "Oh, I don't think you're really an atheist, Stephen. Not truly," he said distractedly.

"Oh, really," Stephen said. "I think I would know. What makes you so sure I'm not?"

Pádraig shook his head. "You're too intelligent to be so sure about something you think is subject to proof, yet can't be proved one way or another, according to your logic."

"No, that's wrong. Have you read any Hume at all?"

"Some. Not much. Probably not as much as you have. I'm more of a St. Augustine man myself."

"Exactly," Stephen said poking a finger at the ceiling. "Where you end up is completely dictated by where you start."

"What do you mean by that? I'll put St. Augustine up against any philosopher of any century on rigor and depth."

"Rigor? I don't think so. All of St. Augustine's proofs of God's existence were reductive. 'There must be a God because all of this is too wonderful to be explained by physical nature.' Basically, all of his work comes down to explaining the gap between the limitations of what we can observe and what else he hopes is out there by saying 'there must be a God.' That's not rigor. That's a leap."

Pádraig continued tidying up the sacristy, absently listening to Stephen. "Sure, I'll grant you that. We call it a leap of faith."

"Right. 'Leap of faith.' I wondered when you'd trot that one out. It's not a leap of faith. It's a keep-your-eyes-closed dive of desperation. It's a way of going through life putting your hands over your ears and humming loud as you can to shut out the reality of biology."

"The reality of biology?"

"Yes. One day each and every one of us will stop breathing, and that will be it. The battery runs out and the lantern doesn't work any more. And can't replace its own battery. The cat dies, and...."

"Enough, enough. I get it. We just don't agree on this. I'm not a lantern, and you're not a cat. There's more to us humans than biology or current. We go on in a fashion after this. That's what the afterlife is all about, even if you don't believe in a throne up in the clouds with God sitting on it."

"Really, Pádraig. For such an intelligent man, I just don't understand how you can ignore the evidence. You really should read more Hume. Now, that man was a philosopher and a scientist. His work Of Miracles, for example. He starts with the laws of nature -- people can't walk on water as a normal everyday event -- and tries to evaluate the possibilities that the laws of nature were bent or broken or suspended in a particular instance."

"By which method he rules out every miracle ever written about, I gather." Pádraig crossed his arms with a sour look at Stephen.

"Well, don't make it sound like he did it with short cuts. It's a thoughtful analysis."

"Thoughtful but devastating. That's how the skeptics always come at us."

"If they're winning so consistently, maybe you should think of switching sides."

"Unlikely at my stage in life, even if I were open to considering it. Anyway, I still don't think you're a real atheist."

"Why not?"

Pádraig opened the curtain on the small ventilation window high on the sacristy wall facing the harbor. The sun was slanting in at an angle that hit high up on the opposing wall. The room was flooded with rose and gold colored light. Pádraig and Stephen stood quietly for a moment, stunned at the sudden shimmering.

"Stephen, did you ever wonder what makes the sunset so beautiful?"

The play of the light had calmed Stephen down from his rant. "Often, I do," he said.

"Hah!" said Pádraig wheeling upon him with a grin. "I knew it! You're not an atheist. You're an agnostic!"

Stephen reddened and clenched his fists by his sides. "You are the most exasperating, pedantic son of a...." Pádraig couldn't help laughing, and it was this that made Stephen run from the sacristy, his rucksack smacking the door frame and splintering the wood just above the strike plate.

39.

Pádraig wandered sleepily through the rest of the day. Foot traffic in the village was down to a minimum. Most of the shops except the newsstand were closed, and even that operating on reduced hours. The pub was closed, but the residents' bar was scheduled to open near midnight, and Ellen's definition of 'resident' was broad enough to accommodate everyone eager for a drink at the end of Good Friday.

Even the tee-totallers had a reason to come out near midnight on Good Friday. To the north, the people of Donegal had a long standing tradition of setting off a moderately impressive display of fireworks at the end of Good Friday, near midnight, sometimes a little later if their prior celebration made them lose track of time.

Pádraig was a little sorry he'd sent Stephen off in a fury and thought of going by the house to make amends, but it seemed like such a long walk. The thought of driving over was even more exhausting at the moment. He holed up in his study with a pot of tea, reading bulletins and periodicals he'd piled up and been meaning to get to for months. With Mrs. O'Flannelly still in and out of the house on various errands, he couldn't safely just go have a lie-down. He forced himself to stay upright, despite the inviting look of the divan in his study. Too short for proper napping for a man of Pádraig's height, but still appealing at the moment.

He started at the sound of a knock at his door. "Father, can I freshen the tea pot for you?" Mrs. O'Flannelly called. Pádraig rubbed the top of his head vigorously to wake himself up. He looked down at what he'd been reading and realized he'd turned the pages to the end of the article, but had no memory of what he'd read. He cleared his throat, "Yes, thank you very much. Please come in."

Mrs. O'Flannelly turned the knob and entered, holding the tea kettle's handle in a kitchen towel. She lifted the lid of the tea pot and poured in more steaming water in a slow stream, meaning to stir up the settled tea leaves as little as possible. She nestled the lid back atop the pot.

"You look a little tired, Father. Are you feeling all right?"

Pádraig smiled as warmly as he could manage. He hoped he looked convincing. "Oh, quite well, thank you, Mrs. Flannelly." She looked at him strangely. He replayed his last sentence in his mind, wondering what had bothered her. "Pardon me, Mrs. O'Flannelly." He laughed nervously, dismissing his own error. "The Triduum is a busy time, as you know, and a bit demanding on a solo priest. But I'm fine, thanks for asking."

"I certainly do see how demanding it is on you, Father. I just wonder whether it might be a good idea next year to phone up Monsignor Hargadon over there in Dublin and ask him if he doesn't know of an extra priest here or there who could come and help at Eastertime."

Pádraig kept smiling and hoped he hadn't visibly recoiled at Mrs. O'Flannelly's well meaning suggestion. "I appreciate the thought, Mrs. O'Flannelly. Let me take it under advisement. Of course, he'd have to stay here, and that would be an imposition on you. I'd have to weigh that," he said, hoping he was building a bridge to her never raising the issue again.

"Oh, no, Father, it'd be no trouble at all to look after another priest. After all, I had two when you were here with Monsignor Hargadon. Even if it meant a little extra work, my sister could help. Maybe the visiting priest would fall enough in love with the parish to stay on. That would be lovely, don't you think?" She puttered about squaring away the elements of the tea tray, clearing away discarded lemon wedges. "And I think you could do with some proper companionship, if you don't mind my saying so."

Through the cobwebs of fatigue, it dawned on Pádraig that something offensive had just been said, but it took his mind a moment to catch up with the instinct to respond. "What ever do you mean by that, Mrs. O'Flannelly?" he asked cautiously.

She laughed nervously, and Pádraig realized that she had not been expecting any disagreement on this point. She wiped with her kitchen towel around the surface of the tea tray, even the clean parts, busying herself. "Well, I just mean that Mr. Attergood is around the rectory and the church quite a lot these days."

"It's Dr. Attergood, just so you know. What's wrong with his being around here? He's a smart fellow. I enjoy talking to him." Pádraig felt the back of his neck growing warm.

Mrs. O'Flannelly concentrated fiercely on the tea tray, then moved with her wiping to the surface of the desk, what little of it lay exposed, free of the fan of papers that Pádraig had spread across it. "Well, he's not Catholic, is he now?"

"No, but we're allowed to talk with lots of people, aren't we now? It's the lack of talking that has the troubles all stirred up in the North, don't you agree?"

"Well, that's debatable from what I hear. But at least they're Christian, or they think they are, the Prods."

"The Protestants?"

"Yes, them."

"And so your problem with Dr. Attergood is that he's not Christian?" He'd never had a conversation like this with Mrs. O'Flannelly. He knew he should cut it off, but was too angry to obey his better instinct.

"Well, no, Father. I think you know what I'm saying. It isn't right."

Pádraig stubbornly refused to let her off the hook from saying what he knew she meant. "What isn't right, Mrs. O'Flannelly?"

She finally tore her focus away from the tea tray and the desk and stood facing him, hands on hips. "He's queer, Father. Everyone in the village is saying it. You must know, too. You see how he is. It's against the Bible, now, isn't it, Father, for like to be with like. Everyone knows that. It isn't right, his spending so much time here, and at odd hours to boot. I'm worried for you, Father. I know, of course, more than anyone, that you're not like that, and I'm telling them when they smirk about it to stop it right away. But it's hard to make people stop talking."

Pádraig took a long look at her. He glanced at his reflection in the window glass against the dark sky outside, his jowls painfully clenched and bulging. Saying anything more, he realized, would be an irrevocable turn for him with Mrs. O'Flannelly and the spokes of gossip that ran from her and deep into the village. He let his breath out very slowly, trying to calm himself.

"It's late, Mrs. O'Flannelly. Why don't you take the rest of the evening off? And don't worry about me, and not about Dr. Attergood. He's a good man and a good friend." He felt relief at the end of this painful conversation. Mrs. O'Flannelly backed out of the room with the used remains of Pádraig's earlier tea. "Good night, Father. I shan't worry about you, but I can't say for others. They're whisperers, the lot of them."

That's one thing to call them, Pádraig thought as he waited for her to make her way through the kitchen and out the back door. He heard her lock the door from the outside and jiggle the handle, as she always did, to make sure it was locked.

He was secure in his aloneness now and bereaved in his loneliness. He reached into the cabinet under the atlas, and pulled out his Cutty Sark and the two glasses with his left hand. He stared at the two glasses for a moment and returned one to the shelf. It had been only a week that he hadn't been drinking alone, but rather in Stephen's company. He remarked to himself on the oddness of his becoming accustomed to his company so quickly. He'd observed the formalities of community life when required in his order, but kept to himself as much as he could without being called out for it. He'd grown comfortable as a friendless man, and having a friend now was a puzzle to him. He put the idea "on the shelf in the study", as he visualized the interior space of his mind, for further contemplation when he wasn't so tired.

He sipped away a good bit at the bottle, but vowed not to drink below the top of the label, then revised this to allow himself to hit the top of the sails of the ship that marked the whiskey's brand. He glanced at his watch and was surprised to see its hands approaching half eleven. Might as well wait outside for the fireworks, he thought. If I don't go out now, I'll fall asleep in here and miss it altogether." He grabbed the long black raincoat he used when he visited parishioners and headed out the door, taking care not to lock himself out of reentry to the rectory's front hallway.

His gait was steady but slow as he crossed the street and looked around for the best place to position himself. He settled on the west-most bench-chair facing the waterfront. He wasn't drunk, he reasoned, but he was extremely tired and might appear so to someone with whom he had to engage at any length. Dressed entirely in black, with even the notch of his collar covered up by the raincoat, and sitting off to the side from where the most of the villagers would gather up, the ones who still had the stamina to come out at this hour, would keep him safe from reprobation. He fell heavily into the chair, the wood now weathered in even the few short years since the Council had donated it and situated it. It was a little bigger than a chair for one; perhaps the Council had envisioned couples' romance or reconciliation on these benches. Pádraig had never seen either in the long afternoons he had spent gazing out his study's window.

Pádraig slouched in the chair so that the back of this head rested on its back. His head tilted back and his gaze softened as he stared into the night sky. A few highway sounds drifted in from the distant N15, truck brakes applied as the village of Cliffony came into view sooner than bone-tired drivers counted upon. A few shore and bog creatures croaked and chirped. Pádraig rested comfortably in this bubble of familiarity, pleasantly suspended in anticipation of the coming show, which was why he was so startled to hear his name called by a strange voice.

"Father Hart, I'm sorry to disturb you. But I wondered if you could spare a few moments of your time."

The voice was soft and friendly, and very close by. Pádraig's eyes flew open; he paused mentally for a second on the strangeness of this: he remembered nothing about deciding to close them.

He sat upright and turned towards the voice. He jumped in his seat at the sight of a man crouched right next to him, hand on the armrest of the chair. He calmed himself at the placid mien of the man; he felt no threat coming from him and applied his usual discipline of seeing a potential parishioner in everyone he met. He let his breath out slowly and gave out a nervous laugh. "I didn't hear you come up."

The man looked around at the ground. "No, the turf is soft here. They've done a nice job with the planting. It's hard to get things to take root with the salt air here. Plus, I'm very quiet by nature. Do you mind if I sit on the bench with you?"

"No, not at all." Pádraig sat up straight in the chair and pulled the tails of his coat close to himself to make room for the man. As Pádraig's visitor moved out of his crouch to take his seat, he stood to his full height. Pádraig couldn't be sure whether it was his own seated position or the man's actual dimensions that gave the impression of gob-stopping grandeur. When the man folded himself into the seat next to Pádraig, though, his knees settled into position as high as his chest, deciding the question.

"It's a beautiful night, isn't it?" the man mused looking out over the harbor.

"That it is," Pádraig agreed. He glanced sideways at the man. "I'm a little embarrassed that you know my name, but I don't know yours. How is that?" Pádraig asked.

"Oh, don't trouble yourself over that, Father. We've never crossed paths. You've no reason to know my name. But your profession gives you a certain celebrity, locally at least. So it's not unusual that I should know your name but you not mine." The man fell silent and returned to gazing out at the distant ship lights along the horizon. Pádraig continued to study him. "What is your name, if I may ask?"

"Of course, Father. In fact, I've come specially tonight to introduce myself." He extended his left hand, which Pádraig gripped cautiously. The man laughed and offered his right hand instead. "I'm sorry. We do things a little differently where I'm from. I sometimes forget to switch over. Anyway, my name is Tan Mithy, and I'm very pleased to meet you."

Pádraig's jaw dropped instantly, then snapped shut in a too-late recovery of amazement. Tan Mithy laughed. "It's all right. I get that reaction a lot. I gather you know who I am, then?"

"Only by second hand reports, which I was inclined to disbelieve until just about now."

"Ah, that must mean you're getting your information from The Four." Pádraig nodded numbly. "Aye, they don't represent us very well nowadays, I'm afraid." Tan Mithy shook his head slowly. "It's a shame you didn't get to talk with your grandfather about me. About us."

"My grandfather...you knew him? He...."

"Consorted with us? That's usually the word that comes up about now. Yes, he went about with us a good deal. He was a good friend and a great and worthy emissary between our peoples. But that's not what I've come about tonight."

Pádraig felt a surge of alertness coming up through his drowsiness. "I'm not in any...danger talking to you, am I?"

"Danger to your immortal soul? Nah, not a bit, if that's what you're worried about. This being Good Friday and Friday the 13th to boot -- coincidences that may make you uncomfortable, I understand. But there's nothing that could be done about the timing. However! Danger to your belief system? That's a different risk. You may be in danger there, I'll acknowledge that. But it's important that we talk. Are you game to continue?"

Pádraig ordered his jaw to return to normal position. "Yes, of course. What is it you say is so important?"

"It's about the girl, Father. You call her Fianna."

"Fianna Gunning? Yes, yes, of course that's what we call her. It's her name. Why should we call her anything else?"

"We'll come back to that. I wanted you to know that she's safe."

"Thank God!" Pádraig exclaimed. "Where is she? Do you know where she is?"

"Aye, that I do. She's been away. She's coming back."

"But where is she now, right now? Can't I go and collect her, bring her home?"

Tan Mithy rested a hand on Pádraig's arm; Pádraig registered his touch as heavy and warm even through his coat. "No, Father, best I take care of that, and I give you my word I will, very shortly. I just think it best that I precede it with a bit of an explanation.

"It's hard to know where to start. Why don't I ask you how much you know about us?"

"Until a few days ago, almost nothing. But I gather, if I can believe it, that you've got ancient attachments here and that you drop in on us from time to time. Mostly in a friendly way, I'm told, and that I really would like to believe at this moment in particular."

Tan Mithy laughed softly. "Yes, yes, always friendly. But we're often misunderstood, sadly. We have what we like to think of as a broader perspective on the world and its continuity. Sometimes what seems like the right course to your folk is quite definitely the wrong one from our vantage point. It puts us in conflict quite unnecessarily from time to time."

"What makes you so much wiser than we are, assuming you're right?"

"We've been at it much longer that your race, for starters. And we've got the advantage of being closer to things. Closer to the earth and what it's saying about the rhythms of experience. The gyre of history, as your man Yeats put it." Tan Mithy shook his head. "A shame they branded him mad for writing about it."

"Were you…in touch with him?"

"A bit, yes. But we're not too fond of being put under a

microscope. Curiosity for its own sake is not a good reason to be coming out to poke at us. We were on speaking terms with him, let's leave it at that. We regarded him as a useful sort. The days are long gone when we could visit your race openly without frightening someone to death or having them call out the pitchforks and nooses. Go betweens like Will were a useful way of confirming that we're still here without the risks of doing it in person."

"Do you have other go-betweens? Currently, for example?"

"Well, your grandfather was one, we've touched on that. But he's gone, bless him, it's Friday."

"You have to say that, too? I thought it was just the humans who had to say that when they mentioned your people."

Tan Mithy laughed heartily and slapped his knee. "So you've heard that one? Truth be told, no one has to say bless anyone on our side or yours. But it's such a charming custom, we've adopted it, too! At least some of us think it's charming. Others may be having a joke at the expense of the gullible. But you were asking about go betweens. The answer is yes. In every generation, we reach out to someone in this area, in Connacht, to establish a relationship, a channel of communication. We're the Connacht host of the gentry, so our go between, our consul, if you'd like to call it that, is always from this area. The gentry up in Ulster have their own, the one in Meath another, and so on."

Pádraig became aware of Stephen standing off to the left of the bench, just within his peripheral vision. He held his notebook like a clipboard and was struggling to position his torch, gripped beneath his left arm, to shine on the page to take notes. "You say you're the Connacht host, and there's one in Meath, too?" he asked.

"Yes, that's right," Tan Mithy responded agreeably.

"But one's a province and one's a county. So are you organized by province or county, generally?"

"A little of both," Tan Mithy said. "Out here in the west, we can spread out a bit. But where it's more populous back east, we gather up by county."

Stephen seemed satisfied with this response, which he noted down. He receded from Pádraig's field of vision.

"So you're rather well organized. But what is it you do, actually? Besides kidnapping people, as it seems you've nearly admitted with respect to Fianna."

"That's not at all the case," Tan Mithy said, but not the least bit defensively. "I'll explain her circumstances in a moment, but let me answer your original question: What do we do?

"Our work in the world was finished long ago, making this place ready for your race. We yielded it to you for your care and stewardship. We watch on you, stop up the gaps when they occur, when the harvest fails or comes in scarce, for example. We step in when death toys with a person, entrapping him or her in the ugly, frightening place between life and demise. That's another example."

"You're saying you engage in mercy killings?"

"Not exactly. We just make death stop taking delight in the end of a life."

"Sound like the same thing to me," Pádraig said with a pout, wondering about his own grandfather's decline and departure.

"Call it what you wish. We provide a necessary function."

"And apart from that? It doesn't sound like enough to keep you busy."

Tan Mithy shrugged and gestured at the night sky. "We enjoy life, day and night. There is so much beauty here. We paint the scenery with music and dancing. We eat and drink what the land gives up."

"It's a good life, then?"

"Yes, very good. Not free of care and worry, but very good on the whole."

"What should worry you when you spend all your time singing and dancing?"

Tan Mithy turned his gaze to the dark ocean. "When we yielded this land to your race, we did it to make peace with another people who loved it almost as much as we did. They were your ancient ancestors, the Milesians. They let us off fairly easy even though they had us at the point of their swords; we were fortunate in that regard. But the bargain came with some strings attached."

"Such as?"

"No children to be born among us. Our population was to remain static for the ages so as not to burden the land with overpopulation. That was their rationale for the demand, and on the surface it seemed reasonable. We didn't have a great deal of time to accept it or reject it; those were the only options offered. There was no negotiation over it to be had. So we agreed. I think their real concern was that if we replenished our ranks, we'd rise up and be trouble for them again one day."

"It doesn't sound unthinkable to make a bargain like that. I mean, myself, I've agreed never to have children. Part of the profession."

"Ah, but you still live among children, don't you? You see them everyday in your profession, at the school, in the church, in the homes you visit. That's the thing we still miss, even more than not having any of our own. When you've lived as long as we have, you're desperate for anything that will make you see things in a new way, help you eke out a different way of turning the prism to see colors and textures and ways of thinking and talking about everything around you." He looked down at the backs of his hands, each one of them large enough to wrap around a football. "We miss it terribly."

"And that's why you steal children like Fianna?" It was an angry question, or Pádraig meant it to be, and he was puzzled at how pacific and drowsy it sounded on delivery.

"I'll have to correct you again on that, Father. We don't steal anyone. Everyone likes to think that -- that their husband or sister has been dragged away in the dead of night. After all, they think, who could love them more than those left behind at home? The fairies have taken them away, kicking and screaming, or else have put the glam-charm on them to trick them into coming away. As usual, it's more self-delusion than truth. They never pause to think that their loved ones are simply unhappy where they are, and long to be somewhere else. For the main part, we just invite them to come home with us and they're only too happy to come along."

"Fair to say that Fianna was lonely, unhappy, made the more so by her father, that much I can say is true."

"Exactly. It was plain as day to anyone who saw her. And spending as much time alone as she did, it was easy for us to approach her, and just ask her if she'd like to come away with us. She said yes with such brightness as none of us has ever seen in her, as if she fell in love with the idea as soon as she heard it. In fact, we had a bit of a contest between the troop up in Ben Bulben and the merrrow based over by the Red Islands. We nosed them out in getting to her first, but I know for a fact that she'd still be welcome there."

"But why did you take her, I mean why her as opposed some other girl or lad? I'd heard that you took away the beautiful and the talented. The best athletes and dancers. I'm fond of her, of course, and more prone to see the gifts in her than most. But what was it that drew you in to her?"

"Well, apart from the opportunity presented, there was another factor."

"What was that?"

"We wanted to protect her, ensure her safety."

"What!" Pádraig shouted. "How could you possibly be more concerned about her safety than her own mother, for example, and her parish? That's just outrageous as an excuse."

Tan Mithy waited for Pádraig's ire to subside. "You know about her writing, don't you?" he asked quietly. "Yes, we found a composition book written in her hand. I'm aware she's written some poems."

Tan Mithy turned to face Pádraig. "Ah, that's just it, Father. It's not just 'some poems'. It's poetry. It's elegy of the sort that hasn't been conceived or committed to ink and page for generations. She needed a safe place to write it. We invited her away to provide such a place, and she accepted in part because of her emotional state. But at some level, she surely knew, and certainly knows now, that she has the talent of a firebrand and the responsibility to go with it."

"What do you mean, 'a safe place'?"

"These words, her words, have power. They're not to be scattered carelessly. They have the power to make things happen. And exercising that kind of power has consequences."

Pádraig shrugged. "I still don't know what you mean. Her words have power, you say. What kind of power?"

Tan Mithy sighed. "I'm a little surprised you're not more schooled about this, the history of poetry in this country. But then again, it pre-dates St. Patrick. I gather your interest in history relates only to what happened from his arrival forward. Maybe that accounts for your unfamiliarity."

"I'm not an encyclopedia," Pádraig said defensively.

"Never mind, I can bring you along to where you need to be," Tan Mithy said patiently. "Once, a long time ago, the poets of Ireland were of high rank in the land. Only the kings themselves were regarded as bearing higher rank. But even the kings deferred to the poets in some matters. They were that powerful.

"Now in that time, there were all different specialties among the poets, each with its particular colors and robes and equated with a rank in the profession of bard. A lot like your church nowadays. You're all clerics with the same basic sacramental authority. But you specialize in orders, like yours, the Jesuits. And I gather that the Jesuits are the top of the heap, or at least most people have come to think that."

"How did you know that I'm a Jesuit?" Pádraig asked.

"Oh, I've heard it said here and there." Tan Mithy's answer left Pádraig wondering what else he'd overheard about him. He pushed the thought aside to concentrate on the lesson at hand. "The reason that the bards were so highly regarded had to do with the responsibilities entrusted to them.

"Some were chroniclers, responsible for memorizing and being able to deliver long and detailed accounts of the generations of the clan, complete with all the branches of the family tree. The precision and reliability of the chronicler were crucial, because it was vital testimony to establish the legitimacy of the lineage of the current king. It wouldn't do for a chronicler to forget part of the recitation or mispronounce a name because the ruler could tumble on the basis of such a mistake."

"An important function in pre-history, I suppose. If you can't write the thing down in a book and carry it with you, better to have someone memorize it and make them tag along with the clan," Pádraig observed. "Having a memory good enough to do it requires skill and practice. But not much creativity."

"No, no creativity at all. In fact, creativity was the opposite of what was wanted in a chronicler. Creativity could get someone dethroned or disinherited. And you're right about this practice being pre-historic. It was centuries longer before a writing culture and a written language emerged. Even then, the writings didn't completely replace the oral tradition of chronicling.

"The absence of creativity in this rank of bards is what put them on the bottom rung of the bardic ranks. Next above them were the entertainers, responsible for being able to perform on feast days by reciting popular stories from a mental library. For these troubadours, memory was an essential tool as well, because the code of the bards required these poets to be able to recite any of hundreds of stories in the catalogue, if you will, at the beck and call of the king. And these were not stories in the sense of an anecdote, not at all. Many of the stories were epics that took hours to recite."

"What sort of story kept the crowds listening for that long?"

"Lots of stories about stolen cattle, very popular, like the Tale of the White Bull and the Cattle Raid of Cooley. The clans never fought so much about land or territory; there was plenty of that to go around. Still is – just look around. But cattle represented wealth and the sustainability of the clan, definitely worth fighting over, and easy pickings during the north to south cattle drives that happened every year to put the cattle in the best meadows of the season.

"But what I'm really coming around to telling you about is the top rank of the poets, the fili. It's hard to explain what they were in ancient society. Usually people describe them as philosophers or seers. They were that, but more than that. They were the thread of tradition across the generations. They were the ones who decided which stories should be included in the catalogue of epics, for example, and how they should be captured. They were also lawgivers. Many of the laws and norms of the time were embedded in the epics – lessons about how wives should treat husbands, how children should treat their parents, fair course of dealing in commerce. All these subjects were covered. Somebody had to decide what the content of those lessons should be. That was the job of the fili.

"They were also the connection between the people and the land. They schooled the people in reverence for the mountains, the sea, the harvest, the forest. They kept the cycle of seasons by marking them with feasts and solemn observances to remind people of their dependence on the earth and the importance of good stewardship."

"So these were the tree worshippers, then?"

"For the glib, it comes down to that. But look at the bigger picture. You had the fili giving the laws, conducting the sacred observances and maintaining the continuity of tradition by committing it to poetry and epics. They built schools to train promising young men and some women to maintain their numbers over the centuries. And this was no summer school. Seven years of training in poetic composition, and none of it on paper. Students composed poetry on assigned subjects lying on their cots in their tiny rooms in total darkness. All of it committed to memory.

"All of this was the padding around the real role of the fili: the dredging up of insights about how this visible world connects with the invisible. They trained themselves to live and work apart, except for periodic forays among the people for ceremonies and instruction. Living apart from the workaday world gave them the freedom to think and meditate and arrive at insights about things that pass most people by."

"So what happened to them all?"

"St. Patrick happened to them. They didn't disappear all

at once, these institutions, the fili and the lower ranks. It was gradual. First, and this had nothing to do with St. Patrick I admit, the fili decided to specialize to get rid of some of the more mundane parts of their work. They gave the druids the ceremonial responsibilities and the brehon the lawgiving tasks. That gave them more time for meditation and composition, which was exactly how they'd planned it.

"Second, it made them more vulnerable economically. Philosophizing and meditating don't pay good wages, so they were dependent upon the local king and his court for their income. They weren't hand to mouth, mind you; they were keen investors and put a lot of capital into their school buildings. Their larders and vaults weren't exactly empty, if you understand me. But as the Christian church got its footing with Patrick and his successors, they converted many petty kings. The Christian priests pressed the newly converted kings for financial support, and that put the squeeze on the fili and the other poetic ranks. But more on the fili than the others. A king can do without a philosopher, but having chroniclers and entertainers around is convenient. Even having a brehon judge in the court, or a druid to head up the feasts could be worthwhile. But no compelling need to pay the philosopher."

"So the filid died out?"

Tan Mithy sighed. "Yes and no. The best talent came from a handful of families, they discovered in the last few generations of the glory days. They concentrated on recruiting from the known branches of the O'Higgins, the O'Clerigans, the O'Conors and the O'Dalys."

A thought floated to Pádraig's conscious mind. "My mother's people…they're O'Dalys."

"I think you're catching on. But there's more to the story of the filid's demise. When funds got scarce, the filid didn't run through their reserves all at once. But when the stores began to dwindle, some of the filid had the nasty idea of making the kings sorry for being so tight with their purses."

"How did they do that?"

"What's the opposite of a blessing?"

"A curse?"

"Yes, exactly. It's said that the first curse in history was uttered by an Irish poet. It was the poet Cairbrey, unhappy with the hospitality served up to him by the king he was visiting. A famous king, too, named Bres, who should have known better. Giving and receiving hospitality were sterling social standards back then. Cairbrey was not just disappointed with the hospitality he received – the small, dark room, the stale bread and no ale at all – he was angry. So he fashioned a curse and cast it upon Bres as he left the court: 'Without food quickly served, without a cow's milk whereon a calf can grow, without a dwelling fit for a man under the gloomy night, without means to entertain a bardic company, let such be the condition of Bres.'

"As it happened, Bres was just as negligent in his kingship generally as he was at hospitality in particular. He was king of my people, the Tuath da Dannan, but his father was from our rivals the Fomorians, and he rather favored his cousins and family on that side. So the Tuath were unhappy with him to begin with and tickled to hear about the curse. They took to lifting it up by repetition. The curse took hold of him over a short time, his stores dwindled, he had no means to support his court and he fell from power."

"Well, but that needn't have been caused by the curse. If he was that unpopular with his own people it was only a matter of time before they got rid of him."

"Who can say whether it would have happened without the curse? But our histories say it happened because of the curse. The fact that people believed it was the cause raised up the power of the filid, too. It made every king in the land afraid of what might happen if cursed or even just satirized by a fili in verse. They called it 'being rhymed up', and it was to be avoided at all costs. The filid knew they were on to something. Sad to say, they saw the blackmail potential in the whole thing: pay up or be rhymed up. They took the kings along in the scheme. Some of it was just plain mean. There's the story of Orlin, a fili in County Leitrim. Just for fun, he told the king to pluck his eye out and give it to him, or else be rhymed up."

"Don't tell me he did it." Pádraig shuddered, too vividly imagining the sounds and sensations that would go with such an act.

"That he did. Or so they say." Tan Mithy shifted in his seat. "The filid weren't all so sinister as things came to an end, just the desperate ones. The ones who remained true to their art dwindled in numbers, but they continued to produce wonderful, moving, insightful works. Some of them even thought to write their poetry down. They saw that the oral tradition of passing things on wasn't going to last much longer. We're fortunate they did that. Otherwise we'd know little solid about them."

"But eventually, they died out, you say?" Pádraig's eyelids fluttered shut for a moment, then open again. He wondered whether he'd brought the bottle out to the waterfront with him. Sometimes a bit of whiskey is what you need to sharpen your perception, he thought. Sharing a drink with a stranger can't be a bad thing, he rationalized. He reached down and felt the ground around the legs of the bench and confirmed, to his disappointment, that the bottle was inside the rectory.

"Eventually, yes. And you can blame your man St. Patrick for that. He did such a compelling job of converting the kings, he and his bishops, that the next most natural thing for the new clergy to do was to ask the kings for financial support. Building monasteries, chapels, decorating them. The kings couldn't afford to support two systems of clergy, in effect. St. Patrick was pretty emphatic about which choice was the right one for the long run and the kings went along. St. Patrick wasn't sorry to see the filid fade away and take the druids with them.

"So the filid profession went away. But the talent for poetry, and the aptitude for insight and expression that inspires poetry that isn't just good, it's sublime those things runs in the clans that trained as filid for over a millennium They didn't disappear. It's in the genes, as they say.

"And lucky for us that it is. It's the only way we have to communicate with your world."

"What on earth do you mean by that? You and I are

sitting here talking, aren't we?"

Tan Mithy laughed softly. "This is highly unusual, though. We usually go through regular channels, very carefully established. Every so often, we manage to find one among you, a descendant of the O'Daly clan or one of the others, that still has the knack. Maybe not a poet, per se, not a writer-down of things. But someone with imagination. And without fear." He hunched forward, knees on elbows. "That part's very important. No fear. Not everyone can sit through a séance like this."

"I suppose I should be honored...or something like that."

Tan Mithy laughed and clapped Pádraig on the shoulder. "Let's see how you feel about all this in the morning. You probably still have questions about Fianna, I'm supposing."

"Yes, I do. More than a cat has kittens. I'm taking in that you made contact with Fianna because she was special in the way you say. Maybe because she's an O'Daly, back in the limbs of the family tree, my mother's side?"

Tan Mithy nodded slightly. "Aye, that's it. The truth is that we fell in love with her poetry. It touched us, called out to us in ways we hadn't heard in many decades, centuries really, dropping the wall between your world and ours -- between our world and all worlds, actually. People may say we glamoured her away, but the truth is she uttered the glamm dicenn, the glamour words and magicked us."

Pádraig scowled and shook his head. "I don't understand. Perhaps I just lack an appreciation of it, but what I saw of her writings, just glancing through her notebooks, was admirable in its imagery and thoughtfulness, but I wouldn't have regarded it as awesome, as you say."

"Meaning no disrespect, Father, but I do agree you lack an appreciation of it. First of all, you haven't experienced the tenth part of what she's produced. I say 'produced' rather than written because much of her most profound work is only in her mind, called forth for recitation on proper coaxing and with appropriate ceremony. We'd heard her read out segments of it when she was alone in her rath, or up on the bluff. We knew right away what she could do in the proper circumstances."

A flicker of connection stirred in Pádraig's mind. "Fianna wanders the bluff? I've never seen her there. I'm up there all the time. I waste a lot of time counting waves, I'm ashamed to admit."

"It's no waste of time, Father. It's lending yourself back to the province and everything that surrounds it and comes with it. Fianna is more of an after dark seeker. Your grandfather liked the afternoon light, just as you do."

"He spent time up there, too? I never knew that. I thought it was my own guilty pastime."

"You'd be surprised how many generations of O'Daly's have spent time up there, staring out from the rocks. How do you think your grandda' met Coomarra?"

"Not you too!" Pádraig protested, then softened when he saw Tan Mithy's impassive expression. "So that's true?"

"Aye, it is. He did the right thing opening all those soul cages, I don't mind telling you. But they still complain about it among themselves. Fianna could have had a home among them, had she wanted, though. They still admire the family and its talents. They'd have been glad to have a fili among them. But we approached her first."

"But how, how did that happen, exactly?"

Tan Mithy let out a long slow breath. "The tradition is that we don't tell any of your people exactly how it happens. We might have a stampede of the curious and insincere banging at our doors. But there's no rule against telling you, someone of your profession and discretion. I can rely on you not to repeat what I say?"

"Absolutely, sir." Pádraig wondered whether he should make the sign of the cross on his shoulder and breast to give the promise due solemnity, but stopped himself on the grounds of piety.

"You know she came out of church that day and got home before her mother."

"Yes, that much we figured out. That and her quarrel with her father."

Tan Mithy snorted. "Rather too one-sided to be a

quarrel, I'd say. He was on her in a flash berating her for her problem, the one you tried to help her with, calling her a liar and an attention seeker. 'I'll give you all the attention you'll want,' he was shouting at her."

"You heard and saw all this?"

"My people did. We'd been fascinated with her for some time, and then worried about her, so we stayed rather close at all times."

"What about when I took her to Dublin?"

"You were out of our jurisdiction, of course, but we asked the Meath host to keep an eye on her for us. Turned out you were there so briefly it hardly mattered. Anyway, you've figured out what happened next. He took the belt to her, held her tight by the arm while he whipped her. She did the only thing she could. She bit him. That made him finally let her go, and she ran."

Pádraig smiled a little to himself. He hadn't been sure whether to believe Ned's accusation last Sunday of Fianna's feral outburst. But Tan Mithy had confirmed. Fianna's resolve and resourcefulness. Pádraig privately cheered her dealing a punishment to Ned that he surely deserved.

"She ran all the way down here to the quay where she pushed Ned's boat off its moor and took it around to the Red Islands. I think she had a vague idea that she'd jump under the waves and be done with it, flogged up against the rocks when she'd worn herself out swimming. But I think she also knew there was something strange and inviting out there. None of us saw this part, but I think she got a greeting from one of the merrow, and friendly though they may have meant to be, their appearance is a bit offputting."

"Green and blue, is it, with a pig's nose?" Pádraig heard himself offer the description with more certainty than he knew he had.

"Quite right. It's as if you've seen one, but I suppose you might just as well have heard a good description."

"The latter. I think," Pádraig toured his memory to decide if he was sure where the image had come from, and came up empty.

"Anyway, they offered her an invitation, we think, but she declined."

"I've heard something about needing the right sort of cap to be able to visit them under the waves," Pádraig said slowly, testing out the bounds of his knowledge.

"Quite right," Tan Mithy confirmed. "A red cap. Some sort of magicked scuba gear, it is. Your grandfather...."

"I know, I know," Pádraig covered his ears. "He had one. I know." He took his hands away from his ears. "We found one, a red cap, in Ned's boat, when we located it, abandoned over there by the Islands."

"Our people caught up with her when she swam ashore. I don't think she was afraid of the merrow, mind you. That's one of the things we see in her, her fearlessness."

"She just found them to be very, very ugly?" He began to laugh. Tan Mithy joined him. "Yes, extremely ugly. I think it's the pig noses that hurt them in the recruitment." Pádraig bent over laughing. Tan Mithy laughed until he could barely speak. "What self-respecting teenage girl," he finally pushed out, "would want to spend eternity with a pig-nosed tribe?"

Pádraig's laughter ground to a halt. "Eternity?" he said. "But you said you'd bring her back. And eternity, that's not for you or the merrow or anyone but God to say what her eternity will be."

Tan Mithy turned sideways to face Pádraig and put his hand on Pádraig's shoulder. "Now, now. I'm sorry I've upset you. I was speaking with a bit too much familiarity. I said I'd bring her back, and I will. And the eternity I'm talking about, well...you can think of it as a suspension of time. Not a judgment about who spends how much time where in the end of it all. Does that sit better with you?"

Pádraig calmed himself and agreed that it did sound more reassuring, put that way. But he couldn't put out of his mind the thought that the medicine had been sweetened, but was still bitter and unpleasant underneath the flavoring.

Tan Mithy smiled pleasantly at Pádraig, then turned his gaze back to the ocean. The moon had come up a bit, and made a soothing shimmer near the horizon blending into the tidal channel then running away from the shore. "I'll be going soon, Father. Thanks so much for your time. Most of my people aren't too keen on speaking to priests, but you're different. I'll have to tell them you're all right."

Pádraig shifted his eyes toward Tan Mithy without turning his head. "Um, does that mean I'd be getting a lot more visits like this, then? Because I'm not sure...."

Tan Mithy laughed heartily and clapped Pádraig's shoulders. "I'll discourage steady traffic. But it's good to know we can count on talking to you in an emergency. You've held up well throughout all this, including my visit, and we thank you for that."

"My pleasure to be of service. I think."

"Let's just enjoy the view for another few minutes, then."

"One more thing, though, if you don't mind," Pádraig said, fighting to hold the thought long enough to ask the question.

"What is it, Father?"

"Why did you agree to bring her back?"

"Very simple, Father. It's because you asked. She's dear to you, and your family has been dear to us through the ages. And we never deny a request from a good vicar."

"How would you know whether I'm a good...."

"Oy! Pádraig!" Stephen yelled far too loudly for whatever time in the pitch black morning it was, Pádraig thought. He jumped in his seat, then turned to shush him.

"Will you shut up!" he yelled back in a hoarse whisper. "People are asleep!"

"Yeah, but we're not." Stephen's steps swerved through the dewy grass as he moved toward the bench. "Or at least I'm not. Are you napping out here? Under the stars?" His hand made an extravagant arc upward and outward toward the ocean.

"You're drunk, Stephen." Pádraig said quietly.

"Aye, I sure am," Stephen said triumphantly. "Spent the evening tippling with Joe. Who I might say holds his liquor much better than I do." He plopped down on the bench next to Pádraig. "Did you know that the Japanese make whiskey? I guess you can't really call it Scotch, the same way you can't call it Champagne, unless it actually comes from there. Still, it's damn good stuff. Yakitori, Yakazumi. Can't remember the name, but...."

"Stephen, please for the love of Mary, will you shut up? We have to discuss what just happened."

Stephen burped and held his breath to stifle a hiccup. "I was just now talking about what happened. To me. Tonight. I discovered Japanese Scotch, and it was wonderful."

"Damn you, Stephen, sober up, at least for a minute. We have to discuss what just happened here, just now, with Tan Mithy."

A visible frisson went through Stephen's neck and skull. He blinked hard, twice. "Okay. Sober now. What the devil are you talking about?"

"Don't fuck with me, Stephen. You were here and you know just as well as I do that he explained the whole thing, that Fianna wasn't really abducted, that she's the best poet in generations and he'll be bringing her back shortly."

Stephen sat bolt upright and laid a hand on Pádraig's forearm. "Wait, wait, wait. You had a whole conversation with Tan Mithy, and you think I was here with you?"

"I didn't think you were here, you were here. You asked him some questions yourself."

Stephen cocked his head and said slowly, "Okay, then. What questions did I ask him?"

"You asked him about the fairy hosts, were they organized by county or by province. And he said some of both depending on population density." Pádraig frowned in thought. "That's the only question I remember your asking at the moment."

Stephen stared at Pádraig for a moment, then giggled. "Honestly, Pádraig, do you think if I'd been here with the chance to interview the faerie king I'd have confined myself to jurisdictional questions?"

Pádraig thought for a few seconds. "Probably not," he growled. Stephen softened his tone. "Do you think you might have nodded off out here, maybe just briefly? I don't mean to put you on the spot, but there's the smell of something on you. Cutty Sark maybe? On an empty stomach after fasting all day?"

"I wasn't dreaming," Padriag shouted, slamming his fist on the arm of the bench. "It was too detailed, too vivid. Too full of things that I didn't know I knew that all make sense now. I couldn't have been asleep." His voice trailed off. "I don't think I could have been."

Stephen patted Pádraig's shoulder. "The most important thing you've said is that he's bringing her back, or she's coming back. If that's true, it's the result we've been looking for. But let's go inside and talk it through. I'll make some notes so we can preserve your impressions and whatever you can remember. If she doesn't turn up soon, maybe it'll be of some use to us."

"Right, we'll have some tea and sort it out," Pádraig said, leaning forward to launch himself off the bench. He stumbled, and Stephen caught his wrist to prevent his fall. They walked slowly and carefully across the grassy berm and up the steps of the rectory where the door stood wide open to the night air.

"I guess that's one way," Stephen wisecracked, closing the door behind them, "to make sure you don't lock yourself out when you go out for a walk half-pissed."

40.

Pádraig looked out the window of his study and noticed the first parts of morning arriving on the flat water of the harbor. He jingled the contents of his pocket and found his redstone, a glob of beach glass the size of a decent eraser. He took it out and rolled it between his thumb and palm. This gesture usually worked to slow down his thoughts and help him march them into order. But this morning, his thoughts were slow enough; that wasn't the problem. They just wandered about, resisting rank and file.

Stephen sat at Pádraig's desk, which looked massive with his small form piloting it. He had pulled the desk lamp close to his notebook and chewed a pencil as he flipped the pages back and forth over the night's notes. His right hand rested on the small stack of Fianna's journals. He looked up at Pádraig.

"I'm on the part where Tan Mithy tells you that his people fell in love with her poetry. And it's funny, that's what Joe and I were discussing last night."

"Hmm?" Pádraig murmured from his post at the window.

"Are you still with us, Pádraig? Or have you learned to sleep standing up?" Stephen called, a little louder than needed in the confines of the small study.

Pádraig lurched forward from the wall of the niche that framed the window and yawned so hard that Stephen could see his neck vibrate.   "I'm awake, I'm awake," Pádraig said unconvincingly.

"This remark that Tan Mithy made about her poetry, it's very interesting. I'm no scholar on the subject, but I know a little bit, and Joe's pretty well read. It's subjective, what makes good poetry. Does it move you or not? Does it call up an image that you never thought of, but fits just right for what needs to be said? But there're some objective measures, too. Things like scansion and meter and rhyme, and she certainly does seem to have it down. Listen to this, from one of her notebooks:

> Where fame and fortune intersect
> Reveal an empty place
> A plaza where the soul can starve
> From simple want of grace"

"That has a nice lilt to it," Pádraig acknowledged, pacing across the room. "It's a little more mature in sentiment than I'd expect from a sixteen year old."

"Yes to that," Stephen agreed. "It's not often you hear a teenager express herself as an anti-materialist. It's almost as if she's tapped into an older voice, some vein of experience not her own. Which makes sense in the context of what Tan Mithy was telling you."

"He said the talent ran in the O'Daly line. I mentioned to him that my mother's people were O'Dalys and he said something about 'now you're starting to catch on'." Pádraig rubbed his redstone insistently as if demanding it yield up confirmation of the connection.

"Here's some more of what she wrote:

> Half a world of hyacinths
> And nothing left for tea
> I'd fill the rest with hyacinths
> If thou wouldst stay with me."

"'If thou wouldst stay with me'?" Pádraig repeated.

"That doesn't sound like a teenager at all, not one in this century anyway."

"No, not at all. But there's something about this one, the hyacinth reference, that reminds me of a poem from one of the Persian poets." Stephen tapped his pencil on the desk. "Not Khayyam. Someone else. I can't remember at the moment."

Pádraig shook his head. "There's not a chance in heaven that Fianna's read or heard of any Persian poet, forgotten or remembered. Where would she see such a reference?"

Stephen tapped the pencil's eraser against his lips. "I don't know. We could ask Terence over at Open Books did she ever ask after poetry books, any ones in particular. Apart from that, I don't know where she would have gotten access. I assume you're saying that the school's library isn't so rich in the poetry department."

"Nope. Whoever bought the books before the buying stopped saw a giant flock of Irish poets, acquired their works, and then topped off the collection with a few English rhymers just to mimic worldliness, I think."

Stephen continued turning the pages, making occasional notes in the back pages of his Yeats text. "There's some wonderful imagery in here. 'I'd draw an atlas of the clouds/ To chart the sun's shadows/ As they touch your face/ In every hour of light.' It's speaking to an intimacy that…well, you know her and I don't. I don't doubt that it's her work. It's in her hand, and there's no reason to think she's copied it out of some other book. But where does she get this perspective, a sixteen year old girl?"

"I'm as flummoxed as you are. She was too quiet, too in upon herself for me to have had any idea what she was thinking, or that she was capable of this type of expression." Pádraig, drawn back to the window, saw Joe sweeping the plaza in front of Luck Boat. "You said you talked to Joe about Fianna's poetry. What did he say?"

Stephen rubbed his temples. "Hmm. That was a lot of liquor ago. But basically, he said that he had been talking with you a couple of days ago about how the others go after people who are the best dancers, the best athletes, the best spinner, the best butter churners. The best anything, apparently. And he said he was wondering aloud with you, what was Fianna the best at that got her taken away."

"I remember that, but only vaguely. I mustn't have been listening very closely."

"Yes, Joe noted that, too, that you brushed by the question. But after we'd read through a little of each of these notebooks, he got around to saying that maybe the poetry is what she's the best at. I mean, we'd need better readers than ourselves to say for sure, but we've got two doctorates between us and a damn well read Chinaman thinking what she's written is pretty fucking good."

Pádraig straightened and turned slowly toward Stephen. "Oh, sorry," Stephen muttered, "I curse when I'm tired." Pádraig continued to stare without speaking. "Okay, I curse even when I'm not tired. I curse all the time, I'm sorry, I'll try to…."

"Shut up! Shut up, will you?" Pádraig shouted. "That's what Tan Mithy said. That's what he said about why they took her. Well, he says they just invited her away and she said yes. But the point is what he said was 'We fell in love with her poetry.' He said it was beautiful and powerful and she needed a safe place to work on it, it was so powerful." Pádraig bounded toward the desk and began reading over Stephen's shoulder, carefully turning the pages, brittle from exposure to the air while in Fianna's rath, between his pointer and thumb. He paused on a page and read aloud: "'I am a patriot of her country/A pilgrim on her shores/Saluting the promise in her smiling eyes.' Who is she writing about, do you suppose?"

Stephen stretched his legs out straight in front of him and arched his back in the chair. He hoped Pádraig wasn't going to ask him to vacate the comfortable seat. "Well, as I understand it, a poem doesn't have to be about someone in particular even if it seems that it is. It might be something more abstract. But if I had to guess on this one, maybe it's the mother, but not Bertie. It's the mother who didn't raise her, her real mother, if that's not unfair to Bertie. She's a 'patriot' because she loves her real mother and a 'pilgrim' because she doesn't know her. And she holds on to the 'promise' that one day they'll be reunited."

"Listen to you. You could be a lit professor yet. Sounds plausible to me. Likely, even." Pádraig paused and looked at Stephen for a long moment. Stephen began to worry again about having to vacate the chair. He was just about to give in and stand up when Pádraig spoke. "There's something else he said. Tan Mithy. About the power of the language."

Stephen flipped forward to some pages they hadn't studied yet. "Well, yes. Her word choice is interesting, varied, precise. All the sort of things you'd expect of a good poet."

"No, no. That's not what I mean." He walked slowly back to the window bay. "Apparently this is just the tenth part of her work. Most of it isn't written down anywhere, according to Tan Mithy. She's a poet in the oral tradition, like the old ones at the poetry schools, composing verse in their heads, lying on prickly cots for hours a day in the total dark. And they did it all in Irish, of course, back then."

Stephen frowned. "Of course, that was the language of the day. Are you saying that Fianna composes and recites in Irish? Is she much of a scholar in it? I wouldn't have guessed so, judging from what you've said about her."

"That's the point. It's a puzzle. If she had any aptitude for the language, she never let on. She'd have passed her O levels, but just barely, hardly anything to sing about. But according to Tan Mithy, she was a past master of it. But the power of it, that he went on about, that's a bit lost on me. An image is an image, isn't it? What makes it better, if that's the right word, in English versus Irish versus Swahili, for that matter?"

Stephen riffled through the books at the bottom of his rucksack. "I think," he said, peering into the dark recess of the bag, "it has to do with the attachment of the image to the place it originated." He nodded in the general direction of the mountain he'd visited with Pádraig the night before last. "How much more powerful is it to write about Ben Bulben in Irish, using the idioms and images attached to the land that roots

Ben Bulben, than in English?"

Pádraig shrugged. "But the most famous poem ever written about Ben Bulben was in English, by Yeats, who spoke not a word of Irish as I understand it."

"But listen to this, Pádraig. Just listen to this and tell me it doesn't put you right back on the side of that mountain, in your mind, the other night." Stephen stuffed his thumb in the binder of a battered paperback to force it open while he read.

"Now they ride the wintry dawn
Where Ben Bulben sets the scene.'"

Pádraig shivered involuntarily. "Yes, I see what you mean. This is the poem where he writes his own epitaph?"

"Yes, he asks to be buried under Ben Bulben and says what he wants on his gravestone:

Cast a cold eye
On life, on death.
Horseman, pass by!'"

"That's pretty grim, even for a tombstone," Pádraig said. He rubbed his head and wished that a pot of tea would suddenly appear. "Does it not strike you that a lot of what he writes doesn't exactly rhyme?"

"I know," Stephen said, studying the stanzas skipped over, "it bothers me, too. But I suppose a Nobel laureate gets some leeway. Anyway, in the old Irish poetry schools, they passed those off as what they called half-rhymes."

"I think it rhymes all the way or it doesn't count," Pádraig grumbled.

"Right, then. I'll dash a note off to the Nobel committee in Stockholm to see if we can get the prize revoked posthumously," Stephen mused as he read on. "But if you can get past that, it's a brilliant poem. It's a full critique of modern ideas squelching the old ways of doing things. It's a rallying cry for poets coming after him. Listen:

"'Poet and sculptor, do the work,
Nor let the modish painter shirk
What his great forefathers did.
Bring the soul of man to God,

"Wouldn't it be wonderful to hear him read that, himself in his own voice?" Stephen ran his fingers down the page as if trying to make it speak.

"It certainly is powerful, when you read it out like that." He walked behind the desk and looked over Stephen's shoulder. "It's a little flat when you just read it silently on the page. You tend to read it too fast, I think, that's the problem. You don't hear and feel the effect of the language on you when you just read it."

"From what you say, I think that was what Tan Mithy was on about," Stephen ventured. "He said Fianna composed and recited aloud, and in Irish. The tradition goes back to the time when there was no written Irish language, not even the precursor symbols for it, that's how long the poets have been at it here."

"But still, I can't catch what's so sacred about saying it all in Irish. All the same…."

Stephen leaned back in the chair, his toes sweeping the floor. "You made the switch, didn't you, from saying the Mass in Latin to saying it in English?"

"Yes, that was quite a while ago at this point."

"Still miss the Latin, do you?"

Pádraig smiled a little to himself. "Aye. I confess I do miss it."

"Why is that?"

Pádraig let out a long sigh. "I can't say exactly. Just a warmth, a familiarity. Maybe a separation of the ordinary from the extraordinary. Back in those days, walking out onto the altar and shifting into Latin, it was like putting on a comfortable pair of gloves that are just right for the job."

"You might not like to think so, but it also made a different kind of separation. Not just the ordinary part of life from the sacramental, for you. It also elevated you to a privileged status, using a specialized language not accessible to most of the faithful," Stephen said. Pádraig opened his mouth to protest. Stephen raised his hand. "I'm not saying it was your idea or that you lorded it over them. But you've got to admit that the parishioners didn't do more than mutter along phonetically when they had to respond. They followed what you were saying not at all. I assume they had an English trot of some sort on the opposite page of the long passages you were reciting in Latin."

"That's what they relied on, yes. True enough for most of them, I'll admit that."

"So far as they were concerned, you were working in a magical language."

"Well, that takes it a bit far. But I'll grant you that it was part of the mystique around the priest and the priesthood. They all imagined we learned a fair amount of Latin at seminary, which was true for some of us. But others of us, myself included, learned only what we needed to get by."

"So you weren't about to spout forth with a whole sermon in Latin, then were you?"

"Hardly. It's not as though you can pick up a conversation class in the language, you know."

"I'm not criticizing you, Pádraig, just observing. You agree with me that there's something special about the language, then?"

"Yes, I agree."

"So what is it that you miss?"

"It's hard to say. Hard to think of an example. But here's one: Agnus Dei just sounds more sonorous than Lamb of God. Agnus Dei. Now that's a phrase you can lift up to heaven. It's even more economical in expression. Or how about 'have mercy on us' versus 'misere nobis'. Doesn't the Latin just sound more abject, more likely to invoke forgiveness than just the limp request of 'have mercy on us'?"

"If you're being picky, it doesn't even really count as a request. It's like a polite command. Pretty risky ordering God around, I should think. If you believe in him, that is."

"Fine, fine. But what's the equivalent here in the Irish

versus English debate you're pushing on about? Irish into English, how much different can it be? Both come from the same part of the world, both modern languages, lots of speakers in common. How much can be lost in the translation between the two?"

"A lot, apparently. Don't take Tan Mithy's word for it. You know your man Douglas Hyde?"

"Prime minister once, wasn't he? My grandfather adored him."

"Yes, eventually he was a politician. But before that, he was a champion of Irish literary traditions and culture. Took great issue with Yeats and his friend Lady Gregory who collected and transcribed Irish folk tales and poetic traditions in translation, not knowing between the two of them more than a word or two of Irish, and even those few words transliterated. He bristled at the idea that anyone could do what Yeats and Lady Gregory were about with any authenticity without understanding the language and appreciating what they were hearing in the language."

Stephen leaned his head sideways to look at the spines of the books he'd unloaded from his knapsack and stacked on Pádraig's desk. "I think Terry loaned me one of his, one of Hyde's books, I mean. Here it is: 'Love Songs of Connacht.'"

"That's this province, then."

"Right. He collected them from around here," Stephen said flipping through the book.

"He wrote the book as a trot, with the Irish on one page and an English translation on the opposite page. So he reproduced the Irish song or poem that he collected, verbatim on one side, then an English version on the opposite side. But here's what he struggled with: The English version had to be too prettied-up to make sense, to seem poetic in English. There were too many nuances and idioms in Irish that he couldn't carry over in the English. He got so frustrated with this that in a few places he drops a footnote and just lets go with a literal translation of the Irish."

"That's a little hard to grasp in the abstract. I mean, I realize that two words that rhyme in Irish might not rhyme when they're translated into Engish, but…."

"No, no. Hyde's problem is much bigger than just that. He does okay with the rhymes, even if he's a little inconsistent in making them work. But just listen to this, The Brow of Nefin. The narrator is a man who misses his love; he's standing on top of Mount Nefin in County Mayo, according to Hyde's introductory note.

> 'Did I stand on the bald top of Nefin
>   And my hundred-times loved one with me,
> We should nestle together as safe in
>   Its shade as the birds on a tree.
> From your lips such a music is shaken,
>   When you speak it awakens my pain,
> And my eyelids by sleep are forsaken,
>   And I seek for my slumber in vain.'

"Idyllic, right? He's crazy about the girl from the sound of it. But listen to the nuance in the literal translation.

'If I were to be on the Brow of Nefin and my hundred-loves by my side, it is pleasantly we would sleep together like the little bird upon the bough. It is your melodious wordy little mouth that increased my pain, and a quiet sleep I cannot (get) until I should die, alas!'"

"Now, that's a real Irishman, I'd say," Pádraig said punching his fist in the air. "Romantic, but not blind to the things about a woman that can drive a man mad." Pádraig laughed, then cleared his throat and composed himself more somberly. "From what I understand from pastoral counseling, of course. I've no actual firsthand experience."

"Here's another example," Stephen said leafing forward in the book, looking for more places with Hyde's asterisk offering a literal translation of something he thought he couldn't get quite right. "This one's called My Grief on the Sea. The narrator in this one's a woman, and her lover has left for America. She can't go with him for some reason. It doesn't say why.

'My grief on the sea,
   How the waves of it roll!
For they heave between me
   And the love of my soul!

"As poignant as that is the way Hyde rendered it, just listen to the literal translation:

'My grief is on the sea,
   It is it that is big.
It is it that is going between me
   And my hundred thousand treasures.

Stephen sat silently for a moment, staring at the page. "Quite a difference, wouldn't you say?"

"Yes, I see what you mean. The first version dresses up her grief. Her grief is rolling like waves, and you can't help but get carried away with the image of the waves and then distracted by how beautiful and powerful they are. But that's not the point of the verse, of course. The second version is primal. You can feel how something's been ripped from her. All she can get out is that it's big, her grief. It's more authentic somehow. You feel what she feels more genuinely."

Stephen stretched his arm diagonally across the desk and lay his head on it. "This is all fascinating. But it must be four in the morning by now. I've got to sleep or at least nap. I'm dead."

Pádraig checked his pocket watch. "You're about right. It's quarter to four. You can stay here, take a nap on the sofa."

Stephen lifted himself out of the chair and trudged toward Pádraig. "Technically, it's a divan, I think. Has only one arm up on the side."

Pádraig chucked. "'Technically', as you say, I think you can still sleep on it. There's a knit blanket on the back of the armchair, should keep you warm enough. I'll close the front shutters, keep the cold from the waterfront out of the room."

"Thanks, Pádraig." Stephen fell onto the divan and Pádraig handed him the blanket. Stephen shook it out and let it billow down on top of himself. Pádraig turned out the desk lamp and crossed the study to the door. He had his had on the door knob when Stephen called after him.

"Pádraig, do you think it still works?"

"What's that now? Does what still work?"

"The Mass, the consecration part. Does it still work to, you know, change the bread and the wine over now that you do it in English not Latin?"

"Why should it not work? It means the same thing."

"Yes, but not exactly, now, does it? What if it's those particular words in that particular language, Latin, that makes the difference?"

Pádraig let out a long sigh. "I'm sure there's a reason I shouldn't worry about this, but I can't think of it right now. I'm reasonably confident that God hears us in English just as well as in Latin and both species 'change over' as you put it."

"Aw, well and fine for you. At least English has some ties to Latin. What about people who've been taking communion at Masses in Swahili? Or Japanese?"

Pádraig banged his head lightly twice against the doorjamb. "You really do mean to drive me to the madhouse. If all those souls have been defrauded of genuine Eucharist all these years, we can't fix it tonight. Go to sleep. It's late. Or early." Pádraig closed the door behind him.

"Isn't that interesting," Stephen said softly to himself in the dark. "It can be both: both late and early. I wonder how many things like that there are." He fell asleep as he started his list and remembered nothing he'd added to it when he awoke a few hours later.

41.

Contempt or horror? Stephen wondered for a moment as he read Mrs. O'Flannelly's face when he turned out for breakfast at half seven the next morning. Both, he decided as he slid out the wooden chair across from Pádraig at the breakfast table.

"Good morning, Mrs. O!" he said with a cheeriness meant to be grating.

"My name is Mrs. O'Flannelly," she replied, her voice a growl.

"Ah, forgive me! My tongue trips on so many syllables so early in the morning." He grinned to himself as she stomped out of the dining room and back into the kitchen. He poked Pádraig's elbow. "Oy, there. Are you awake?"

Pádraig snapped back to the present moment. "Technically, yes. But only technically. My body's upright, but my brain's back on the pillow. Pour me some more tea, will you please?"

Stephen filled Pádraig's cup and pushed the milk over toward him. "Your housekeeper's not keen on my being here."

"Hmm?"

"Did you see her face when I walked in? Hear the little skirmish when I said 'good morning'?"

"No, not really. But I'm not surprised. She had some nasty things to say about your...people a day or so ago."

"Par for the course," Stephen sighed. "I just don't want to get be't up."

"If it comes to it, my money's on you, my friend. Just try not to throw the first punch."

"Thanks for the vote of confidence," Stephen said, stirring his tea. "What's the plan for today, by the way?"

"Well, Tan Mithy said he'd bring her back soon. What do we do with that? Do we just wait for him to deliver her?"

"Um, we could do that Pádraig. If you're willing to see whether your dream comes true."

Pádraig slapped the table. "We've been over and over this. It was not a dream. It was too real. Too specific. I've never read anything about the Tuatha da Dannan or the Milesians. Now I know their whole damned history. Explain that."

"Look, a lot of dreams are highly novelistic, sucking in information you didn't remember ever acquiring. Something someone mentioned to you a long time ago pops back and shows up in a dream. It sounds a lot like some recreational chemical experiments I did when I was...."

A commotion launched in the kitchen with the sound of a chair skittering sideways across the floor. A dish or two hit the floor with a ceramic explosion. Mrs. O'Flannelly's soprano scream completed the mix. Pádraig and Stephen stood and rushed to the kitchen door. Stephen felt himself thrown back into the hallway by a boy, twelve or thirteen years old and solidly built, who landed on top of him. The impact knocked out his wind and left him speechless. Pádraig looked down with concern and pulled the boy back to his feet.

"Aidan, what's the meaning of this? What's happened?"

Aidan doubled over to catch his breath, then looked up at the priest.

"She's back, Fa'her. Fianna's mum sent me. She's back."

42.

Within a few minutes, Mrs. O'Flannelly and Pádraig, between the two of them, had pulled chairs into the hallway and hauled the two crash victims into them. Pádraig patted Aidan on the shoulder and handed over the glass of water that Mrs. O'Flannelly fetched from the kitchen.

"Are you all right, Stephen?" Pádraig called over to him.

"I think so," Stephen said tentatively. Looking over at Aidan, he said, "Don't I get a glass of water, too?" Mrs. O'Flannelly glowered at him and disappeared to find another glass. She remained in the kitchen and extended a hand across the threshold with a grudging quarter-glass of water to Pádraig, who passed it over to Stephen.

"I'm sorry, Fa'her. I ran all the way here," Aidan said, still gulping for breath. "Downhill, most of it, but still a long stretch. I should have slowed down at the kitchen door, but my legs were on fire and I was afraid if I slowed down I'd just stop altogether."

"That's okay, Aidan. Nothing's broken." He glanced into the kitchen where Mrs. O'Flannelly was cleaning up with a broom and dustbin. "Nothing important, anyway. Tell me what Mrs. Gunning told you."

"She came running over the hill to our place this morning. My da' and me, we were just after the milking. She comes running in, hard to do it in the Wellies. Almost knocked over the milk can. My da' was just about to lash out furious at her for almost spilling a whole morning's work, when she starts crying and yelling. She needs help, she says, Fianna's turned up in the yard in the middle of the night, asking can she come in for her supper. Ned, I mean Mr. Gunning, he won't have it, he won't let her into the house. So Mrs. Gunning took out some blankets and bread and tea once he was asleep and stayed with her in the dairy barn til it got light. That's when she ran over to our place."

"Well, we have to go over there at once, is that what she wanted, Aidan? I imagine it must be," Pádraig said, sizing up Stephen and his fitness for duty.

"Yes, she said to tell you, ask you, could you please come right away with the car. She can't keep Fianna there, she said, not without making the mister fly off the handle. She said you'd understand what that means?"

"I'm afraid I do," Pádraig said gravely. "Stephen, we have to go right now. Are you able to travel? There may be some running involved."

Stephen pushed himself up out of the chair and stumbled for a moment. He shook his head to clear it and took a deep breath. "I'm ready. Let's go."

Padriag turned back to the boy. "Aidan, you did a good job in difficult circumstances. Stay here until you're rested. Mrs. O'Flannelly will make you some tea and toast." He looked over to Mrs. O'Flannelly, who nodded curtly.

"Thank you, Fa'her. I'll be all right. I know you've got to hurry, but could I ask you something, Fa'her? A small favor?"

"Yes, Aidan, of course. What is it?"

Aidan accepted a mug of warm tea from Mrs. O'Flannelly and cupped it in his two hands to warm up his fingers. He took a small sip. "Well, I wonder, would you mind calling me just Dan instead of Aidan?"

Pádraig looked at the boy and judged his request to be sincere. "Of course, Ai..., Dan. Assuming your parents have no trouble with it. But why do you want a different name?"

"I visited my cousins in America last summer, the ones in Weston, near Boston. They made fun of me, Fa'her, my name.

313

They said it was too Irish, too old fashioned. They said Dan was better."

Pádraig patted the boy's shoulder. "I don't think anyone or anything can be too Irish. Our people have given up too easily on Irishness in the past, I've come to think. We'll talk about it later."

Stephen was already waiting by the Escort when Pádraig jogged down the kitchen steps with his keys. Pádraig threw the car in reverse and spun out of the carpark and down the street toward the waterfront. "So Fianna's back, Stephen," Pádraig said, grinning with satisfaction. "Still think I'm a barmy dreamer?"

"Look, it's wonderful that she's back. But that doesn't mean that the king of the faeries had anything to do with it. Let's just be rational about this. We'll go up there, talk to her, make sure she's all right and ask her about everything."

"Oh, bloody fine. When you're up in the garret with your university friends, talking to ghosts, all bets are off and sure as hell there's something supernatural going on. But when something happens to me, you want to be all scientific about it."

Stephen ignored Pádraig's rant. "Is that Sister Alex?" he asked, squinting at a diminutive figure walking across the Council lawn in front of the water at an admirable pace. She wore a red parka with the hood pulled up tightly around her face.

Pádraig looked over as attentively as he could consistent with keeping the car on the road. "Yes, that's her red coat and I see the rosary beads swinging over there, see, on her right hand?"

"Oh, right. Must be her. Say, just stop up for a quick minute while I tell her the good news."
"Stephen, we really haven't the time. We must get up there. Bertie's obviously in distress."

"Well, Sister Alex has been in distress, too, over the whole thing. It won't take five seconds to tell her she's back and everything's going to be okay." To prevent Pádraig's saying no, Stephen pushed open the passenger door and made as if getting out with the car at full tilt. Pádraig slammed on the brake and Stephen held on to the useless seat belt until the car came to a stop. He hopped out and jogged toward Sister Alex. Pádraig pulled the car to the sidewalk.

He watched from a distance as Stephen caught up with Sister Alex and gave her the news. He was puzzled, though, when Stephen fell back a step after speaking with her, and even more surprised when Stephen turned back to the car and began gesticulating furiously that Pádraig should come over and join them. Pádraig turned off the engine and walked over, fuming at the delay Stephen was causing. He forced himself to be pleasant, though, in front of Sister Alex.

"Stephen, you know we're in a hurry." He smiled through clenched jaws.

"Pádraig, I mean Father, you have to hear what Sister Alex told me. I came over here and told her that Fianna was back, and she said –"

"I said 'I know'."

"So I said, how do you know? Did you run into Aidan on his way to the rectory? And she said –

"I said, 'no, I didn't'."

"So I said, 'well how then?' And she said –

"I said, 'because I saw Tan Mithy dropping her off in front of the convent at three this morning.'

Pádraig's eyes went wide. He wasn't sure whether Sister Alex had just validated him or joined his delusion. A third possibility crossed his mind, that Stephen had put her up to a joke. But as he looked at Sister Alex, her face serene and guileless, her demeanor totally matter of fact, he realized she was serious.

"Sister Alex," he said quietly, I want to hear everything you remember about what you saw. But right now, Stephen and I have to get up to the Gunning place, urgently. Could you possibly come with us?"

She looked at her rosary, where her thumb and pointer held her place in the decade she'd been praying. "Why, yes, I can do that. I'll come back to this later. The rosary is like a recorded symphony; you can always come back and pick up where you left off." She coiled the rosary in her left hand, kissed the crucifix at its end and tucked it into her pocket. Pádraig strode off toward the car. Sister Alex put her hand on Stephen's arm and they walked along behind Pádraig.

"Sister Alex," Stephen mused, "if I hadn't hopped out of the car to tell you Fianna was back, when is it that you would have mentioned to someone that you saw Tan Mithy dropping her off? I mean, it's a fairly unusual, even shocking thing to see in the middle of the night, isn't it?"

Sister Alex smiled and shrugged. "I'd have gotten around to it if it came up. Otherwise, I'd have kept my tongue still. I've lived a long time, most of it right here or not too far away. It's a deep place, Stephen, as I think you're coming to see. So 'unusual' and 'shocking' are relative things for me. Especially if you've got the habit I do of staying up and staring out the window from midnight til four in the morning."

"Ah, right," Stephen said. "Your old prayer shift."

"Right." She pointed back at herself with her thumb. "Old dog; no new tricks. If I went on about half the things I've seen, they'd invite me to the padded room."

They arrived at the car, and Stephen pulled the seat forward for Sister Alex to ease herself into the back. "Sister, I know it's a little inconvenient to get in back there, but it's safer. The seat belt in the front doesn't even work. I'm used to it; I'll sit up there."

"That's very gallant of you, but unnecessary. If I fold myself in back there, you may never get me out. I'll ride up front with Father." Stephen opened his mouth in protest; Sister Alex patted his cheek. "Really, Stephen, it's all right. I'm the one with a rosary in my pocket, remember?"

Pádraig thrust the car into gear a little too eagerly in his excitement to get to Bertie's and to interview Sister Alex at the same time. The Escort stalled out and it took Pádraig a few tries to start it up again, a special trial since Sister Alex's presence prevented him from giving voice to his frustration with his favorite string of curses. In a few minutes they were sailing up the hill toward the Red Islands overlook and on to the Gunnings' home.

"So, Sister Alex, tell us what you saw. I'm eager to hear."

"Well, about three in the morning, a few minutes before, I'd say, I heard a little clipping sound outside the visiting room window. I couldn't tell exactly where it was coming from, so I got up and went to the window. I saw them ride into the square, coming from the road on the east, she behind him."

"So there were two of them, Fianna and a man, riding in on a horse?"

"Well, I thought at first it was a horse. But the sound of the hooves wasn't quite right. A horse, especially one that's shod, makes quite a racket, you know, especially on pavement or cobblestones."

Pádraig frowned. "But if it wasn't a horse, what was it?"

Sister Alex smiled. "It looked like a horse at first, but it turned out to be Orlando."

The car had just reached the beginning of the giant curve that took the road around to the north and safely away from the cliff above the Red Islands. Pádraig turned to Sister Alex, his mouth agape. "Pay attention!" Stephen shouted from the back seat and lunged forward to correct the steering wheel before the car hit the protective railing.

"Sorry," Pádraig said.

"Who the devil is Orlando?" Stephen shouted. Sister Alex flinched. She looked over at Pádraig, who cleared his throat almost imperceptibly. Stephen saw the priest's Adam's apple bob twice before Pádraig spoke, so softly he almost missed it.

"Orlando is…a dog. Willie's dog. You've seen him yourself, lying out there in the sun in front of Beach Club."

"Orlando, like Orlando Furioso?" Stephen asked.

"No, no. Like Orlando, Florida. In America. Willie went to Disneyworld once back in the '60s," Sister Alex said smiling, as though she herself remembered the trip fondly. "Or maybe it was Disneyland. Anyway, it was definitely Florida. And that's why Orlando is Orlando."

"Sure, but meaning no disrespect, Sister, you've just said that Orlando is not Orlando. Or wasn't at three in the morning today when he was apparently a horse. Is this making sense to you, Pádraig?"

Pádraig was by now afraid to blink for fear of sending the car over the railing. He was driving very slowly, his eyes fixated on the road ahead of him. "Nothing is making any sense right now, Stephen."

Sister Alex turned halfway around in her seat. "Stephen, you're well read in Yeats, I take it, or becoming so. Have you not read the stories he collected about the faeries' night escapades?"

"No, haven't come to that section yet, I confess."

"They're quite charming and heroic. One I remember is the story of a man named Tumaus, sent away by his family to drive the cattle to the south. The drive path intersected with the high road at a certain point, and it was there he crossed paths with the caravan of a wealthy Spanish family, royalty by the looks of things. As he stood there, holding back the cattle, his herding dog, Bran, doing the best he could to help, he caught just the briefest glimpse of a beautiful young woman, a princess, peeking out of one of the carriage windows. In a moment, he knew that he loved her and that she was terribly sad.

"He had nothing else on his mind for days and nights after that encounter, wondering why she was so sad and what he could do to help her. Only Bran's wet-nosed nudging at meal time could get him to move about to feed the two of them. It was only a matter of time that his melancholy and broodiness would draw notice from the others, and about a week after his distant encounter with the princess, a leprechaun showed up at his campfire."

"I thought the leprechauns were the cobblers of the faerie world. Why would he walk up to a cattle driver's camp?" Stephen asked.

"You're right about their being the cobblers, but that doesn't mean they like it," Sister Alex answered. "Imagine if people were always loading off their shoes for you to fix, and you had no choice but to do it, even if you'd rather go fishing. They get a bit fed up by the end of the day, the stories say, and they want to have a bit of fun at night. So they did, like this

318

particular leprechaun did: approach someone to inveigle in an adventure.

"So the leprechaun comes over to Tumaus and says, 'You have the distant look of someone separated from his true love, friend. What be's the matter?' 'I can't say she's my true love, sir, only that I think she is and it's her melancholy I want to relieve. But she being so far away, I cannot guess where, not a thing can I do about it.'

'Not so!' says the leprechaun. 'We'll take my fine steed and gallop through the wind and over the water to find her. I know just the one you mean, and we'll find her in the court in Sevilla. And we'll do it tonight.'

'That's impossible!' cried Tumaus. 'Not if you'll believe me and come along,' says the leprechaun. 'See here,' he says and gestures at Tumaus' dog Evergreen. Suddenly, humble Evergreen is a stallion, snorting and stamping, eager for a good romp.

"They climb onto Evergreen, Tumaus behind the leprechaun because the faerie rider must always be in the lead to maintain the magic when it meets the wind, and fly across the land and ocean and to Sevilla where they find the princess, melancholy as ever, brooding on the balcony of her chambers.

"Tumaus says to the leprechaun, 'Many thanks to you, kind sir, for bringing me into sweet proximity with my true love, for I know she is that now. But she will never have me, being as I am in cattle driver's garb with the odor to go with it. 'Look again, friend,' says the leprechaun, and Tumaus looks down at himself in gentleman's clothing.

"Tumaus calls up to the princess, whose name is Narvida, and she is shocked and pleased to see him, she having remembered her glimpse of him as poignantly as he remembered his of her. She explains that her melancholy is caused by her father's decision that she must marry a man much older than she from a rival family, this to keep the peace between them. The leprechaun was nearby, listening from the shadows. 'Friend,' he whispered. 'Ask her will her father release her from the betrothal if another gentleman can guarantee the peace.' 'Who will do that?' Tumaus whispered back. 'You will, friend,' the leprechaun said. 'Just do as I say.'

"So Tumaus asks the lady, will her father agree to it, and she says, 'aye, he will, I'm sure of it.' So Tumaus says good-bye and he and the leprechaun mount Evergreen and ride back to the pasture where the cattle have been standing at sleep all the night. Tumaus falls asleep and when he wakes at first light, there's Evergreen the collie, curled up on the ground beside him.

"That night, he makes his campfire, same as always, and just when it's hot enough to heat his tea, here comes the leprechaun again. 'Time to go!' he says, and he waves again at Evergreen who once again becomes a golden stallion. He likes the change, it appears, because he cavorts and dances on his back legs, which makes Tumaus laugh in pleasure.

"But tonight is different, because the magic doesn't stop with Evergreen. The leprechaun puts up a great wave of effort, and each and every steer becomes a stallion. The pasture is crowded with the most handsome herd of horses ever seen in Ireland. 'Off we go!' yells the leprechaun, and they fly into the night, the whole lot of them.

"It's still the dark of night when they clatter into the courtyard of Narvida's family in Sevilla. Evergreen's arrival the night before had been more stealthy, he being a dog in truth, but the herd of night stallions, being steer by day, arrived with the full orchestra of hooves. The whole family turned out to see what was the matter. The leprechaun pushed Tumaus off his mount and whispered, 'Swear your love to her and your loyalty to her father!'

"So Tumaus does this, and the father, bedazzled by the show of force represented by the beautiful steeds populating his courtyard declares Tumaus a worthy suitor and protector of his daughter and the entire family. A priest is summoned, the banns are waived, and Tumaus and Narvinda are married then and there.

"The two retire to the marriage chamber and the father makes off to arrange for a grand feast the next day. Late into the night, though, the leprechaun falls asleep under the bush in the courtyard where he'd been lying and whispering out instructions to Tumaus."

"Then what happened?" Stephen asked, as enthralled as a boy at a campfire.

"Well, the magic collapsed, of course. Evergreen was a dog again, and every one of the night stallions became a lowing steed, milling about in the courtyard and making a great racket in their confusion as to where the pasture had vanished to.

"Back in the marriage chamber, Tumaus looked no different to Narvinda, of course, they having traded clothes for bedclothes. But the noise in the courtyard made them rush to the balcony where they saw the mishmash parade. Tumaus looked down in horror and could do nothing but spill out the truth to Narvinda."

"So did she toss him out? What did the father do?"

"Well, she might have tossed him out or set her father upon him. But she was touched by his honesty and pure motivation in coming to save her. She laid her hand upon his breast and said, 'I forgive you.'

"Just then, the leprechaun rolled out from under the bushes where he'd been sleeping. He held his hat and hung his head when he saw how his work had gone awry. He began to tremble when he thought of what terrible punishment Tumaus might mete out to him for his colossal mistake.

"But Tumaus was generous. "Kind sir, you've brought me this far and done me this well that I've become tonight the happiest, most contented man on earth. I bid you stay here with us, make your magic at home here.

"The leprechaun, glad for the reprieve, agreed to stay, and shared his gold with the court as well. His magic had made the court of Narvinda's father strong and secure, and they abided in peace with their neighbors in the rival clan for many decades until after the father's passing, and Tumaus' becoming the gray sage of the court."

"So that's a happy ending, I suppose?"

"I think so. What's unhappy about it?" Sister Alex asked, turning in her seat.

"The poor leprechaun is stranded in Spain!"

"It's always a happy story when the faerie gets outmaneuvered!" Sister Alex exclaimed. "Anyway, he gets his due. I forgot to mention the way the story is referred to, the title generally given to it."

"What's that?"

"It's called 'The First Spanish Leprechaun.'"

"That's pretty slim consolation, isn't it, for his being permanently separated from his people and his family?"

Pádraig glanced at Stephen in the rearview mirror. "Aren't you taking this on a little too passionately, Stephen?"

Sister Alex reached back and patted the back of his hand. "You're very kind to worry after the others, but in this case, entirely unnecessary. The leprechauns are solitary faeries, not the trooping kind that might miss home. Put your mind at rest, dear." She turned toward the windbreak. "Isn't that the Gunning drive just up there, Father?"

Pádraig slowed the car down further still and eased it into the ruts of the road. He pulled the gear shift into low and tried to minimize the bouncing in consideration of Sister Alex. "I'll get as far down the lane as I can without risking getting stuck, Sister Alex."

"Oh, that's fine, Father. I have my walking shoes and I'm along for an adventure."

"I guess it's inevitable that we'll have to deal with Ned," Pádraig said as they pushed out of the car. "We can't exactly sneak up on the dairy barn without his noticing."

"Well, here's an idea, Father. Why don't you engage him when he comes out and Stephen and I will quietly go off to the barn and see what's what."

"Good idea, Sister. Let's go."

They'd just closed the car doors when Ned emerged from the hallway onto the porch. He hooked his thumbs in his braces and cocked his head. "Now, Father, I've made it plain about your being up here. I won't have you trying to provoke me to disrespect, so I'll just ask you and the sister and your little friend to turn around and go."

Pádraig walked slowly toward the porch steps, showering calm on the situation. "Ned, I'm here because Bertie sent for

me. I know Fianna's come back. She asked for my help."
Stephen and Sister Alex walked slowly to the left side of the
yard and back toward the dairy barn. Pádraig took a few more
steps toward Ned.

"I understand you've disallowed her in the house, Ned. Is
that true?"

Ned nodded slowly. "Sure, it's true. I know where she's
been. I won't have glamoured going on in the house. It's a bad
precedent. Once they've taken her, they'll be back and greedier
and greedier until there's no one but me left. And then they'll
come for me. But they won't take me. I've made
arrangements, taken precautions."

Pádraig leaned in and squinted. Ned wasn't a religious
man, but Pádraig had always known him to wear a scapular,
like most men in the parish. He suspected it was more of a
charm than a sacred element to them, but Ned had always
worn it. Now, in its place was a leather cord with a rusty nail
hanging down from it.

"Ned, what's that you're wearing around your neck?"

Ned glanced down and fingered the pendant. "Oh, this?
It's an iron nail. The others, they can't abide iron, makes them
shriek and run. If they come around here again, I'll be ready
to run them off."

"Okay. Sounds as though you're prepared. What makes
you think they'll turn and run at the sight of the nail?" Pádraig
asked, extemporizing.

Ned rolled his eyes. "It seems you paid no attention at all
when you were growing up here, Pádraig. You know as well as
I that the grandfathers held this to be true and reliable. Did
you not listen at all when they gathered over there at An Post?"

"No, I didn't have much time for that."

Ned straightened up to his full height, impressively over
six feet when he bothered to stand up on his own power. "No,
you didn't have time for much of anything but yourself, did
you now."

"What do you mean by that, Ned?" Pádraig felt the
question stir up something uncomfortable in the back of his
mind and the pit of his stomach.

"You know what I mean. If you'd given a tinker's damn about your own sister, your mother wouldn't be grieving her now, would she?"

"Look, Ned, I did the best I could, I…"

"Bloody shite you did! You should have been here, protecting her from….everything. Everyone. Instead, you were off kissing arse to earn that ring around your neck, bloody little good it does anyone around here."

Pádraig froze for a moment as an unexpected picture flashed across his mind. Eileen, outside the newsstand, age fourteen perhaps, framed in his mind as he passed through the village, getting dropped off in front of Beach House on a visit home from seminary. A lorry driver delivering supplies to the pub had given him a lift on the Green Road in from Cliffony. It was a candid shot of Eileen in his mind; she not expecting him home that weekend at all, and not arriving in the unfamiliar vehicle. She didn't see him in the passenger seat as he passed by. But she wasn't alone, in the memory floating through Pádraig's brain. There was another person, a boy, a little older, dancing a hornpipe for her, she all smiles and applause, he grinning and whirling, basking in her sweet attention. He hadn't thought about this scene in more than twenty-five years and now he focused on the face of the boy and brought it closer to him in memory to see who it was.

"Ned," Pádraig said quietly. "You loved her, didn't you?"

"Yes, I loved her! You ruined her life, letting her go off with that Terry Johnson. And you ruined mine!"

Pádraig cast his eyes down. "I had no choice, Ned. I couldn't make her come with me. She insisted, I begged."

"Bollocks, Pádraig! You make out around here as if you're pure as the April rain. The angels make your bed in the morning and fluff your pillows." His voice was high and sarcastic. "It makes me sick to call you 'Father'. I'll no longer do it." He turned to go back into the house. Pádraig called after him. "Ned, you know why I'm here. I have to take Fianna with me. Bertie thinks she's not safe here."

Ned wheeled toward him and staggered off the porch. "Take the little witch! I never wanted her here in the first place. I only gave in because Bertie had her heart set on having her, and I couldn't explain why I couldn't abide it without breaking Bertie's heart." He snorted and shook his head. "I once cared about that sort of thing, can you believe it? But having the girl here, it's knocked the caring out of me." He paused to catch his breath. "I know who she is, Pádraig. You made a point of refusing to tell us. But I know who she is."

Pádraig blinked and waited. Ned took a menacing step toward him.

"How could you, Pádraig? Saddle me with the daughter of the only woman I ever truly loved. How could you?" Tears welled from Ned's eyes. Pádraig's stomach dropped as the weight of Ned's long pain fell upon him. "This is the daughter," he said, pointing in the direction of the barn, "this is the daughter I could have had with Eileen," Ned gasped between sobs, "had you not ruined it all with your selfishness and neglect. And then for you to thrust her into my home as though I'd be fine with it." Ned doubled over, his hands on his knees. "Damn you to hell, Pádraig. Damn you to hell."

Pádraig stood frozen, sure a pat on Ned's shoulder would elicit a blow. "Ned, I didn't know, I didn't realize until just now how you cared for Eileen. I'm so sorry."

"You should be sorry, you ignorant bastard! The whole village and half of Bundoran knew I loved her. You had your head in your books and up your own arse. You should be sorry!"

"Why didn't you tell me when I came to you and Bertie about Fianna? Just tell me privately that it wasn't a good idea?"

"And just how the devil would you think I could do that? You know Bertie was heart-breaked over having no babies. She was already nearly thirty when we married, worried she'd be an old maid with her mother's house her only home. A man needs a wife, and she's a good woman. No need to be letting on that she was a better than nothing choice after my own heart was broken." Ned shook his head. "I cared about things like that once. I was careful about them."

Pádraig looked over to his left and saw Stephen and Sister

Alex with their arms wrapped around Fianna, Bertie close behind them. Stephen's eyebrows urged a quick departure. Pádraig nodded slightly in acknowledgement. .

"Ned, I have to go now. We'll be taking Fianna with us, and we don't want any trouble about it."

"Ha! Take her!" Ned waved dismissively. "Good riddance of her!" He laughed bitterly to himself. "At least I'll have Bertie back to myself, now."

Stephen and Sister Alex hustled Fianna to the car. Bertie tore at her hair and wept, but silently. Pádraig backed away from Ned, dove into the Escort and revved the engine in reverse to complete the escape.

43.

The four rode back to the village in exhausted silence, with worried glances over to Fianna from time to time. She sat in the back seat between Stephen and Sister Alex, her head lolled back and letting out an occasional giggle for no reason at all. Pádraig rolled the car into the car park behind the rectory and turned off the engine.

"Fianna, dear," Pádraig said turning to the back seat and trying to get the girl's attention. "You wait here a moment. The grown-ups are going to step out and have a talk." Her eyes met his for a moment;the only acknowledgement he got.

Pádraig, Sister Alex and Stephen clustered behind the car. "What the devil is going on with her?" Stephen said. "Is she in shock?"

"Maybe so. We'll have to get a doctor in to see her. But in the meantime, where can we put her? I'd have her in the rectory, but that's improper by any measure, an unrelated female under the same roof as a priest."

"Even though she's your niece?" Stephen asked.

Pádraig shook his head. "True, but not publicly known, and the appearance would be just as bad. Sister, how about the convent?"

"Normally, yes. But you'll never believe what our superior has dreamed up. The convent is becoming a retreat center. Can you believe it? We've gone from being cloistered in full

327

time prayer to running a bed and breakfast, for goodness sakes. They're calling it Our Lady's Star of the Sea. Our Lady would redden and stamp at such a misappropriation, if you ask me. But It starts filling up tonight at tea for the Vigil Mass. So I'm afraid it's out of the question."

"I suppose we could have her out at Mother's house," Stephen said. "But I'm not sure we could handle her if things get rocky, and I'd hate to put Mother in harm's way. Do you think she's dangerous?"

"No reason to think that," Pádraig said, "but she's not herself, that's for sure. I wouldn't want to have her so remote from me and whatever help we might need from Cliffony or Bundoran. But thanks for considering." The three stood silently for a moment.

"What about Joe and his wife?" Stephen asked. "Could they give her a room for a little while until we figure things out? Maybe she could even help out in the kitchen or with the washing up."

"That's an idea," Pádraig said, brightening up. "Could you trot over there and see if they're amenable? Lay it on that I'm asking personally for a favor but can't come over to do it myself at the moment."

While Stephen went off to make entreaties to Joe, Sister Alex slipped back into the car to sit with Fianna. Pádraig leaned back on the boot of the car and tried to collect himself. It was hard not to see Ned as partly right, but he defied the waterfall of guilt he felt pouring down on him. He thought of all the people he'd helped over the years, weighing the good he'd done against Ned's accusations. What's the better part of life? he wondered. To make small differences in many lives, or great ones in a few? Didn't Jesus admonish his disciples to leave their parents and families to follow him? If I were meant to stay home and look after Eileen, why was I called to the priesthood? He lifted his face to the wind coming off the water to dry the tears he felt coming.

Stephen came jogging around the corner. Pádraig gulped to regain his composure and pushed himself off the boot of the car. "What did he say?"

"He said he'd do it. His wife was there, and he checked with her. She seemed rather shocked that the father would toss her out like that. I didn't go into the relationship details, but I have the sense the Joe knows she's related to you."

"That's fine news. I'm sure I never told Joe outright about Eileen and Fianna, but he's probably picked up enough clues to figure it out. He's definitely got that sixth sense about him."

"I know what you mean, I think. Anyway, he said drive her around the back door of the Boat and he'll see her in that way. No need to give Ellen and her crowd something to talk about."

"Agreed. Let's go."

Pádraig pulled in behind the restaurant and Joe threw open the door. Pádraig walked Fianna up the metal steps. She smiled vacantly at Joe and his wife. "Now, Fianna, love, you'll be staying here with Joe and Wendy for a little while until we get things better arranged. Are you all right with this?" Fianna nodded, or Pádraig thought she did. "Wendy and Joe can help you get sorted out with a comb and toothbrush and such." He turned to Joe. "If there are any expenses involved, you'll please let me know, Joe, and I'll take care of them." Joe smiled warmly. "I remember someone a long time ago and very far away from here who got me sorted out with a comb and a toothbrush and such when I wasn't welcome in my father's home. I am honored to repay in kind." He bowed slightly from his shoulders and neck. Pádraig felt his throat giving in to a sob and took a deep breath to postpone it. "Thank you, Joe." He nudged Fianna toward Wendy, who opened her arms. Fianna fell in toward her, her arms at her sides, silently accepting the embrace.

Stephen and Pádraig clattered down the metal stairs. Sister Alex pried herself out of the back seat and unspooled her muscles until she was mostly upright. "Ach! I thought I'd be a permanent resident of that back seat! Well, cheers and blessings, Father, Stephen. I think I'll finish my walk. And my rosary. You know, before the tourists arrive." She looked over at Stephen. "You wouldn't like to come over and serve up the tea bread, would you, Stephen?" He shook his head in horror. "Ha! I didn't think so. You're a sensible young man. I'm going to try to dodge it myself. See you at Vigil, Father," she called over her shoulder as she pushed off toward the waterfront, arms pumping and fingers pinching the beads of her rosary.

"I don't know about you, but I'm exhausted. Are you up for an early dinner?"

"Yes, but the question is 'where?' Joe has his hands full; seems wrong to ask him to make dinner, too. Beach Club is out. Mrs. O'Flannelly has seen enough of the two of us for one day."

"Let's go to Mother's house. I can make something for the three of us. She loved meeting you and it will be a change of pace to get out of the village."

"Fine, that's a lovely invitation. But if you have any notion of getting me liquored up to tell funny priest stories, forget it. I have to work late tonight. Vigil."

"Right, right. Everyone keeps mentioning that. I get that it's supposed to replicate waiting for the resurrection, but what's the ceremony all about?"

"Get in," Pádraig said, opening the driver's side door. "I'll tell you on the way."

44.

Despite his best resolve, Pádraig had in fact taken a few drops at dinner, and now, preparing for the Vigil, he was in regret. It wasn't that he was too drunk to function, just that his fatigue, layered on with the small dose he'd taken, was a weight on him. The first sips had been invigorating, made him smooth and gracious with Mrs. Attergood. Now he yawned in the sacristy and rinsed his mouth with the minty liquid that didn't count, he assured himself, as taking water within the fasting hour before communion.

He'd said the Vigil Mass on his own at least two dozen times, he calculated, as he flipped through the lectionary, and had participated as a congregant or a concelebrant every other year of his life since first Communion. Still, the ritual was complex enough that he required a refresher every year before the start. He scanned the pages quickly, hoping he hadn't cut himself too short on time to preview the whole service. He heard the doors to the sanctuary open and close once or twice, then hushed whispers, signaling the arrival of the first churchgoers. He sighed and accelerated his run-through.

A clatter in the hallway startled him out of his concentration. Timothy and Terence tumbled in, breathless. "Sorry, Fa'her," one of them said; Pádraig thought it was Terence, but hedged his bet. "It's all right. You're not late yet! There's a lot to do, though, so hurry and get dressed. Then go out and light the fire pit. Can you do that by yourselves without me having to call the doctor or the fire brigade?" The other twin smiled broadly. "Of course, Fa'her. We're thirteen now! Just had a birthday only yesterday."

Pádraig thought back to their puzzling absence from the Good Friday service, and felt a surge of relief. "Ah, so is that why I didn't see you yesterday at the service?"

The brothers looked at one another, perplexed. One of them spoke. "Yes, Fa'her, do you not remember, we mentioned a week ago we'd be going to Sligo Town with the whole family to see the cathedral and have tea as a celebration." He grimaced and looked down at the floor. "No cakes, though, it bein' Good Friday and all."

Pádraig thought back on his consternation; he was certain he'd been stood up for some unexplained reason. He had no memory of their saying they'd be away, but put that away to think about later. It was at least something, knowing that he hadn't been silently shunned by the whole parish, even the altar boys. He clapped them both on the shoulders. "We'll make it up to you, the not having any cakes on your birthday. Thirteen is a big milestone; your confirmation year, assuming the bishop makes his way out here. We'll celebrate tomorrow after the Masses."

Pádraig returned to his perusal of the order of the service. He sighed. This was a long one; seven readings from both testaments before he even got to the regular part of the Mass. He'd read the short versions, of course; no use antagonizing people. But even that would streamline the evening by only a few minutes. At least there aren't any catechumens this year, he thought, disturbed at himself for being glad there was no one new to baptize. Still, there would be the renewal of the baptismal vows and the reading of the liturgy of the saints, both of which he found grand in their solemnity.

It was nearly ten after nine o'clock when Pádraig next looked up and realized that the twins hadn't come back from lighting the fire pit outside the church's front door. He'd just made up his mind to go and see what had happened when they dashed into the sacristy, out of breath again.

"Everything all right?" Pádraig asked cautiously.

"Oh, yes, Fa'her, only it's windy tonight and we used up all the matches trying to get it going. Terence had to run across to the pub to ask could they spare a book." Pádraig tried to grasp what he could of Terence's face, vainly hoping to remember which boy was who. "Well, thank you for the extra effort, Terence. And Timothy. We'd better get started before the natives get restless." They smiled as if they knew they should, though the expression seemed lost on them.

Pádraig briefly reminded the boys of the order of the service; they went out into the sanctuary together, Terence bearing the Paschal candle, Timothy, the crozier. The congregation rose on their entrance and followed the three to the back of the church and out into the tiny courtyard. Timothy had been right about the wind; Pádraig took care to keep his vestments wrapped close to him and away from the sparks of the fire pit.

"Dear friends in Christ," Pádraig began, his arms outstretched at a safe distance from the pit. "On this most holy night, when our Lord Jesus Christ passed from death to life, the Church invites her children throughout the world to come together in vigil and prayer."

The light of the fire played on the faces of the parishioners fanned in front of him and gave them an intensity he missed in the usual massgoers. Sister Alex passed among them, making sure each had a taper. Pádraig felt a warm satisfaction in the connection of this moment, this ritual to the first days of the church when Christians huddled in secret, overcoming their fear together in the dark.

"This is the passover of the Lord," he continued, arms outstretched. "If we honor the memory of his death and resurrection by hearing his word and celebrating his mysteries, then we may be confident that we shall share his victory over death and live with him for ever in God."

Gradually, he realized that his parishioners' collective gaze was drifting from him and his outstretched arms to some

333

unseen attraction behind him. He pressed on with the liturgy; it was an unwritten rule of the ritual that once begun, it must be finished. I can't exactly wheel around and peek at what they're gawking at, he thought. He pushed forward with the ceremony, working from memory now that even Terence had dropped concentrating on holding the lectionary where Pádraig could read it in the firelight. He anchored his gaze on Stephen, asking with his eyebrows what was happening behind him. Stephen's eyes went wide as he mouthed, "Fianna."

45.

Pádraig abbreviated the blessing of the new paschal fire, hoping that no one besides Sister Alex would notice or mind a slightly shorter service. He leaned over to Timothy. "Let's get the candle inside now." He touched the boy's shoulder lightly. Timothy looked back quizzically. "But we haven't carved the year into the candle yet, Fa'her." Pádraig stepped forward to encourage the boy to match his step. "We'll do it later. Come on now, let's get everyone back into the church."

He hurried, not too indecorously, he hoped, to the altar and turned to get his first look at what had so entranced the congregation looking back at Fianna. He wanted desperately to have a word with Stephen or Alex. He looked over at Terence, the one person on the altar with him who had apparently seen what had absorbed everyone else's attention. Terence was wide-eyed as Stephen had been. "What is it, Terence? What is it that has everyone agog?" Pádraig whispered as loudly as he dared, hoping that the hymn would last long enough for him to fill himself in. Terence replied, eyes straight ahead without a turn of his head. "It was herself, Fa'her, stumbling down the hill, not even on the road, coming down over the field, swinging a lantern. Waving her arms and twirling all at once. She was like a madwoman, Fa'her, though I'm sure I've never seen one. Except tonight."

And then she was there, pushing through the doors of the

sacristy, Stephen slightly behind her. Stephen approached her gently and placed a hand on her shoulder. She twirled away, her arms flailing like useless wings. Stephen fell back, unsure of making another approach.

The entrance hymn ended; the last sound trailed from the organ bellows and the church was silent for a long string of seconds while Pádraig assessed his options. He'd never interrupted a Mass, never discontinued one once started. Even a fainting parishioner, all too common on the summer Sundays, was ministered to by a pew neighbor and the ushers while Pádraig would shoulder on. He had just nearly decided to press on when Fianna bellowed out a sharp laugh.

"Hah!" she shouted. "Hah!" The syllables wound together and soon she was laughing uncontrollably, doubled over in the aisle. No one moved.

"Fa'her, what should we do?" Terence asked in a loud whisper. The parishioners in the front pews were paying attention. "Shall I run and get her mum?"

"Excellent idea, Terence." Pádraig could feel the perspiration beading at his temples. "Run. Pick up the hem of the suplice and run. You don't have time to change."

"Yes, Fa'her." Terence dashed through the door toward the sacristy. Pádraig heard the soles of the boy's dress shoes slapping the linoleum floor as he raced on his mission. Timothy remained on the altar, still as a statue, his hands dutifully clasped in imitation of Pádraig's, the two of them a bulwark of calm in the unfolding chaos.

Fianna continued to make her way down the aisle of the sanctuary and her laughter turned to keening. She gestured broadly to the opposite sides, stretching her arms up to salute the arches of the stained glass windows, past St. Bridget, St. Kevin and St. Molaise himself. As she grew closer, her words grew more distinct, but were still unintelligible to Pádraig.

There was no turning back to the routine of the Vigil Mass now; Fianna's performance overtook the church as she strolled and spun her way down the aisle. Her eyes were dark pools; she moved as if entranced. Stephen followed at a distance, matching her steps from an arm's length behind.

None of the parishioners moved to block or embrace her; some gaped and smirked. Then, Sister Alex pushed past the massgoers between her seat and the aisle to intercept Fianna just as she reached the step where the communion rail had once separated the priest from the congregation. She embraced her gently from the side and whispered something, softly, for Fianna only to hear. The girl smiled slightly and relaxed into Sister Alex's arms. Sister Alex tottered briefly as she adjusted to the girl's weight. She eased Fianna down to the floor with Stephen's help and pushed herself upright, leaning on Stephen's arm.

Pádraig stood for another moment assessing the scene and gave up trying to think of a helpful precedent for what to do. He cleared his throat.

"Dearly beloved," he intoned, raising his arms in blessing, hoping this would enhance the authenticity of his improvisation. "God has called us tonight to sort out the difficult circumstances of this girl and her family." The congregants continued to stare at Fianna, craning over one another's heads to see what was happening in the aisle. Pádraig raised his voice. "Go in peace. The Mass is ended."

A few paid enough attention to mumble, "Thanks be to God." Pádraig recessed down the main aisle toward Fianna, shooing the parishioners in the forward pews toward the side aisles. They reluctantly tore their gazes away as they filed toward the back of the church.

"Does it still count, Father?" whispered Bridget O'Neill. "I mean, there being no communion as such."

Pádraig patted her shoulder, "Yes, yes. It counts as Vigil. There's no communion at Vigil in any event. You're still to come tomorrow morning, right?" She nodded. "Make sure the others understand, will you?" She smiled and slipped away with the ranks, happy to be entrusted with a mission that served as an excuse for a little gossip.

He collected the edges of his vestments and crouched down next to Fianna, who writhed and giggled intermittently. Stephen joined him; Sister Alex bent as low as she could to hear and help without committing to a position she couldn't extricate herself from. Bridget Johnson leaned in close over Alex's shoulder. "Is she possessed?" she whispered in a shaken voice. "She looks possessed, don't you think so?" Stephen rolled his eyes and looked up at Sister Alex, pleading for help in making the woman go away. Sister Alex turned halfway toward Bridget. "No, dear, probably just exhaustion. If it were possession, we'd likely have been hurled against the walls." She smiled pleasantly at Bridget, who drew back in horror. "But that gibberish she was speaking, wasn't that tongues, wasn't it? I'm sure it was." Sister Alex rolled her eyes looking back at Stephen, then turned around to address Bridget. "No, dear," she said, taking the woman's hands in her own. "Tongues is a gift from the Holy Spirit, not a message from Satan. And anyways, she was speaking Irish, dear, nothing more exotic than that. It only sounded like tongues because you've no inkling of your own culture." She smiled warmly and tilted her head to one side, dismissing Bridget, who withdrew in confusion, but with the prize of a few extra nuggets of information for the gossip cauldron.

"What do we do now?" Stephen asked, looking down at Fianna. Pádraig repeated her name several times and patted her cheeks lightly. She made no response, but continued to laugh intermittently, her gaze distant and unfocused.

Terence came flying into the sanctuary, breathless and red-faced. "She's right behind me, Fianna's mum." He ran back to the doors of the church and peered out. Bertie entered at a light jog. Pádraig hadn't known she was capable of such speed.

Bertie joined Pádraig next to Fianna's outstretched body. "She's had a fit of some sort, Bertie. I can't make it out. It may be exhaustion, it may be a nervous breakdown. We'll have to take her into Cliffony to hospital." Pádraig put his hand under Fianna's shoulders to help right her. She came to sitting and looked around at the gaggle surrounding her. "What's happened?" she said, her puzzlement sounding genuine. "You...fainted," Bertie said. "I'll bet you haven't had a thing to eat today, have you?"

"No, sure I have. They give me all I can eat, Joe and

Wendy do. But what happened?"

"Nothing at all, really," Bertie insisted. "Nothing at all to worry about. Here, now, let me help you stand up." She tugged at Fianna's arm until she was upright. Fianna stumbled a bit and blinked hard.

"How are you feeling?" Stephen asked.

"A bit queer, to be honest." Fianna rubbed the crown of her head.

Pádraig whispered to Bertie, "I really think she needs the doctor. I can drive the two of you into the town."

"No, no, Father!" Bertie's whisper was fierce. "She mustn't leave the village! I just know, if she does, I'll never see her again. I just know!" Pádraig shook his head and opened his mouth to protest. Bertie lowered her voice. "I know you think of her best interests, Father. But I'm her mother. I'm ashamed I can't bring her straight home, but Ned won't have it. I'll bring her back to Joe and Wendy; they're saints; they'll take care of her. I can sort it out after that, with a little time, a little more time."

"Bertie, let me call him, then, call the doctor and see if he'll make the trip out here. I don't know it he will, but we should ask," Pádraig pleaded.

Bertie shook her head. "No, Father. You know I defer to you in all matters of faith. But this is a mother's heart speaking to you. If he comes out here, though he probably won't, he'll want to take her away. I can't abide it, Father!"

Timothy appeared from the sacristy, now changed into his street clothes, but still looking shaken. Wendy and Joe hurried in from the back of the church; Terence had disappeared again, Pádraig noticed, apparently to fetch the two of them.

"Is there anything else, Father?" Timothy said softly. "I mean, can I go home now?"

"Yes, Tim. On your way home, though, give a hand to Wendy and Joe to get Fianna back to their flat, would you please?" He clapped Timothy on the shoulder. "You did a fine job tonight. Very brave."

46.

Afterwards, none of The Four remembered Fianna coming into Beach Club; she just appeared suddenly, half an hour after closing time. She walked to the end of the long bar where Ellen was holding court, hunched conspiratorially with the rest of The Four. Ellen looked up, startled. The others turned to look at Fianna over their shoulders.

"How did you get in here?" Ellen shouted.

"Oh, the service door was left open," Fianna said quietly. "Very careless of a publican. Possibly illegal, too. It might seem you're open after hours when you shouldn't be."

"You're not welcome here." Ellen threw down her polishing rag. "Now, get out!" She gestured angrily at the door.

Fianna smiled and moved closer toward them. "Not yet. I have something for you. A poem. Let me recite it to you." She closed her eyes and began to speak.

"Who thinks they know the best for all
Sees nothing but raging, hot temper.
Pretense of authority, arrogance
Makes blind to justice and kindness
'A Vision' my precursor wrote in these hills
Uniting present to enduring consciousness.
These Four have no claim to vision

And deprived of it may reflect better in darkness
On the harms their actions wreak."

Ellen laughed loudly. "That's a terrible poem! It doesn't even rhyme, not even close to it! Now, be gone with you before I have the gents rush you out of here." She took a few steps around the end of the bar toward Fianna. Fianna reached one hand into the sachet slung across her shoulder and flung her hand in an arc across the end of the bar in the direction of The Four.

Martin howled first and clapped his hands to his eyes. Ellen shrieked as she dropped to the floor. "You witch! You are a witch! I'm blinded, I'm blind." She blinked her eyes open and turned her head side to side. "I can't see anything! You've blinded me!"

The other two followed quickly in the same way, bellowing and rubbing their eyes. They called out to Fianna to curse her, then to beg her to help them, but she had already slipped out the back door.

47.

It was Terence who came running to the rectory early the next morning, then over to the sanctuary when he learned Pádraig was in the church making ready for Easter Mass.

"Fa'her, Fa'her," he yelled breathlessly from the back of the church, starting Pádraig so badly that he almost pulled the crucifix down off the wall as he removed the Lenten wrap from it. He ought to have done it the night before, but nothing had gone according to plan.

"What is it....." Pádraig silently regretted not being able to tell one twin from the other.

"Terence, Fa'her, I'm Terence. Timothy can't run worth a penny. They told me to come and fetch you at once, to go up to the houses."

Pádraig made the boy sit down in the front pew. "Which houses? Who sent you?"

"Up to Ellen's house. They're all up there, scared to go home to their own houses, or can't because there's no one there to take care of them." Terence turned and looked back at the entrance of the church. "Fa'her, you've got to hurry. They'll wonder if I didn't deliver the message if you don't come right away."

Pádraig put his hand on the boy's shoulder. "Terence, I promise, I'll come with you straightaway. We'll drive up in the Escort. But first you must tell me what's happened."

Terence swallowed hard.   "They're all blinded, Fa'her. The four of them.   They say Fianna did it.   They say she's magicked, she's glamoured, she's a witch -- terrible things about her Fa'her."

"How did she supposedly do this, Terence?   Do you know?"

"I don't know exactly.   She said a poem to them, but it didn't rhyme, then she cast a spell or something, and they all fell down blinded!"

Pádraig saw the fright in the boy's expression and knew that more questions would not produce useful answers. "Come on, Terence.   Let's go up there.   Where shall we go first?"   He hoped the practicality of the logistics would calm the boy.

"I told you, Fa'her.   They're all hunkered down at Ellen's house.   Her niece is there, she's a nurse, or almost a nurse or something. She's trying to help them.   They can't find a doctor yet, it being Easter and all, and they don't want to leave the house for fear of running past Fianna again. They think she'll do them ever worse if she has a chance."

The door at the back of the church opened quietly, shoving a sliver of daylight into the sanctuary.   As the door closed, Pádraig recognized Sister Alex making her way down the aisle.

"I see Terence found you, Father."

"You knew I was looking for him?" Terence asked.

"I surmised it, yes.   There's only one thing in the village that could ignite such furious running, and it's got to have to do with what I saw over at the Beach Club early this morning." She sat down in the pew behind Terence.

"What did you see, Sister?" Pádraig asked, concealing his growing panic that Fianna actually had been involved in something injurious.

"Well, it was Leonard that came and got them.   It must have been half two in the morning when he pulled the panel truck 'round the front and helped them out, one at a   time, putting them in the seats of the van, closing it up, driving away. They looked in awful shape.   Couldn't walk on their own, not at all. At first, I thought it was just another night of...well, just another night at Beach Club. As I understand it from a distance, of course."

"Of course," Pádraig added reassuringly. "But what made you think it was different, whatever you saw?"

"Well, they were making a terrible racket. I could hear it clearly from behind the glass in the sitting room. And they were wailing about their eyes, their eyes, they couldn't see. Now, I understand that that kind of thing can also be a consequence of too much imbibing, but this seemed different. They were clutching at their faces as if their own eyes were jellyfish, stinging the daylights out of them."

48.

Pádraig concentrated as best he could, moving through the Mass, anxious about the turn of course he'd planned with his last ounce of energy early Easter morning. He wondered how many would notice it; not everyone dragged a Missal to Mass any more.

"A letter from the Apostle Paul to Timothy," he intoned. He saw a handful of confused faces turn upward to the altar as he switched out the Epistle instructed by the lectionary cycle for one that suited him better as a vehicle for his homily.

"'We know that the law is good if one uses it lawfully, knowing this: that the law is not made for a righteous person, but for the lawless and insubordinate, for the ungodly and for sinners, for the unholy and profane, for murderers of fathers and murderers of mothers, for manslayers, for fornicators, for sodomites, for kidnappers, for liars, for perjurers, and if there is any other thing that is contrary to sound doctrine, according to the glorious gospel of the blessed God which was committed to my trust.

"The word of the Lord," he concluded. He moved as quickly as decorum allowed through the Gospel The homily was what he was determined to get on to.

He waited for the noise of the congregation reseating itself to subside. He leaned forward on the lectern. "My friends in Christ: He is risen." He raised his hands and smiled

345

broadly, inviting their response in kind. Not a smile flickered among them. He pushed on.

"Every year at springtime, when the world blossoms, giving us full of tangible evidence of God's promise of renewal, we commemorate and celebrate the central mystery of our faith: Christ died, and by the grace of God the father, our father, he rose from the dead. I've preached for many years on Easter about this miracle and in preparing for today, I humbly came to the conclusion that there is little I can say that adds to what Easter says for itself.

"Now, you're probably surprised to hear a priest volunteer to give up a chance to repeat himself." He paused for a moment to accommodate the quiet laughter that rippled among the pews. "But don't start toward home just yet. I want to talk about the Epistle. Some of you who follow along in your Missals noticed that this particular letter from Timothy was not scheduled for reading today. But it has much to teach us.

[1 Timothy Ch.1]

"Centuries ago, before written records even existed, our village and out county were ruled by kings, some high, some petty. When I say 'petty', I do't mean that they were venal or absorbed by trivial concerns. They were petty in the sense of smaller or lesser to the high kings. My own ancestors, the O'Harts, were petty kings here in Sligo. And let me assure you, not a penny left of whatever they once accrued." He smiled to reassure the congregation that it was all right to laugh a bit. He needed to bleed out a little of their nervousness. "The kings were top of the mountain back then, with many, nuanced social ranks cascading down below them.

"But as powerful as they were, these kings were not fearless. There were running battles among the clans, not over land, which was abundant then, plenty for all. What they fought over was cattle, in the form of cattle raids. Cattle were mobile wealth and having more at the expense of your rivals gave a clan the upper hand in the fight for survival.

"But there was an even greater threat, more constant and

close at hand for the kings. You might be surprised to hear who it was that struck such fear in their hearts, the one rank in society whose anger and displeasure they most feared to earn. It was the poets. Surprising, yes?" He waved a level hand across the podium and arched his eyebrow. "Now why were they so afraid? It's simple. Obvious. The power of words. Satire. How afraid were they?

"It's said that the first Irish curse was written by a poet who felt insulted at the way he was treated as the house guest of a petty king. That's an odd thing, isn't it? Ask anyone what they've heard about the Irish and they'll go on and on about our hospitality, how freely it's given and so genuinely extended. They'll always mention that, in my experience." He paused for effect. "Well, that and the Guinness. That gets mentioned a fair amount, too." The few gents who had made their way to the mass, standing in the back of the church nodded and chuckled.

"But why should poor hospitality inspire a curse? If it's a gift, freely given, then just be grateful for whatever you get and leave it at that, why don't you? But society was different then. People traveling across our vast island on foot had to rely on the last house they could see by light of day for succor and support and protection from whatever threats the night might disgorge.

"On the occasion I'm referring to, the guest was a poet. He was disgusted by the cold food, sour wine and hard bed that the king offered. When he left in the morning, he turned back to the castle and said, 'May your life be as cold as the victuals you offered, as sour as the wine you served and as hard as the bed you provided.' It is said that the king's household suffered under this curse for decades until no other clan would conduct commerce with them. The king's clan was forced to disperse to avoid starvation.

"Take this story, for example. Will Yeats, whose name a few of you recognize, I hope, writes about a legendary king whose court poet blackmailed him. The king feared that the poet would 'rhyme him up' in satire, as the phrase went back then, and stir up his people against him. 'Anything but that,' the king apparently said. 'Let me make you a gift to change your mind. What can I give you to persuade you?', the king asked.

"Well, this naive king made a grave mistake opening himself up like that. The poet thought for a minute and said, 'Give me the right eye, plucked out of your head, and I'll hold my tongue.' The king felt, of course, that he'd been tricked, but knew he'd lose more than his job if he refused the poet the gift he demanded. And so...." Pádraig mimed the plucking of his right eye with a loud cluck of his tongue. The women in the front pews gasped; the teenage boys in the back elbowed each other and juggled imaginary eyeballs among themselves.

"These are ancient examples of the power of words and the depth of our people's belief in the power of words. The belief is not just ancient. It is modern. It is contemporary and is the linchpin of our faith.

"In a few moments, I'll turn to the Liturgy of the Word and recite the consecration over the gifts. The words I say will transform the bread and the wine into the body and blood of our Lord and Savior Jesus Christ in a miracle that we call transubstantiation. It is our creed and our doctrine not that the eucharist and the cup merely represent Christ, but more profoundly that as a result of the consecration, these two worldly elements become Christ in the two species of body and blood. These are powerful words, then, aren't they. The Church has eschewed and condemned magic for centuries, so this is not magic. But this sacred transformation is at the heart of our Catholicness.

"These words I say every morning, and will say in a few moments, are unique to my ordained office and ministry. Even the most devout, the most pious among you cannot substitute for me in the consecration. And why is that? It is because of another powerful set of words that were spoken over me by his eminence the bishop at my ordination over a quarter of a century ago. Those words conferred upon me the power to say other words that are nothing short of a daily miracle, drawing Christ into our presence.

"All of our sacraments are powerful in this way. The

348

utterance of blessing words at baptism cleanses original sin from the infant's soul and opens the gates of heaven to that child. The union of man and woman is adultery the day before the sacrament of holy matrimony is administered, but a consecrated act of love on the wedding night, made so by the recitation of vows and the conferring of matrimonial blessings." Pádraig ignored the indignant sighs of the women in the first three rows who bobbed up from their rosaries for a shocked instant before darting back to their devotions.

"Words are powerful, which is why we must wield them carefully." He gathered himself for the difficult part now directly ahead of him. "We know God by many names. One of them is simply 'the Word'. Jesus is 'the Word made flesh', John tells us in his Gospel. And the Bible is, as we know, the Word of God. His words are even more powerful than the ones we utter, and we owe them the duty of careful hearing and deferential interpretation.

"The Holy See cautions Catholics against interpreting the Bible, but not because it doubts that the faithful have the intelligence and insight to do so. Rather, interpreting the Bible can be a thicket where context matters as much as the words themselves and the choice of a translator centuries ago to adopt one word instead of another can have a ripple effect across the generations."

He looked out across the congregants and met Mrs. O'Flannelly's eye. He leveled his jaw. "We are well counseled to avoid taking upon ourselves construction of verses to judge the character of others. Take the lessons you will to instruct your own behavior, to lift yourself up to the standards of the Apostles and the Epistolaries. But take great care in wielding the words of the Bible to judge others."

He flipped through the lectionary and lifted the pages with the yellow ribbon marking his place. He squinted at the text and thought that it wouldn't be long before he'd have to accede to the optometrist's suggestion that reading glasses might serve him well.

"I want to take us back to the Epistle reading we had a bit earlier. You might have noticed that this isn't the one in your missal. It's a bit irregular for me to change it out, but please indulge me for a few moments.

"What stands out to most lay people who read or hear this passage is the part about how the laws are not for the upright but for the wicked." Pádraig glanced back at the lectionary. "'On the contrary, they are for criminals and the insubordinate, for the irreligious and the wicked, for the sacrilegious and the godless; they are for people who kill their fathers or mothers and for murderers, for the promiscuous, homosexuals, kidnappers, for liars and for perjurers -- and for everything else that is contrary to the sound teaching that accords with the sound teaching of the gospel.'

"It's a source of satisfaction to some that homosexuals are thrown in there along with patricides, matricides and kidnappers. It makes it easy to toss them off, make them different from us.

"It's a caution to us, though, in our understanding of this passage that the liars and perjurers are in the line up, too. How many of us can stand apart from that group on a full-time basis? Truly, now, in the light of good conscience on a bright Easter morning?" He shook his raised arms at the congregation. His hands returned with a slap to the lectern.

"And I'll tell you something else. One of the rites of passage in ordination as a Jesuit is studying the Bible not only in English, but in its ancient languages. And this passage is not about homosexuals who mind their own business and live quiet lives in privacy. Let me not shock you with a candid translation, nor bore you with a vocabulary lesson. Trust me, this is about people of a predatory mindset.

"While, we're on the subject of sins and their punishments, let me bring you news about a favorite pastime around here that ought to bring you second thoughts. Gossip. Not thought of as a sin, I suppose. Let me inform you: It is a well-knighted sin. St. Paul refers to gossipers in one of his letters to the early Roman Christians, part instruction, part rebuke, as "whisperers." And what is the nub of the sin of gossip? Is it only a sin when what you pass on about isn't true? No. The sin of gossip occurs when you pass on information that isn't yours to share, even if you know it to be true. It's a confidence passed on, outside its rightful circle. It's a betrayal of trust, as suggested by the origin of the word: A god-sib is a confidant, a sibling in God, a sibling in Christ. And so gossip is the passing on of a confidence so dearly held that it is entrusted to a brother, a sister in Christ, and then betrayed.

"Why is it so injurious even if it be true? It is injurious by its intention, to put the subject in a degraded, negative light.

"Even worse the sin when the gossiper passes off information that is known to be false or is unverified by the gossiper."

Pádraig paused a moment, his arms extended on the lectern, his head bowed. He lowered his voice.

"There was a woman once, they told us in seminary, who went to confession. 'Father, forgive me, for I have sinned,' says she. 'I had a row with my neighbor and took the Lord's name in vain. But she started it, for no good reason.' The priest asks her, 'What started the argument?' The penitent says, 'She was angry I told the ladies at the public house that her daughter was flowsing about in Dublin town.' The priest asks her, 'Why did you tell them that?' 'Well,' says she, 'I heard it and just mentioned it to them.' There was a bit of a silence then, and the penitent asks, 'Father, am I pardoned?' The priest says, 'Not yet, not till you do your penance.' 'And what is that, Father, how many Hail Marys and so forth?' The priest says, 'No, I've something else in mind. I want you to go home and collect all the newspaper in the house. Make sure it's a big pile. If it's not as high as your forearm, ask the neighbors for their old papers.' The woman says, 'Yes, Father. And then what?' 'For every two sheets of paper, fold them together in the shape of a boat. You know how to do that?' 'Yes, Father, I did it with my Donny when he was little.' 'Good,' says the priest. 'When you're finished, take the whole lot of them, use a wheelbarrow if you have to, and take them down to the beach.' 'Yes, Father,' the woman says, a bit of puzzlement in her voice. 'And then what shall I do?' The priest tells her, 'Launch them all, one by one, on the waves.' The woman was silent for a moment. 'Yes, Father, I'll do as you say, but that'll be hundreds of little paper boats on the water.' 'I know,' the priest says. 'When you've finished, bring them all back to shore and come back to tell me about it.'

"So the woman goes off and does as the confessor says. Near the end of the confession hours, she comes back to the priest. 'I did as you said, Father.' The priest says, 'And what happened to the boats. Did you bring them all back safely?' The woman hesitated a moment, 'Well, no, Father. You must have known when you set me out to do it...' He interrupted her, 'Just tell me, in your words, what happened.' The woman sighed and said, 'Well, Father, the most of them never came back. None of them, truly. The paper got waterlogged and they sank, or they were fetched out beyond the harbor by the waves and the wind.' 'So you brought none of them back?' the priest asked. 'No, Father, it was impossible.' 'Ah,' says he. 'And so it is with gossip. What our words unleash wreaks damage that can never be recalled.'

Pádraig looked out at the congregation, a mural of faces hanging in disbelief at the directness of his rebuke. Almost enough said, he thought, but not quite.

"I am not deaf. I am not unaware of what is said in this parish about me, and about Dr. Attergood. I leave you to reflect on where my story touches you."

49.

Pádraig sat in the kitchen alone, for once, since Mrs. O'Flannelly's decampment. He knew his sermon made it more likely than not that she'd never speak to him again. He leaned on an elbow and thought about the prospect of more meals at Luck Boat now that no one would be looking to take Mrs. O'Flannelly's place. The thought cheered him up; tea and toast would do for almost any meal he couldn't get from Joe's kitchen and that he could make himself.

He wasn't sure what to think of what had happened and had no clue of what to expect next. After his homily, he had moved through the liturgy of the eucharist as if in a daze and he thought he had noticed fewer parishioners coming forward for communion than usual on an Easter Day mass.

He was still tired; he wondered whether there were enough hours in the week allowed for sleeping to erase his fatigue. He let his mind wander in a semi-wakeful way, uncurtaining his own interior as a cinema screen, himself ensconced in a velvet armchair there in his mind, looking on.

The bench across the street came up on the lower part of the screen and his mind's camera took his gaze across the harbor and over toward the boggy moors that separated the town from the caravan village of the Johnsons. A figure emerged from the trees stepping over the stones and into the bog as though muddy, wet shoes and feet soaked through them were not a care at all. Her skirt ruffled in the breeze and she walked impossibly, confidently across the rocky terrain as though skimming over the treacherous surface.

She paused and turned west to face the harbor. A small rowboat, invisible to Pádraig until now, bumped against the shore-rocks. A nimble figure, a girl, climbed out. Her leap to the shore pushed the boat back into the harbor, soon unretrievable, soon abandoned. She carried nothing with her. She approached the woman on the shore. Pádraig heard nothing; he couldn't be sure at his distant remove whether words were exchanged, but thought the greeting was silent. The two joined hands and walked north along the moor as far as Pádraig's eye could follow until they disappeared around the curve of the head that led inland toward Bulben.

He roused himself a few minutes later and was surprised, glancing over at the oven clock, how much time had passed. Late enough, he thought, for a lonely lunch. He thought of calling Stephen, but decided he preferred a walk and some silence.

He stumbled out the kitchen door, his legs uncooperative in repayment for his refusal to sleep. He walked across the empty road; Easter Monday was a second-class holiday but a day with no work nonetheless. He dropped into the bench facing the quay and Stephen appeared from nowhere, perched on the arm, his hands deep in his jacket pockets.

"Jesus, Mother of God," Pádraig startled. "Where did you come from?"`

"What are you talking about? I've been coming down the road watching you since you crossed the street, calling hello at the top of my voice. Are you in a daze again, then? We need a plan."

Pádraig shuddered; wished he'd brought a jumper out with him. He crossed his arms and rubbed his shoulders warm. "A plan about what?"

"Um, your sister? And your niece? What do we do next, help them get situated, whatever they might need. I imagine Joe and Wendy will want to be helpful, but the rest of the village is getting pitchforks and pikes ready."

"Oh. You're probably right," Pádraig said. "But it doesn't matter."

"What? How can it not matter that they'll be drawn and quartered next time either one of them tries to buy a tin of tuna or take a walk in daylight?"

"It doesn't matter. They're gone." Pádraig looked softly out over the water. The waves here were smaller, tamer, but lately they had the same hypnotic effect on his as the bigger ones near the Red Islands.

Stephen turned to face Pádraig. "What do you mean they're gone? Did they come and say 'bye, now, and sorry for all the kerfluffles'?"

"No, not that. I didn't really see them at all, though it felt as though I did, and I'm as sure as if I did. They've gone up the coast together, hand in hand as they should be." Pádraig nodded toward the soggy strip that threaded along the edge of the head near the wooded area that housed the Johnsons. "Gone up the mountain, I've the impression," Pádraig said.

Stephen looked at Pádraig, incredulous. "Up the mountain? You're saying they went to live with the fairies?"

Pádraig turned to face Stephen. "Stephen, you're a learned man. I'm surprised at you. There's no such thing as fairies." His eyes smiled and narrowed. "In any case, they prefer to be called 'the others.'" He turned back to the waves.

"Bless them, it's Monday," Stephen mumbled.

"Amen," Pádraig added.

Stephen dropped onto the seat next to Pádraig. "So what's next, then?"

"Next?"

"Yes, what happens next for you?"

Pádraig sighed. "Not sure. Nothing good, I imagine. No use trying to stay here, I'd say."

"Have to agree with you on that. I think your sermon -- I think you burned the bridge and shot the horses with that one. Good luck getting them to take communion from you now."

"They'll have to put up with me on that for a little while yet. But you're basically right. I'll have to ask for reassignment."

"Where will you go?"

"No way of telling. Could be anywhere, technically, but I've been around long enough to have some influence over the decision."

Stephen laughed. "Yes, and you've made so many friends along the way who'll be dying to help you. What was the name of that bishop you said you slapped a little while ago?"

"He wasn't a bishop, just a monsignor."

"Oh, well then. Not nearly as serious as I thought."

"But bad enough, as you suggest. I'll aim for America and see where I end up."

Stephen waited the space of a few waves, thinking. "America. Never lived there. But I'd like to one day. At least visit."

They sat quietly for a moment. The afternoon had passed somehow as they sat there. The dying light made it difficult for Stephen to read Pádraig's face, but Stephen imagined a trace of sadness there in the gloam.

"Well. Who knows where I'll land," Pádraig finally said. "But wherever that is, it would be a welcome thing to see you turn up."

Stephen smiled toward Pádraig's dimming profile. "Thank you for that. Being welcome somewhere, even in concept, is a new sensation for me."

"Ah, yes. But it's easily extended, my friend. I figure this, based on what we've just been through together: Surely somewhere in the world there is trouble that needs to be caused by us."

"Surely that," Stephen agreed, as Easter Monday's last sunlight squeezed past the horizon and into the harbor.